Enchanted dreams

Erotic
Tales
of the
Supernatural

National Bestselling Author

NANCY MADORE

Enchanted
dreams

Erotic
Tales
of the
Supernatural

Spice

Recycling programs
for this product may
not exist in your area.

ENCHANTED DREAMS EROTIC TALES OF THE SUPERNATURAL

ISBN-13: 978-0-373-60534-7

Copyright © 2009 by Nancy Madore.

www.Spice-Books.com

Printed in U.S.A.

For Michael Hulbert, with my utmost gratitude and love for all the encouragement and inspiration, for putting up with me and for so many other things, like slipping into characters' heads for me and bringing them to life. I couldn't have written this without you.

EROTIC TALES OF THE SUPERNATURAL

The
Enchanted
Forest

Catherine stopped again to catch her breath. She couldn't believe how out of shape she had become. There was a time when she was always outdoors getting exercise, whether it was camping or playing volleyball or running. How long had it been since she'd entered a marathon? Lately, all of life's many demands kept her busy running an entirely different kind of race. She couldn't seem to find time for herself anymore. There was little enough time to sustain the barest existence. These musings caused a pang of anxiety to rise up in her. She closed her eyes and took a deep breath, willing her worries away. How had matters of basic survival come to absorb her every waking moment?

But these were precisely the thoughts Catherine came here to forget. She had not suffered an anxiety attack in nearly twenty-four hours. She was determined to enjoy her brief escape from the rat race, if only for a few days. She tipped her head back and breathed in as much as she could of the crisp, cool air that surrounded her. It smelled of earth and life. She looked around then, suddenly aware of the strange silence. As her nostrils drank in the sweet and pungent aroma of the forest, her heartbeat could not help but slow down. The beauty and tranquility were having their effect. Why couldn't all of life be this simple?

Catherine picked up her overstuffed backpack and hefted it up onto her shoulder, resting it on the left side now because the right shoulder was beginning to ache. She felt another wave of annoyance at this reminder of how poorly things were constructed these days. The strap had broken within the first hour of her using it, unable to withstand the weight of her camping gear. She should have chosen a more practical pack, she thought, but she had been swayed by the colorful design—and the sale price—of this one. Besides, its bright orange-and-yellow pattern gave her a feeling of security, just in case there were hunters in the woods. Not that it was hunting season, but one never knew. But as it happened, she had not encountered anyone at all since setting out on her little excursion. There was a lonely, isolated feeling to the place that convinced her no one else was around. At first it was disconcerting, and she had been tempted to turn around. But it was not an overly exhausting hike to the campsite, and she was sure to find someone there.

With her racing heart calmed, Catherine resumed hiking, but at a slower, more manageable pace. She was nearing a high point in the mountain and veered closer to the steep edge so that she could observe the views below. The trees were thinning out now, perhaps because of the elevation, and this made the sight even more spectacular. Clumps of trees gave way to fields of green, spotted here and there with patches of wildflowers.

As Catherine gazed at the scene below her, she was once again struck by the curious silence surrounding her. Listening more intently, she noticed that there were actually sounds to be heard, such as the twitter of a bird or the rustle of a squirrel, but these seemed to blend into the background as seamlessly as the foliage. There were no conspicuous sounds, no noises that would indicate purposeful activity or any other synthetic clatter clashing with the natural progression of things. Catherine pondered this, marveling at the perfect harmony that seemed to exist among the plants and animals compared to the chaos associated with more intelligent beings.

Even as Catherine was thinking these thoughts—ironically, right in the very midst of them—a bird suddenly flew out at her from a nearby bush, startling her. She lost her footing and, unable to catch herself, stumbled over the edge of the mountain. There was a split second of absolute clarity where she realized she was not going to be able to stop her fall, and in the next instant she noticed the thick, solid branch peaking out from beneath the fallen leaves that was rushing up to meet her. She only had time to perceive these things, not to react, or to move, or even to feel alarm. And then everything went black.

Catherine opened her eyes and looked dumbly around her in utter confusion. Where on earth was she? Something was not quite right, yet she felt remarkably calm. She sat up tentatively, remembering the fall and aware that she had sustained injuries.

The very first thing she noticed was that all of the forest—from the tiniest blade of grass to the tallest tree—appeared to be buzzing with life. She was suddenly struck with how curiously vibrant the colors were, and how pungent the aroma around her. It was almost as if the trees were speaking to her, even as the gentle wind rustled their leaves. Things seemed more distinct and noticeable than before. She wondered if she had suffered a concussion.

As she observed the forest around her, Catherine had the oddest sensation that she was no longer alone. She looked more carefully at the plants and trees, scanning them for signs of life. But aside from the foliage, she saw nothing.

She got up slowly, brushing off her shorts and checking for injuries. Her wounds appeared to be minor, as she was able to move about without suffering additional discomfort. Yet she couldn't shake the feeling that something had changed. She still had the impression that she was being watched. She called out, "Who's there?" but there was no response. She wondered vaguely why whatever it was didn't manifest itself. Yet for some reason, she still wasn't afraid. In the midst of such radiant harmony, it was hard to conceive of any real danger.

Her voice, when she had cried out, sounded foreign to her ears. Something about the valley she had fallen into called to mind the enchanted forests of her childhood fairy tales. She realized that she ought to make her way back up the mountain and find the trail, but she was captivated by the little forest nook and didn't want to leave. What would it hurt to look around for a few minutes? Just off in the distance, she spied a field of brilliant colors that begged to be explored. She spotted her backpack on the ground nearby, and had half a mind to set up camp right there. Why should she leave this enchanted spot to set out for a public campground? This would be *real* camping, where she could open the flap of her tent without nudging a tent right next to hers.

As Catherine considered this, she walked toward the field, surveying the area around her with a great deal of curiosity. A prettier campsite could not be imagined. There was a tranquility to the place that seemed to promise sanctuary. It had everything the public campground had except electricity and, perhaps, water. But even as this thought occurred to her, she suddenly perceived a very faint sound—so faint she could only just identify it as the sound of rushing water. As she followed the sound, she discovered with joy that it was, in fact, a waterfall.

Catherine stared at the waterfall in amazement. It was just like something from an exotic island. She could smell the water as it exploded over the cliff's edge. She approached it timidly, almost wary of its incredible magnificence. At any rate, she thought, she could wash the many scrapes that dotted her arms and legs in the sparkling spring. She removed her shoes and socks and tentatively dipped her toes in the little, churning stream at the bottom of the falls. It was cool but not cold, so she plunged her feet in. She bent down to scoop water over her bare legs. The flash of a silver trout caught her eye as it passed and she jumped, half expecting it to pause at the surface on its way by to speak to her, just as the one in the Brothers Grimm *Tale of the Fisherman* had. She laughed at the thought. Yet it would not have surprised her.

Catherine let the water, cool and soothing, trickle over her legs. She gathered several more handfuls and splashed them over the cuts and bruises on her arms. She realized that she was thirsty, too. Carefully, for the bottom of the stream was lined with sparkling rocks, she stepped closer to the falls, leaning forward to scoop some of the freshly falling water into her cupped hands. It tasted as sweet and refreshing as she imagined, and she swallowed several mouthfuls in large gulps. She was surprised how thirsty she was and drank until she had her fill. Then she simply stood there, admiring the majestic beauty of the waterfall. It was truly enchanting. But if she was going to make camp, she knew that she would have to find her way back to the trail soon.

Catherine cautiously stepped from the stream and looked toward the forest from which she had come, when she suddenly noticed that the sun was unusually high in the sky. This seemed strange. Wasn't it later in the day? She tried to remember roughly what time it had been when she fell, but she couldn't. Yet she had already eaten lunch and was fairly certain that the better part of the day was behind her. By all counts, it should have been late afternoon. How, then, could it now be coming on midday? Surely she had not lain unconscious overnight! But just then it occurred to her that her stomach was empty. She once again had that strong sense of unreality and wondered if she had suffered more serious injuries in the fall than she originally thought. Perhaps she had a head injury. She vaguely remembered the large stump sticking up out of the ground. She felt around her head for bumps.

But at present it seemed more important that she eat something. Her backpack was stuffed with food, but just at that moment she spotted shimmering patches of red scattered about in some of the bushes nearby. Upon closer inspection, she saw that they were raspberries, and they were so plentiful they were practically falling off the branches. Looking around, she could see that the lush bushes were growing everywhere all along the little stream. Catherine tentatively picked one of the berries and touched it to her tongue. It was tart and sweet, just like a wild raspberry. And the bushes were overgrown with them. What a find! There were so many berries that, without ever taking a single step in either direction, she was able to eat her fill.

While Catherine was gorging herself on raspberries, a strange notion came into her head. She began to think that the berries had appeared as a result of her desire to eat. But after considering it, she rejected the idea as preposterous. The berries had been there all along; she had simply not noticed them before. The waterfall had absorbed all of her attention.

But there was no denying that there was something special about the place. Contented by berries, she returned to the stream and sat down on the bank. She watched the running water flash and sparkle as more gleaming trout passed by. The sight of them pleased her. She stretched out on the bank lazily, resting on her side so that she could gaze down into the gurgling stream. How pleasant it was to simply watch the water trickling over the glimmering rocks as it rushed along its merry way. How benevolent its cheerful sound, tinkling contentedly as it hurried off to—where? Catherine felt peaceful and serene as she pondered this. She suddenly couldn't remember what those things were that had bothered her before. After a while, she rolled over onto her back and looked up at the sky.

But what madness was this? Suddenly the sun was sinking into the horizon!

Catherine jumped up and looked around. She was yet again assailed with a nagging sense of unreality. How could high noon so quickly have turned to dusk? How long had she been lying by the bank, staring down into the water? How was it possible that she, Catherine, a person who normally couldn't sit still for a moment, had wasted an entire afternoon looking at water?

She decided it was time to leave the strange little forest glen and quickly surveyed the area one last time, looking for the direction from which she had come. She wandered all around, searching for something familiar or for some evidence of her footsteps. But try as she might, she was unable to find a pathway out, and it was quickly getting dark. She would have to wait until morning. She was surprised to find that this did not disturb her overmuch, but she regretted not bringing her backpack with her when she had wandered off. At least then she would have had supplies. How would she manage to get through the night now? In a little while, it would be too dark to see and she would be left fully exposed to the elements.

Or would she? With a surreal sensation of awed disbelief, her eyes fell upon a little nook at the base of the foothill that rose up to one side of the waterfall. At first glance it appeared to be a shallow cave, just the right size for her. Catherine approached it with interest. It was indeed a small alcove that had formed out of the earth. Upon closer inspection, it appeared to be the result of erosion, for there was a large tree sitting directly above it. All along its inner cavity could be seen smooth, wooden roots, jutting out here and again over the ceiling and walls like sturdy brown beams. The cave did not recede so far into the earth as to frighten or alarm, but was just enough to protect someone from the elements. The floor was covered with large, crisp leaves that had apparently fallen from the tree above. Finding the little alcove filled Catherine with a sense of well-being. She was beginning to believe that this forest really was enchanted. It was certainly the most enchanting place that she had ever been. She went to work immediately, gathering more leaves from the ground outside the cave and stuffing them into the corner where she planned to sleep. As she rushed to prepare her little nest before it became too dark, she suddenly caught, from the corner of her eye, the sparkle from a lightning bug. In that same moment, the last bit of the sun disappeared behind the mountain.

It was fully dark now, but look! More lightning bugs were— one after the other—coming alive, blinking so brightly (for her benefit alone, she now believed) and so frequently that her campsite was kept in a steady stream of soft light. Catherine stared, openmouthed, at the wondrous spectacle.

She began to think that somehow, in the course of her fall, she must have landed in some kind of enchanted world, perhaps even crossing over into an entirely different dimension.

Catherine snuggled comfortably into her cozy little bed inside the cave, but sleep was not quick to come. She was plagued by gently rising waves of restlessness, brought on, no doubt, by the extraordinary things that had occurred. Her mind drifted aimlessly, gliding through random memories of enchanted forests and fairies. As her thoughts meandered over the folklore, her exotic surroundings remained uppermost in her mind. She thought about the peculiar events of her day, unconsciously allowing her hand to trail over the length of her body and lazily letting it come to rest between her legs.

The fireflies continued to light up the sky around Catherine, and stars blinked at her from far off in the distance. She was mildly surprised to find that she was aroused. Her fingers had been absently—and very lightly—circling and caressing her body, and they were having an effect. She tried to recall the last time she felt aroused. It was not since she had started taking the antianxiety medication. That, too, was tucked away in her backpack, she suddenly remembered. She hadn't taken one since before the fall. But how long ago had that been? She had lost all track of time. She remembered how quickly the sun seemed to set from its midday position; she would have sworn that no more than a single hour had passed in that space of time. But was it time that had changed, or was it her perception that was skewed? Had she fallen into some kind of trance while gazing at the gleaming water?

These speculations passed through Catherine's consciousness offhandedly. She wondered that she could feel so calm and serene in the light of so many uncertainties. How did she know, for instance, that she wasn't actually suffering from some kind of head injury? That would certainly explain her peculiar perspective of the things that were happening around her. And without her medication, even for a day, she would normally have been so terrified of an anxiety attack that she would have brought one about. But at the moment, even this realization that her meds were out of reach did not rattle her. It simply felt too good to have her body responding like this again. She felt excited, and terribly alive.

Catherine's fingers kept encouraging her arousal, stirring it up and up as they circled and massaged her engorged little bud of pleasure. Soon, her desire was taking over all other thoughts. She suddenly, recklessly, wished that this enchanted forest would bring her some magic now!

By this time, Catherine's body was lightly swaying back and forth in time with the steady, circular motion of her fingers. The activity caused her hips to sink farther into her leafy bedding, settling deeper and deeper into its softness.

But what was this? Suddenly, Catherine was disrupted by something solid that was buried beneath the leaves of her bed. She tried to ignore it but that only seemed to make it more pronounced. With a sigh of frustration, she sat up and carefully pushed aside the bedding to find out what lay beneath it. When she saw what it was, she gasped. She blinked several times to make sure she wasn't imagining things.

Examining the object more closely, Catherine perceived that it was most likely one of the tree's roots, which had circled back around toward the direction it had come in order to be unearthed in this alcove. This, in and of itself, was not especially unusual perhaps, but the shape of the root was. It rose up out of the ground at an angle, thick and gnarly and long. That it happened to be there, coming up out of the ground in that particular place and jutting out at that particular angle, was certainly no coincidence. The longer she stared at it, the harder it was for Catherine to believe that she hadn't noticed it sooner. And then her last thought before she discovered it came to her and she blushed. She was now, more than ever, convinced that she was in a magical place where all her wishes would become a reality. But who was behind it? What was the presence she kept sensing?

Intrigued, Catherine could not resist reaching out and touching the lanky root. It seemed to tremble and pulse in her hand, startling her and causing her to instinctively jerk her hand away. As she gazed at it, she noticed that it was precisely the size, shape and texture she preferred. Although it was a bit rugged and rough, she thought ironically—playing the devil's advocate for the moment as she skeptically examined her most secret wish come true—and then smiled at her own ungraciousness. But the smile instantly froze on her face. There, and there again, all over the root in fact, there oozed a clear fluid—perhaps a sap of some kind, she immediately suggested to her disbelieving mind—seeping out from its many crevices. Was it possible that the fluid had been there all along? It was, and yet Catherine felt that it was not.

She suddenly thought of Eve in the Garden of Eden. Was the proverbial apple this impossible to ignore? Already, her body was trembling with desire and anticipation.

Catherine made her decision in an instant. There was still the disconcerting sense that someone—or something—was watching her. Yet she felt that, whoever or whatever it was, be it fairy or plant life, it watched with approval and meant her no harm. Maybe it was the source of all her good fortune, her benefactor in this enchanted place, granting her every wish like a kind of fairy godmother. All around her there appeared to be nothing but loving energy. In fact, all of the encumbrances of her normal life, which had always been at war with her instincts, were starting to fade, diminishing in importance by the hour. She kept forgetting that she needed to find her way out of the forest, and even what it was that she needed to get back to.

All of this was a mere fleeting thought in the back of her mind as she excitedly took off her clothes. Uppermost in her thoughts, overruling everything else, was her desire, pure and raw and true. She was unabashedly grateful that the root protruded so far out of the ground as she carefully moved herself over it. The angle, too, could not have been more suitable. All she had to do was ease herself back, little by little, opening herself to the object of her desire in small, slow increments as she inched backward onto it. The clear, sappy fluid that was released by the root not only made the entry smoother, but it seemed to heighten her pleasure as well, increasing the friction as she slid back and forth. It felt as if it seeped into each and every crevice of her silky folds, filling her completely and creating a delightful resistance with its sticky texture, which intensified her pleasure as she slid along the long, gnarly shaft. She struggled to take it deeper and deeper with each thrust backward.

The root, meanwhile, continued to throb and pulse as Catherine shamelessly used it. She trembled with pleasure, relishing the exquisite feel of it inside her body. Every part of her felt as though it were alive. She went back farther and farther on it as she picked up her pace, delighting in the loud, squishing sounds of her juices as they mingled with the thick sap from the root. And even the forest all around her seemed to stir, pulsing and throbbing right along with her. The fireflies lit up the sky, bringing even her shadow to life where it moved over the cave's wall in time with her thrashing body. Birds and other wildlife called out to her from the distance. When at last she cried out with intense pleasure, she could not say for sure whether it was her own scream or that of another creature of the forest.

Almost instantly afterward, Catherine fell into a deep sleep. It was a sleep filled with fleeting visions of strange, sensual places filled with curious and wonderful things. In these dreams, what once was irregular was now ordinary and proper. Plants were living things in the truest sense, with thoughts and feelings of their own as they fulfilled their objective to please those whose lives they touched. All was perfect harmony, where desires were meant to be satisfied. Catherine sunk deeper into the spell of the forest as she dreamed, without the slightest thought for what she was leaving behind. She slept effortlessly in her leafy bed, content and satiated, yet always teetering on the edge of her newfound arousal.

When Catherine awoke the next morning, she was first conscious of how refreshed she felt. The next thing she noticed was that her injuries of only a day before seemed to have completely disappeared. She was still vaguely aware that there was something she ought to do, but the forest repeatedly distracted her from this awareness each time it threatened to emerge. These distractions took many forms, and in the process Catherine discovered a variety of interesting plants that she had never heard of before, some of which seemed to offer themselves up for practical use. She was drawn to one plant, for instance, for its extraordinary size and spectacular color, but upon closer inspection she found that its huge petals were actually similar in texture to silk. The thick, durable petals were abundant, too, with the ends curling up into themselves like large bolts of fabric. It was impossible to resist making use of these petals for this purpose. She found many unique plants with too many useful functions to mention. It soon became apparent that the highest purpose of the forest and its plant life was to please her. The flowers and plants not only served, but they did so in such an extraordinary and delightful way that they couldn't fail to please, and Catherine was completely charmed out of her former life.

In her enchanted forest, time quickly lost all authority over Catherine. She was no longer even aware of the passing days and weeks. Catherine busied herself with taking advantage of the many joys and opportunities the forest offered her. In time, she was able to fashion beautiful attire from flowers and leaves—stunning clothes that seemed to caress her skin while allowing her to move more freely. Everything she needed to sustain her life grew out of the enchanted soil, and they consisted of the most appealing and beneficial properties she had ever known. All of her senses were constantly awed and enchanted.

The only thing missing from this tiny paradise Catherine had stumbled into was a companion. In all of the time that she had been there, she had never seen another living soul. There was plenty of animal life that she encountered but never a trace of another person. Catherine had been talking to the plants almost from the beginning, and over time she started to believe that they could hear and understand her. There were moments when she doubted her own sanity, but she could swear that whenever she opened her mouth the plants seemed to, ever so slightly, lean in her direction and listen. And there was something else out there, too, it seemed to her—some other being that watched over her and listened. Sometimes it seemed so close that she thought she could actually feel its breath upon her neck. But when she turned her head to look, there would be nothing there. This was not overly frustrating for her, though, because she was perfectly willing now to believe in those things she couldn't see. She trusted that she was sensing something that was actually there. She began to think of them as fairies. Recalling everything that she had ever learned about fairies as a child, they seemed to offer the most likely explanation. She had read in Irish folklore that fairies were actually spirits, wandering the earth in between lives. They had a reputation for being kind and generous overall, although at times they were said to be impish and mischievous. This made sense to her, and it seemed to fit with what she felt about the invisible beings that filled the atmosphere all around her. In time, she was speaking to them as if these suppositions had been confirmed.

But whatever benevolent spirit or fairy or enchantment it was, one thing that Catherine came to know for certain was that no matter what she might wish for, it would inevitably appear. This was something she had not only learned to accept, but came to expect. If she, for example, craved something sweet, she would instantly catch the scent of nectar from some utterly delightful fruit. Or, if erotic thoughts tempted her consciousness, the wind was apt to suddenly bring a stray flower to lightly caress the eager flesh between her legs.

All of her senses were heightened. Her hearing, in particular, seemed keener than ever. She was becoming more and more aware of sounds she had never even noticed before, whereas the noises she had heard all of her life—particularly those that crept in from outside of her enchanted forest—were suddenly strange and unfamiliar to her, and even a cause for fear. Any such noise would send her deeper into the woods to hide. Her existence before discovering her magical forest was no longer of interest to her. She had finally found peace in this place where she could exist in perfect harmony with the world around her. There was much of intrigue and humor and even romance in the life-forms she now communicated with. She began to equate all good fortune with the entities she had come to think of as fairies, and blame any misfortunes, such as storms or other mild discomforts, on "demons." She spoke to both as if they were right there beside her at all times, for she believed their existence was solely centered on hers. She adapted to her new life fully and seamlessly, even dressing like a woodland nymph, in the stunning shades produced by the wildflowers of the forest. She designed her clothing purely for amusement, and it always left her fully exposed to the elements and open to the whims of whatever chose to please her. She could not imagine hiding her breasts from the numerous plants and flowers that seemed to take pleasure in caressing and clinging to them, any more than she could close up her own grasping flower from the various woodland life-forms that would sample the nectar that flowed forth from there. She kept that part of herself always ready and exposed, her trembling, delicate petals always ready to unfold and open to new pleasures. Even the rain possessed the power to arouse her; she would lie in the soft grass and raise her hips up toward the sky, relishing every single droplet that fell.

Catherine looked up at the sky, aware that a storm was approaching. Angry molecules crackled in the air all around her. Her skin prickled in response. She was decked out in a colorful outfit she had crafted that very day. The top consisted of dried strands of grass held together at the top, just above her breasts, by a band of stunningly bright flowers, and the bottom, which just barely fell to her thighs, was the same. Every now and then, a gust of wind would whip through the dried grass, exposing bits of pink flesh and causing the slightly roughened edges of the grass to scratch and tease her tender flesh. She shivered in anticipation as she rushed out toward the open field.

The sky was quickly turning darker from the approaching storm, but the golden field glowed brightly as she entered the clearing. The wind picked up considerably without the trees of the forest to block it, and her grass coverings whipped frantically over her skin. There was a tree in the midst of the flowers, and Catherine ran toward it eagerly. When she reached it, she embraced it. The rough edges of its bark were abrasive against her skin. She caught the sweet, familiar smell of honeysuckle from high above, and looked up to admire the willowy vine that had laced its way in and around the many branches throughout the entire length of the tree. But the tree did not mind, or at least Catherine felt this to be so.

She let her hand roam over one of the long, sinewy vines of the honeysuckle. It had clung to the trunk of the tree for so long that it seemed a part of it now, imbedded so deeply into the bark that it was hard to tell which was which. Her fingers trailed lightly over it, and she was not surprised when one of the younger, more malleable parts of the vine reached down from out of the tree and deliberately circled itself around her wrist. She ran her free hand over one of the vines on the other side and waited for it, too, to restrain her in the same manner. The rubbery appendages wrapped round and round her wrist, three times each, bending their leaves courteously to cushion her tender flesh from its unyielding hold. A few of the honeysuckle's tender white flowers dropped to the earth with a sigh. Their sweet scent filled Catherine's nostrils.

Before she had time to wonder what would happen next, a root came up from out of the earth beneath her feet and curled itself around one of Catherine's ankles. Another root popped out almost immediately after the first and captured her other leg. Catherine watched the scene in ecstatic amazement. No matter how many nights she would spend in this enchanted little paradise, these events would always fill her with wonder and excitement, even as she waited in delicious anticipation.

The roots began gently spreading her legs apart, and the honeysuckle loosened its hold just a bit on her wrists. She allowed herself to be maneuvered so that she was sitting on a large mossy rock, situated just off to one side of the tree. She sat on the soft, cushiony moss with her legs spread and held wide apart by the deeply embedded roots that had been unearthed for this event. Her hands were allowed to rest on the rock behind her, but they remained lightly restrained by the honeysuckle vines.

In this position, Catherine sat leaning back at a slight angle, with her arms resting behind her, her breasts jutting outward and her legs spread apart. A gust of wind came sweeping through the valley and ravished her grass garments, causing them to fly in all directions. Two hardened nipples peeked out from the top portion of her dress and the bottom half was completely blown off to the sides, leaving her fully exposed.

Catherine struggled against her restraints, not trying to escape, but simply squirming in anticipation. She waited with excruciating impatience, wondering agitatedly what intensely pleasurable delights were in store for her this time. She did not have long to wait.

Here, already, moving in her direction in steady line, Catherine could see the fiercely colored heads of the tall wildflowers that littered the open field. They approached her in smooth, sweeping waves, seemingly brought about by the wind, but apparently being moved by some power underground, too, for their roots remained intact. With each new gust of wind the wave of flowers came nearer and nearer, until at last the blooms began to brush against her opened legs. Closer and closer they came with each new breeze, until they were being whipped across the sensitive flesh of her inner thighs, making them tingle and smart. And they kept advancing even more, causing her thighs to turn from a pale beige to a bright pink, and the little lips of her sex glands to part in surprise.

Catherine now writhed against her bonds, but not at all wishing for them to release her. If anything, she wished they would hold her more rigidly. She was terrified that they might come loose and bring this fantastic event to an end. There was a pleasing sting to the flowers' thrashing that clashed delightfully with her arousal and created a most intense ache. She was so preoccupied with the sensations brought about by the gentle whipping that she did not even at first realize that the flowers might be doing anything other than simply being swept against her for that pleasure alone. The wind, meanwhile, began to howl as her body strained and shuddered under the exquisitely relentless assault from the brightly colored blooms as they one right after the other slapped against her quickly heating flesh. She wondered at their remarkable strength, for not one of them appeared to lose so much as a petal.

But eventually a slow dawning came, even as Catherine felt the oppressive weight of something heavy and thick coating the little petals of flesh that surrounded her aching hole. She peered down between her legs and noticed that each and every bloom, while brushing across her trembling nether lips, cleverly turned its face toward them and thrust out its heavily coated stamens for a thoroughly intimate kiss that doused her with their nectar! She noticed, too, that each wave of flowers that passed her continued to move forward in the same direction, so that with each new burst of wind an entirely new group of flowers assailed her. In this way, each flower that struck her was fresh and full of more of the thick nectar to leave with her. But why? Her little lips trembled to be so laden.

Catherine's inner thighs were becoming more and more inflamed and even raw, and her labia was weighted down with the heavy nectar of literally thousands of flowers. She was trembling with an agonizing mixture of pleasure and need. She arched her back and thrust her hips up in an effort to escape the next wave of flowers, but each and every one caught her regardless, striking her pulsing flesh with even more vigor, and hampering her poor little petals with even more of their nectar. Although the nectar was administered one tiny bit at a time, it was astounding how much she had accumulated so quickly. The heavy discomfort was almost completely giving way to desire. Catherine could feel her arousal welling up, strong and full. She whimpered helplessly, wishing suddenly that it would never end.

But already her bonds were tightening and the wind was dying down. The flowers at last receded. Catherine closed her eyes for a moment and tried to still her disappointment and quiet her trembling limbs. Her flesh stung and her legs quivered violently. Her nether lips struggled and quivered under the burden of the nectar.

Her attention was suddenly caught by a peculiar, high-pitched sound, seemingly far off in the distance. She opened her eyes and saw that there was a dark but luminous mist of something moving in the sky in the direction of the sound. Whatever it was, it was quickly approaching. Catherine hardly had time to consider what it might be when the first of its arrivals landed.

The shrill whistling had actually been the fluttering of hundreds of tiny wings in flight; once the swarm arrived the noise immediately quieted. Butterflies touched gently down, elegantly and politely, and immediately began to dine on the nectar. There were so many of them, each smartly dressed in their own individual mixture of bright colors so that no two sets of wings were precisely the same. Catherine stared with wide, disbelieving eyes as they each, in turns, feasted on the banquet that had been so painstakingly spread out before them. Their activity tortured her in the most delightful way. The already oversensitive flesh had been made even more so by the extraordinary whipping she had received. She could now keenly feel each and every little butterfly that tapped relentlessly upon her flesh in an effort to capture the sweet taste of nectar through its sensors. Then, slowly, their tongues emerged, unfurling to nearly three times the length of their bodies to painstakingly begin lapping up the sticky nectar. Catherine was acutely aware of the butterflies' wings as they fluttered and moved, gently battering her with their sheer numbers.

Catherine moaned loudly, straining once again against her bonds, which seemed to tighten in response and draw her legs farther apart. The multitude of butterflies produced a rainbow of lush, colorful activity between her trembling thighs. But they were gracious and well-mannered; they did not battle over the sumptuous meal that was spread out before them. Rather, they each in turn feasted elegantly and leisurely, while the others fluttered their wings and tapped their little feet as they patiently waited. Seven or eight could partake in each sitting, and it tantalized Catherine's burdened labia when they supped on the sticky nectar. Those that finished moved graciously aside but still lingered, loitering so close as to be nearly on top of one another, but comfortably so, nevertheless.

Catherine's sensitivities were so acutely awakened by these events that she was keenly aware of every single touch, no matter how feathery light or minute. The butterflies dined enthusiastically but unhurriedly, cleaning their little appendages meticulously as they ate so as not to waste a single drop of the precious nectar. They each worked at her flesh mercilessly with their feet and tongues as they feasted, prodding and kneading her inflamed labia in an effort to remove the sticky nectar from her body. They roamed freely over every part of the feasting area, clinging agilely to her sticky slit and meandering restlessly over and around her clitoris.

Catherine's hips bobbed and jiggled as much as was possible under her restraints. She felt as if hundreds of tiny hands were actively massaging and stimulating her. But each time she came within a feather's breath of relief, either the intensity or the location of the stimulation would shift and change, taking her opportunity for release with it. Yet the relentless buildup of desire never stopped; it kept building and growing until she feared that she might burst.

In the course of all this activity, even with such refined diners as these, the nectar could not help but be spread even farther over the area. As this occurred it allowed more butterflies to partake. Catherine knew all of this without actually seeing it, for she could feel them feeding over every part of her, from her clitoris to her anus, and she could do little more than shudder violently as the sensations of pleasure their feeding gave her racked her body. Each little tap from the butterflies' feet felt like dull little pins pricking her flesh as they tapped and tasted and tapped again, until she had endured thousands of the agonizing little touches. Her body was a living, quaking mass of frothing desire, churning inward from where the butterflies gathered.

It was late afternoon and the wind had died down for the feasting, but the sky was still darkish. Catherine's body was held at an impasse between desire and euphoria as she was obliged to await the pleasure of the butterflies, who remained maddeningly leisurely at their meal. In the end, it took them the better part of an hour to accomplish their goal, but they left her without a single trace of nectar left over from the incredible flower thrashing she had endured. The wind suddenly picked up again and the butterflies left Catherine in a fluttery explosion that was no less spectacular than when they had arrived.

Catherine's exposed flesh was now bright red and burning hot; the cool wind upon it caused her little lips to shiver uncontrollably. They were parted slightly from all the activity and a bit of her own nectar was squeezing out between them. Catherine waited eagerly, trusting that she would be given relief at the determined time—and no sooner—and knowing that that time would be designed for her optimum pleasure. It seemed that this forest was dedicated to giving her the very best delights that the world had to offer, and it simply would not allow for less.

The sky was coming alive once again, and now, in her present state, even a stray breeze was enough to give Catherine a tantalizing thrill. She arched her back and tried to thrust her hips upward, delighting in the cool air touching her overheated flesh, even as she caught sight of the next portion of her pleasure approaching.

A single bud was coming up out of the ground and growing, right before her eyes, into a broad stem with massive leaves. Within a blink of her eye, it sprouted and grew and now, at its tip, a large flower was blossoming. The plant was approximately four feet high in the end, having grown that entire length within a single moment.

The flower looked something like an oversized iris and was covered all around the outside edges in rich, purple fur. She saw that it was opening, and held her breath as she waited to see what was inside. The accelerated speed with which the flower was coming to maturity suddenly seemed terribly slow to Catherine.

From deep within the iris's center, perhaps coming out of its very stem, there sprung forth a thick shaft that Catherine immediately recognized as its stamen. This stamen was like any other in that it had a bulbous pollen sack at the end of its stalk. But aside from this, Catherine saw that it was not like other stamens at all. First and foremost was its exceptional size. As Catherine eagerly watched, it continued to grow and thicken to the incredible length of nearly a foot, and expand in diameter to the thickness of a ripe plum. Catherine's back arched reflexively. She had no uncertainty about what the stamen was for.

The flower had risen out of the ground from a spot that was centered directly between Catherine's legs. All it had to do was to lean toward her, bending slightly in the direction of her hips. Her labia was still quivering, and it seemed as if they suddenly parted in anticipation. The flower continued to lean and tip in her direction until the stamen touched her. The pollen sack at its tip was pliable to a point, but it was so large and protruding that this did not help much as it began to push its way into Catherine's body. She moaned loudly as it entered her, and her flesh continued to burn and pulse. Yet there was palpable relief just to have it inside her, pressing its way through her inner walls, filling her. She felt almost depraved in her desperation to have it. It inched its way in slowly, backing out a hairbreadth periodically before advancing farther. Catherine relished each and every advance, gasping and moaning in time with its movements forward or back.

Soon Catherine was taking more of the stamen inside her than anything she had ever taken before, and her body bucked slightly against the intrusion. But she could do little to escape in any direction so she remained rooted to the spot, with her hands still held firmly behind her and her feet held far apart and firmly attached to the ground. There was nowhere for her to go, but she wiggled and squirmed as best she could anyway. Her body arched and contorted, and she moaned and whined as the flower continued to advance. Her hips were lifted off the protruding rock, for she was obliged to raise them in her frantic effort to accommodate the impossible stamen, and it held her there, impaled in midair.

Just when she thought she would be torn in half, the flower made its final advance. She was amazed to see that she had managed to take the full length of the iris's stamen inside of her, and now, suddenly, its stiff, leafy head was brushing against her throbbing clitoris. She cried out when she felt it. The rough surface of the petal, heavily coated as it was with the stunning purple fur, provided just the right intensity and motion to further inflame her passion and assist her in her climax. Each time the flower withdrew and advanced again, the thick petal stroked her. Yet it was not as repetitive as she would have liked for a quick release but, rather, it was of an intensity to bring her to her satisfaction slowly—easing her into it.

Catherine strained against her bonds and cried out loudly. Her hair was flying from side to side as she railed against the most intense and exquisite pleasure she had ever experienced before or, in truth, ever imagined she could endure. The thick stamen drove into her with an intensity and tirelessness that caused her insides to flutter, while the flower's furry head kept repeatedly teasing and titillating her from the outside. Wave upon dizzying wave of desire and pleasure combined to make her feverish. Her gyrations became one fluid movement, and her cries became one long moan. The wind picked up around her, cooling her overheated flesh, and causing her skin to tingle and her nipples to grow hard.

Up and up Catherine's desire circled and grew within her, like a whirlwind building up to a storm. The iris appeared to remain unaffected and determined, dutifully thrusting into her deeply while relentlessly brushing its stiff petals against her. Higher and stronger her feelings of lusty passion kept building until Catherine felt them spin into a crescendo of pleasure that exploded within her. The violent eruption released a tremendous flood of euphoric ecstasy trickling through her. The ecstasy quickly faded into a gently swelling bliss.

The stamen now stopped and withdrew somewhat, but it did not yet retreat from her body. It remained persistently inside her, hovering halfway in, without moving. Catherine did not wonder over this. She knew, by this time, that there was still more pleasure to come. In fact, she had learned that this strange and wonderful forest would continue to provide pleasure until there was simply no more pleasure to be had.

She waited delightedly for what would come next, and already she could feel fresh little tingles of awareness rising up within her all over again. Her body was swollen and drenched, and she could feel herself spasm lightly around the portion of the stamen that remained inside her. Her insides seemed to be grasping at it with each little tremor of pure delight.

In response to her newly awakening passion, the enchanted forest once again seemed to come alive. Catherine noticed that the roots that were holding her ankles were beginning to move, shifting slightly from within the earth below. The honeysuckle vines also began to loosen their grip on her wrists. Catherine sucked in her breath and yielded as Mother Nature carefully maneuvered her body to a position that better matched her newest innermost desires. But which of her fantasies was it playing out now? She felt the enchanted forest knew her better than she knew herself.

Smoothly, with only the slightest disturbance that had almost no effect on the stamen that was still firmly imbedded inside her, Catherine found herself suddenly facing the ground, hovering just above the rock she had previously been sitting upon, but this time she was held suspended in midair. During this maneuver, other honeysuckle vines had been busily weaving themselves into some kind of web that surrounded her, so that she was not obliged to simply hang there, struggling under her own weight, but was actually enveloped in a kind of leafy hammock that cradled her in a delicious aroma that reignited her senses. It offered support where needed, while leaving her bare where it would provide the most pleasure to be exposed. When all of these machinations were accomplished—in the space of a mere moment or two—her body was situated so that it resembled an upside-down V, with her hips at the peak and her torso and legs slanting slightly downward from there in both directions. Her legs were still held open wide and the stamen had not budged an inch from where it was lodged inside her simmering body.

Catherine felt the whirling desire building up inside her all over again. It was not achingly acute like before; now it was all just simple, unadulterated pleasure. The hammock allowed her just enough freedom of movement so that she could enhance her own pleasure as she wished, but no more. She noticed suddenly that there was a little knot in the flowered netting that protruded and rubbed against her swollen clitoris. All she had to do was jerk her hips in a little rocking motion to increase the friction between herself and the little honeysuckle knot. And already the stamen was steadily advancing again. She gasped in surprise as it once again filled her. It felt as if it was even larger in this position. Her body instinctively moved forward in an effort to escape the intrusiveness of the stamen's powdery appendage as it thrust itself against her insides. But when the hammock's constraints were reached, they recoiled, acting like a spring and forcing her back even farther onto the stamen. She cried out in exquisite agony, realizing that each and every reflexive attempt to escape would actually bring her back with double force!

Catherine struggled to remain motionless, but with every advance from the thick, sturdy stamen her body would instinctively jerk forward, causing the soft, pliant hammock to thrust her backward again and again. A momentum was building that she could not control. Her breasts popped out from between the web of flowers, and a stray honeysuckle vine that was whipping in the wind slapped at them mischievously. And neither the wind, nor the vines, nor the stamen—nor even Catherine's wayward body—could ease the delicious tension or slow its raging pace, so that it kept building and building, with all the elements working in perfect harmony to achieve a crashing crescendo. There was little more that could be done, other than to endure the torturous pleasure until that moment was reached.

This time, the iris's stiff petals tickled her nether hole mercilessly with each thrust home. And with faultless rhythm, the stamen's thrust forward always met her reflexive spring backward. She cried out with each explosive impact, and even the sound of her screams added to her exquisite desire that kept spiraling out of control. Her pleasure was so acutely intense that she felt oppressed by the knowledge that it would end, even though she knew there would be more pleasures to follow, perhaps even more intense than what she was experiencing now. She struggled to hold back her quickly approaching release, wanting to prolong the sweet agony for as long as possible. The elongated pleasure tore through her body, leaving her raw and inflamed, yet still crying out for more.

And it suddenly occurred to her that the entire universe was centered on her. Hadn't she known this, even when she was just a tiny babe, crying out for her mother? Then, she thought it out of ignorance, but now the thought appeared to be a result of a higher knowledge, and possibly all she had to do was acknowledge that it was so.

But none of this was important at the moment. All that mattered was that the forces around her kept giving her this pleasure. She could think of no more important endeavor than the one she struggled with now, and every part of her strained to keep her body from succumbing to the overwhelming sensations. But the pleasure assailed her from every angle—from the gently chiding whipping of the vines against her swollen breasts, to the excruciatingly deep penetration of the stamen that she was forced to not only endure but to meet head-on, to the little knot in her honeysuckle hammock that kept rubbing against her clitoris, to, finally, the coarse chafing of the iris's bristly bearded head as it teased and tickled her anus beyond what she could endure. All of these stimuli Catherine had to fight against in order to prolong her pleasure, and her efforts caused her desire to build with an intensity she had never felt before. The sky above her appeared to darken in response to the growing storm within her. It seemed to mirror her frustration in its angry countenance, and the wind also increased its energies as if to join in. Her nipples began to sting smartly from the whip of the punishing honeysuckle vines.

Like a clap of angry thunder, her satisfaction struck her, loud and deep and harsh. Her body shook with large, quaking tremors that startled her. She screamed in protest, but already the stark pleasure was waning into trickling waves that fluttered through her. But the force of it left her sated and content and subdued.

The wind died down, and Catherine now found herself

resting unencumbered in her flowery hammock. She turned onto her back and allowed it to rock her gently to sleep.

And so it happened that Catherine took up residence in the enchanted forest, without ever sparing a single thought to the life she left behind. The forest kept her so captivated that she could no longer remember that there was anything to go back to. Had she kept a memory of her other life, it would have only pricked or irritated anyway. But even this much was spared her. She could no longer call to mind even the smallest detail.

This new life consisted only of pleasure. Like the fairies she imagined to be all around her, Catherine flitted from one end of her enchanted forest to the other. She had developed a sort of primitive communication with these beings she believed were fairies. They did not speak, yet they were there with her. She felt she understood them. She had come to respect their reserved silence, believing them to be timid and skittish because she, too, now preferred to be kept hidden from others. Yet she acknowledged their presence in a number of innocuous little ways, such as leaving them treats here and there—much as she believed they did for her from time to time—and in wishing them the goodwill that she felt they had likewise brought upon her.

Yet real communication, as she had formerly known it to be, did not seem possible. That there was intelligence and reason around her she could not, for a moment, doubt. But there was no one to speak her language to, no one to address her in her native tongue.

One day, perhaps it was months or possibly even years after she had first discovered the enchanted forest, Catherine stumbled upon something peculiar that captured her attention. She instantly recognized it as something coming from the other world outside the forest, although she didn't know what it was or how she knew this. It was a strange object, something not indigenous to her forest. There was something about it that caused it to stand out from the rest of the surroundings, like something alien. Its colors were what she noticed first, for they had an unnaturally dull tint, completely void of the brilliance she had become accustomed to seeing in the wildflowers of the forest. These colors seemed a poor imitation, and she wondered how they had got there.

Curious, Catherine reached down and picked up the foreign object. It was not terribly large but it was quite heavy. It was orange and yellow, with orange bands coming out the sides of it. One of the bands appeared to be broken. It seemed that beneath its outer casing, it held more objects inside. She noticed that there was a strange seam all along the edge of it, and an eerie sense of déjà vu crept over Catherine as she grasped hold of the little tab at the end and slid it backward along the seam, opening the outer casing. She fished through the many different objects that were inside but, try as she might, she couldn't figure out what they were. The peculiar feeling stayed with her as she stared at them uncomprehendingly. But eventually she lost interest and laid the objects back down where she found them. Yet there was undeniably something strange in all of this, if only for the unusual effect it was having on her. Catherine stood up and looked around. And then she noticed something else—something she did recognize—in the plush woods nearby. More curious than ever, she moved nearer. Upon closer inspection, she saw that it was, in fact, hair. But it was hard to tell if came from an animal or human because, whatever it was, was hidden in the bushes nearby. Something stirred in Catherine.

She moved carefully, not really out of fear as much as instinct to be cautious. She tentatively moved some of the branches aside to get a better view, but then abruptly jumped back. The hair was attached to a skull! Just as Catherine had instantly recognized the overabundance of life stirring all around her in the forest, she now instantly perceived that life had gone from here. A haunting sadness welled up in her. She moved the branches away again and carefully brushed aside some of the fallen leaves and other debris. There was another brief moment of a kind of general, vague recognition, but Catherine was far too detached from the faded thing disintegrating into the earth to actually own it. She shook off the discomfiting stirrings. But she could not help feeling a powerful compassion for the woman who had died there.

Looking up, Catherine noticed that dusk was coming. For the first time since that day when she had first discovered the enchanted forest, she was afraid to be wandering alone in the dark. Yet she was hesitant to leave the poor girl alone. Acting on instinct, she carefully replaced the leaves and brush over the body, mindful this time to cover the woman's hair, as well. Next she darted off to a nearby field to collect a handful of wild-flowers. Uttering a small prayer for the woman's soul, Catherine placed the flowers on top of her leafy grave. With one last pause, she got up, brushing the leaves and the strange melancholy off her. Then, with the adroitness of a spirit, or a fairy, she flitted out over the flowery field, fluttering toward home and the pleasures that awaited her.

Disenchantment

Everything was going wrong and now, on top of everything else, she was late. Maryanne skittered over the wet cobblestones, rushing to get to the restaurant. She would be a mess by the time she arrived. But she'd had to drive four blocks away just to find parking!

Why was she even bothering? She tried to silence the pessimistic voice in her head but it would not relent. It reminded her that she had no reason to expect this guy to be different from any of the others. There was nothing special or noteworthy about him that made it worth the effort. Even by online-dating standards he had offered little intrigue, and with all the embellishing that takes place in preparing one's online profile, that was rather dismaying. She tried to recall what prompted her to go out with him, and then she remembered that he had caught her in a weak moment when, feeling unsettled and lonely, she suddenly longed for a normal life with an average guy. So here she was, on a Friday night, rushing around to meet this average or—more likely—less-than-average guy.

She took a deep breath and tried once again to assume a positive outlook. At least she was getting out of the house. It could be interesting. She might as well try to have a good time. There didn't have to be any entanglements. She couldn't hide forever.

And perhaps this one would work out differently. But she couldn't count on that and she knew it.

She dashed through the restaurant doors and found him waiting for her. Just as the little voice in her head had predicted, he looked nothing like his picture and yet she recognized him instantly. Something in his present look was more like what she would have expected anyway. Within their casual online correspondence, she had detected an inherent gentleness, a kind of considerateness in his demeanor that had initially captured and ultimately held her interest. While these qualities had not been evident in his picture, she recognized them in his face, and her reluctance eased up the tiniest bit. "I'm sorry I'm late," she murmured.

Dan stood up from the bench where he had been waiting and smiled warmly at Maryanne. Clearly he had embellished his height in his online profile, as well. She resented this; she could have at least worn lower heels to minimize the difference had she known. She tried to hide her annoyance. Yet he did not seem to mind so much; she noticed that his eyes were looking over her slender form with approval.

"Maryanne? You're so much more beautiful than your picture!" he said earnestly. Then he blushed slightly, as if embarrassed by this outburst. She had the impression that his comments, at least, were spontaneous and genuine. "Don't worry about being late," he said good-naturedly. "I figured you were having a tough time finding parking. I did get us a table, though."

He led her to their table and pulled out her chair for her. "Wow," he remarked as he sat down across from her, "those are some guns you're packing there!"

Maryanne drew back, startled, and Dan quickly gestured to her arms, once again embarrassed. "I mean, you must work out," he clarified.

"Oh…yes!" she said with a laugh, feeling the tension leave her. "I practice yoga," she explained.

"Yoga's quite the workout," he surprised her by saying. "I tried it myself a few times, but I found it difficult to hold many of the poses. I get distracted too easily. Let's see, what was that one? You stand sort of crouched with your hands high up in front like the bug…the locust, was it?" He put his hands up in front of him in an exaggerated simulation of the pose.

"The praying mantis," she corrected, laughing.

"Yeah," he agreed amiably. "That's it. Nearly snapped my hamstrings trying to do that one."

Maryanne tried to imagine this stocky, seemingly unsophisticated guy attempting yoga and suddenly burst into loud laughter at the thought of it. But when she recovered, she changed her tune, eyeing him sideways and saying, "Actually, you look like you could handle it." And it was true. Although he was a burly man, she could see at a glance that he was all muscle.

"Well, I might have exaggerated," he conceded. "I actually only strained them a little."

"That seems a bit more plausible…" she teased, surprised to find that she was flirting with him. The realization made her suddenly shy, and she tilted her head slightly downward in a reserved gesture she was in the habit of assuming to conceal her face. She could feel her cheeks growing warm and knew she was blushing. If Dan noticed her discomfort, he was considerate enough to pretend that he did not.

"I'm built mostly for hard work," he continued with a

matter-of-fact shrug. "Like an ox. That's how I manage to keep in some kind of shape. But you look like you live at the gym."

"Not really," she said, tilting her head a little bit more. But she was pleased.

"I'm sorry," he told her. "I'm gushing here. I'm really not obsessed with appearances. It's just that you're so toned and in amazing shape. I have to admit I find that attractive. Even your cheekbones. Wow!" He gestured around her face without touching her. "It's like they're chiseled out of marble or something." It was an earnest compliment, and it wasn't the first time Maryanne had heard it. But whenever anyone mentioned her amazing bone structure, all she could think of was the way the boys in grade school used to tease her, calling her "alien" because of the way her large eyes and high cheekbones dominated her face. If only she could get those children's cruel voices out of her head.

Dan casually reached over and brushed aside the loose hair that had fallen down over her face. From anyone else, this would have been too forward a gesture for Maryanne, but Dan did it with such simple aplomb that she hardly noticed that he had done anything at all.

"So what are you hungry for?" he asked, turning his attention to his menu.

"I don't know," she said disinterestedly. She picked up her menu, trying to think of something clever to say.

"I chose this restaurant because their food is exceptional. You mentioned in your profile that you were a finicky eater."

"I did?" she asked.

"I think you did," he replied, considering. "I'm not sure exactly what you said. Something gave me that impression."

Maryanne wondered what it was. He certainly was intuitive. She realized that she felt considerably more relaxed with him than she usually was on first dates—particularly blind dates—but even so, she had the urge to rock gently back and forth in her chair, another nervous habit she had picked up. Most people didn't mind it once they got to know her, but she knew it would be disconcerting for a man to see her do it on a first date. Yet with Dan, she wondered. He seemed to be the sort of man who would make a person feel comfortable no matter how odd his or her behavior.

"Well, anyway," he continued, "the food here is first-rate. The chef grows a lot of the vegetables in his own organic garden nearby. You can really taste the freshness. I figured you were probably into health food."

"Well, sort of," she said noncommittally.

Maryanne ordered a salad and Dan ordered a steak. But she showed no interest in her food when it arrived. Having consumed her second drink by then, she was finally loosening up.

"So have you ever been married?" Dan asked. Maryanne had been wondering when the conversation would come around to that. People were so obsessed with past relationships. She disliked talking about them. Besides, whoever told the truth when it came to that? Had a man on a date ever said, for example, "Yeah, I just couldn't seem to stop sleeping with other women"? Or would a woman ever admit, "Everything he did just made me want to bite his head off"?

"No," she said without elaborating.

"Did you never want to?" he persisted.

Maryanne felt she was treading in dangerous territory. Yet the drinks had loosened her up considerably so it didn't seem to matter so much.

"Yes," she replied honestly. "I'll admit I have thought about it a time or two. But…"

Dan waited a long moment before responding. When he did, Maryanne was surprised that he was still waiting for her to finish her thought. "But…what?" he prompted. She looked at him, impressed. Most of the men she encountered had the attention span of a fly.

"It's hard to explain," she began. "I've never really put my thoughts about marriage into words before." She thought about it for another minute. He was looking at her with keen interest, as if he really wanted to hear what she thought about it. His seeming interest encouraged her. "I believe marriage is impossible," she said. Then she shook her head vigorously, causing her hair to shift back and forth over her face. "No, not impossible. That's ridiculous. People get married every day. What I mean is, it's hopeless…and destructive and doomed to fail."

He seemed genuinely taken aback by her comment, although there was a little smile playing about his lips upon hearing it. He appeared to find her vehement passion over the matter charming. She was surprised, too. She had never admitted her true feelings about it to anyone before. "Hopeless and destructive and doomed to fail?" he repeated, following it with a low whistle. "I could maybe see hopeless and destructive, or destructive and doomed to fail, but all three together…" He shook his head as if to say she'd gone too far. She could see that he was trying to make her laugh—and perhaps he wanted to minimize the severity of what she'd just said in the process—but now that she had confided in him she felt like explaining what she meant.

"It's hopeless and doomed to fail because it can't possibly succeed, and I think it's destructive to the people who have to learn that the hard way. The truth is that marriages don't succeed, not in the truest sense of the word. People stay married sometimes, it's true, but is it really what they thought it would be when they walked down the aisle together?" She said this without the slightest bitterness, which only seemed to give credence to her words.

Dan put down his fork (she had not yet picked hers up), giving Maryanne all of his attention. Both were now fully intrigued and absorbed by the topic. "But how could you possibly know this if you've never been married yourself?"

"I don't have to go through something myself if I am able to learn from watching others," she replied. "Have you been married?" she asked suddenly.

"Yes," he admitted.

"Well..."

"Yes, but even having failed, I still believe in the institution of marriage. And I liked being married, for the most part."

"For the most part?" she said.

"There were moments..." He paused, at a loss for words to explain.

"Of disenchantment?" she asked with a smile. "A slow, ongoing letting go of expectations, like gradually sliding down a not-so-steep hill?"

Dan looked at her with curiosity. "So, if not marriage, what then? Living together? Dating?"

She was feeling strangely reckless. And Dan was somehow drawing her out in a way that other men were not usually able to do. Something in his demeanor put her at ease. "To be perfectly honest, I don't think it's possible for a man and a woman to stay together for any significant amount of time. Relationships seem to have a shelf life."

He jerked back in surprise. "Isn't that supposed to be the guy's position?"

She laughed. She wondered what he was thinking about the things she was saying and was surprised to discover that she cared. In fact, she wanted to make him understand. She thought for a moment of how to illustrate her point.

"See that couple over there?" she began, exclaiming immediately afterwards, "Don't make it so obvious!"

Dan nodded conspiratorially and tossed his napkin on the floor with an exaggerated flourish. Maryanne struggled to contain her laughter as Dan made a show of casually bending over to pick up his dropped napkin while surreptitiously stealing a glance in the direction she had indicated. The straightforward, uncomplicated person that he was made the scene all the more comical.

"The woman who looks like she's been sucking on a sour ball?" he whispered after a long and lengthy ordeal just to get a glimpse.

Maryanne giggled. "That's her," she confirmed. She leaned in and lowered her voice, growing more serious. "Her husband has been staring openly at me all night."

Dan looked momentarily confused. "Well, you're a beautiful woman," he said in a matter-of-fact manner, as if to add, "What do you expect?"

"Right in front of her!" she added more adamantly.

Dan drew back and paused, but there was a light coming on in his eyes. "Oh, yeah, women hate that."

"Women hate that," she echoed, "because it's destructive. It causes them to deteriorate inside. Don't look at me like I'm being overly dramatic. And I realize that it's in a man's nature to constantly observe women. They can't help it, as they're so quick to point out, but that's exactly what I'm saying. That's why it's impossible for relationships to work."

"But it seems like a rather small thing, considering…"

"Well, of course, I'm not just talking about *looking* here. What I'm referring to is that *interest,* that overabundance of attentiveness and courtesy that men show to the women they have not yet been intimate with. In and of itself, even that might be tolerable if not for the utter *lack* of interest they show to the women they *have* been intimate with!"

"Do you really think it's as bad as that?"

"It's often worse."

"Well, if women know this about men, and it's the way men are, as you say, can't the women work around it?"

"They can and do work around it," Maryanne replied. She was completely relaxed now and spoke conversationally, explaining her philosophies without the slightest rancor. Her eyes were wide, and she even felt a bit excited. "But that doesn't mean they're not deteriorating while they're doing it."

"Forgive me if I seem a little callous here, but aren't you blowing this a little out of proportion? Most of the guys I know would never do any more than look."

"Whether or not he acts on his interest in other women is irrelevant." Maryanne was pleased that Dan wasn't simply patronizing her, or, worse yet, trying to steer her away from what some men might consider an uncomfortable topic. He was taking her seriously enough to disagree with her, and she appreciated that. "Because the damage will already be done. See, women also have instincts that appear to favor more short-term relationships."

"Okay, now you definitely have my attention."

"A woman's most fundamental need, at her core—and I'm not talking about human survival here but *female* survival, something she needs to keep her femaleness alive—is to be desirable." She paused for effect, noticing that he was hanging on her every word. She let this first idea sink in before completing her thought. "Almost every single natural behavior of a man—*after* he's had sex with a woman—is designed to diminish her belief that she is desirable. I think it is an unconscious effort to ultimately destroy her desirability to other men."

Dan sucked in his breath. "Wow!" He turned discreetly to look at the woman she had singled out before, this time observing her more carefully. Maryanne casually observed the woman as well. The couple had clearly been together a long time; the wife was even beginning to resemble the husband. She had little, if any, visible signs of femininity or sexuality left. There was a sadness behind her eyes that somehow softened the bitter twist of her lips. She was staring past her husband indifferently. Dan had caught the husband ogling Maryanne when he suddenly turned, and the man looked guiltily away. Dan turned back to Maryanne, his expression tragic. She smiled.

"You see?" she asked, knowing that he did.

"You make an interesting point," he conceded. "But I'm not ready to accept defeat just yet. Let me think about it a minute." He picked up his fork and knife and cut off a bit of steak. Maryanne watched him as he chewed on it thoughtfully. She couldn't help chuckling as she watched him, a bit too gleefully for the occasion perhaps, but she was so delighted to be able to have this kind of open discussion with a man. She had always known that her observations were different from those of other people, men and women alike; hers were much more cynical and pessimistic. She couldn't help seeing things for what they were, but she had learned to keep most of these observations to herself. She tried her best to acquiesce to the accepted viewpoint, seemingly agreeing with all that was politically correct in an effort to fit in with those around her. At times she felt like a chameleon, always changing her own brilliant colors to mimic the much less appealing ones of those around her. There were times when she even doubted herself, wondering if she really was viewing things correctly after all, but her efforts to change only gave more credence to her original viewpoint and she was obliged, however reluctantly, to keep it. So now, to actually share that viewpoint with another person—a man, no less—and actually have it cause him to stop and think was terribly exciting for her. Dan, for all of his optimistic thinking—she had spotted that in him immediately—was not one to ignore a strong argument that had merit. She waited eagerly to see what he would do with the ideas she had shared with him, sipping on her drink in the interim.

Dan swallowed his steak and looked at her. Just as Maryanne expected, he was cleverly going to place the ball back in her court by pointing out some similar inconsistencies in women. "You know," he began tentatively and thoughtfully, clearly enjoying the conversation as well, "there are plenty of women out there who lose interest in men, too, after they've had their way with them…playing all kinds of cruel games and generally screwing with their heads."

But Maryanne had already thought of this. "If you think about it for a minute," she countered, "you will realize that that actually proves my original point. A woman who plays head games with a guy usually isn't all that interested in him to begin with. She either wants something from him or she's giving in to his persistent advances for some other reason. She doesn't have any genuine feelings for him. And this is the point—a woman's disinterest is the only thing that can hold a man's interest. He's still interested in her because *he really hasn't had her yet*. She allows him to hang on because it satisfies her need to feel desirable, but since she doesn't really love him, she'll just keep using and abusing him. And for as long as she doesn't care about him, she will keep his full attention. But if she falls in love with him, what happened to that woman over there will eventually happen to her. Even if a man tries to fight this instinct, his soul will be crying out for someone new. He might not have the guts to act on it, like you said—but *instinctually* he will become more aware and interested in almost every other woman, and she will *know*."

Dan was shaking his head, but his mouth was full of food so she continued. "Just think about it. It's true."

He forced his food down with a gulp. "So if you really believe this, you go out with a guy, what? Once? Twice? How long before it starts to go to shit?"

"I don't know," she replied thoughtfully. "I haven't figured that out yet." She dipped her head, suddenly shy, and tapped her long, glossy fingernails together in front of her nervously.

Dan gave her a funny look, but he was smiling. "Come on," he teased. "You must have an idea. How many dates does it take to get to the jerk inside the man?" he asked with the same rhythm and inflection as the cartoon owl who asked, "How many licks does it take to get to the center of a Tootsie Roll lollipop?"

Maryanne laughed. "Remarkably few, if I were to guess."

"So how am I doing?" he asked. "Will I even make it through the night?" Maryanne looked at him in surprise, and he cleared his throat. "I'm sorry…I didn't mean that like it sounded. Jeez!" He shook his head. "We *are* jerks!" But his eyes still sparkled with humor.

"I don't think of men as jerks," Maryanne told him. "I just think that relationships between men and women have a short life. Does it have to be somebody's fault? Women are just as responsible."

She once again had his full attention. "Go on," he said, narrowing his eyes dubiously.

"I'm a realist." She shrugged. "But most women aren't. They stubbornly deny what is happening and ignore their inner voice that is crying out for attention—attention that can only be found in a new relationship. Now both of them are ignoring her and she really starts to deteriorate. Perhaps women are too sensitive. Perhaps our feminine egos are too fragile. But there it is. Many women just go with it, like that woman over there seems to have done. But you can see by looking at her that something is missing, right? You can see that the life has gone out of her? Probably she's moderately healthy otherwise, and lives a fairly normal life. But her femininity and passion are utterly gone."

Dan snuck another glance at the woman and seemed dismayed to find her husband eyeing Maryanne yet again. "Why doesn't she leave that bastard?" he asked, perturbed.

Maryanne laughed. "When she married him, it had probably already started. That's why women are so hot on marriage. They think it will bring his interest back. When it doesn't, I'm sure these women are devastated at first. That's why *Cosmo* sells so many magazines with nine hundred different ways to get his attention. But, by then, who knows? Maybe there were kids on the way, or perhaps she depended on him financially. And if you push a part of yourself aside for long enough, it will eventually die." She looked at him. "You see, he couldn't help that her loving him took all the intrigue away, and she couldn't help that having no power to intrigue made her unappealing. Both were simply responding to what was."

"And you still date, believing this?"

She laughed. "Like most women, I am a hopeless romantic."

"Do you believe in love?"

"I do! That's just it. But I think that sometimes love means letting go."

Dan sat there for moment, thinking. "You know," he said, "what I'd like to do is prove you wrong. I really would. But in order to do that, I'm assuming I'd have to come up with some evidence. Maybe find some shmuck out there who's actually still enamored by the woman in his life. That's really what we're talking about here, right? She wants to feel special. She wants him to treat her like she's special, even though the instinct inside him is saying, 'Been there, done that, losing interest,' right?" He waited for her to nod her head. "I think there *are* men out there like that. Men who are more interested in the woman they're with than any other women."

"Well!" said Maryanne, impressed. She couldn't help finding his optimistic, I-would-like-to-fix-this attitude extremely attractive. "You thinking it and it being true are different things," she reminded him.

"Okay, but, come on now," he said in an extremely reasonable, almost reproving tone of voice. "*Your* thinking that you're right doesn't necessarily make it true, either."

And in that moment Maryanne knew that she was hooked. What she was going to do about it, she hadn't yet decided. But what she had discovered in him so far—his intelligence, his open-mindedness and now, his strength of character—made him suddenly seem irresistible. She knew that her instincts had already singled him out. And in that instant, in that sudden moment of realization, she felt joy—but only for that single instant. For in the next, she had already begun to mourn the inevitable loss.

"Touché," was all she said.

As if he already sensed his victory, Dan settled back in his chair and relaxed. Was it just her imagination, wondered Maryanne, or was he, too, already aware of it?

"Mmm," Dan murmured thoughtfully. "So now all I have to do is find a man who is smart enough to override this... instinct, as you call it, and continue to show an interest in the woman he's with. Is that it?"

"Well, that would definitely be a good start."

"Mmm," he said again. His lips twitched to hold back a slight smirk that was struggling to be set free on his features. "Where could I find such a man?" Encouraged by her growing smile, he continued on this theme, making a pretense of looking around the room curiously. "I wonder where," he murmured.

Maryanne decided to play along. She, too, began to look around the room, but more skeptically than he was doing. "I don't know," she said doubtfully. "It doesn't look promising."

"Well, then," he suddenly announced with conviction. "I guess I'll just have to prove it to you myself!"

Maryanne threw her head back and laughed. Game, set and match! she thought, admiring how he'd handled it. But when she recovered, she looked him over doubtfully, one eyebrow raised high. "You?" she asked. But she was only teasing him, and they both knew it.

"Sure, why not?" he replied with a casual air. "I always say, if you want something done right you have to do it yourself."

"So who's the lucky girl?" she now wanted to know.

"Ooh." He tried to look a little put out. But he recovered quickly. "You realize the only way you're ever going to know for sure whether or not I'm proving you wrong is if you're right there, seeing it for yourself."

"Mmm." Now it was Maryanne's turn to consider. "I guess that seems fair." But truthfully, aside from this bantering, which was engaging and fun in and of itself, she really had no idea if he was serious about it. Was this just a line to get her home for the night? Probably. But what did it matter? If it was just a line, it was certainly one of the more original ones she'd encountered.

Just then, the waiter came to offer them dessert.

"You've barely touched your food," Dan observed. "Was everything all right?"

"It was fine," Maryanne told him. "I just wasn't very hungry."

He looked at her suspiciously for a moment, but didn't say anything more. But she knew what he was thinking. People accused her all the time of being anorexic. But she loved her body the way it was.

As they left the restaurant together, she was suddenly filled with that jittery excitement that comes with a new romance.

"How about a little dancing?" Dan suggested. "Would you be into that?"

Maryanne smiled. "I would."

She was not, however, a confident dancer, and she was pleased when Dan seemed content to slow-dance. Being close to him and having all of his warm, undivided attention directed at her as he led her across the floor acted like a cathartic for her libido. She felt ready and even eager for a more intimate embrace. But he appeared to be in no hurry and she, too, felt remarkably at ease and relaxed. Before she even realized it, they had danced and talked and laughed the night away.

She was surprised when he drove her back to the restaurant.

"Where did you say you were parked?" he asked.

"Oh! Uh, let me see." She had fully expected him to want to take her home, or at least somewhere private. She was so taken aback by his casual manner that she momentarily forgot where her car was. She glanced at him, confused. She knew she had given him all the right signals. She was certain he was attracted to her. What on earth was going on? "It's that street over there. Yeah, that one. And it's the black car, a few blocks down." She was completely flummoxed, and not a little disappointed.

"I had a wonderful time," Dan told her, and she noticed that there was surprise in his voice. She wondered if he had felt some of the same misgivings about their date that she had.

"Me, too," she said, blushing when it came out sounding like an accusation.

Dan chuckled knowingly. "Believe me," he said with emphasis, "I would love nothing more…"

Maryanne stared at him, surprised that he had read her mind.

"Oh!" she said again. It was disconcerting—albeit refreshing—to be confronted with such honesty.

He parked behind her car and shut off his engine. "If I'm gonna get around this whole male instinct thing and prove you wrong, I'm going to need a strategy," he told her. "My plan is to let the anticipation build for a while, you know, kind of work my way up to sex. I actually believe in the old adage that the harder you work for something the more you appreciate it."

She stared at him, stunned. "Are you serious?" It was hard to tell because he was grinning at her.

"Sure. Kind of. Yes!" He opened his car door and got out. She didn't even reach for her handle, knowing him well enough already to realize he was coming around to open her door for her. He even took her hand and helped her out of his car. But once she was outside, he blocked her from going anywhere. "Of course there's another part to my strategy, too," he admitted.

"Oh? And what might that be?" she asked, a little breathless.

"Well, I figure if I kiss you—and I'm not talking about a tight-lipped little prim-and-proper good-night kiss here, but a full-fledged, no-holds-barred, French, Italian and Portuguese all in one, make-out kiss—it'll help build my anticipation and keep me on pins and needles until the next time I see you."

"Portuguese?"

"Don't question me," he said, gently cupping her face in his hands.

She was still laughing when his lips touched hers, brushing them ever so lightly at first, but the laughter suddenly died in her throat, because he really did kiss her then, just like he said, with a full-fledged, no-holds-barred, French, Italian and Portuguese all in one, granddaddy of a kiss. She clung to his shoulders for support. His strong arms held her up as his hands moved possessively over her back and hips. His lips and tongue seemed to be consuming her. When he finally pulled away, she stared up at him in surprise.

And later, as Maryanne tossed and turned in her bed into the next morning, she wondered if it was for himself or her that he was building anticipation.

Whatever Dan's intention, they were both eager to see each other again after that, and they made plans for the following night and then the night after that. It went on like this for several weeks. They spent more time together than Maryanne had ever spent with a man, and yet they had still not become intimate—at least not in the truest sense. Dan always refused to take her home. Sometimes he would even go so far as to please her right there in his car, when what started out as one of his good-night kisses ended with her trembling in absolute pleasure after he somehow managed to get beneath her clothing and find just the right places to touch her.

"But I want to please you, too," she'd say, really meaning it, and not just offering herself because she felt that she ought to because he'd pleased her.

"Not yet," he'd tell her. "I want you know how much I appreciate you. I want you to *believe* it."

And she did. By the time he finally took her home for their first real night together, she was utterly convinced that she had somehow breached the ordinary parameters of relationships as she had come to know them and discovered something truly different and exceptional.

Dan had shown the ultimate self-control up to this point, but when at last she presented herself to him in a little silk negligee she picked out especially for the occasion, he finally lost control. With a strangled groan of anguish he embraced her, moving his hands all over her, trying to touch her everywhere at once and, in his enthusiasm, tearing the delicate fabric.

Maryanne laughed delightedly. She was filled with feminine arousal. She had never in her life felt more desirable, and she knew that because she felt so lusty and desirable, she *was*.

"God, how I've wanted you," he moaned. He suddenly picked her up, holding her close in his warmth as he carried her to the bed. She could not wait to feel him inside her.

They made love their first time in a kind of frenzy, with Dan holding back for as long as he was able, trembling violently with his effort. He came to her in the ordinary missionary position, but there was nothing ordinary in the way he held her, cradling her shoulders and head in his strong arms, and gazing down into her eyes in between bouts of passionate kisses. He had that wonderful feel and smell of a clean-shaven man, and Maryanne wrapped her limbs around him in eager delight. A kind of aggressive passion welled up in her, and she dug her fingernails into his back. This seemed to push Dan over the edge, and his thrusts began to quicken with his impending release. But suddenly he stopped short, holding himself very still to recover his control, and shaking violently with the effort. Maryanne looked up at him in wonder and he smiled into her eyes.

"Almost lost it there," he groaned. "You've got me in knots."

"Go ahead if you want!" she encouraged.

"No. You first."

And once again she was reminded of how much she meant to him, and her own arousal soared to be so valued and so desired. She kissed him with all the passion she felt. He moved with her, assisting her, maintaining control and using his hands and lips and everything else he could think of to please her. When she finally cried out with her release, he lost the last bit of his control, crying out with her.

Afterward he was not quick to release her, but held her quite close, remaining firmly embedded in her as he spoke in a low, intimate voice. "You're an amazing woman," he told her, and his eyes seemed to be trying to communicate something more to her as his gaze burned into her.

It was not long before they were both aroused all over again, and this time he had no difficulty prolonging their lovemaking, switching positions numerous times before Maryanne found herself being taken the way she liked best, on her hands and knees. With this she went wild, flinging her hips outward toward Dan in a most enticing erotic dance. Her sudden abandon roused him beyond what she had seen thus far, and she was once again struck with her own femininity and allure. She felt exceedingly sensual. All her inhibitions melted away, and she audaciously continued her dance until the pleasure finally became too much for her and a thousand little sensations exploded within her. Meanwhile, Dan paused to allow her to achieve the full spectrum of her release.

Maryanne smoldered in the aftermath for a few moments. But then, craving a more intimate embrace, she lifted her body up against him, so that she was on her knees and leaning back on Dan's chest. He immediately acclimated to this new position, wrapping his arms around her body to offer support while lunging upward into her body. He moved his hands over her, squeezing her nipples with one while gently stimulating her clitoris with the other. Filled to overflowing with tender affection, Maryanne reached her lithe arms behind her to reciprocate the embrace, gliding her long, manicured nails up and down along his firm backside. Every now and then she would dig her nails into his flesh—just hard enough to stimulate but not to hurt—egging him on as he tirelessly thrust up into her. The lust was consuming her yet again, and she nimbly turned her upper body toward him suddenly, clutching his face in her hands almost violently so that she could kiss him. A kind of euphoric aggression reared up in her with her sudden awareness of her feminine power, but the soft, warm contentment that she was blanketed in overruled all.

"Why do you never eat?" Dan asked her later.

"I eat!" she replied.

"I haven't ever seen you eat," he countered. "And you're so thin." She was quiet, so he carefully maneuvered himself to look at her face without disturbing her much. "I'm not trying to stick my nose where it doesn't belong, or fix you or anything like that," he said. "I just want to make sure you're okay. And to let you know that I understand if you ever need a friend."

"You understand?" she asked curiously. There were myriad things she normally said when someone brought the subject up, but at the moment she was too weakened by the intense lovemaking to get sufficiently worked up to a defensive status.

"My sister is anorexic," he told her. "She's a beautiful woman and I can't stand that she suffers so much simply because she doesn't know it."

Maryanne stared at him, speechless.

Dan kissed her lips tenderly, holding her face in his hands. "I would hate it just as much if you didn't know how beautiful you are."

She smiled. "You certainly know how to make a girl feel beautiful," she admitted. And it was true. Maryanne suddenly felt like a goddess with a body as supple and sensual as a cat's. In the days that followed, she basked in the glow of being one with another and having it mean everything to him. She raced to see Dan at the end of each day, longing once again for that intense pleasure of being accepted and adored and desired. Within a week, she was struck with the astounding realization that she was in love.

When it first occurred to her, Maryanne was alarmed. What about all her philosophies about love? What about the conclusions she had reached about relationships over her lifetime?

But she told herself that this time was different. She could clearly see, even in this incredibly short period of time in which she had known him, that Dan was different than any other man she had known before. He had already exceeded everyone else in her heart.

She had no choice but to try, she told herself. She must find the courage to see it through.

And already, she harbored secret little fantasies and dreams of their life together. They kept growing and building deep within her mind and heart. Her long, lonely past was behind her. A life with Dan was in front of her.

A month had passed since the night she first met Dan, discouraged and stressed and apathetic. She had hardly put her best foot forward that night, but he had looked past everything else and discovered something special in her. And unlike any other man she had ever known, he had proven himself to her. Tonight she would show him how much *she* appreciated *him*. Tonight she would prove herself to him.

Maryanne trembled with anticipation as she went about her day. She took the day off work so that she could accomplish all that she planned. She began with an arduous trip to the salon and, by the time she left, there was not so much as an inch of her body that had not been buffed, waxed, filed, exfoliated, styled or in some other way enhanced. She could hardly afford it, but all that she had to do was picture Dan's face and suddenly she knew that it was money well spent. Besides, she could tell by the way she was tingling inwardly that she had to be positively glowing outwardly. She couldn't wait to see Dan's expression when he saw her.

But then, having gone to so much trouble and expense already, she felt that she ought to have something fabulous to wear, both in and out of the bedroom. After all, with this being the anniversary of their first month together, it was important that she show Dan that she was willing to make the effort to please him.

The day flew by in a haze of anticipation at the prospect of delighting a loved one. Everything was a success. Maryanne not only found the perfect dress to complement her slender figure but it just happened to be in Dan's favorite color. Suddenly feeling a bit naughty and bold, she followed this purchase up with stockings and a garter belt. She would wear that—and nothing else—under her dress. She debated with herself over whether she should tell him what she was wearing ahead of time or let him discover it when he undressed her. She could imagine teasing him with it at the restaurant. But then again, the surprise when he discovered it himself would be memorable as well. She tried to make up her mind as she headed home to put on her makeup. Glancing at the clock, she realized with a start that she was actually running late.

They had agreed to meet at the same restaurant where they first met in person. Maryanne felt a strange sense of déjà vu as she rushed through the streets to get to the restaurant. Once again, parking had been impossible.

But none of that mattered when at last she reached the restaurant, cheeks flushed and a brilliant smile on her face. She felt such keen excitement that the mere sight of Dan, sitting in the same spot where she had seen him for the first time, caused her heart to flutter unnaturally and her breath to catch in her throat. But when he turned to face her, the smile died on her lips.

"What's wrong?" she whispered breathlessly.

"Not a thing, now that you're here," he replied with his usual, good-natured manner. But before Maryanne could even accept or reject this, he stood up and turned toward the hostess without having given her more than a cursory glance. "Here she is," he said to the woman apologetically. "I really appreciate you holding the table."

And with that Maryanne was suddenly being ushered along behind the hostess, with a little nudge from Dan to the small of her back. She felt trapped between the two of them and suddenly terribly claustrophobic. In the back of her mind, she had a premonition of something tragic about to occur but she ignored it, turning her mind angrily to the moment instead, and thinking that she didn't really care whether or not the hostess had to hold the table. That was what hostesses were paid to do, after all. Why must Maryanne be flung around like a rag doll, without even so much as the courtesy of a greeting just to make life easier for the restaurant staff?

Maryanne kept walking but she turned her head toward Dan as she went, prepared to toss a flip remark along these lines in his direction. But the remark instantly died in her throat. She saw that his eyes were glued on someone else, and she knew without even following his gaze who it was that had captured his interest. It was a woman that she had barely noticed a moment before, except perhaps in that way women do tend to notice other women. She suddenly remembered her in vivid detail. She could almost visualize each and every feature at the same moment that Dan was seeing it, just by watching his eyes move up and down over the woman with keen interest.

And then Dan's eyes met Maryanne's.

They arrived at their table. The woman in question had passed by and was gone. Maryanne fumbled with her chair and clumsily seated herself. She felt awkward and ridiculous. She dug her nails into her palms and tried her best to appear nonchalant.

She noticed with another wave of humiliation that Dan's eyes were full of remorse.

"I'm sorry," he said solemnly. Maryanne merely looked at him with a confused expression, as if she had no idea what he could possibly be sorry for. Her lips were formed into a small, humorless smile. She wanted to brush the matter aside but she didn't trust herself to speak. "Look, I know that you're upset. You saw me looking at that woman, right? I'm sorry. It was like…I didn't even realize I was doing it until I saw your face."

"You have nothing to be sorry for," she told him, praying he would drop the subject. But she could hear that her voice held that tone; the tone was a dead giveaway that there *was* something to be sorry for. She tilted her head to hide her face and pretended to examine the menu. Above all, she desper-

ately hoped that he wouldn't humiliate her further by patronizing her with some perfunctory compliment. She far preferred
him to continue to not notice her at all. She tried to think of
something to say to change the subject.

"You look beautiful tonight," he said, immobilizing her in
horror. Every word he uttered drove her further away from
him. "You're the most beautiful woman in the room."

"I worked late so I didn't even have time to change," she
lied. "I almost didn't show up at all, so you see your compli-
ments only make you appear less sincere." She definitely didn't
want him thinking she had gone to any trouble.

"Well, what I mean is that you look beautiful without having
to lift a finger."

She was in turmoil, but the smile remained stubbornly fixed
on her lips. Inwardly she was comparing this night with their
first date, when he had been indulgent over her tardiness and
took note of every detail about her with keen interest. But this
was really no surprise, she reminded herself. Hadn't she predicted this very outcome that first night?

"You're thinking that this is a sign that I am beginning to
do the guy thing and lose interest in you."

"What I was thinking was that I wish you would change
the subject."

"You see!" he exclaimed. "That's what I mean. If this didn't
really upset you, your eyes would be flashing with excitement
right now while you pointed out how right you were."

Maryanne was momentarily taken aback. He was perfectly
right. And she was impressed with him all over again in spite of
what had happened. She sighed. It was so disconcerting to
know that as she grew more attracted to him, he would only
grow less attracted to her. The waitress came and they ordered
drinks.

Maryanne was becoming more composed.

"Okay," she conceded, pulling her thoughts together. "Although I am hardly upset, as you suggest, I will admit that I was thinking that the disenchantment has already begun. Just as I predicted that it would. Just as I knew it would. I never for an instant believed it would be otherwise. So why should I be surprised or upset?"

"All because I looked at another woman?"

She shrugged. "That and other things."

He looked at her sideways, confused. "Other things?"

She was careful to phrase her words so that she didn't give her true feelings away. She would discuss it with him—she found that she was intrigued by the prospect of doing so—but she would never let him see how much he had hurt her. She could never let him know that she'd been fooled by him, even for a single moment. That would be the worst thing she could do.

"When I met you here tonight, every detail of our meeting was precisely the same as it was the first time, right down to how late I was." *Except that I worked ten times harder to impress you tonight,* she added to herself. "I planned it that way so that I could compare how you behaved tonight with how you behaved back then. Suffice it to say, you were more considerate, attentive, and much more intrigued with me when I was a stranger. So yes, I would say that it's already starting."

He stared at her, momentarily speechless. In the meantime, their drinks arrived. He sipped his thoughtfully.

"Maybe this…thing that happens with guys isn't what you think. Maybe it *seems* one way to you, but that's not the way it really is. I know, for example, that I have been thinking about you nonstop all day. Every minute that I waited for you in the front of this restaurant tonight was pure agony. My feelings for you are stronger than a month ago, so the only thing I can think is that somehow my behavior is not showing you how I really feel."

"That may be true," she said. "But what does it matter? I'm not a mind reader, so your behavior, not what you're thinking, is what has an effect on me." She suddenly remembered the way his eyes had moved over the woman earlier. It was precisely how they had traveled over her the first time he saw her. And now, for all of her efforts that day, he had yet to really look at her.

"Well, I'll just have to be more aware of it and try harder," he said. He took another sip from his drink. But he was suddenly anxious. "Will you allow me that—the chance to become a better man?"

She felt a tug at her heartstrings in spite of her unhappiness. Yet she couldn't help wondering why men clung so tenaciously to women when their instincts were telling them to let go. And she couldn't help being irritated with him, either. Why was he so intent on selling her something he had no ability to deliver? This could have been so much more fun if he had just allowed her to remain indifferent. But he had to push her for more and now she had stupidly allowed herself to fall for him. She found his disenchantment utterly despicable. And the worst part was, *her* disenchantment was the one thing that had the power to intrigue him all over again!

She was once again struck by the utter hopelessness of relationships.

She couldn't bring herself to answer his question either way, but luckily the waitress came by at that moment to take their order. For dinner, she ordered another martini.

With Dan once again the attentive pursuer, his eyes seemed to open suddenly and he really looked at Maryanne for the first time that night.

"If this is how you dress for work," he observed thoughtfully, "I think you should switch to a career in modeling."

She downed the rest of her martini in a single gulp and shrugged. "What, you think I look good tonight?" She said this as if it were the most absurd thing she had ever heard.

Dan laughed. "Yeah, I think you look good. Too good." He picked up her hand and carefully examined her perfectly manicured pink fingernails. "Mmm," he remarked thoughtfully. "I don't think they're working you hard enough over there."

"Well, you know how it is," she countered nonchalantly. His playful mood was catching. "Some of us make it look easier than others."

"I guess so!" he agreed emphatically. He turned to her hair, picking up a lock and examining it as he twirled it between his fingers. "And I would say that the air-conditioning in that place is set to the perfect temperature and humidity for hair. Just look at the condition of this curl!"

She turned her eyes as if to examine it with him. "Humph," she said, pretending to ponder the matter as if she had no idea that there were at least four different hair products forcing it to perform in such an exceptional matter. "I never noticed that before."

"Yeah. Those are some great working conditions you've got over there." His attention now turned to her face. She watched his eyes as they took in everything from her delicately shaped eyebrows to her shimmering lips. "Great working conditions," he repeated thoughtfully.

While it delighted her to hear these things, every single word only served to prove that she had been right. But she only smiled.

"I think I fucked up more than I realized," he said quietly. And she could feel herself melting for him all over again in spite of everything. But the little voice inside her head cried, "Don't! You'll only make it end faster!"

And she suddenly realized that it was not his fault or hers. It simply was. And she no longer wanted to talk about it. Why rail against what is? To accept things as they were was to truly live and experience life. To fight against those things was to prevent it. She looked at Dan with appreciation. The least she could do was accept him, and in order to accept him she must forgive him. And for the first time in her life she was able to accept and forgive herself, as well.

"What are you thinking?" Dan asked her.

"I was thinking that you look pretty good yourself."

"Well, unlike you, I actually had to work at getting present-able," he joked. "Shaved and everything, see?"

Maryanne laughed.

They were back on good terms again, and they flirted and talked and laughed just like always.

But even so, later that night, when it was time to go home, Maryanne felt like being alone.

"Can I just come over and tuck you in?" he asked.

"I don't know," she hedged. "I'm not sure I'm up for it."

"Listen," he told her. "I really want to be with you tonight—no, it's not about sex, I don't even want sex—but I want to be near you…to hold you. Come on. Can I, please, can I, huh?" He began to whimper like a puppy until she relented, laughing.

"Okay, maybe just for a little while."

And he was true to his word, simply wrapping her in a blanket of warmth as he snuggled up next to her in the spoon position.

"Shhh," he interrupted when she tried to move or speak. "I don't care how much you beg or plead, you are not getting sex!" She laughed, all the more amused because his raging erection was conspicuously poking into her back. "Now just settle down and go to sleep."

But all of a sudden Maryanne didn't want to go to sleep. She wanted Dan. And she was in a dangerously indulgent mood regarding wants; it was a mood to not only satisfy those wants but to surpass them.

She wiggled her backside into him enticingly and smiled when he groaned.

"Come on," he begged. "Play fair."

She moved against him again, more persistently this time. His hips automatically jutted forward in response. She continued to rub up against him rhythmically, slowly maneuvering herself until his erection found its way in between her legs. And still she kept undulating her hips back and forth over him, enjoying the exquisitely tantalizing foreplay.

She could feel his heartbeat pounding in time with hers, but neither of them was in a hurry to put an end to the delicious torment. They knew the moment would come when all of their movements and gyrations would at last cause his erection to find its own way into her. And when it finally did, only then did Dan clamp his arms and legs around her body to hold her firmly in place as he mindlessly drove himself into her. Their bodies, which were entwined together as one and still lying down sideways, were periodically propelled forward in time with his thrusts. Maryanne couldn't move so much as an inch, Dan held her so fully restrained. But she was content, for the moment, to simply bask in the pleasure of having him exactly where she wanted him. All of her instincts rose up within her, curling and mingling with her most intense desires. "Listen," her instincts seemed to be saying. "Listen to your heart and accept what is."

She passively allowed him to hold her during this exquisite assault for as long as she was able, relishing each and every deliciously agonizing moment of delayed gratification that it brought. The pleasure she would gain from prolonging and extending her own satisfaction would be immense. And in the meantime, she enjoyed every single thrust of his body into hers, delighting in the feel of him as he took her with reckless abandon. And she could tell that he was in no hurry, either, but, rather, he was in a mood to take his time and savor every stroke right along with her. She let her hands run over his strong, muscular arms, reveling in the way they so fully restrained her. She loved the feeling of being momentarily powerless and completely surrendering to the man that she loved.

Their bodies moved together in perfect harmony, with hers gracefully arching upward in time with his thrusts like a well-choreographed dance, and neither one wanted it to end. They remained entwined this way for the better part of an hour. But Maryanne's desire, which had merely been simmering so far, was suddenly about to erupt into a boil.

She began to struggle against him. Her hips were first to buck and thrash, and then her arms and legs followed. When he loosened his hold on her, she moved up onto her knees, clutching his hips to hers as she went so he would not leave her for a single instant. Her growing excitement as she now took control spurred him on even more. He glided his hands lovingly over her body, caressing her breasts and teasing her nipples. He let his fingers roam lower until they found her swollen clitoris and began prodding and teasing it mercilessly. She used her thighs to propel her body up and down on him in time with his thrusts. As his hands moved over her, so, too, did hers reach behind to caress him.

Maryanne moaned loudly with pleasure as she pumped her hips over Dan's rock-hard erection. She felt the giddying sensations of her impending orgasm rising up in her, causing her to become even more reckless in her utter abandon. She clutched his hips in her hands, pulling him into her even as she pushed backward, making his thrusts go deeper. Her nails dug into his flesh as she held him, but her aggressiveness only further inflamed Dan. He, too, became more impassioned, and his fingers on her clitoris became more forceful, coaxing and prodding the little swollen nub relentlessly. With his other hand, he pinched her nipples ruthlessly.

Maryanne's hips kept thrashing violently, even as the heady sensations of her orgasm began to erupt within her. In a sudden frenzy, she turned her face toward Dan's, and he immediately captured her lips in a passionate kiss. Her hands flew up around his neck and she clung to him so that she could kiss him more passionately. Her cry of pleasure was muffled by the kiss, but suddenly Dan's head flew back in ecstasy as his own release hit him. In that very instant, Maryanne's fingernails bore into the back of his neck, effectively paralyzing him. His body continued to ejaculate even more vigorously as she plunged her teeth into his neck and ripped out a large portion of his flesh. He could do little more than stare in disbelief as she began to devour him. She ate with relish, suddenly oblivious to everything else but her incredible hunger. Dan could not move or speak. His final moments were spent in an unfathomable paradox between the ultimate pleasure and the most unthinkable horror.

When Maryanne's hunger finally waned, Dan's head had all but been severed. She moved away from him, strangely at peace. It was, she told herself, for the best. There was no more self-loathing or regret. She had finally learned to accept herself, and ironically she had Dan to thank for that.

Maryanne sat on the edge of the bed, slender and straight-backed, with her head tilted slightly forward in that timid way that she had, and her hands clasped in front of her as if in prayer. She allowed herself to rock lightly from side to side, now that she was alone. She thought about the future. Unfortunately, it meant that she would once again be obliged to change her appearance and move on. But even that did not worry her overmuch. A chameleon who could blend into any environment was also an integral part of who she was. She could suddenly see the wisdom and harmony in everything that occurred around her. She would never again struggle against her own instincts or pine for a different existence. This was how things were, and from now on she would accept her reality for what it was. To struggle against it was, to Maryanne's way of thinking, living in denial. She smiled humorlessly when she thought of the myriads of sad, empty females who allowed their inner selves to be depleted by this fallacy of holding one man's interest and affection forever.

But she would never share her insights with anyone again. Doing so had only accelerated the process and brought about a quicker end. At all costs, she must learn to enjoy love for as long as possible before it was inevitably lost to disenchantment.

Dying For It

For the most part, they're like you'd expect. Or at least I found this to be so. I followed one of them for weeks and, although I was often shocked, I was hardly ever genuinely surprised.

Vincent was friendly, agreeable and bright. I always observed him from a safe distance, it's true, but his magnetism could be felt from far off. And you could see it, too, from watching those around him. They were always perfectly at ease and utterly charmed. Men and women alike found him irresistible. He had a healthy glow in his cheeks that belied any pernicious habits, dietary or otherwise. He might have been taken for a vegetarian.

I started following Vincent the very first night I discovered him. Before I was even fully conscious of it, parts of me were already tracking him from across the room.

Over the years, I had become quite a recluse. Not that I was ever the sort of person to win a popularity contest, but lately

I had become more withdrawn. It wasn't by choice, really, but more from a lack of social skills—in this field I had potential that never really got developed. I was too shy. And I was never any good at casual conversation. The trendy topics always seemed inane to me, and I could never think of anything to say when they came up. And even on those rare occasions when I did manage to think of something clever to contribute, I could never get it out successfully. My timing was usually off, so that my comments came too early or, more often, too late. Either that or I would suddenly become so timid, speaking so self-consciously and with so much anxiety, that the whole point would become lost in the utter awkwardness of my manner. In those moments, it was actually a relief to have my voice drowned out by someone louder and more confident. Eventually, I gave up. And my quietness, which might have made a more attractive woman appear demure or mysterious, rendered me all but invisible. I blended into the woodwork as inconspicuously as any ordinary knot or other imperfection. But although I am painfully shy and awkward around people, I still enjoy being around them. My need for human companionship is so strong that it doesn't even matter if no one notices me. I'm usually content to simply watch those around me.

This, and other more recent developments, had created a great restlessness in me by the time I found Vincent. I still remember the moment I first saw him with a vividness that has more clarity than the actual event, which took place in a kind of haze of orange lighting distorted by wispy vapors of cigarette smoke. I was sitting in a dim corner of a crowded bar. It was a noisy, run-down little hole-in-the-wall with low ceilings and outdated acoustics. On that particular evening, I was glad for the noise. Every now and then a waitress would stop and say something, which always surprised me because I had come to believe that I really was becoming invisible. I was halfheartedly sipping at a lukewarm hot toddy. The jukebox, which carried a wide variety of pop songs from every culture, was playing a tune that caught my attention. With each chorus refrain, it kept repeating the same unsettling idiom over and over again, and I felt my face grow warm with mortification as I waited fretfully for it to end. The strong, male voice, with its rich Southern twang, crooned out—rather insensitively, I thought—the words, *Lonely women make good lovers.*

As I listened to the song I couldn't help wondering how this popular country-music star, who no doubt had his choice of beautiful women, happened to know this. It was true, of course, which was why the song caused me so much discomfort. I knew firsthand how rare and extraordinary a thing a lover is to a lonely woman. All of her pent-up fantasies and cravings only grow stronger with the long periods of privation, building an enthusiasm in her that is difficult to contain. Naturally she's eager, as the country singer so aptly pointed out. She cannot help but feel appreciative. She is able to feast sumptuously on trifles scarcely capable of tempting more fortunate women. At least that was something, then. How could a woman who receives more than her fair share of attention comprehend the pleasure of, say, simply being noticed? Can the mere *thought* of a lover's touch cause her to tremble when there are men reaching for her at every opportunity? I have seen women turn away from a lover's caress in contempt, and it is the men, in those cases, who know of the pleasure I speak.

The men in the bar that night, however, did not appear the least bit interested in the country singer's advice. As always, they clustered deferentially around the most desirable women. I recognized their yearning enough to sympathize. But the women were distracted, although they laughed and flirted mechanically. One man in particular had fully captured their attention. He had captured mine as well. The influence of his charm was inescapable. I had been watching him with interest throughout the night.

There wasn't any one thing that was especially unique or exceptional in Vincent's appearance or personality. He blended in with other men brilliantly, and even had a peculiar ambiguity about him that caused you to wonder, after the fact, what it was that impressed you so much. In his manner—and I came to know it well in the weeks that followed—there was something completely and utterly charming. As well, I found his character to be extremely well-rounded. He was in every way confident, yet often humble. He was kind but not susceptible. He was amusing but never foolish. Of his attributes I could go on and on. The closest thing to a flaw that I was ever able to detect in him was his penchant for shallow relationships. He had an untiring aptitude for developing new acquaintances, but he never allowed anyone to come close to seeing the full spectrum of his personality. I understood the necessity of this, mind you, but I wondered that he never seemed dissatisfied with these fleeting connections, realizing, as he must have, how easily someone like him could have developed a closer bond. That he could capture a woman's heart was certain. If he were ever known, he would most certainly be loved. Isn't that what every living thing desires?

From among the beauties that were eyeing Vincent that night, he selected a rather—I felt—shallow and insipid woman. She had little to offer of either charm or substance. Even worse, there was a meanness about her that should have offended a man like Vincent. She was rude to those around her and even cruel to the waitstaff. I didn't know Vincent at the time, of course, but even so, she seemed so opposite to him that I wondered how he could tolerate her.

This was what triggered my curiosity, and it held my interest throughout the night. Watching Vincent interact with the woman, I became more and more convinced that he felt little more than antipathy, if not outright dislike, for her. He was, of course, charming and courteous—Vincent would never be needlessly cruel—but his aversion was evident. I could see it in his expression and detect it in the ironic tone of his remarks.

When they finally left the bar, together, I found myself following at a leisurely pace. I had no particular plan, nor was I working very hard to keep them in my sight. I was not in the habit of following people. I just kind of hovered in the distance, drawn as if by some kind of invisible force. I think I sensed that something peculiar was about to happen. The two of them being together seemed to foretell it.

It was remarkably easy. The woman happened to live in a nearby apartment and, it being a balmy night in the densely populated city, it was not surprising that they walked. Many times since that night I've hailed cabs and actually uttered the words, "Follow that car," which illustrates the strength of the force that drew me to Vincent. But there were usually other people scattered about, livening up the dark streets. Just like at the bars, I blended in seamlessly on city streets, with hardly ever a soul noticing me.

I wish I could tell you something novel and exceptional about the way it happened, or to perhaps add some small nuance to the legends and folklore. But it *is* novel and exceptional to actually watch it happening in real life, right before your eyes! I can assure you that the event was abundantly exceptional and even shocking as it is. I suppose people will always need to embellish an event, no matter how extraordinary it is. To the folklore I have nothing to add. The most remarkable thing, from my point of view as I peered in through a small opening in a curtain, was the ease with which it was carried out.

There is a remarkably powerful force at work, a force that,

once begun, is absolute and unstoppable. The force seemed to emanate from Vincent, seeping from his pores and fluidly engulfing the woman in its influence. Vincent became like something not from this world once his desire was unleashed. It would consume everyone and everything, even Vincent himself, in its ultimate need to be satisfied. And that's really what it appeared to me to be—some kind of inescapable, raw and powerful need. I was awestruck by the intensity of it. In my ignorance of what was about to occur, I remember scrutinizing the woman again and again, studying her to see what I had missed, but I could find no reason for the incredible animal passion that suddenly overcame Vincent. It was as if his very entrails had been clenched in a grip of iron until the passion was appeased. A red-hot fire burned behind his eyes, and his breath poured forth from raging nostrils. Oh, how I envied the woman in that moment!

But as Vincent's passion continued to escalate, I became alarmed. The intensity of his desire was frightening to see. It was clear that it was not just sexual desire that I was seeing, but some kind of rapacious need. It would consume her; of that I was suddenly certain. Even she appeared to recognize this, and she seemed to acquiesce under the inevitability of whatever it was as she simply handed herself over to him. It was as if she said, "Here, you need me more than I." How can words express what I witnessed that night?

I wasn't surprised—I was expecting it by this time, actually—when I saw the first flash of descending teeth, milky white and flawlessly sharp. Vincent held his victim wrapped securely in his arms, fully captive, albeit willing, as he spread precarious kisses over her lips and face and throat. There was a frightful light in his eyes. The woman was flushed bright pink from her forehead to her breasts. She clung to him in a kind of passionate frenzy. He paused for a moment, appearing to undergo some inner struggle, but it was easy to see that he had long since lost the battle. Even his features appeared to harden and congeal, making his gestures and movements seem forced and beyond his control. His fangs once again captured my eye, shimmering ominously in the light. At first, Vincent only brushed them lightly over the woman's skin—so lightly that it caused tiny goose bumps to rise over her flesh and a shiver to run down the length of her. A large vein was pulsing conspicuously from her neck to her temple. Although she could not possibly have known what was coming, she seemed to tremble with premonition. A single thread of saliva traced a shimmery trail behind the deceptively gentle fang as it caressed the throbbing vein for several long moments.

Vincent appeared to be falling under some kind of a hypnotic spell, and I saw his eyes roll up into his head as a look of pure euphoria came over his face. Then, in one quick, fluid movement, he buried both fangs deep into the engorged vein in the woman's neck. I could hear his groan of satisfaction from where I stood outside the window. He drank deeply, pulling in with his jaws and gulping greedily in an incredible feeding frenzy such as I had never seen before.

I have since learned that the human body can lose up to forty percent of the ten or eleven pints of blood it holds before shock sets in. At that point blood flow and oxygen is reduced, causing organs to break down and malfunction. Among the first of these organs is the brain. Consciousness is altered as a kind of lethargy blankets the brain. This is when the victim truly capitulates to the will of the vampire, readily and even eagerly. I have seen it time and again since that night, and I've come to believe that there is no more pleasant way to die.

With that first bite, Vincent fed for a period that was about as long as a person can hold his breath. I know this because I had inadvertently stopped breathing when I saw his fangs pierce the woman's neck, and I remained that way while he drew her precious lifeblood out of her. About the time that I was compelled to resume breathing or else faint, he, too, suddenly threw his head back and gasped for air. In time, I was able to estimate that these first feedings comprised somewhere between two and three pints of blood, which was not enough to kill the victim.

The woman had neither struggled nor uttered a sound. She appeared shocked and dazed. Dark red droplets of her blood shimmered on Vincent's lips. With his initial thirst momentarily quenched, he was once again composed, although still highly impassioned. He bent forward to kiss the woman's lips. This time, he kissed her more gently, almost tenderly, as he slowly and smoothly stripped away her clothes. She acquiesced to him entirely, yielding to his will as if she were under a spell. It was as if she had but one objective, and that was to honor his every last request. With what life she had remaining, she seemed determined to do her best to achieve this, and she only stirred when it assisted his efforts for her to do so.

At last she lay sprawled out before him, bare and pale and beautiful, as he, in turn, undressed. Naked, he took her to him, gently at first, but more savagely as she egged him on. She, too, was becoming more impassioned, seemingly reviving with her desire. She clung to him fiercely, provoking and urging him in turns, and becoming increasingly demanding. In a sudden turn of events, it seemed that she was now the aggressor, thrusting herself violently against him and digging her fingernails into his back. And Vincent, temporarily sated, acquiesced to her every whim, feeding off her responses and allowing her to dictate his movements. She struggled against him with her arms and legs, thrashing and tearing at him one moment and then clutching him in the next. He yielded to her completely, becoming deceptively patient and tender and sweet.

But I could see that his passion, which appeared to rise and fall in ever ascending waves that rushed and flowed like moods, was escalating again. He began to assert himself once more, grasping her hips to hold her still while he bartered for a kiss, or teasing her mercilessly until she did whatever else it was that he desired. I could see the terrible hunger steadily building in him throughout their lovemaking, and I became apprehensive as I continued to watch. He leaned down to kiss and lick her breasts, lapping hungrily at them with long, lingering strokes of his tongue. I knew his need could overtake him at any moment and I shuddered as I waited for what was to come. The woman, too, seemed to sense something approaching, and she clung to him with a desperate little cry. But he kept both of us in suspense for much longer than I expected, taking his sweet time while leisurely lapping at her breasts and circling his tongue aimlessly round and round the pink tips. It seemed that he would wear her skin away with his tongue, he worked at her breasts so fervently. I watched anxiously for that glimmer of white to descend from beneath his rosy lips yet again, and it did shortly thereafter. But this time, Vincent only grazed on the feast spread out before him, carefully piercing one nipple and then the next for a small sampling from each. The woman writhed beneath him, overcome with what must have been incredible sensations, I supposed. I waited breathlessly for her response, but to my surprise, all I saw in her countenance was pleasure. The incisions from his bites appeared to be so clean and precise that they hardly even left a mark, and the bleeding stopped almost immediately after he withdrew.

Meanwhile Vincent's passion still kept mounting and rising, and with each advance it seemed to me the woman was in a more and more precarious state. She had somehow revived, but was too caught up in the pleasure to notice the subtle changes in her unique lover. She pressed herself against him almost violently, crying out several times as her body shuddered and convulsed with the power of her orgasms. She appeared oblivious of any impending danger. Perhaps she thought, after all, that she had stumbled into the arms of an especially wild and adventurous lover. I bit my lip as I watched him get nearer and nearer the brink of that terrifying need that would erase the last of his control. But as for his victim, the closer he got to the edge, the more her pleasure seemed to intensify.

I gazed at them in a kind of aroused stupor, tormented by the conflicting sensations of envy and lust and horror. Strange, unimaginable thoughts raced through my mind. My very life seemed to flash before my eyes with the ideas that were filling my head. They were the fancies of a madwoman and yet I could not halt them. But I was distracted from my thoughts by the sight of Vincent picking the woman up and, with superhuman strength and swiftness, flipping her body so that she was now lying on her stomach. Without missing a beat, he jerked her up onto her hands and knees and smoothly reentered her from behind. In this final shift, he was now once again the aggressor, and I watched him struggle against his wild, insatiable hunger with the last vestiges of his control. It was clearly beyond him, even I could see that. I think he realized it, too, as he reached his hands around her body and captured her breasts in his hands. He pinched the nipples teasingly, causing her to cry out with delight, before clasping on to them for leverage. With her now so fully captive in the most erotic of embraces, he suddenly let loose with long, powerful thrusts like those of a piston from a powerful machine. With each plunge forward he seemed to gain power and momentum, so that he was driving into the woman with impossible force. And she encouraged him, crying out with pleasure and actually meeting his thrusts head-on! I watched, transfixed, as they thrashed about like something in the wild, both mindlessly pushing toward the dreaded crescendo. And then I saw that terrible light appear in Vincent's eyes. I gasped at the sight of it. His hips bucked savagely one last time as he threw himself into her all the way, and in the same instant he buried his fangs in the back of her neck. She stared at the wall in front of her with an expression of astonishment. She appeared to be both surprised and euphoric, all at once. I had never seen pleasure shape the features in just that way. Her body rose up in a kind of ecstasy as he simultaneously filled and emptied her. His buttocks continued to thrust spasmodically with his orgasm as he drained the last of her life from her body. When he finished, he withdrew both his penis and his fangs at the same time. Her final breath was released like a whispered sigh of satisfaction. After a stunned second, she dropped in a heap. Vincent gazed down at her before turning abruptly away.

Suddenly he appeared to be angry. I hid farther in the shadows as I watched him dress in furious, jerky movements. As for me, my mind was once again bustling with strange thoughts and sensations.

I was alarmed and distraught and enthralled, to the point where I thought I might lose my mind. Somehow I was able to accept what I had seen. But as time wore on I realized that I had done more than simply accept it, I *appreciated* it. I began to consider my discovering Vincent's secret incredibly good fortune. It seemed to me like something nearing divine intervention. I would not go so far as to suggest that it was of a heavenly nature, but I was sure that it came from some otherworldly realm. Warnings of souls lost to the devil came to mind, but for me, the source of this fortune was not even a consideration. There had been so little of opportunity in my lifetime that I felt it would be foolish to look this gift horse in the mouth. Some may consider me evil, but perhaps by the end of my tale they'll have formed a different opinion.

During those weeks when I followed Vincent, I barely existed. It was as if I was living in the space that separates two worlds. I rarely went home, and then only to address the most pressing details, such as to shower or change. I did little to maintain my life—or what I had now come to think of as my former life—abruptly and without notice leaving behind employment, household chores and so forth. I had long since lost interest in that life anyway, so I suppose it was not surprising that I would so quickly latch on to anything new. I had no idea how this strange discovery of a whole other existence was going to affect me. For all I knew, embroiling myself in it might well end my existence altogether, and put me in yet another dimension of which I knew nothing. But this, too, was fine with me.

Up to this point, I was only acquainted with the legends. I began reading everything I could get my hands on about vampires, the undead and anything else that might explain what I had seen that night, and yet I was aware that most of what I read was only speculation. Even so, I could not get enough of it, and I would read late into the mornings, too exhausted and exhilarated to sleep after a night of following Vincent. The stories and legends put my mind at ease as I cut off the last of my ties, and slowly filed away at my softer edges, filing and filing until the pain was too acute to endure.

Watching Vincent was addictive. As I grew to know him better, I felt myself becoming more and more infatuated with him, obsessed even. I sensed a certain kinship with him, accompanied with a strange belief that he, too, would feel it for me. For all of his charm and outgoing nature, he was, I thought, as lonely as I was. And yet, somewhere in the back of my mind, I knew this was foolish. What I understood were his passions.

I could relate to the desire and hunger that drove him. But, what he felt in those brooding, melancholy moments after his passion was spent, I never truly understood. At times, it seemed as if he hated his existence, but perhaps, in my desire to understand him, I had begun to confuse his thoughts with my own. And yet I could plainly see that he, like me, suffered.

The notion that vampires feed exclusively on blood, or that they kill multiple victims in a single night is false, or at least it was in Vincent's case. He had a varied diet, and he particularly favored French cuisine. He only fed on human blood out of necessity, usually about once every three to six days. I could always tell when he was ready again. There was a visible deterioration, a sort of rapid aging process that began to take effect. It affected him like a kind of depression, but perhaps only I noticed this because I knew him so well, for even in his weakest state he was still always the liveliest figure in any room. But after he fed! I often wondered that those around him were not frightened by the intense aura of power and energy that radiated off of him.

It might have gone on this way forever, with me lurking in dark shadows behind Vincent for the remainder of my life. I was never one to take action. Life always had to force its will on me. Those things that didn't simply happen to me didn't happen at all. It was the same with Vincent. Who knows what would have become of me if he hadn't intervened.

Like a car accident, it happened in an instant. It was so sudden and unexpected that my strongest desire became a stark terror for me when it finally arrived. In a swift turn of events, the follower was being followed. In a moment he was upon me.

I cried out in surprise. But I made an immediate effort to compose myself. Inwardly I tried to recall what I had planned in this eventuality, until I realized with dismay that I hadn't yet settled on anything definite.

"Who are you?" Vincent demanded in outrage.

"Ana," I said, dipping my head slightly in a nervous habit I had developed to hide my face. It was unnerving to have him standing so close that I could inhale his masculine scent, and even more so to have his fiery gaze fixed on my face. My heart was pounding so rapidly that I wondered if it would burst. It was becoming difficult to breathe. I began to feel faint. But with effort, I willed my heart to slow and I felt myself calming. Beneath the initial shock and alarm, I felt excitement…and even joy.

"That's not what I asked and you know it," he hissed angrily. He grasped hold of my arm but held it without hurting me. His hand was cool, but not deathly cold like I had expected. "Now, *who are you?*"

I was struck with a sudden fear. What if he simply ended my life right there in the street? I was the furthest thing from the women he normally chose. How on earth was I going to convince him to take me with him?

Yet I instantly disregarded this fear. Vincent was not a cold-blooded killer who would end a life for naught. And aside from this, I happened to know that he was hungry, and I had acquired a strange confidence from having seen some of his choices.

He was looking at me with a great deal of annoyance. Yet he appeared uncertain about what to do next. I searched for the words that would get him to take me with him to his house.

"I will tell you everything," I promised, speaking in the shy manner I had adopted of keeping my voice low and scarcely moving my lips. I struggled to overcome my nervousness enough to assert myself. "*If* you will take me to your house," I added firmly.

"How long have you been following me?" he whispered, looking me over suspiciously. It was clear that I had taken him by surprise, and he had no idea what to make of me, my manner, or how I spoke. I might have been Frankenstein to his Dracula, for the look he was giving me.

"I will tell you everything," I repeated more emphatically. *"At your house."*

I had no idea how much he knew. Had he sensed that someone was following him all along? Or had he just discovered me this night? My mind swam with uncertainty as Vincent, still having hold of my arm, nearly dragged me through the streets toward his house. I knew the way by heart, and as we progressed I had to hold myself back so that I wouldn't overtake him and actually lead him there.

His house felt curiously unfamiliar from the inside. It had appeared much brighter when I was looking in from the outside, but I saw now that the lighting was actually calm and soothing. Vincent tossed his coat on a nearby chair and approached me.

I abruptly turned away, looking longingly out one of the windows into the black night. I was assailed with so many sensations and doubts that I suddenly wished I were still only a spectator.

"What are you hiding?" he asked.

"I'm not used to being around…men," I admitted.

He was silent, but he continued to scrutinize me.

"Please," I said impulsively. "This will be easier for me if you look away. I can't think with your eyes boring into me." I could not believe my audacity but it was suddenly more than I could bear to have him staring at me like that.

"You will talk whether I look at you or not!" he exploded, causing me to jump. But seeing my discomfort, he reiterated more civilly, "I have no idea who you are. I would be a fool to just turn my back on you."

"But it's not like I could hurt—or kill—you, is it?" I replied without thinking.

A smile played at his lips, but he appeared to think better of it. "You see," he said, wagging his finger at me. "That's exactly the kind of thing I want *you* to tell me. When you're lurking around out there in the streets, you're not, by chance, calling yourself Buffy, are you?"

My lips gave in to a tight smile in spite of my anxiety. This was the Vincent I had come to know. I suddenly wanted to extend these precious moments with him for as long as I could. I realized in that moment that I had fallen in love with him, and my smile disappeared as I felt a sudden pang of devastating grief.

"I've already told you that my name is Ana."

"And you promised to tell me who you are and why you've been following me," he reminded me.

"I know," I said with a little sigh. "And I will." I smiled again and to my horror, tears came to my eyes, although I quickly blinked them away. "I'm just taking my time because this…this…moment, is…" I tried to think of how to describe what being here with him meant to me, but words failed. "Momentous," I finished feebly.

He appeared somewhat moved, or at least curious, so I continued.

"And," I added, "what I have to tell you is rather difficult to say." I had mulled over many different strategies and approaches, but it wasn't until that moment that I knew what I would do. I had decided to simply tell Vincent the truth—or as much of it as I could—and let the chips fall where they may. I felt a strange conviction that he would understand. Yet when I looked at him, my heart ached. What if he responded to my request with contempt?

"I know what you are," I began nervously. "I mean, I know that you drink…blood." I peered up at him cautiously through the strands of my hair that had fallen over my face and acted as a kind of shield for me. "I know you can't help it," I added quickly when I saw the bitterness in his eyes. "It doesn't matter how long I've been following you. The important thing is why I followed you."

"Why did you?" he asked.

"The night I first saw you—right before I saw you, actually—I was thinking that I wanted to die."

He stared at me, incredulous.

"I had my reasons," I went on. "I'm not depressed or insane, or anything like that. I have my reasons."

Vincent stood but he did not speak. He seemed anxious and uncomfortable. I decided to go on.

"When I saw you, I was distracted from these thoughts. There was something about you that instantly captured my attention. I think it was your energy. You seemed to me like the very essence of life and all that it could be. That's what I saw. I wondered how you came about it. Was it simply good luck or some mystical discovery? I tried to discover your secret as I watched you. And I saw that the other people in the bar noticed it, too. It was almost as if your…vivacity was catching, and everybody wanted it." I paused a moment, caught up in the memory, before continuing.

"You had your choice among the women there, but when I saw the one you selected my curiosity was piqued even more." I looked up at him suddenly and was surprised by the attentiveness in his expression as he listened to me. I half expected him to be impatient for me to get to the point. His obvious interest in what I was saying encouraged me. "The woman was…well, you might say that she was the direct opposite of you. It wasn't just her lack of charm or intellect, either. There was a crudeness in her manner that became even more noticeable when she was with you. It was clear that the two of you didn't fit. Before I even realized what I was doing, I had followed you to her house."

"You followed me to her house?" Vincent interjected. "When was this?"

"It was about six weeks ago," I admitted. "She took you to an apartment on the first floor and I was able to see everything through a small opening in a curtain."

He just stared at me in astonishment.

"Afterwards, I followed you here," I went on. "And I've followed you regularly ever since." I once again peeked out at him through my hair.

"So what do you want?" he asked suddenly. "You must want something, right?" He suddenly stopped. "Oh, God," he murmured. "You want me to assist in your suicide."

I took a deep breath and released the words in a rapid gush. "I want one night with you in exchange for my life." I realized, of course, even as I said this, that he could easily take my life whenever and however he chose. But I knew, too, that he would have an aversion to that kind of violence. And yet, perhaps he would feel that a night with me would be even worse.

I had no idea what he was thinking. I had been standing in the darkest corner of the room that I could find while he stood calmly in the very center. He took three steps in my direction and then stopped, as if he were about to speak. But after simply looking at me for few seconds, he abruptly turned and took several steps back. Then he turned again and took another three steps forward. My fear that he would refuse me was growing stronger.

Yet having said my piece, I was all of a sudden remarkably composed. "You seem upset," I observed. "Are you only able to kill women who want to live?"

When I saw his expression, I wished I had not said that. "But why are you upset, then?" I asked.

"I'm not upset," he said. "It's just that you've caught me off guard. I don't know what to think. How do I know this isn't some kind of trick?"

"Why would you think it's a trick?"

"Because people don't usually go around asking vampires to kill them!"

"So you *are* a vampire! That's officially what you are, then?"

He just looked at me, shaking his head in disbelief.

"You would be doing me a favor," I said, trying, oddly enough, to make him feel better.

"You said that first night I captured your interest," he interjected. "Okay, so now you've captured mine. I have more questions I want answers to. There are things I want know, like what your 'reasons' are, for starters. You're the first person who I've ever had the opportunity to discuss this with, so let's just slow down a minute, okay?"

I was surprised and delighted by his words, but I was apprehensive, too. What if I had nothing more of interest to offer? What if this first, strange confession was all there was? Who else had ever shown an interest in me?

But I knew that, within my depths, there was stored up a lifetime's supply of thoughts and sensations and passions, all of which I could now offer up as sustenance to this man who I still thought of as a kindred soul. This realization hit me with joyful excitement, although I remained somewhat uncertain. If only I could have erased our physical differences, it might have been easier to believe. Nevertheless, this was, so far, the most romantic moment of my life, and I embraced it with anticipation. But I wanted to know for certain that Vincent was not, in the end, going to refuse me my request.

"I will happily share with you all that you wish to know," I told him. "But I feel compelled to say that, having seen the women you've brought here before me, I can tell you that I am at least as worthy as they were to suffer their fate." I blurted this out before even considering my words.

"No! You are not as worthy as they!" he argued adamantly. "I can tell you that already, although I have only sampled your worthiness so far. I couldn't wait to quiet their tongues, while I am anxious to hear more from yours. Here, I will pour us some wine and we will sit and drink it together as we talk. You will answer my questions, and perhaps then I will decide whether you are worthy to join those women in the afterlife, after all."

This was not exactly the assurance I was looking for, but I smiled in spite of that. To simply be with him was a pleasure that I would gladly die for. He led me to a small couch and motioned for me to sit. Then he gathered up the wine and glasses and settled himself—a bit too close to me—on the couch. After he poured our wine, he surprised me yet again by picking up my free hand and holding it in his. He still seemed somewhat agitated.

"I will be joining those women in the afterlife with or without your assistance, I'm afraid," I began in my shy, matter-of-fact way. "I found out that first day I saw you, although I had been sick for a while—nearly my whole life, really. I left the doctor's office and went straight to that little pub where you were."

"I don't remember it," he interjected. "Where was it? Who were you with?" I was surprised by his interest in these minute details. They didn't interest me. "It was some little pub over on… I can't even remember the street. I was sitting alone and I'm sure you never even saw me. You were surrounded by people—women, mostly—and ended up with a very beautiful, although, as I mentioned earlier, rather horrible—if you'll forgive me saying so—woman."

"Oh, that tells me nothing!" he complained with exasperation. "That could have been any of the nights I went out."

I laughed. It was true. I was surprised that he so readily admitted it. "Well, it was your terrible taste in women that caught my attention and prompted me to follow you in the first place."

"That's the other thing," he continued. "How did you follow me? Did you simply walk out the door behind me, as easy as you please?" He seemed genuinely bewildered by this but I couldn't tell whether it was that I would dare to do such a thing to begin with, or that I had managed to do it without him detecting me.

"I just kind of followed you. I don't know. There were often other people on the street as well. It wasn't that hard. I was careful never to get too close." I tried to read his face. Having watched him for so many weeks now, I could often guess what he was thinking by his expressions. On this night, however, I was discovering expressions I hadn't seen before. I looked him over leisurely, trying to decipher the meaning behind this particular expression. I decided it was skepticism.

"So do you mean to say," he began thoughtfully, "that you've been following me all this time—and in quite a clandestine manner, I might add—in the hopes that I would discover you, bring you here and finish you off?" He looked incredulously around the room while he said this, as if he were expecting Ashton Kutcher to suddenly pop through one of the doorways and shout, "You've been punked!"

"Look at me," I said in my most earnest tone. "Do I appear to be anything other than what I've been telling you I am?" He really looked at me then, and in spite of it being my idea that he do so, I blanched. I did not really want him to look at me so closely. And I was suddenly struck by my own duplicity and filled with shame. But I forced these feelings aside and pressed on. "I happen to know that you haven't fed in five days," I told him. "Knowing how weak you must be, I don't understand your reluctance. I must be at least as 'contemptible,' as you put it, as those other women were." But in truth, I was flattered by his apparent reluctance, even though it was counter to my purpose.

Vincent, meanwhile, was still examining me closely with narrowed eyes. He appeared to be weighing my words against what he was observing. I tried to remain as calm and impassive as possible, but it was difficult, and I had a sudden urge to escape—an impossibility at this point. Yet I could still feel that inexplicable kinship with him, too, and I tried to focus on that. Aside from his overpowering good looks and charm, he was actually very easy to talk to, and I found myself wanting to confide in him. But his nearness was overwhelming. Feeling rather trapped and claustrophobic, I wriggled my hand, which had all this time been securely confined in his, out from within his grasp. He allowed me this little freedom with an amused look. I couldn't bear the silence any longer, so I continued to speak what was on my mind.

"I've never had a lover," I confessed. "I don't even know how to attract a man in that way." I shrugged my shoulders as if I wasn't concerned over this, although that was another little deception. "And it is not likely that I will get the chance now." I looked into his eyes, so warm and kind and unbearably beautiful. "Being with you would be...it would be the best night of my life, with a...tolerable ending."

The silence after this little speech from me went on for far too long. I was becoming desperately anxious. When he at last scooted closer to me on the snug little sofa, I think my heart actually stopped for an instant. I'm sure my expression was utterly piteous as I stared up at him with my heart on my sleeve. I felt as if I was waiting for him to strike.

Vincent smiled.

"Would you care for more wine?" he asked politely. I looked down at my glass in surprise. I had not even realized that had I finished mine.

"Yes...please."

He calmly poured the wine. I noticed that he had finished

his, as well. I had no idea what would happen next. But as I waited I knew that I had never felt so excited or alive.

When our glasses were full, he took a sip from his and then absently rotated the goblet in his hand, causing the wine to circle within.

"I was only twenty-four when it happened," he said. "I was hunting, and I had wandered deep into the woods." He watched the wine as it swirled round and round in his glass. "It came from out of nowhere, and to this day I have no idea what it was. At the time I thought it was some kind of a wild animal. But it all happened so fast that my memory is a little fuzzy." He paused, taking another sip of his wine. He took a deep breath before continuing. "I laid there for days, half-dead. The pain was incredible, although I couldn't find any injuries aside from a small bite to my neck. I felt weak, so weak my head throbbed with the slightest movement. I kept thinking I had been poisoned. It was like I could feel it—the poison—working its way through my system. I figured that whatever bit me must have had rabies. And as I lay there, I became more and more convinced that that was what I had. I couldn't get out of the woods. I could hardly move. I was sure I was a dead man."

I listened intently to every detail, literally hanging on to every word. Until that moment, I'm not sure I ever completely believed that any of this was real.

"There was another hunter," Vincent continued after a long, thoughtful silence that I did not want to disrupt, in spite of my eagerness to hear the rest of his story. I could see that it was difficult for him to look back on this part of what happened. "When he discovered me out there, he came rushing toward me to see if he could help." He shook his head. "It was like something took over my body. Something like…instinct. I honestly couldn't stop myself. Somehow I knew that there was only one way I was going to get out of there alive. And I wanted to live!" His eyes seemed to be searching mine for understanding. "I don't know how I managed it. I was incredibly weak, but all of a sudden it seemed like I had the strength of ten men. He didn't give in easily, and I was…inexperienced. I think I took him by surprise mostly." He shuddered at the memory. "It was horrible, and in those first wretched moments I wished I had died out there. I drained him, like an animal, stopping only to vomit in disgust before guzzling down even more. What I managed to keep down revived me enough so that I could make my way home. I recuperated alone, too terrified to go to a doctor. I stayed in bed and got lots of rest, popping Vitamin C every chance I got and looking up rabies and similar diseases in medical journals." He laughed, in spite of his obvious misery. "And as I got better, and was eating regular food and everything, I figured that maybe what happened with that hunter was just a freak, near-death kind of thing, you know." He shook his head and laughed again, but without any real humor. "But in a few days I felt myself growing weaker again. And I felt the craving. I wish there was a better word for it than that. Craving doesn't quite explain it. It's like I'm starving and having withdrawals and being eaten alive from the inside, all at the same time. I really do think I would die if I didn't get it, and although that might not be a bad thing, the poison, or whatever it is that's inside me, won't let that happen."

When he finished, I looked down at my wineglass, unable to meet his eyes. Although I had listened to every word with interest, for some reason I wished he had not told me all of this. We sipped our wine in silence. He did not speak until I looked up and once again met his eyes.

"We will take this as slow or as fast as you want tonight," he told me. "We can make it last all night if you wish." I was both thrilled and terrified by his words.

"Thank you," I tried to say, but my words came out like a croak. I could not seem to locate my voice.

"Come!" He lifted the wineglass from my fingers and once again took my hand firmly in his. "Tell me what I can do to make you feel more at ease. Can I draw you a bath?"

I looked at him in surprise and then, unable to find my voice, simply nodded.

I could not believe this extraordinary turn of events. Not even in my most brazen and imaginative fantasies had I dared dream of such a night as this was turning out to be. Everything was happening in my favor. Yet I was feeling more and more ill at ease.

As I was settling restlessly into the warm, sudsy water of Vincent's bathtub, there came a tap on the bathroom door.

"Yes?"

The door slipped open a few inches. "Would you like more wine?"

"I would, and company, too, if you care to stay," I heard myself responding. The warm water and wine were having their effect.

He closed the lid of the toilet and sat down there.

"How old are you?" I asked him.

"Eighty-five," he said with a smug smile. He looked like a man in his early thirties.

"Still in your prime," I murmured. He laughed.

"Is it true that vampires live forever?" I asked.

"Whatever it is that I am, I don't believe I'm going to live forever. I seem to age much more slowly than other people, but I'm certain I have aged in the last sixty years."

"I wonder what you would look like right now if this had never happened to you."

"Probably I'd be dead," he said. "Or worse—bald and on Viagra."

I laughed. Then I shook my head. It was impossible to imagine Vincent like that. "This suits you better," I told him.

My bubbles were slowly shrinking away, causing me to feel self-conscious. With his usual perceptiveness, Vincent stood up to leave. "You finish and I'll see you out there."

I was strangely calm, in light of everything. My excitement was tempered by a sobering dread of certain things to come, and I wondered how I would manage. But it was what I wanted, and I would not waver. As I slipped into the oversized bathrobe that Vincent had so thoughtfully set out for me, I knew this would be the defining night of my life.

Vincent was waiting for me on a lavish, king-size bed. I couldn't help smiling to see him there, wearing nothing but a robe himself. I did not feel beautiful but I did feel desired, and I suppose I was, if you looked at it in a certain light.

He immediately drew me into his arms when I approached him. I struggled to maintain control over my growing excitement, only too aware that as I became more impassioned my heart rate would increase. I certainly didn't want to push Vincent over the top just yet. But even this chilling inducement couldn't seem to slow my thrashing heart. It was beating so vigorously that I could actually feel the blood rushing through my veins. And I saw the gleam of awakened hunger in Vincent's eyes. I knew he would need to quench his first, undeniable need before anything else. But for the moment, he merely kissed and licked my lips, then moved on to my face and chin, spreading deliciously wet and lingering kisses all over my feverish flesh. I could feel my blood quickening, and I knew the artery in my throat must be pulsing with life. I felt his lips and tongue right there on the spot, lightly tickling it. His breath was hot, scorching a trail along the length of my neck. I felt the pointed edge of a rigid tooth; it brushed lightly across my skin, once, twice, thrice. I arched my neck for him and braced myself, clutching his shoulders with trembling fingers.

The fangs of a vampire are as sharp as a surgeon's scalpel, so you hardly even feel it when they first break the skin. But as they settle into the vein there is a distinct awareness of a terrible intrusion, accompanied by a heavy, unsettling discomfort. A small cry is automatically released from your lips, like a rush of air. It's a cry of surprise, mingled with confusion over what just occurred, and added to that is the wonder that it is so absolutely bearable. But then, as you feel the blood being drawn from your body, you are suddenly struck with a kind of alarm. And there is uncertainty, too. Is this even really happening? And instinctively you know not to move—not while those razor-sharp fangs are still engaged.

I had come to believe that, in his first feeding, Vincent consumed only enough blood to leave his victim weakened, but not yet in shock. There appeared to be a certain dwindling of the spirit brought on by the loss of blood, along with a kind of lingering disbelief—both of which must have contributed to the docility, and even enthusiasm, after the fact. *Whatever just happened,* the victim reasons, *I'm still here and I feel incredible.* Now I was experiencing it firsthand.

When Vincent disengaged himself from my neck and rose up over me to gasp for air, I stared up in awe to see my blood still glistening on his teeth. It was quite an incredible moment for me. His beauty and omnipotence suddenly overwhelmed me. It was as if I were watching my own lifeblood working miracles within him. It was a peculiar feeling indeed.

As for me, I felt light-headed and deceptively invincible. Yet I knew I had merely passed into an altered mental state brought about by loss of blood. I was hovering precariously near, but not yet at, the point of physical shock. Oh, but I never felt so alive! Part of it was no doubt the combined thrill and horror of the event. And, of course, the biggest part of it was Vincent himself.

How can I explain those first moments?

When I was a child, I recall feeling something like what I experienced with Vincent, although on a much smaller scale. It was something that would come over me when I was very sick, usually when I had a very high fever. As the fever was building, I would sometimes get the sense that I was outside of myself, and it would seem to me that time suddenly stood still. It's not easy to describe, but when it happens, all your pain subsides and your worries dissolve in a hazy fog of well-being. Consciousness becomes awareness and nothing else. It's as if you can suddenly hear your insides at work as they throb and pulse out a rhythm that calls to mind dreams not yet realized. It's a kind of euphoria that rushes toward you like the ground when you fall, only to meet you in the end like a loving embrace.

What would you give to find the ultimate bliss? Is there any price too high?

Vincent was opening my robe, and he spread his hands over my skin tenderly. I had never been touched that way before. My body seemed to curve toward him instinctively, eagerly meeting his touch like steel turns toward a magnet. I shuddered with exquisite desire. My every molecule seemed to be swelling with pleasure.

Vincent was taking great pains to go slowly with me, and I adored him all the more for that. I could see that he was highly aroused, and that he was fully focused on our lovemaking now that his first, inexorable need had been satiated. But my passion was quickly exceeding his. My arms reached out for him and, with a strength I had not realized I possessed, I pulled him to me and held him there fiercely. He acquiesced, chuckling. I clung to him, trembling slightly when I felt his rigid arousal brush against me. Instinctively my hips bucked upward and moved against his hardness. He groaned. But why was he delaying for so long?

Sensing my impatience, he spread apart my legs and moved in between, but he moved too slowly, maddeningly slowly, kissing and stroking me leisurely as he went until I thought I would surely be driven insane before ever realizing the pleasure I had so long awaited. And even when he was finally settled snugly between my legs he lingered still, simply holding himself right there at my entrance as if he were waiting for an invitation. Instinctively I wound my legs around him. I could feel him pressing restlessly against my barrier, and I saw that he was struggling for control as he looked down into my face. His eyes blazed dangerously but I stared brazenly back, wide-eyed and transfixed, like an animal in a trap. His eyes held mine as he pushed himself all the way into my body and I—my entire being—was awakened from head to toe. The pleasure was almost unendurable. I had waited so long to experience it, but now I was glad I had waited. I was pleased that this would forever remain my first, and perhaps only, impression of love.

I was overwrought with sensation, and Vincent's repeated filling and stretching of me brought me over the top. I felt the need to move all of a sudden and I did so, grinding and thrashing my hips against him like I had seen those other women do but without fully understanding why. Something was welling up inside me, building and growing. It seemed to have control over my actions and, trusting the instinct, I allowed it to lead me where it would. Vincent continued to move within me, but I could tell that he was holding back and allowing me to take the lead, also trusting in whatever force was driving me. I clung to him as I bucked my hips wildly against him. The pleasure just kept building and building until I thought it would burst. And that's exactly what it did, suddenly releasing an enormous wave that flooded my insides and then exploded into a million tiny sensations. I cried out, oblivious to everything but the pleasure. But it subsided far too quickly, and I cried out again, this time in protest.

"No, please, don't stop!" I objected.

"Shhh," murmured Vincent in my ear. "I won't stop." But in the very next instant he, too, let out a tremendous yell, and I felt another wave of satisfaction in the knowledge that I had given him pleasure.

I nearly lost myself in that moment. And truthfully, if I had, I would not have felt I had lost anything at all. But Vincent's words suddenly came to my mind, from when he had been dying in the woods, and thought to himself, "I want to live!"

"I want," I began.

"What do you want, darling?" he asked, so tenderly I thought I might have died already, after all.

"I want...more. I want...all!" There was so much I wanted to experience of life before I died.

Vincent tried to quiet me and I had a strong temptation to just lie back passively and enjoy whatever came, but somehow I found the strength to sit up and carry on. I was determined to finish what I had started. I saw that Vincent was still hard, and I was pleased. I pressed my hands forcefully against his chest.

"I want to look at you," I said, pushing him backward. He acquiesced eagerly, lying back on the bed and spreading out before me.

"Mmm," I murmured happily, feasting first my eyes and then my hands over his body. Next came my lips and tongue. I was determined to cover every inch of him. He was lean and hard. I worked my way down slowly, languishingly, leaving lots of tiny, feathery kisses over his chest and belly before reaching his hips. He was still raging hard.

My eyes kept wandering over him, examining and admiring him as if I were committing him to memory. I dropped kisses everywhere I looked. He moaned in pleasure, especially when I dipped down and flicked my tongue over his hard-on. Seeing that he liked this, I began to lick it from its base to its tip, running my tongue over the various engorged veins that swelled up all around it. There was one in particular that I noticed bulged and throbbed more than the others. I let my tongue linger over it a moment, fascinated and thrilled and terrified by it all at the same time. Up and down I kept sliding my tongue, sighing gently as I poured my breath out over him.

With sudden, irreversible decisiveness, I raised my lips up over my teeth and swiftly and deftly drove one of my highly sharpened incisors deep into the large, bulging vein I had just seconds ago been lustfully running my tongue over. I was able to pierce it flawlessly in that first, precise thrust, and instantly afterward clamped down over him with my lips while pulling vigorously with my jaws. Vincent's blood gushed forth instantaneously, shocking me with how quickly it filled my mouth. I had a strong urge to gag, but I forced myself to swallow the blood in huge gulps, trying desperately to ignore the sickening, coppery taste of it. I knew that the poison—or whatever it was he had infected me with—had not yet had time to take effect in my system, but this was my one and only opportunity. Before poor Vincent had even had time to cry out in surprise, I think I must have swallowed over a pint.

Vincent was taken utterly by surprise. Just as I had anticipated he would, he froze, uncertain about what to do. He could hardly jerk away or strike me while I was still so precariously attached; even in his shocked state, he was aware of the dangers in that. But it was actually much longer than I expected before he was even able to cry out for me to stop.

I released him after his second cry, immediately scurrying off the bed and retreating to a neutral corner of the room. I don't know if it was his second cry that stopped me, or the fact that I simply couldn't take any more. I was struggling to keep down what I had swallowed, fighting wave after wave of the dizzying nausea.

Once I had disengaged myself from Vincent, he, too, jumped up from the bed. However, he was clearly still quite vulnerable, falling down once before managing to secure his footing. He awkwardly cupped his hands over his groin with a look of distress. His eyes shone with rage, but he was disarmed—for the moment.

"What the hell are you?" he yelled. He kept glancing down distractedly, opening his hands periodically to examine himself. As far as I could tell, it seemed as if the bleeding had nearly stopped. The incision had been remarkably small and clean, just penetrating the vein.

"I'm sick, remember?" I said. "Like you, I want to live."

"What?"

"I want to be a vampire."

"So you bite my *dick?*"

"I was afraid you would be too strong to restrain if I bit you anywhere else," I said sheepishly. "I am sorry."

"You're *sorry?*" He appeared to be too astonished for words. "Get out."

"But…"

"Get out!" he yelled again, louder this time. "I should kill you." But he was paler than usual and seemed weak and woozy. Even as he said this, he leaned back on the wall for support.

"I was careful not to hurt it," I said, picking up my clothes from the chair where I had left them and moving toward the bathroom so that I could dress in private.

He was examining himself again. "How did you… What did you pierce me with?"

I stopped to look at him. "I filed my teeth down."

"You *what?*"

I sighed. "I filed my teeth down. You know, with a nail file."

"Let me see."

I took a deep breath and then raised my lips up over my teeth. My two incisors were shaped into two frighteningly pointy fangs, more terrifying even than those of the vampire. I had filed so much of them away that all around the nerves were exposed. That's how I was able to learn to talk while barely moving my lips. The pain when the air hit those nerves was an excellent reminder.

"When did you do that?"

"I did it after I saw you that first night."

"You went home and filed down your *teeth?*"

"No, I...well, yes, I began filing them down a little at a time. It hurt too much to do it all at once."

"With this in mind?"

"Well, yes, actually, I was hoping it would happen something like it did." I looked at him regretfully. "Does it hurt much?" I asked. "I didn't want to hurt you. That's why I filed them down so much."

He was still too angry to worry about making me feel better, although I could see that I hadn't hurt him as much as might have been expected. I had only used the one incisor, and it was a precise, smooth cut that pierced the artery just right.

"I'm sorry," I repeated, moving once again toward the bathroom so that I could dress.

"What's wrong with you?" he asked suddenly.

"I have leukemia," I replied, assuming he was referring to my terminal illness.

Vincent allowed me to leave there alive.

I trudged home in the dark, feeling sick and tired and miserable, and without any knowledge of what would happen next. I was getting weaker by the minute. Doubts filled my head. Had I ingested enough of Vincent's blood to become a vampire? But I wondered if that even mattered. If what Vincent told me about his own account of what happened was true, then my plan to drink vampire blood may not have been necessary at all, although it was most certainly the thing that got me out of there alive. And perhaps it had provided enough sustenance to get me through. But was I a vampire? And what about my disease? What if being bitten by Vincent didn't rid me of my disease? Would I simply remain sick for a longer, perhaps indefinite period of time? Clearly I had not thought all of this through. The night I first saw Vincent I instantly and thoughtlessly clung to the idea of what he was. But I suddenly felt that, no matter what I did, I would never be like him. And I was more depressed than I had ever been before in my life.

By the time I got home, I might have done away with myself then and there if I had had the strength.

I've been sick all of my life, as I have already indicated, but even so I was not prepared for the incredible pain I would feel in the days that followed. I was certain that I would die, and wished time and again that I had just allowed myself to die that night in Vincent's arms, happy and sated. I wondered about him continually in between the bouts of anguish.

Next came the hunger, and that's when I knew I would live. But I realized once again that I had not really thought through the details of my plan. Where was I supposed to get someone to feed on, for example? And would I actually be able to pull it off? Biting Vincent had been one thing, for I was careful not to actually harm him, but to take a life? Of course, as my hunger grew, this problem vanished. How long, really, can a person fast when sustenance is everywhere around them? I grappled with the idea of leaving the first one alive, to live if he was able. But in the end I could not. Another instinct warned me that this would be compounding the wrong. Perhaps that is what Vincent felt, as well.

I have always been rather pale and drawn, but not in the

flawless, youthful way of the vampire. I nearly fell in love with myself in those first weeks. I'm ashamed to admit that I would look at myself in the mirror for hours. Not that I was beautiful, even then. But my skin, without the sickly tinge, was lovely! My drab green eyes suddenly seemed bright and fierce. My lips and cheeks were rosy with health. Oh, to have good health! Are you healthy? Rejoice! I virtually skipped when I walked from the exuberance I felt.

And suddenly, men were approaching me! I never did get used to that. I continued to be reserved and uncertain around them, but now my shyness seemed to make me more desirable. And that suited my needs. But unlike Vincent, I wasn't able to be intimate with them. I found that I always ended up killing them before we were able to consummate it. It would end in a kind of relief for me. It may be a good thing that there aren't more women like me out there, or I think men would be dropping like flies. Perhaps it was the men that I chose. Like Vincent, I felt the need to single out someone who seemed a bit more killable. It is a terrible thing to decide who to kill, and I would have preferred, if I'd had the know-how, to scout around for child molesters or other evil beings but, then again, who am I to judge?

I hated it, but I needed it. Like Vincent, I went as long as I could between feedings.

I thought of Vincent all the time. He had become such a huge part of my life. He was the one who gave me life, in a way, for this was the first time I had lived. I wondered morning, noon and night how he was and what he was doing. But I was afraid to approach him. I couldn't bear to see hatred in those dark, beautiful eyes.

Oftentimes, out of habit more than anything else really, I would find myself standing on his street. But I always picked up my step when I passed by his house. I could no longer watch him through windows. Sometimes I would wander into a nearby park and sit, for a while, on the swings—something I was never well enough to do as a child. Other times I would walk up and down the side streets, wondering what he was up to. I could almost imagine that I was with him, by just being in the neighborhood where he lived.

"You're alive!"

I whirled around at the sound of his voice one night and suddenly there he was!

"Wow!" he exclaimed. "And you look great! So…healthy." Vincent shook his head in amazement. "So it actually worked, then?"

"Yes." All of a sudden, I couldn't breathe. His eyes shined on me with pleasure. With *pleasure!*

"I wondered," he went on. "I've been going crazy wondering, actually, but I had no idea where you lived or even what your last name was."

I finally found my voice. "I know. It was kind of…odd." I couldn't help laughing suddenly. "I was just thinking of you," I told him honestly.

"You don't say."

"Yeah, I, ah…just came from your house, actually." I laughed again. It was so wonderful to see him that I felt as giddy as a teenager.

"No kidding!" He laughed, too, and raised one eyebrow ironically. "Funny, that's the last place I would have looked."

"Are you…I mean, did your…cut…heal up okay?"

"It did! It really wasn't even that bad, you know, just kind of shocking. You're the first girl who's ever done that to me. I never expected you to be so…resourceful."

I laughed again, amazed and so very happy that he was talking to me.

"I know this whole thing started out kind of weird," I began, and then when I saw his expression I quickly amended, "Okay, *very* weird. Extremely weird. But, you know, we have this…thing in common now, and…I don't know, it might be nice…I mean, it would be nice—for me especially—if I could see you…once in a while. Or a lot." He was smiling again, which encouraged me, so I pressed on brazenly. "A lot would be better than once in a while, but either one will do."

"Well, what are you doing right now?" he asked.

"I already told you. Returning from your house."

We both suddenly burst into laughter. And we laughed throughout the rest of that night. I was surprised and unbelievably happy. For all I knew, I could have been his mortal enemy after what I had done. But it confirmed, too, what I had believed all along actually, which was that Vincent was the sort of man who would really blossom on a second date. Just as I suspected, he did yearn to be known for more than just a few hours. He wanted to be known well and appreciated for his many subtler qualities, and was actually quite demanding in this regard. What great companions we made, in the end!

And as it turns out, there is something I can tell you about vampires that you probably haven't heard before. I only discovered it myself because of my jealous nature, which made it torture for me to be alone while Vincent went out to feed. Of course, feeding did not have to involve a long and lengthy seduction, but it seemed that the two went so well together. And neither did Vincent want me out roaming the streets looking for blood. We wanted to be together. We began seeking a single victim, to share between us. It was never really necessary, after all, to drink more than a few pints during our feedings. But even this presented its difficulties. Should it be a man or a woman?

It all came about because Vincent needed to feed more often than me. He grew weak faster than I did. On this occasion I was not quite hungry enough yet. It never got easier for me to kill, so I had to have that desperate feeling in order to do it. Poor Vincent would nearly starve to death waiting for me. I could see that he was growing visibly weaker, although he still had the strength to make love. I was riding him from on top. This seemed to revive him somewhat, but I could still see the hunger in his eyes.

In that moment I wanted to be everything to him. I wanted to fulfill all of his needs, even the hunger. At the mere thought of it, my blood began to flow a little faster. I was suddenly aware of it, coursing through my veins. A new thrill filled me over what I was thinking. I squeezed him from deep within me, closing in all around his hardness, as the excitement continued to build in me. Vincent became more excited, too, and that strange, fiery light came into his eyes. I felt a rush of adrenaline as I slid my hair to one side, exposing the pulsing artery in my neck to him. There was a look of surprise on his face as I lowered my neck to his lips. I brushed it back and forth over his opened mouth, and I heard the faint hiss of his sharp intake of breath. I kept on, simultaneously moving up and down on his erection as I brushed my neck over his lips, again and again. Finally, he could no longer resist, and with a low groan he grasped hold of my head and buried his fangs in my neck, causing me to cry out. But even as he drank his fill, my hips continued to move up and down on him, and I shuddered violently as my orgasm shot through me. He took what he needed and then jerked his head to one side, gasping for air as he released himself inside me.

I had no idea what effect my vampire blood would have on him. I would have to wait to find out. In a maneuver so quick I hardly knew what was happening, he threw me beneath him and took me again—solely lovemaking this time—with a wild abandon that I had not seen in him since our very first night together.

Later, while I looked on nervously, he paced the floor. He was wild with energy and excitement. Every now and again he would stop and look at me.

"Are you sure you're all right?" he'd ask.

"For the hundredth time, I feel fine," I assured him. "I'm no more affected than if I'd given blood."

"Amazing!" he reiterated again. For all my bravado, I was excited, too. If we could exist like this, feeding off each other every few days, it would negate the need to kill.

"But what about you?" I asked. "Do you think it will suffice?"

"Suffice? Suffice?" he nearly yelled. "I feel like a god!" He threw his arms out and let out a yell. Mostly, I think, he was as happy as I was at the prospect of never again having to kill.

And as it turns out, vampires fare even *better* on vampire blood than human blood.

Oh, and becoming a vampire does cure leukemia.

Expecting

Emilie stared in disbelief at the clear, indisputable blue mark on the indicator. Anxiety gripped her insides, and she was assailed by the pungent taste of metal as another wave of nausea rushed through her. Beads of perspiration coated her upper lip. She closed her eyes a moment to wait for the nausea to pass.

Seeing the result—she had known it all along, really, and feared it from the very first—so conclusively displayed in the little plastic window instantly transformed her fear into a concrete, vigorous horror so powerful that it struck her like a physical blow. The implications jarred her to the core, shattering her reserve and opening a whole new dimension of potential terror. Her life suddenly yawned out before her in a vast expanse of dread and uncertainty. She knew now that there was no stopping the terrors that awaited.

But in spite of this, there was, at least, no doubt over what to do. There was only one thing she could do. That was the principal horror, really, that what she must do was the only certainty she had at the moment. Intensifying that principal horror was all the years of striving for this end, only to have no choice in the matter now. And of course, there was the horror of not really knowing for sure (although she *knew*). And all of this was compounded by the biggest horror of all, which was the unbearable waiting. She could feel her anxiety growing as rapidly as *it* was growing. With each day that passed while she waited in secret, she felt she was losing a little more control, and this left Emilie feeling more and more helpless and afraid.

It had been only six days since the event, but Emilie felt as if she had suffered the trauma of six years.

In the meantime, her feelings for David had completely changed. A wide gulf had developed between them, in spite of the short time elapsed. It had begun with a kind of shattering fracture at the time of the incident and expanded with each and every moment Emilie spent trying to hide it from him. Her efforts to keep it hidden seemed to push David further and further away, just as his attempts at discovery increased her own need for secrecy. This was not something a person could speak about freely with anyone, but with David in particular, it was impossible! Emilie knew this because she had been just like David once. But now, the man who had up until six days ago been her soul mate, had become someone she couldn't relate to at all. He was foreign to her. The characteristics she had formerly admired in him now seemed terribly annoying.

This sense of disillusionment was magnified during intimacy. It had become torture for Emilie to endure her husband's touch. Guilt-ridden and terrified of exposure, she forced herself to go through the motions because, although they had been married for eight years, they were still in the habit of making love nearly every night. But it was exhaustive for her and extremely difficult. Worst of all, sex with David triggered memories that she spent every waking hour trying to erase, for with the memories came strange yearnings that still mortified her. Those yearnings, above all, she must rid herself of. They were disturbing and offensive—as disturbing and offensive as the overpowering taste of metal that accompanied them.

But in spite of her best efforts to forget—or perhaps because of them—the memories reemerged in Emilie's dreams. The dreams she could not control, and sleeping became a kind of torment. They were always the same, so that for all their perverse peculiarity they were inevitably becoming more and more familiar—and perhaps even a bit more acceptable—to her.

Sometimes the dreams were fleeting and distant and at other times a single detail seemed to encompass an entire night. The images in particular were vivid and moved her greatly. Her body would shudder and jerk from the force of them. All of her senses, deadened as they were throughout her stilted days, seemed to suddenly come alive once she drifted into unconsciousness, so that to simply close her eyes could sometimes cause the hairs to rise up all along her sensitive flesh, and instigate the taste buds at the back of her tongue to rise up and alert her to the pungent taste of metal.

As the dreams crept over her—or *into* her, as it seemed more like to Emilie—she would at first feel fear. But with each consecutive dream the fear would become steadily surpassed by an unwelcome yet overpowering sense of longing and expectation. It was as if the dreams were answering a call that Emilie herself had sent out. The darkness would suddenly become infused with a light so intense that Emilie could actually feel the heat of it warming her skin. Her heart would skitter wildly in response to the rush of adrenaline that flooded her system in preparation of what was to come. Soon the adrenaline had its effect and, temporarily sedated, Emilie would wait breathlessly for what was to follow. She knew that no matter how many times she relived it, each and every detail would still have the power to shock her. She could never be fully prepared for the creeping, slithering, clinging feel of them, weighty and slick as they moved sluggishly over her. The intrusiveness of their touch, so all at once eerie and repulsive, caused all of her senses to come startlingly alert. Unable to do more than to simply lie back and observe in those first frozen moments, she would be trapped in a sea of sensation that thrust her to and fro, shifting through shock, fear, agitation and arousal.

In her dreams, just as during the actual event itself, Emilie's vision was always impaired by intensely bright light. But even so, she could still make out their tall, gray shapes looming over her, and particularly the shiny, black orbs from which they appeared to observe her. She would stare up into those dark depths—into seeming nothingness—uncomprehendingly, mildly aware that something was being communicated to her but grasping little more than that it was having a paralyzing effect on her.

Their silent communication was not the only influence with which they were capable of subduing her. They also, in their slow, pervasive way, steadily enveloped her within their tentacles—so many tentacles—all of them contracting and pulsing as they enclosed themselves around her limbs in an effort to hold her. The tentacles, which appeared to be shape-less masses at first, were actually powerful and vigorous instruments beneath their oily surface, able to hold and subdue her with the same unyielding force of a boa constrictor. And just as with the boa, any movement at all would cause the tentacle to constrict. Emilie could not keep herself from shuddering in response when the tentacles tightened around her, even though she knew it would cause them to tighten even more. A kind of panic would build up in her—not born of fear but of frus-tration—and at last she would attempt to grasp hold of them.

She felt that they were closing in on her but she couldn't actually reach them. When the frustration became too much for her, she would begin to struggle and thrash about in her effort to hold them. But in her panic she would feel herself getting farther and farther away from them. Even the light seemed to slowly get dimmer. Then she would cry out for them to come back. She would scream and struggle and grasp at them until she jerked herself right out of her dream and beyond their reach. She would awaken with a jolt, and in the next instant find David close beside her, shushing her and pulling her close in an attempt to comfort her. Trembling violently, Emilie would shrink away from his touch with revulsion. His warmth, his caress, his soothing voice—even the comfort he offered—to Emilie, seemed *alien*.

The memories of her dreams made her afraid. But ignoring them left her emotionally destitute. What did anything matter?

During her waking hours, Emilie began brooding continually over what she had to do, even as she continued to do nothing. She worried over the right time to act. It seemed to her that whatever it was inside her was growing at an unusually rapid pace. There were times when she believed she could actually feel it getting larger. What if the right time, by human standards, was too late?

Terrifying thoughts and images troubled her day and night. But she was reluctant to contact a doctor. What if he discovered the truth about what was inside her? What would happen to her then?

The days ticked by slowly in a haze of mortification and dread. Emilie continued to withdraw into herself in an attempt to avoid confrontation. At all costs, she must hide the fact that anything was amiss. But in spite of her efforts, she had the sense that she was standing out like a sore thumb. Her silence seemed stilted and awkward. Her attempts at conversation seemed forced and contrived. She felt that action and inaction alike came out like a scream for help.

"What the hell's going on with you?" Ironically, it was her mother, the person she had always been the most distant from—the person who Emilie always felt knew her the least—who first noticed that something was wrong.

"What do you mean?" Emilie asked, feeling a disconcerting mixture of alarm and hope. In that instant, the thought of someone sharing her secret seemed all at once comforting and terrifying.

But then, in the next instant, the hope dissolved and there was only alarm. She knew she could never let her mother know about this. And yet, she wondered what it was the woman perceived.

"You're like a vampire lately," her mother went on. "Even more than usual. All secretive and spooky. You never were the most forthcoming of my children, but lately it's like you're hiding a deep, dark secret. Is he abusing you?"

"Mother…no! God, why do you always jump to conclusions like that? You know perfectly well that David doesn't abuse me." Emilie was immediately annoyed—which was a relief in her present state of mind. She realized then that she would rather almost anyone discover her secret other than her mother, who would never listen to reason because she preferred to make the most ridiculous assumptions.

"Well, that's a matter of opinion," her mother continued, undaunted. "Ever since you married him you've become more and more introverted and withdrawn. You've been living like hermits! And now, since you got back from the cruise, you've been like a different person altogether. Each time he gets you all to himself, it seems like he destroys another little piece of you."

"I live how I want, Mother. I wish you would give that a

rest!" An old resentment flared up in her and Emilie suddenly had the urge to defend David. She imagined, just for kicks, blurting out the truth to her mother, if only to prove her wrong for once. That would set her back for a few minutes.

"Well, what is it, then? Even your sisters have noticed that something's not right with you."

So! Her sisters had discussed her with their mother! It must be obvious that something was wrong with Emilie for them to have gone to their mother. She felt the panic attack welling up inside her.

"I have to go, Mother." Emilie hung up the phone without waiting for her to reply.

Emilie suddenly felt as if she were encased in a glass tomb, visible to the world around her but unbearably isolated from it. She longed for support but was terrified of exposure. Anyway, she knew that support would not be forthcoming in her case. To begin with, she would never be believed. The truth about what happened would be neither heard nor comprehended. People were not inclined toward the truth because they were adverse to listening. Anything that startled, frightened or disgusted was rejected almost immediately and substituted with conclusions—scathing, condescending, ostracizing conclusions that built a wall around the source of truth in an effort to protect others from what they feared most. Emilie would get little opportunity to explain anything before everyone would be lost to their conclusions about *her*, without a thought for what actually had happened.

But in the meantime, her situation was getting worse. There was something she couldn't explain growing inside her! She was suddenly in a full panic. She swallowed two of her little blue pills and then concentrated on her breathing while she waited for them to take effect.

Talking to her mother caused her thoughts to turn to David.

Everyone had come to the conclusion that he was controlling, simply because Emilie had become more reclusive since she met him. What nobody seemed to realize was that Emilie was the one who had instigated that isolation. She simply hadn't wanted to be with anyone but David since falling in love with him. She had needed only him. He was like an extension of herself, they were so much alike. They understood each other perfectly. No matter how many hours they had spent together, it was never too much. Indeed, it didn't seem long enough. They could talk for hours on end without ever running out of things to say. It was a delight to find someone so much like her and to feel so understood. She used to believe she could tell David anything. But since the cruise, he seemed different, changed. Yet she knew that she was the one who had changed. But what did it matter? She could no longer relate to him in the same way she had before. How could she? There was this huge thing between them now that they could never talk about. David would never be able to sympathize with her in this. She knew this because she would not have been able to sympathize with him if the situation were reversed.

Given how close they had been, David could not fail to notice the change in Emilie. He was, of course, being patient and understanding, which she would have found comforting before but now only made her feel more caged in and agitated. He tiptoed carefully around her, advancing only with the meekest of gestures, offered up like tender little peace offerings. So far he had not confronted her directly or pushed her for answers. But she could tell that he was becoming frustrated.

The conclusions he had drawn, when at last David confronted her, surprised Emilie. It was the same day her mother had confronted her, just later that afternoon.

"Just what happened between you and the bartender on the ship?" he asked.

Emilie stared at him, speechless. She struggled to remember any of the bartenders on the cruise and failed.

"I woke up and found you missing from our bed that night," he explained patiently. It almost seemed as if he had already had the conversation several times in his head. He spoke with an odd calm, Emilie thought, as she watched him. "It must have been about two in the morning," he continued. "I went out to look for you and finally found you in the lounge with the bartender. You were sitting in a booth in the back and you were all over him." He spoke completely without anger. It struck Emilie like a rehearsed speech. Yet she felt it cost him quite a lot to pull it off. She was particularly shocked that he hadn't mentioned it before this. A strange feeling of unreality came over her. She felt like a character in a play.

"You're mistaken, David," she told him truthfully, mimicking the same calm tone that he was using. "I never spoke to any bartender on that cruise ship, other than to order a drink. And I certainly wasn't 'all over' anyone."

"Are you telling me I don't know my own wife when I see her?" he asked, his voice rising the tiniest little bit.

"What I'm telling you is that I never left our cabin in the middle of the night to meet a bartender or anyone else on board that ship. Maybe you only dreamed you saw me." She spoke the words with conviction but the hairs were rising up along her neck. What exactly had happened that night? She only remembered the one incident, but how had she managed to get into the bright room to begin with? Where was she? She had originally assumed that she had been taken from their cabin in her sleep. She had come up with that scenario through a series of deductions that seemed to her the only possibility.

"Then where were you that night?" he demanded.

"What night?" she asked.

"The night you disappeared from our bed. The night that changed everything between us!"

"What do you mean?" she asked, blushing slightly. She wondered if he actually knew something that could enlighten her as well.

"You know perfectly well what I mean," he said, allowing his frustration to show at last. "I'll be honest. I figured you had a little fling that you regretted afterwards. I suppose that's why you've been so strange lately. I thought I'd give you a little time to get over it, but frankly my patience is running a little thin here, Emilie."

She stared at him, aghast. "A little fling?" she repeated, truly astounded now by his composure. For an instant, she felt the old stirrings of admiration and love for him. His love for her was humbling. She was thoughtful for a moment, genuinely touched. "So you thought I had an affair and you said nothing?"

"The first time I got up and found you in the bar, around one-thirty, I figured you were just having a good time, so I left you alone. I went back to bed. I actually managed somehow to fall back asleep. But when I woke up again around five and you still weren't there, I got a little concerned. I went back up to the lounge but neither you nor the bartender were anywhere to be found. But then around five forty-five, about the time I got back to our cabin, you were there in bed, asleep. I don't know…" He paused a minute, apparently too choked up to continue. Emilie waited breathlessly for him to recover. He looked at her when he had composed himself again. "It was so out of character for you, I decided to just leave it alone." After this both of them were silent. In a while, he added, "It wasn't really us. That whole vacation…I just figured we could put whatever it was behind us and get back to normal, but that doesn't seem to be happening."

"I did not have an affair with anyone."

"Where were you, then?"

She was silent for a moment, wondering what to say. "I don't know."

"You don't know?"

"I don't remember getting up and leaving our cabin that night," she told him honestly.

"What about going to the bar?"

She shook her head. "No."

"You don't remember *anything* about that night?"

"No," she said again, thinking to herself, *Not anything I could tell you about.*

David looked at her for a long moment. He seemed to sense that she was keeping something from him, although it appeared he wanted to believe her.

"Well, then, would you kindly explain why have you been so…different ever since that night?"

"I don't know, David," she said. "I really don't know." There were so many things she didn't know. She didn't know why she felt so different about him now. She didn't know how she got out of their bed that night and ended up in the bright room. She was alarmed by the possibility that David might really have seen her with one of the bartenders. She had no memory of being in the lounge or talking to anyone. Was she there before or after the incident? Could the bartender have had something to do with what happened? Perhaps someone had slipped something into her drink. Did something really happen in a bright room or was it all just a hallucination of some kind? Could she even be certain that the events she remembered ever really happened?

But she almost immediately rejected the idea that the incident might not have been real. It had happened. The memories were too vivid. The taste of metal was still in her mouth.

And she was pregnant. That was no hallucination. Yet, she and David had spent most of their time on that cruise holed up in their cabin, until that night. Even before they left for the cruise, they were intimate nearly every night. It was not entirely impossible that the child was his. The odds were probably better that it was. There had only been that one incident on the cruise, and she couldn't even remember all of the details. Given what David just told her, there surely was some question about what happened that night. And even if it did happen the way she remembered it, she reminded herself again that it was only the one incident. What were the chances that a single incident would result in pregnancy?

But on the other hand, after four years of trying to get pregnant with David, wouldn't it, in fact, make more sense that the isolated incident must have resulted in pregnancy, given that David's efforts had thus far failed?

No, the baby was not David's. Emilie could not say why but she knew it. She tried to convince herself that once she rid herself of it, she and David could return to the way they were. In the meantime, she would just have to make more of an effort to hide her present feelings and go through the motions of married life as if everything were normal. Clearly she would have to try harder.

Her talk with David seemed to act like a cathartic. The realization of what she had to do next was there all along, but until now it had seemed to exist in her subconscious exclusively, lingering as if from quite a far distance off…so far that she had not felt compelled to act on it as yet. Everything was happening so quickly. But now, suddenly, she felt an incredible urgency to act.

Surprisingly, there was no hesitation or regret. Everything that Emilie had believed and held dear up to that point instantly disappeared. Things like choice and guilt were luxuries that no longer existed for her. That little voice inside her—the one that had always held her to standards based on a life of longing for a child of her own—had been silenced in a single moment. Her terror, pure and solid and more real than anything she had ever known before, was growing as rapidly as the creature inside her seemed to be. It obliterated every other emotion.

First thing the next morning, with the episode with David still fresh in her mind, Emilie opened the phone book. She was unsure who to call. She could hardly contact her regular doctor, who had spent the last few years trying to help her and David conceive. Flipping through the pages, she was surprised to find that there was a category for abortion. She dialed the first number listed.

"You have options," the woman at the other end of the phone told her in a gentle, understanding tone. Emilie had made several botched attempts to articulate her situation. The woman, however, appeared to need no explanations or excuses. She seemed satisfied to simply provide the information in a kindly, indifferent manner and allow the nervous callers, of which she clearly had many, to choose the course best for them. "We have both the pill and the procedure available at this clinic."

"There's a pill?" asked Emilie, surprised. She had not kept up with what was happening in the world of women's rights, being so committed to her life as wife and prospective mother.

"Indeed there is," the woman informed her brightly. "Shall I schedule you an appointment for a consultation?"

Emilie felt a sudden wave of panic. In that instant, her morning sickness kicked in and a ripple of intense heat flooded her insides, followed by an upsurge of nausea. She swallowed the taste of metal. "What happens during the consultation?" she asked.

"Nothing too traumatic," the woman assured her cheerfully, perhaps sensing her discomfort or maybe just accustomed to these questions from women riddled with unwanted emotions and distracted from fighting down their nausea. "We will, of course, do a pregnancy test and if there's any confusion about how far along you are we may do an ultrasound. Other than that, the consultation is pretty much just to inform you of your choices and offer any other support you may need."

That might not seem traumatic for most women, thought Emilie, but the idea of a pregnancy test—and especially an ultrasound—terrified her. What might they discover if they prodded too closely? "I already had a pregnancy test," she told the woman. "And I know the day of conception."

"Of course," the woman replied smoothly. "We have to do our own pregnancy test on our patients, but it's possible we may not need to do an ultrasound on you. But those are the things we can discuss when you come in. Which day is best for you?"

After a long pause, Emilie finally said, "Any day, the sooner the better."

And in spite of her fears, the pregnancy test did not reveal anything except that Emilie was pregnant. The doctor's expression held nothing but simple courtesy as she confirmed Emilie's condition. Emilie sat stiffly on a table, shivering in her examination gown. The doctor asked her to lie back and began pressing on her lower stomach. "Tell me if you have pain anywhere," she said. Then she lifted Emilie's feet into stirrups that had fuzzy socks attached to the ends. Emilie tried to think of an appropriate objection to being examined.

The doctor slipped two gloved fingers into Emilie's vagina and pressed a little more. Her eyebrows rose. Emilie held her breath when she saw the change in the doctor's expression.

"I think you may be wrong about the time of conception," the doctor told her. "You seem farther along than one to two weeks."

Emilie's heart seemed to stop for an instant, then it resumed beating with heavy, racking thuds. She tried to breathe normally but was only able to take in very small, unsatisfactory breaths. There seemed to be a blockage about midway into her lungs, preventing her from taking in enough air. She felt dizzy, but fought the urge to faint. Terror was ripping through her.

"Not to worry," the doctor continued, slipping the gloves off her hands and throwing them into a nearby trash bin marked Hazardous Materials. "We can do an ultrasound."

"No!" Emilie exclaimed.

The doctor looked at her with mild surprise. A strange sense of events spiraling out of her control enveloped Emilie. She felt that she positively could not risk the doctor actually seeing whatever it was growing inside her uterus. She berated herself inwardly. She believed all along that it was growing at an abnormally rapid pace, and she realized now that she could have averted this by giving the doctor an earlier conception date. She felt more desperate than ever that she should not allow the doctor to perform the ultrasound. "Please..." she began, trying to speak calmly. "It cannot be much farther along than what I told you," she pleaded. "I swear that I had my last period."

"That could have been spotting," said the doctor. "An ultrasound is not painful or—"

"But I know I can't be that much farther along," Emilie protested. "I know I couldn't be nine weeks anyway, and you said they give women the abortion pill up to nine weeks!"

"Yes, that's correct," said the doctor. "And I do agree that you are not yet nine weeks." She paused a moment, examining Emilie's face. "Are you certain that you want to terminate this pregnancy?"

"Yes." Emilie nodded her head vigorously. "I am absolutely certain."

"Well—" the doctor sighed, picking up Emilie's file "—your blood work came back okay, so in that case we can begin your treatment today."

Emilie hadn't realized that she had stopped breathing until she heard these words from the doctor. Her breath came out in an explosive rush. She didn't dare speak. The relief temporarily overwhelmed her.

But three days later, after having taken her first pill in the doctor's office that day, and then following up with the rest of the pills at home exactly as she had been instructed to do, Emilie was devastated to find that she was still pregnant. Not only had the pregnancy not been terminated, it seemed to her that whatever was inside her was still growing at an accelerated pace.

She was afraid to call the doctor and tell her the news. Surely now they would insist that she have the ultrasound.

Emilie sat down miserably in front of her computer. Opening the Internet, she typed in the search box the words *pregnant by an alien*. More than four million results came up.

One by one, Emilie began following the links and spent the rest of that day reading. There was a lot to sift through. Most of the links consisted of insane chatter that offered no real enlightenment, but from the seemingly more reliable sources she found some consistencies that she herself could attest to. There were apparently many other women out there who had similar experiences to hers. Some people believed that the "grays," as she now believed she had encountered, often impregnated women in an effort to produce "hybrid"—half alien, half human—children. Why these hybrids were being bred Emilie could not find a satisfactory answer to. But she found great comfort in the fact that other women had been through an encounter that was remarkably similar to her own. In particular, she became hopeful when she read that many of the impregnated abductees reported having a second encounter shortly after the first, where the aliens returned to take the fetus from the mothers. Some women claimed to have gone through this entire process several times with the aliens. Others claimed to have experienced a kind of communication with them, where they were provided the "knowledge" that these hybrids were necessary for the continuation of the aliens' civilization. Emilie read all that she could find on these hybrids and their mothers, but in spite of the large number of hits she had gotten, there appeared to be precious little useful information to be found.

But the mere suggestion of the aliens returning gave Emilie cause for hope, and she fervently clung to the possibility that the aliens would come back and relieve her of her burden.

And yet, she knew that she could not rely on this. She must do something. But what?

She had already been informed by the nurses at the clinic that, in the event that the treatment did not work, she would be obliged to follow through with the procedural abortion. There were several problems associated with this, both of which seemed insurmountable to Emilie. First, the procedure they recommended was best performed between six to twelve weeks. She would never be able to endure carrying it another four weeks. But it was even worse to imagine going through the procedure. What kind of matter would they find when they extracted the contents of her uterus?

It was preferable to imagine that the aliens would return. But how could she be certain that they would? Yet the idea, once conceived, took hold of her consciousness, and Emilie suddenly found herself waiting. Every moment, with every movement and sound around her, she realized that she was only waiting. Even when she seemed to forget that she was waiting, she would suddenly remember again when she jumped to attention at the slightest noise, or flash of light, or anything else that captured her attention. But always she was disappointed to find something other than what she was waiting for. During this time, a kind of shift took place in her consciousness, so that she lived in state of constant expectancy that was shattered by thousands upon thousands of little disappointments.

Imagining the aliens' impending return, Emilie's entire being would become alive and alert, tingling with an unwelcome and discomfiting anticipation. Yet now she had good reason to accept, and even desire, their return. Recollections, fleeting but powerfully persuasive, would tease and torment her consciousness. Images of the tentacles—massive and encroaching in damp, colorless gray—flashed before her eyes, capturing her, holding her, penetrating her. With every passing hour her sense of expectancy grew, so that the slightest indication of something approaching would cause her hair to stand on end and her flesh to tremble and pulse. In those moments she was frozen with expectation and need, although she was repulsed by her own desire. She was alarmed and mortified by the jarring response of her body to the memories, which should have left her petrified with dread, not aching and wet with yearning. She tried to focus on the many negative and frightening aspects of the experience, but like a moth hovering too near a scorching flame, she was already trapped in the hypnotic spell of the bright white light, and she fluttered about in a frenzy as it continued to draw her in, closer and closer to that which frightened her most. In accepting her fate, she had come to expect it, even look forward to it, and in the meantime a terrible yearning took over all of her consciousness, creating an aching discomfort deep in her womb.

During this time of expecting, Emilie's dreams became even more intense and detailed. Often when she awoke, she genuinely believed the dreams really had happened. She would sit up in bed, excitedly grasping at the details of her vision, until she felt the familiar morning sickness well up, and her mouth watered from the offending taste of metal. Then she would lie back down in bed and close her eyes, trying to recapture the dream and retreat back to the state of mind that took her there. There was little left of actual terror now, for she had come to realize that they were not going to physically harm her. They were, underneath their alien exterior—she felt—harmless and peaceful creatures. There was even a kind of gentle beauty in their eyes as they silently watched her. They never spoke, not even to each other. The only sounds she ever heard were the slick, fluid noises coming from her body and her own echoing cries. The aliens, in spite of their absolute silence, somehow managed to convey a sense of calm so potent it would have taken drugs to produce the same effect by human standards. She had a sense that their every movement was calculated and controlled and significant. Her mind always seemed to go back to her memory of the tentacles, and she thought about them continually, imagining them caressing her, restraining her, penetrating her.

The dreams left Emilie weak with longing.

With the passing days a kind of frustration began to develop. Although Emilie's sense of waiting and expectation intensified, her fear that the aliens would not return also grew. This frustration kept her in a constant state of irritable touchiness and, everyone, especially David, kept a wide berth between themselves and her.

After a while, the fear caused her sense of urgency to reemerge. The alien thing inside her was still growing at an accelerated pace. She realized that she couldn't wait any longer. She reluctantly scheduled a second appointment at the clinic. But she was actually more terrified of what might happen at the clinic than anything she might be subjected to in an alien encounter. The events that had taken place in that encounter had been shocking and traumatic, but the thought of being exposed was unimaginable. Her life would be over.

This time there were protesters at the clinic. Emilie sat in her car, silently watching them. She did not feel that she possessed the strength to walk into the building. But with a sudden burst of anger, she got out of her car and approached the building. She saw that the protesters spotted her, but she refused to retreat. She must get to the other side. She could hear their angry voices shouting out messages and was seized with a full-blown fury of her own. What right did they have to try to stop her? Their conviction was suddenly terribly oppressive to her. She struggled to control her rage as she brushed off the pamphlets and flyers they flung at her.

But a dizzying confusion was coming over her. The crowd seemed larger than she originally thought. In which direction was she going? She was suddenly disoriented. Panic seized her as she struggled to find her way out of the crowd. She longed to scream but couldn't find her voice. Someone had hold of her. They were leading her, talking to her with soothing little sounds. A strange heat moved through her, searing upward, and filling her head in a sudden rush. She felt light-headed and realized she was going to faint.

And yet she did not lose consciousness. Somehow, the crowd just suddenly disappeared. Emilie didn't move—she couldn't move. It was as if she were paralyzed. But she was moving. There was no tangible movement that she could detect and yet she was certain that she was being moved. A strange sense of déjà vu crept over her. She realized that she was floating. Her last thoughts were of the white room with the bright lights.

Emilie woke up with a start, believing herself to be at the clinic, but there was an instant awareness of unreality all around her. And there were bright lights! She wondered hopefully if she had finally made it back. Perhaps her trip to the clinic had forced the aliens into action. Had they intercepted her? She looked around and suddenly there was no doubt that she was back in the white room. But was she only dreaming it?

She realized that she was naked and the anticipation filled her in such a rush that it jarred her on impact. A slow, tingling upsurge of stinging desire seeped tenaciously through her veins, meandering along each of the various pathways toward her womb. Her heart thudded heavily in her ears. Her legs had been lifted and were being held far apart. She could feel the cells all around her womb rising and swelling and moistening in readiness. Each one seemed to be pulsing with its own pounding, stinging ache. She squinted as she looked around her. Her eyes were slow in adjusting to the unnaturally bright light, but she desperately wanted to be certain that it was really happening this time.

Emilie felt something cool on her leg and jerked her head in that direction, still struggling to see. The heat of the light penetrated her, radiating inward, with so much potency that it felt like a physical touch. Yes. She believed that she was truly awake and that they had returned. Full remembrance of what happened came rushing back as Emilie felt the first tentacle creep insidiously upward along the inside of her leg. The tentacle clung to her flesh as it moved, causing goose bumps to rise up in alarm. It felt like hundreds of tiny, podlike suction cups clinging and grasping at her skin as it worked its way over her, reminding her of an immense caterpillar that clutches as it moves. The tentacles gently kneaded and pinched with every advance, sending all of her nerve endings into a flurry of sensations, ranging from revulsion to arousal. She felt another tentacle moving over her, and then another, and she could just make out the dusky formations against her pale skin. She did not resist, although she did have the presence of mind to feel an instinctual terror. But after the weeks of terrified brooding, with all of her senses held hostage by the dread of them *not* returning, her relief gave her body the freedom to suddenly come alive. Recalling her dreams, she brazenly reached her hands out to inquisitively touch the alien tentacles. The feel of them on her sensitive fingertips brought a fresh horror to the experience, as well as sending an alarming thrill through the center of her. They were real. It was going to happen again. A powerful surge of arousal flooded her womb, causing her vulva to swell painfully under the force of it. Her body ached with need.

Emilie turned her head and tried to capture a glimpse of them. Their visages were dim and difficult to make out in the harsh light, but she could clearly see their large, vacant eyes peering at her. She stared into the impenetrable orbs in open-mouthed wonder as the tentacles continued to slowly advance on her, kneading and pulling at her quivering flesh as they inched their way up and wrapped themselves around her arms and legs to hold her steady for what was to come. She shook with impatience.

This time, having the terror of not knowing what to expect behind her, Emilie's senses were more keenly in tune with each and every nuance. She noticed in particular that their tentacles seemed to secrete something liquid as they moved over her, clasping and pulling—perhaps even penetrating—her tingling flesh in the process, and afterward leaving traces of the mysterious residue behind. She could distinctly feel the flurry of activity all along the undersides of their tentacles, constantly shifting and grasping as thousands of tiny fingers seemed to break through her skin with their continuous barrage of little clinging pinches. It suddenly occurred to her that this residue could be having some kind of tranquilizing effect on her; although her skin seemed to come alive under its influence, a sense of well-being seemed to be seeping into her, releasing her inhibitions and enhancing her desire. She felt all at once paralyzed and alert, so that, although she could hardly move, she could most definitely feel, and more keenly than she could ever remember feeling before. Spread wide open and immobilized as she was, she could not help but think of a fly trapped in the web of a spider. She reminded herself that she was not the aliens' prey. And yet, she was also keenly aware that they wanted something from her.

All of this was happening at an excruciatingly slow pace, as if in slow motion, reminding Emilie of her dreams. But this was much more vivid than any dream, and unlike her dreams, it was not somewhere off in the distance but right here in front of her, acutely real. And now, at long last, she glimpsed the other appendage—the very one that always evaded her in her dreams—approaching. Wobbly and thick, it moved toward her like something massive being conveyed on the end of a tenuous wire. It appeared even broader than she remembered—it was oh so thick—and grayish in color, just like the tentacles. Emilie watched, transfixed, as it advanced. Her arms and legs were still spread wide and held gently but firmly in place by the clinging, moving tentacles, allowing this new appendage full access to her body. She strained painfully against her lively restraints, not in an effort to escape the appendage but struggling to bring her body forward, to meet it head-on, hardly able to wait for it in its excruciating slowness. She sucked in her breath. She could no longer see the tip of it but she could suddenly feel it, there, at the entrance!

She wanted it, God help her. She wanted every alarming moment of it. She couldn't wait for it, in fact. She tried to open herself even more in an effort to accommodate the appendage but her limbs remained paralyzed. It was as if she had no limbs. Only those sensations that allowed her to *feel* what was happening remained active and keenly alert. Yet the tentacles continued to hold her down in spite of her paralysis, and all the while their undersides kept ceaselessly kneading and clasping at her flesh with what felt like a thousand tiny suction cups.

Emily moaned loudly as the appendage, pulsing and gyrating thickly, wriggled in between the folds of her labia, parting her lips with its broad head and coercing her to open. She was stunned momentarily by the intense pleasure she got from having the alien inside her again. The appendage worked its way in slowly, urging her to accept its gangly fullness leisurely and persuasively, throbbing so vigorously that she could feel the reverberations throughout her womb. Inch by painstakingly slow inch, it advanced farther up into her, easing the painful ache that had been building in her during the weeks of waiting and expecting.

Meanwhile, the vibrating thing that was filling her continued to inch forward and expand. It, too, released a kind of slick substance as it pressed onward, but this made its advance only slightly easier, since the sheer size of it caused every forward thrust to stretch and graze her tender inner flesh.

As the appendage approached her womb, Emilie readied herself for what was to come. Even in the throes of ecstasy, she was aware of what was happening. She understood what was expected of her and knew what they had come to do. She all at once comprehended the images around her, even with her vision blurred by the too-white light. She suddenly recognized the odd, grayish blotches that spattered the white-walled background for what they were—hybrids, the women online had called them, in various stages of development, that were kept in jars on the wall. Why Emilie had been chosen for this she didn't know, but she would do what had to be done, and with this thought she felt a sense of purpose. She could feel their need for her as acutely as she could feel her own.

One of the tentacles that had been holding her legs had begun moving steadily upward while it held her, winding and massaging its way to the very top of her thigh and then resting its tip on the inside edge. Emilie edged her body alongside it so that she could rub her clitoris vigorously against it in an attempt to relieve the exquisite agony that continued to steadily rise up within her. Her body was throbbing with sensation, and she began to rock, moving her hips back and forth with anxious little jerks, struggling to create the right friction between her and the wayward tentacle. She was too wrapped up in her immediate need to think of anything else. There was nothing else but the enormous, pulsing appendage that filled her.

But just as the ache was nearing what she felt was the most intense pleasure of her life, her euphoria was interrupted by the approach of a second appendage that she suddenly caught sight of. She cried out when she saw it, instantly recalling its purpose from the previous encounter.

This new appendage came at Emilie just as agonizingly slowly as the first one had done, and she felt equal parts desire and dread as she waited for it. But when she eventually felt it pulsing at her anal entrance, pressing and whirling against the tightly puckered hole, the anticipation from the extended wait made her long for it. It pressed into her patiently but persistently, releasing more of the tantalizing fluid as it ultimately breached the opening and snaked its way inside. Like the first appendage, it kept pulsing and vibrating as it worked its way into her body. But it was not as large as the other and, once inside, it appeared to act as yet another restraint to hold her still while the aliens completed their objective. Without words, the aliens had managed to communicate this to her, and she now knew this and many other things, such as that she had been specifically selected to be impregnated, and that the hybrid that she carried would end up with the others on the wall. She remembered everything from the previous encounter, and other things besides, but none of it mattered, except that she was now able to comprehend and anticipate the events as they were taking place.

Emilie waited for her body to adjust to the intrusive feeling of being so completely filled by the aliens' appendages. She knew that immediately after the discomfort, incredible pleasure would follow. And sure enough, her first orgasm exploded within her, and she shuddered in the realization that it would set off one right after the other, like an avalanche of pleasure that once began could not be stopped. She was prepared and even yearning for all of it now, and she looked around for the third appendage, even as she saw that it was approaching her from the side. She opened her mouth to accept it, shuddering as another orgasm ripped through her. She savored the pungent flavor of its metallic fluid this time, at last understanding that it would amplify her pleasure. And she could already feel the intensity of her orgasms increasing.

Emilie closed her eyes and tried to contain the steady waves of ecstatic pleasure that were overtaking her. It seemed as if her entire being was throbbing and pulsing in perfect time with the aliens. She must appear like something alien herself, wrapped in their tentacles, with their enormous appendages extending from every orifice. She moaned in exquisite agony at the image of her white skin amongst so much of their sallow gray. The lower half of her body felt invaded and filled and immobilized, even as every molecule screamed with tingling, agonizing pleasure. She eagerly swallowed the mysterious fluid, feeling her mouth water from the sharp taste of metal as she delighted in the sensations of being penetrated and stretched and restrained from all angles. Wave after wave of orgasmic euphoria burst forth in her like the concrete blocks of a dam giving way in a storm. And even in between orgasms, the pleasure continued to trickle through her in little gushes that made her quiver and jump.

The appendages extended out perhaps eighteen inches or so from the aliens' bodies, but how much of this she was taking inside her body Emily could not have said. She could feel the first appendage pressing and vibrating determinedly against the opening of her womb. She sucked more enthusiastically on the appendage in her mouth, preparing herself for what she knew would be coming next. Meanwhile, her orgasms kept intensifying as she choked down the taste of metal.

With slow, deliberate precision, the first appendage began to expand and contract, spreading its tip out over her womb and filling her with a thick, heavy pressure as it clamped itself onto it. She could feel the pressure in her anus increasing as well, while that appendage expanded also in an attempt to hold her even more still in preparation for what was to come. With her so fully subdued, she could no longer rock her hips back and forth to further stimulate herself but this was no longer necessary anyway, as she could not stop the orgasms now if she tried.

Emilie braced herself as she felt the appendage gently force open her cervix. She felt a giddy sense of unreality, in spite of the thick, swelling cramps that overtook her. She willed herself to open wider, and she could feel herself opening. She swallowed more of the mysterious fluid, and the cramps seemed to contribute to the pleasure she was receiving, making each delightful wave feel heavier and stronger and more penetrating.

In spite of the pleasure Emilie was receiving, she could not help feeling a flash of fleeting alarm and mild resistance with each new phase of the experience, but she knew that it would disappear just as quickly as it had come. She felt it again when she perceived that something was permeating her womb. It must have come from inside the appendage, whatever it was that was making its way into her womb. It worked at its objective diligently, opening her even wider as it went. The cramping continued in thick, rolling, waves that seemed to catch hold of her orgasm and make it swell and pulse throughout her abdomen. She moaned loudly, staring up into their vacant depths as orgasm after orgasm washed over her. And the aliens just kept silently watching her with their expressionless eyes.

Emilie now felt a cool, sticky fluid being expelled into her womb. She was beginning to enjoy being used by these creatures to propagate their species, and she was more than willing to accept all that it entailed. The only fear she felt at that moment was that, once they finished what they were doing, it would be over. The emptiness that she would feel then, she could not bear to think about. She must focus on the present. Already, her body was showing signs of exhaustion and she knew that once they were finished in her womb it would be over. She focused on the appendages that penetrated her as wave after wave of intense pleasure assailed her. They filled her so completely, expanding and stretching her so absolutely, that she could hardly focus on anything else. She had reached a state of euphoria, aroused beyond anything she could have imagined.

Emilie moaned in ecstasy as another wave of pleasure rushed through her. The wetness was now seeping out of her, soaking her inner thighs. It was almost too much to endure, being so utterly ravished by the hoary, pulsing appendages that twisted and ground inside her. She wondered vaguely as she stared up at them what they were thinking. Did all of their other abductees behave the same as she did? Did they wonder about her as well, while they silently watched her squirm and moan? Did they know the pleasure they were giving her? Did it please them, or did they find her peculiar? She suddenly wanted to speak to them but her mouth was still filled with the appendage and the taste of metal. She stared into their black, seemingly vacant eyes, and tried to communicate her thoughts to them. With her eyes she kept silently pleading with them. She wanted them to know that they could come back for her. She wanted to assure them that they could use her again and again. The fact that other women claimed to have repeated encounters gave her hope. Since she couldn't communicate through language, she wanted to show them with her body that she was willing. She was willing to populate their entire planet if only they would keep filling her in this way.

But even as she kept silently pleading with them, a slow, menacing despair began to creep over Emilie. The pleasure was beginning to subside. She knew that her body was exhausted, but her mind wanted to go on. Yet she knew that she could not glean any more pleasure from the experience than she already had. As the orgasms faded, they were replaced by a dull sense of emptiness. They had expelled the contents of her womb. It would soon be over.

Another substance was being released, and Emilie could feel herself drifting off to sleep. She halfheartedly struggled against it, but the desire was too powerful to resist. She tried one last time to communicate with them before she finally lost consciousness.

Emilie came to slowly and reluctantly. She made several attempts to open her eyes, blinking them shut again repeatedly against the sharp, bright lights. Hope filled her as she struggled to gain her vision and confirm the meaning of the bright lights. Had her attempt to communicate with them succeeded, and her wish to remain with them been granted?

She fought to contain her sudden anxiety as she waited for her eyes to work. She squinted as they slowly became adjusted to the light. Her vision returned quickly once the initial shock of light had been absorbed, and she scanned the room she was in quickly, searching for signs of them. But the disappointment was already upon her before she fully recognized her surroundings. Although she was in an unfamiliar place, it was in a familiar realm. She was no longer with them.

She realized gradually that she was in a hospital room. She tried to sit but realized that she was being restrained. Something held her arms to the bed!

Before Emilie could so much as open her mouth, there was a nurse at her side, already quieting her before she had uttered a sound.

"Where am I?" she asked. "Why am I tied to the bed?" There were so many questions that Emilie needed answered.

"Everything is going to be fine," said the nurse. "The doctor will be here in a moment."

Emilie struggled against her restraints. She wanted to touch her abdomen, to see if the little bubble had gone. "Is it out?" she asked, her voice rising.

But the nurse was intent on keeping her calm. "The doctor will be here in a moment," she kept saying to Emilie. Her evasiveness, combined with her constant efforts to quiet Emilie, only served to increase Emilie's tension. She was quickly becoming hysterical. She turned her head this way and that, looking around frantically for a clue to what was happening.

Movement just outside the doorway caught her eye, and Emilie noticed that there were several people right outside her door, talking. It was difficult for her to see who they were because of a curtain that was partially blocking her view, but she could just barely make out David talking to someone in a white jacket. The doctor?

She watched David's face anxiously, trying to decipher his words as he spoke. She was afraid to call out to him. He looked pale, and when he finally turned and met Emilie's eyes, she saw that there was an expression in his that she had never seen before. He looked at her as if she were something abominable. Emilie stared back at him in silent alarm, frozen with mortification.

"Please," she whispered, turning back to the nurse. "Please help me."

"Shhh," the nurse said soothingly, patting Emilie's hand. "It's going to be okay. The doctor will be here any second."

And just then a woman in a white coat turned the corner into the room, followed by a man who looked vaguely familiar but who Emilie could not place. Last to enter was David, who remained several steps behind the others, as if he were afraid. He refused to look directly at Emilie.

"How are you feeling, Emilie?" the woman asked, but she resumed speaking before Emilie could answer. "I'm Doctor Rozzi, and this is Doctor Meade from the clinic." She indicated the man who came in with her. "Do you remember what happened?"

Emilie looked at David. She wished he wasn't there. She struggled to remember the questions she had wanted to ask a moment ago. "I…I'm not sure what happened," she said, choosing her words carefully. "Why am I here? Why are my hands tied to the bed?"

"That is only a precautionary measure," Dr. Rozzi assured her. "We wanted to make sure that you didn't hurt yourself."

"Hurt myself?" Emilie looked at the doctor, stunned. "Why would I hurt myself?"

"Do you remember what happened this morning?" the doctor asked her again, but she removed the restraints from Emilie's hands as she spoke.

Emilie brought her hands to her chest self-consciously. She remembered everything except how she came to be in the hospital, but she was not about to discuss it with these doctors or David, so she shook her head in the negative. "Please just tell me why I'm here," she said. She sat back in her bed, suddenly calm although a nagging sense of something horrific churned painfully in the pit of her stomach.

"Do you remember visiting the clinic?" Dr. Rozzi asked her in an exaggeratedly patient tone.

Emilie looked at David at the mention of the clinic. He watched her from behind the doctor with the look of horror still fixed in his expression. Emilie's sense of dread and foreboding increased every time she looked at him. "I remember…protesters," she began, struggling to recall what she could about the clinic.

"Okay. That's a start," Dr. Rozzi encouraged her. "And do you remember being inside the clinic?"

Emilie shook her head. "I didn't go inside the clinic," she told the doctor.

There was a pause as Dr. Rozzi appeared to consider this. "Do you remember why you went to the clinic?"

Emilie glanced at David again. Her heart was beginning to beat faster. It was strange to be able to feel it and see it on the computer monitor, all at the same time. She nodded her head.

"That's great, Emilie," Dr. Rozzi told her. "You're doing fine. And can you tell me anything about the procedure you had at the clinic?"

Emilie blinked and then shook her head. "I…didn't have the…procedure," she said adamantly. A strange, unidentified dread was creeping over her. She had been clasping the blankets to her chest while the doctor questioned her, and now she slowly pulled them even more tightly to her, as if to prevent someone from removing the blankets and proving Emilie wrong, right there in front of everyone.

"Emilie," Dr. Rozzi continued in a tone of polite firmness combined with patient understanding, "a procedure was performed on you today at the clinic."

Emilie looked at the monitor above her head. She stared at it, mesmerized, as it traced the erratic pace of her heart.

"Do you understand, Emilie?" Dr. Rozzi asked, speaking to her as if she were a child.

There was silence for a long moment. "They took it," Emilie whispered suddenly.

There was another pause, during which Dr. Rozzi appeared to be grappling over how to proceed. "Okay, Emilie," she continued in her patient tone. "That's good. And then do you remember what happened?"

"I fell asleep," said Emilie.

"And after that?"

"Nothing. I woke up here." She suddenly became upset. "That is all I remember, Doctor. Now, please, please, just tell me what happened!"

The other doctor cleared his throat and Dr. Rozzi turned to him expectantly.

"Hello again, Emilie," he began awkwardly, clearing his throat again before continuing. "You slept through most of the procedure. We had to sedate you because you were further along than we originally thought. You seemed fine until you woke up in the recovery room." The doctor paused here to clear his throat again. "At that point you became quite hysterical."

"Do you remember any of what he's telling you?" Dr. Rozzi asked.

Emilie shook her head, and the other doctor went on. "You kept screaming and demanding to see the…fetus," he said. "You had quite an episode, tearing things off the walls…breaking them. We had to call an ambulance and that's when you were restrained and brought here."

Upon hearing the doctor's words, Emilie suddenly recalled thinking, as she drifted off to sleep, that she must see the baby before they took it away with them. She wanted to be certain that it was really theirs before she let them take it. But how had she ended up inside the clinic with this doctor? Had the aliens come to her there? "But…I don't understand," she said to the doctor. "How did I get inside the clinic?"

The doctor sighed. "The clinic is where you came to have the abortion," he reiterated impatiently.

"But I didn't have an abortion!" Emilie cried. She looked at David, then at the doctors again. "It wasn't an abortion."

Dr. Rozzi put her hand on Emilie's. "It's perfectly all right," she told her. "We are going to help get you through this."

"No!" Emilie cried, jerking her hand away. "You don't understand. I didn't have an abortion."

Dr. Rozzi gave the nurse a look as if to say, "Get ready," and then she turned to David. "She's going to need your support now," she told him. David moved reluctantly from behind the doctors to stand at Emilie's side. He reached down unenthusiastically and took her hand. Their hands remained flaccid and lifeless, as if the connection was equally repellent to both.

"I didn't have an abortion," Emilie repeated again, but this time it came out more like a plea.

"I'm sorry," Dr. Rozzi said. "Doctor Meade is one of the resident doctors for the clinic and he was there with you at the time."

Emilie turned to him and paled. "You were there with me while I…while I…you…"

"Performed the abortion, yes," he told her. "We had no idea that you were so troubled about it. You seemed so determined to go through with it beforehand."

"You're sure there was an abortion?" Emilie was incredulous.

"I'm quite certain, yes," the doctor assured her.

"Was it a…?" The doctor became a blur as large tears suddenly filled Emilie's eyes.

"The sex of the baby is not something you should concern yourself with," he advised.

"Human?" she finished.

The doctors exchanged glances. David gasped. Everyone was clearly taken aback by her question.

"Emilie," Dr. Meade began after an uncomfortable pause. He was clearly choosing his words carefully. "What did you mean at the clinic when you kept saying that you wanted to see if the baby was theirs? Who are 'they'?"

But Emilie suddenly realized what the doctor had said before. Her eyes grew wide with horror. "The baby had a *sex?*"

Dr. Rozzi tried to interject. "Emilie…"

"Did you *see* the baby?" Emilie demanded. Her mind was racing as she now struggled to remember the details of what happened. She had not actually *seen* the aliens take anything out of her. She had only assumed that's what they were doing. But everything seemed suspect to her now. Why had they come for her, if not to get their hybrid from her before the doctors at the clinic got to her? But if that were the case, why did Dr. Meade keep insisting she'd had the procedure? She looked at him with suspicion. He had to be lying. Was he in on it with the aliens? Was he one of them?

"Why was I brought here?" she asked, her voice turning hard.

"I already explained that to you, Emilie," Dr. Rozzi replied patiently. "We're going to keep you here on the fourth floor for a few days," she continued. "For observation, and to make sure you aren't going to hurt yourself or anybody else."

"You can't keep me here!" Emilie said, her voice rising. She looked at David, but perceived immediately that she couldn't expect support from him. Once again, Dr. Rozzi looked meaningfully at the nurse, who now jerked into action, retrieving a little vial from a nearby table and hurriedly attaching it to a syringe.

"David," Emilie began, knowing it was hopeless, but needing to try. "He must be one of them," she said quickly, realizing there would be no way to explain everything before the nurse finished preparing the sedative. "It wasn't yours," she continued. "It wasn't even human, David." She turned to the doctor suddenly. "Bring it here, then," she screamed. "Show it to me." The nurse was preparing her arm for the needle. Emilie knew better than to struggle. "Please, David," she cried. "Please don't leave me here with them."

"This is only temporary," Dr. Rozzi said in an even tone. But Emilie wouldn't listen to her. She felt the prick of the needle in her arm and winced. Dr. Rozzi continued speaking in soothing tones. "Given your history, I think it's likely that all of this is a one-time episode brought on by prenatal stress and hormones. I've run some blood tests to confirm if this is the case. For now, there is nothing more you need to do other than rest."

Emilie remained in a state of drugged bliss for several days. When she next saw David, he was supportive and attentive, more like the husband he had been before the incident. He had recovered from the initial shock, Emilie supposed, and forgiven her "temporary insanity," as Dr. Rozzi called it. The doctor explained that the insanity was brought on by a condition Emilie had—something to do with extreme deficiencies of iron in pregnant women causing the kidneys to malfunction. It was often accompanied by a strong taste of metal in the mouth.

Recovery was slower than Dr. Rozzi expected, and Emilie remained on the fourth floor for several weeks, not days as she had originally predicted. During those weeks, Emilie underwent intense therapy where she and Dr. Rozzi discussed the various details of Emilie's life, most of which led to Emilie's mother. What happened at the clinic was concluded to be a tragic but isolated incident of extreme anemia. Although Dr. Rozzi often questioned Emilie about her feelings about her lost pregnancy, she never mentioned the strange "hallucinations" Emilie had suffered from again.

And tomorrow Emilie would be going home.

Emilie looked upon the coming day with mixed feelings. Things would never, she knew, be the same with David. Going back to him and their life together would be difficult now.

Perhaps their marriage would end. The thought of being alone with him filled her with dread.

Emilie sighed, wondering what lay ahead for her. She supposed that she would just have to wait and see, feeling a strange sense of acceptance for whatever it was. There was little she could do to change it anyway, she now realized.

But she had a sense that it would all work out. What did it matter what any of them thought? *She* knew the truth. And she knew better than to tell anyone about it, too. Quite obviously, this world was not ready to accept what she knew to be true. And even among those who would accept it, there were plenty who would fight it if they could. There was good reason for her to keep quiet.

But aside from all of this, Emilie knew now that they were watching her. She had known it all along, really, but she became consciously aware of it her second day in the hospital. And once she'd figured this out, she went back over her behavior in the days prior and decided it hadn't been that bad. She had said very little, even in her worst moments, and afterward she had denounced every word. And since then, her behavior had been exemplary. Everything she said now, especially in her conversations with Dr. Rozzi, was really meant for their ears. She was determined to prove that she could be trusted. Next time she would handle things better. She promised this to herself and to them. She hoped they heard her. Hadn't they communicated to her telepathically in the little room? She was certain they must be able to hear her now, as well. They simply must.

And so tomorrow Emilie would go home, to David, and wait. She knew she would have to trust them if she expected them to trust her. She would keep their secret hidden deep inside her, releasing her memories of them only in her dreams. This would have to suffice until they returned. In the meantime, Emilie would remain…expecting.

Flowers for Angela

Tuesday, July 21, 2009

The addition of Eleanor Dobbs to my patient list puts an end to my Tuesdays off, but I couldn't comfortably fit her in any other day. I will see her at eleven, and then, for now, spend the afternoon catching up on office business. It looks as though all my hard work has finally blossomed into a successful, full-time practice!

My new patient is a middle-aged woman dealing with issues of loss from the death of her husband (he has been gone for nine months). I'll begin grief therapy initially, until I ascertain if she has any other issues. I had a brief consultation with her today, where we went over the basics. Incidentally, she and her husband had been seeing Dr. Michael Czernick in couple's therapy right up until he died.

Meanwhile, the tension at home continues to escalate.

Tom's attempts at reconciliation are cursory and unsatisfactory. Things got a little heated last night, and sure
enough, I find flowers in my office this morning (carnations!). Every gesture from him seems calculated to
annoy me. His lack of genuine effort makes it impossible
to take him seriously.

Tuesday, July 28, 2009

I encouraged Eleanor Dobbs to simply express her
feelings about her loss today. As is the tendency with
grieving spouses, she appears to be exaggerating his attributes somewhat and admits to no negative memories
of him whatsoever. This is fine for now, but it will be
important later on in therapy for me to help her to
accept the man he was, so that she can grieve properly.
I sense this may be difficult with her, as she seems a bit
more rigid in her denial than what is typical. Perhaps
there are issues of guilt? She currently expresses feelings
of loneliness, lethargy and depression, and says she has
the most difficulty at night. I prescribed a mild sedative
to help her sleep.

Tom was distant and sullen last night. When I am
around him lately, it's like there's a constant pressure
weighing me down. He was upset because he made
dinner and I was late and didn't feel like eating. But here
again, his gestures are thoughtless and rarely hit the
mark (he knows I'm watching my weight and he makes
pasta, of all things). So I guess I'm supposed to choke
down the meal he prepared whether I want it or not?
Everything always has to be on his terms.

But even when he's not moping or complaining, he's
bombarding me with questions—always his incessant

questions about everything! The smallest query from him grates on my nerves like a dripping faucet. I'm not sure why this is. I know he's trying to be civil and it's not like I have anything to hide. But I get the impression that he's only asking these things to gain some kind of advantage over me. Even the simplest inquiries about my day, my practice, my health, even my feelings—when coming from Tom—feel like the most frightful invasion.

Tuesday, August 4, 2009

Last week, as Eleanor Dobbs was preparing to leave my office, I asked her to write down some of her most cherished memories of her husband as she thought of him throughout the week. I was looking for examples of their more memorable moments together, some nice things he had done for her, special gifts he given her, etc. The list Eleanor brought me was astonishingly deficient. I felt it so lacking as to be mendacious, but she appeared to be quite sincere.

We then proceeded to discuss her list—one item in particular was especially perplexing for me. Her husband had brought her a "gift" of a half-eaten chocolate cake. When she asked him about it, he admitted that it was leftover from a party at his office. I mentioned to her that it seemed a strange thing to include on her list, and as we discussed it further, I learned that Eleanor is actually allergic to chocolate! I questioned her repeatedly about why she would include this on her list, but she appeared to be unable to explain it. Yet she remained strangely fixed in her belief that it was a nice gesture, and also that the memory of it makes her feel "happy." Very odd.

Tom brought up sex again last night. In his usual passive-aggressive manner, he "wondered" out loud how long it had been. I wanted to say, "It's been four months, one week and two days, Tom." It's truly irritating the way he tiptoes around a subject. He doesn't see that he's making me the responsible party for the sex that *he* wants! It's so typical. I deal with this all of the time with my patients, and yet it doesn't make it easier to cope with in my personal life. I must say that it does shed a new light on many of my concepts about therapy. I have always encouraged both partners to make an equal effort on issues in their marriage. But what if both partners don't *want* change on a particular issue? Surely the party with the stronger interest should do the lion's share of the work. I can understand why some patients might resist therapy if it means working toward a solution they may not necessarily want.

Tuesday, August 11, 2009

Today Eleanor Dobbs and I discussed her marriage in more detail. Mainly I wanted to know more about the treatment she and her husband received in couples' therapy with Dr. Czernick. I have been hearing his name pop up more and more in the industry. He is purported to having somewhere in the neighborhood of a ninety-three percent success rate with couples—naturally I disregarded that for the absurdity that it is. Most therapists, I am certain, would agree that most of these couples should be encouraged to separate. Instead of assisting his patients in this natural progression of things, Dr. Czernick appears to be convincing them to stay together at all costs. But what I'm wondering is how he manages to do this. I tried to gain insight from Eleanor but she is still so steeped in denial and grief that it is difficult to get to the core of her ideas and beliefs, and locate their origins. Time appears to have little or no effect on her grief. She suffers as much, if not more, with each passing day. Her memories of her husband have not only been transformed into exclusively happy experiences, but they seem to be getting more and more distinct instead of fading, as would be expected. And when we discuss these memories in greater detail, the anticipated epiphany never comes. Whether she is describing a "wonderful moment" she shared with her husband or a "proof" of his love for her, she doesn't seem to notice that the incident does not come close to living up to her impression of it.

This is the case with all of Eleanor's memories of her husband, even those pertaining to sex. She mentioned several times that this part of their life was exceptional, so today I encouraged her to talk more openly about it. She proceeded to describe to me how, in the months preceding her husband's death, they had begun to share "intimacies" she had never before known existed.

I asked her what had prompted these new intimacies, to which she replied, "The efforts he was making toward our marriage made him seem so much more appealing to me." I let this pass without comment and encouraged her to continue.

"He had always called me his 'pet,'" she began with a strange little half smile on her lips. "I liked it when we first started dating, but after we were married it began to get on my nerves. It just seemed kind of degrading and annoying. But then, I don't know, it was like we were dating all over again and I liked it."

"And this was *after* you went to see Dr. Czernick?" I asked.

She thought about this for a minute and then nodded. "Most definitely after."

"All right...go on. So he would call you his pet?"

"Yes." The strange little smile settled over her features again. "And there were other things, too." She grinned sheepishly, somewhat embarrassed. "He wanted me to do things and I discovered that I liked doing them. It seemed to bring us closer together."

"What sort of things?"

"You know," she replied, apparently feeling awkward to be discussing it so openly. "I think it's called S and M."

"Oh," I said, catching on. I attempted to put her at ease. "It's very normal, Eleanor, for couples to experiment with sexual fantasy and role-playing. It's quite healthy for the relationship."

The expression on her face still struck me as peculiar. I found that I was becoming a bit ill at ease as I waited for her to continue.

"Yes, well, it all started kind of suddenly and then it just escalated from there," she said, becoming more distant as she retreated inward, focusing back on those memories of her husband. "One day he came home with a present for me." She spoke slowly. Tears came to her eyes, but she digressed here for a quick moment to add, "I didn't mention it on my list before because, you know, I thought it might be hard to explain it at the time."

I nodded for her to go on and she continued.

"It was beautifully wrapped," she said serenely. Her gaze drifted past me and attached itself to a picture I had hanging on the wall. "I remember the paper was yellow with little pink daisies, and there was even a bow on it.

Inside there was a black velvet box. I was so excited when I saw it because it had been so many years since he bought me jewelry." She paused, seeming to savor the details of the moment as she related them to me. "Inside the box was the most gorgeous, white, shimmering gold-and-diamond-studded collar, with a tiny gold ring for a leash and an engraved ID tag and everything."

I was momentarily taken aback, but she went on, not noticing me at all now.

"He fastened the collar around my neck," she said, closing her eyes dreamily in remembrance. "I remember it felt cold on my skin, and a little heavy at first, but it fit around my neck perfectly. He asked me to wear it for him every night from then on. So I did." She opened her eyes to look at me. "I wear it sometimes still," she whispered.

I was having difficulty finding my voice. It was not the collar that disturbed me. Many women—and men, too, for that matter—find the symbolism of wearing a collar tremendously thrilling during various kinds of sexual play. But there was something in Eleanor's demeanor as she confided these things that bothered me, although I could not yet pinpoint what it was. I worked to keep my face impassive as I debated over how to proceed. It is not unusual for me to hold back commenting with patients, so Eleanor was not overly disturbed by my silence. At any rate, she was still too caught up in her memories to notice what my reactions were. Tears that had been filling her eyes began now to spill over as she resumed staring at the picture behind me on the wall.

"After that he began to jokingly call me his cute little pet doggie," she continued. That peculiar smile kept reappearing on her face in spite of her tears. "And then, like I said before, it just kind of escalated. Before I knew it, I was pretending to be his little dog, you know, getting into it. He liked me to crawl around on my hands and knees like a real dog does, and of course, he preferred I didn't wear clothes when I did it."

"Did you enjoy doing that?" I asked, finding my voice at last.

"I loved it," she said automatically, still staring at the wall. "I loved being his pet doggie."

"Were you… I mean, did *you* contribute any ideas for these…new intimacies?" I asked.

"Sure," she answered. "I was always trying to make it more real for him. I'm the one who came up with our nightly routine when he got home from work." She chuckled at the memory. "He laughed so hard the first time I barked. He was so pleased with me, so I started watching for him out one of the windows every night, and when I heard his car drive into the driveway, I would bark as loud as I could through the window so he could hear me. Then I would jump all over him and bark again when he came through the door." She snapped out of her stupor suddenly to look at me directly. "I would wag my tail and everything."

"What were you feeling while you pretended to be his dog?" I asked her, feeling more and more ill at ease.

She stared at me, as if my question momentarily stumped her. Then she crinkled her nose. "I suppose it was a little weird at first. But after a while, it began to feel normal. More normal than being me, even, in a way. I guess it was hard sometimes. I remember gagging a few times before he got me the kind of dog food that I liked."

The expression on my face must have jerked her out

of her reverie, because she blushed suddenly and hastened to explain.

"He thought it would be more real if I didn't eat people food."

I felt myself growing pale as she continued with a nervous laugh. "People food isn't good for dogs."

This was considerably outside of my scope of experience with sexual fantasies involving sadomasochistic behavior. And here again, I knew that I wasn't hearing anything too terribly extraordinary in that sphere. Yet I was struggling to get to the root of Eleanor's behavior. I was curious to know what she was feeling during all of this, and what was driving her. I was looking for indications that she was deriving sexual pleasure from these activities with her husband. And yet, in the world of sadism, there are many motivations.

"So, at times you felt repulsed by the things your husband wanted you to do?" I asked.

"Repulsed?" she repeated, instantly becoming defensive. "No, I don't think I said I was repulsed…"

"Okay, but you mentioned that you gagged at one point. Would you say that you were somewhat repulsed while you were gagging?"

"I was immersed in playing the part. Even real actors sometimes do things they don't want to in order to be more convincing!"

I could think of no reply to this, so I simply persisted with the same line of questioning.

"But overall, Eleanor, while you were playacting at being a dog, what feelings were you experiencing?" I asked.

"I was happy," Eleanor replied straightaway. Perhaps even she noticed how mechanical this sounded, so she went on, struggling somewhat, but more thoughtfully this time. "I needed to do it," she said. "I felt like I *really was* his pet dog…like that was my purpose." After another moment, she added, "The sex was incredible."

"In what way was it incredible?"

"The same," she said. "It was the thrill of being his pet and doing everything to please him. That's what dogs do."

"So you continued to play the part of a dog during sex?"

"Yes!"

"Can you describe the pleasure you experienced during sex?"

"I… It's hard to describe."

And as I continued to question Eleanor, my sense of foreboding increased. I felt we were touching upon issues here, but it was difficult to get to the source of them. The conundrum, of course, is that sexual motivation is pretty subjective to individuals, especially in the realm of sadism. The submissive will always struggle to please the dominant partner, often in even more disturbing ways than what Eleanor has described. But generally speaking, their underlying motivation is not simply to please their partner. In a true submissive, there is a motivation beneath this motivation. Being dominated arouses the submissive, most often sexually. Each act of domination excites them further. The more difficult the challenge put before them to "please" their partner, the more excited they become, which is why many of them will submit to extraordinary things, including pain. The euphoric sensations they get from submitting are more gratifying—and even, in some cases, empowering—than anything else they can imagine. And they are usually able to describe these euphoric sensations in great detail.

I cannot say for certain that Eleanor was simply playing the part of a submissive, yet my gut reaction to her responses is that a crucial element of their little "game" was missing, leaving me to wonder why she would go through the motions night after night. What was her motivation, if it wasn't sexual? The desire to please one's partner, in and of itself, is not normally enough to induce one to eat dog food.

And yet, her desire to please her husband seems to have been as genuine as her grief now appears.

My initial impression that Eleanor is delusional seems more probable than ever. But why or how these delusions have come about I am not yet able to determine. I wonder how Dr. Czernick fits into all of this. At some point in their marriage, Eleanor was so unhappy with her husband that she sought marriage counseling. The happiness that she now describes must have come out of that counseling, or else it developed later, out of guilt following her husband's death. Eleanor has stated that her husband became more loving and committed during their couples' therapy, but I see no actual evidence that this is the case. Her sudden happiness seems to have miraculously appeared out of nowhere.

I have learned that Dr. Czernick is a big advocate of hypnosis. I wonder if this has affected Eleanor's impressions about her husband. The power of suggestion can be strong in some people. His high success rate with couples also comes to mind. I can't pinpoint what it is exactly, but I feel that there is something not quite right here.

Meanwhile, my fights with Tom are growing worse.

He will not be put off, and I haven't the energy to deal with him. There's just so much on my plate right now with my growing practice; the last thing I want when I come home is confrontation. It might sound clichéd, but I need space. Tom, more than anyone, should understand this. Where was he all those years when I wanted to work on our marriage? He actually had the nerve to suggest we go to couples' therapy, and even mentioned Dr. Czernick, of all people!

Tuesday, August 18, 2009

Today I confronted Eleanor Dobbs with two lists. The first was a list of her husband's behavior before they went to therapy and the second was a list of his behavior after. The lists were so similar as to be almost the same. The only apparent distinction between the two, in fact, was that Mr. Dobb's efforts appeared to become even less genuine *after* therapy than they had been before.

To illustrate this, I reminded Eleanor what she had told me about her sex life with her husband. She had stated that one of the issues she had *prior* to counseling was that his overbearing manner left her feeling demeaned and turned off. She named several things in particular that bothered her, such as pushing her head down toward his penis in an effort to get oral sex from her, or often wanting to tie her up during sex. Her response to this behavior at that time was to avoid sex with him altogether. This is shockingly inconsistent with what she told me last week, and even today when we discussed it. She said that she began to intentionally wear her hair in pigtails so that her husband could grasp hold of them and force her to take more of him into her mouth and throat whenever he chose to do so. Furthermore, in the months preceding her husband's death, they were almost never intimate without her being restrained in some way, whether she was chained to a wall by her gold-studded collar, or tied up with her nylons, ankles to wrists, to make her body more accessible to him. She not only cooperated with all of his requests, but actively conspired with him over them—all for the pleasure of pleasing him!

When challenged with these examples taken from her very own statements, Eleanor was at first confused, but then became angry. In spite of my efforts, she remains obstinate in her delusion that her husband did change for the better in therapy and that he had begun to make her "happy."

My curiosity finally got the better of me, and this afternoon I ran a background check on Dr. Czernick. I'm not sure what I expected to find but I was a little disappointed when there wasn't much there. He's achieved most of his acclaim through his recent success in couples' therapy. He published a few articles about his philosophies on treating couples, which I found somewhat interesting but not enlightening in Eleanor Dobbs's case. About a decade or so ago, he had been associated with a research facility by the name of Cyndo-Kline Laboratories. I couldn't find much on them—they have since gone out of business—except that a drug they created was turned down by the FDA. Probably it's nothing, but I have an old acquaintance at the FDA—Monte or Mick, is it? He may remember something about Cyndo-Kline and their drug. I'll put in a call to him.

Last night, out of boredom more than anything else, I finally gave in and had sex with Tom. My emotions throughout were strangely mixed. At first, his touch actually repelled me; I have so much resentment stored up against him. His hands felt prying and intrusive, particularly when he reached under my clothing. There was an assertiveness in his manner that seemed antagonistic to me. He touched me with a kind of ownership that caused my skin to recoil under his fingertips and every fiber of my being to be repulsed.

Yet I was strangely aware of it from his vantage point, too. Here was the man who had married me believing that this would be one of his regular conjugal benefits. Back then I couldn't get enough of him, although things have changed so much since then. I could tell that he was filled with resentment, too; I could feel it in his probing touch as he moved over me with an air of entitlement. And I understood him perfectly in that moment. I knew that the greater part of his pleasure was in getting me to submit.

Meanwhile, the repulsion I initially felt from his touch quickly transformed into a strangely powerful sensation that was more erotic than anything I could remember experiencing with Tom before. It seemed as if we had reached a temporary breaking point, where Tom finally asserted himself and I acquiesced. It would have been equally exciting for me had it been the other way around, which is why I understood how Tom felt and was able to appreciate it for what it was. But the knowledge that Tom would never comprehend my need sometimes to dominate as well, made the moment bittersweet.

The sex, once I fully submitted, was actually pretty good. It was as if I had crossed a threshold from the old habit of holding back into a new dimension of giving up all that I had to give. The decision to actually let go and accept it was the hardest part, because it meant letting go of my anger and resentment and putting aside the belief that I am right and have been wronged. It meant allowing myself to take and give pleasure to the person who has been causing me all of this anguish. It was quite liberating and gave me a bit of insight into the world of sexual submission (I couldn't help but think of Eleanor). I was still aware of each and every hurt, but these only made the pleasure all the more poignant when I, for example, took him in my mouth while remembering all his cruel taunts about how I rarely gave him this pleasure and, when I did, how miserably I failed to please. Recalling these experiences seemed to actually enhance my pleasure as I made the extra effort to please him now. I found these thoughts so exciting that I wondered if my submission would have been half so pleasurable without this bitter edge to it!

Tom did not appear to notice any struggle within me, being too caught up in taking full advantage of the situation. This, too, suited my sudden need to have him be the strong, dominant male. He ravaged me completely and this morning I awoke with a few mildly aching reminders.

Immediately after it was over last night, Tom instantly returned to his weaker self, complaining petulantly that we weren't intimate like this more often. My resentment returned with renewed strength, along with a strong regret for having submitted to him. But strangely, all of this that is happening with Tom only manages to absorb the tiniest bit of my attention. It is no more than a distraction, really (perhaps that was why I was able to submit to begin with). I find that I am immersed in my

patients' lives much more than I am in my own. There
are simply too many issues on my mind at the moment
for me to worry about Tom.

Tuesday, August 25, 2009

Eleanor Dobbs and I continue to discuss the discrepan-
cies between her memories of her marriage and the
reality. Perhaps I should be more indulgent in light of her
obvious grief issues, but I am trying to find out how her
therapy with Dr. Czernick works into all of this. I am convinced that Eleanor is delusional, but I don't know if Dr.
Czernick has a part in it. Eleanor defends her husband's
behavior with the mechanical single-mindedness of a
Stepford Wife.

I finally reached my friend (Mortt) at the FDA. He was
very curious to know why I was inquiring about the
research conducted at Cyndo-Kline, but I was careful to
tell him as little as possible. He remembered the
company and the drug they submitted called Zeldane.
It was presented as a treatment for insomnia. Mortt
could not recall all of the details, but he did remember
that it was rejected due to side effects.

This will all probably amount to little more than a
huge waste of my time, but for some reason I want to
know more about Dr. Czernick and his drug. I asked
Eleanor today if Dr. Czernick had prescribed anything
during her treatment with him and she said that he had
not.

Tom has reverted back to his usual passive-aggressive
self, brooding and morose, playing the part of the long-
suffering husband to the hilt. Every now and then, he
makes some feeble attempt at an appearance of concilia-

tion but I have come to believe that he does these things only to add credence to his belief that he is the victim. He sent me flowers again today! No matter how many times he sends them, it never quite loses its ability to irritate me. And this is the crux of the matter between us. Tom will not capitulate to me on any single thing, not even when he is giving me a gift! I would rather he assert himself in other ways, instead of stubbornly clinging to his outdated modes of pleasing a woman which *this* woman does not find pleasing.

Tuesday, September 1, 2009

I continue to attempt a breakthrough with Eleanor Dobbs, even though I realize I may be pushing her too hard. She seems frustrated and discouraged when I persist in questioning her over the lists. But I can't help reminding her that, at one point, these behaviors bothered her so much that she sought counseling. How is it that those same behaviors suddenly became a source of happiness for her. However, I cannot get her to explain or even acknowledge these inconsistencies.

It calls to mind the psychological journals I read in college about propaganda and mind control. Eleanor's responses to my questions are too automatic and mechanical, reminding me of victims of brainwashing.

These impressions I have in Eleanor Dobbs's case have been amplified by the recent information I found on Dr. Czernick's research drug. I was finally able to learn that Zeldane came from a distant strain of the popular "Z-drugs," nonbenzodiazepines that act within the central nervous system like the benzodiazepines, but without the addictive properties. Zeldane, it seems, also has many of the same properties as sodium pentothal (truth serum), and was originally thought to be a better, nonaddictive choice for therapists who use that drug in therapy. However, in clinical tests, Zeldane was found to cause amnesia and promote acute hallucinations in the patients that participated.

I feel that I am onto something important here, and yet it is hard for me to accept what I'm thinking. Both amnesia and hallucinations would be useful tools for brainwashing. But this fits together rather too neatly, which makes me think it could all be a bizarre coincidence. I'm not confident that I'm altogether objective about this, either. From the onset I have distrusted Dr. Czernick and his methods in couples' therapy, and my skepticism has likely clouded my judgment. I must proceed carefully. While my instincts are almost frantic with alarm (another reason to proceed with caution), my more practical side tells me that my assumptions are preposterous. What is the likelihood that there is a connection here (it would be tantamount to mind control!)? And aside from all of this, I know that I am obsessing over this too much.

I can't even think about Tom right now. And of course, with his usual self-absorbed sense of timing, he wants resolutions right this minute! I find it impossible, sometimes, to remember why I ever married him.

Tuesday, September 8, 2009

My focus today with Eleanor Dobbs was to try and pinpoint the exact moment when her feelings about her husband's behavior began to change. When did his actions stop annoying her and begin to make her happy?

It was extremely difficult to get answers from her because her memory of her sessions alone with Dr. Czernick is almost completely erased. Of course, this is often the case with hypnosis. Although I could not locate a specific time or event that would enlighten me on what caused the change to come about, it has become apparent that it began to happen after about three of Eleanor's sessions alone with Dr. Czernick. I questioned her again about any medications administered or prescribed, but she insists that there were none.

Meanwhile, I've been trying to find out more about Zeldane. It's difficult with the research lab closed down and disassembled. I would have liked to have spoken to some of the patients who participated in the test studies, but I have no way of knowing who they were. I remember Mortt mentioned a competitive pharmaceutical company being involved in this, as well. They were opposed to Zeldane coming onto the market. It's very possible that their opposition was prompted by their own interests as a competitor, but clearly they must have had some information about the drug. They were instrumental in getting the FDA to reject it. It's hard to say whether or not their information will be reliable, given the source. These drug companies are extremely competitive, and the actual performance of the drugs can be secondary to the interests of the big companies invested in them. Even so, I would like to take a closer look at the actual clinical data on the patients who used Zeldane. I was fortunate enough to get an appointment with Dr. Lang, who prepared the clinical findings on Zeldane for the opposing company. I will speak with him the beginning of next week.

Tom seemed different when he confronted me last

night. He was angry and forceful, issuing ultimatums. I can see that he is getting more and more frustrated, and I am, too. The tables have certainly turned since a few years ago! But now that I am the one engrossed in my work, I find it ironic that Tom is so unsympathetic. He suddenly and unexpectedly decides he wants to work on our marriage, and now I'm supposed to drop everything and jump in line? I couldn't do that even if I wanted to, and I'm not sure that I do. All the former neglect has forced me to become more invested in my work and I actually find it much more gratifying than being Tom's wife. Tom claims that his preoccupation with work was out of necessity, whereas mine is merely an escape. Very profound for an engineer, but I couldn't help reminding him that I am the trained psychotherapist! And of course, he couldn't resist pointing out that it was his working overtime that put me through school in the first place. Everything is always about him!

Tuesday, September 15, 2009

I think I may be nearing a breakthrough with Eleanor Dobbs. She seems to be susceptible to deprogramming therapy, such as used on victims of brainwashing. This is experimental at this stage. If she responds to the therapy, it will confirm my suspicions. But the therapy is tedious and time-consuming, so a definitive answer may not be soon in coming. As well, it is clear that Eleanor's case is different than most cases of brainwashing. More than enough time has passed for a kind of natural deprogramming to have begun to take effect— even without therapy, it is inevitable that her own thoughts will begin to assert themselves again once the source of the brainwashing has been removed. Whether the source was her husband or the counseling, she is going on a year now and her delusional thinking appears to be gaining in strength. This seems to support the idea that the problem lies within her, rather than with an outside influence.

This brings me to my discussion with Dr. Lang yesterday. He referred to his notes throughout our conversation, offering no speculations of his own about how the drug Zeldane might be used. He very simply reiterated what I had already learned about the drug up to that point. I questioned him in particular about the hallucinations, but the data was not very detailed. He did recall one man who had taken Zeldane as a sleep aid just before his house caught on fire. For a long time after the incident, the man's wife claimed that he would wake up during the night with hallucinations of the fire—exactly as if it were happening—over and over again. He had no memory of these hallucinations in the morning.

This has got me thinking, but I want to do some research before I form a hypothesis about what might be happening.

Tom was once again issuing ultimatums last night and before I even realized what I was doing, I had agreed to seek counseling with him. But it was not really for our marriage that I acquiesced. While Tom was ranting, I had an idea. I happen to know that I am not susceptible to hypnosis, but if I were to go through the motions and allow Dr. Czernick to believe I was hypnotized, I might be able to find out how he achieves such incredible influence over his patients, if, in fact, this is the case. I will, of course, record the entire session in the event that I do, at any point, lose consciousness, and then I'll examine the tapes after the fact. This is perhaps a bit unorthodox, and no doubt risky, but I'm too excited to worry about the risks. I have to admit I'm enjoying the intrigue of this mystery that could potentially become a scandal of monumental proportions. I can't even say why, but I have a strong feeling that there is something very scandalous beneath this blanket of "happy" couples. I am surprised, frankly, that Dr. Czernick's success has passed without closer scrutiny so far. Anyone who works with couples would agree, I am sure, that even the most loving couples can grow apart and, more often than not, it becomes healthier for them to move away from the relationship if they are to reach their true potential as individuals.

I have already scheduled our first appointment with Dr. Czernick! I did it first thing this morning. Since I still have some time open on Tuesdays, it looks like that will be the best day for it. Tom appeared shocked when I called to tell him I scheduled the appointment. Naturally, I have not mentioned any of my suspicions about Dr. Czernick to Tom.

Tuesday, September 22, 2009

I'm continuing the deprogramming therapy with Eleanor Dobbs until I have a better diagnosis. I must say I see very little result from it so far, but then again, it is too soon. I will have to watch and see how things proceed.

Tom and I had our first session with Dr. Czernick today. I have to admit that I felt rather foolish about my suspicions while sitting in the very ordinary-looking office of this plainspoken older gentleman. I felt a sense of impropriety toward a fellow psychotherapist, as well.

The session itself began as it might have in my own office. Tom and I each, in turn, had an opportunity to voice our grievances against the other. Tom went first, droning on and on about how selfish I am and then he went into his tirade about how I don't appreciate anything he does and so forth. There wasn't anything he said that I hadn't heard a million times before. But when my turn came, I was surprised to find that I had no shortage of complaints about him, either. There was no need to embellish or make things up; my antipathy for Tom has escalated to the point where his every action has become a source of irritation for me. Voicing my feelings out loud to Dr. Czernick made me realize that Tom and I should most definitely separate. I said as much to Dr. Czernick.

This took up about forty minutes. Then, Dr. Czernick gave us a brief overview of his therapeutic methods, all of which I was aware of already. He then set up a few ground rules—nothing out of the ordinary—such as that Tom and I avoid discussing these issues at home from now on and so forth. He told us he would be seeing us separately for the first month or so, alternating between us each week. We each signed a consent form to be hypnotized. It was agreed that I would have the first appointment on the following week.

I've been second-guessing my speculations quite a bit since my meeting with Dr. Czernick. I want to look more carefully at Eleanor Dobbs in the sessions to come. My assumptions about her psychosis could be influenced by my first impressions of Dr. Czernick. As a psycho-therapist, I know that it normally takes much longer to effect a change in a patient than the amount of time she and her husband saw Dr. Czernick. I must explore other aspects of her background that may be critical in her delusional behavior. I could very well be missing a deeper issue. This is not to say that my suspicions have been alleviated, only that I see now that I have been too fixated on my suspicions about Dr. Czernick to be objective.

Tuesday, September 29, 2009

After listening to the tape of my session today with Dr. Czernick *twice* since coming back to my office, I still can't say for certain what happened. I was able to be hypnotized after all. For that period of time, at least, I am forced to determine the events from what I can hear on the tape.

But first I want to review the entire session so that I will have it documented. I'll also note here that I once again felt a sense of impropriety over "spying" on Dr. Czernick in this way. He has a very simple, matter-of-fact manner that leaves me feeling rather irrational.

Dr. Czernick was all business, immediately instructing me to lay back on a very comfortable lounge-type divan. My tiny, high-frequency tape recorder, which is made to look like a cell phone, was already running, smoothly and silently where it was strapped to an outer pocket of my handbag.

Dr. Czernick sat in a chair about a foot away from me, to my right, and asked me to relax. There was a very low-volume music playing in the background. He attached a blood-pressure check to the middle finger of my right hand. So far, all of this was standard.

Once I had settled in, Dr. Czernick began to instruct me on my breathing. I obeyed his commands and felt myself gradually relaxing. Throughout the process, he continued his instructions for me to breathe slower, breathe through my mouth, then through my nose, etc., also offering phrases of affirmation in between, such as "all is well," "life is a journey," "you can feel your problems floating away," and so forth. Some of these I felt were a bit clichéd, but of course, these comments do have their effect, and I found myself becoming more relaxed and developing a more positive frame of mind. In listening to the tape afterward, I recalled feeling very open to suggestion. However, this is not only normal but acceptable in therapy, so nothing Dr. Czernick said could be, on the surface, construed in a negative light.

Throughout the encounter, and even after I had reached a fully relaxed state, Dr. Czernick never let up with the gentle commands relating to my breathing, posture, etc. In between these commands, which were designed to distract my conscious mind so that he could probe my unconscious, he would ask me leading questions. For example, he began by questioning me on the matter of the flowers, saying, "Please breathe out through your lips as you answer. Why do you *think* Tom brings you flowers?" I concentrated on my breathing and responded, "Tom knows I don't care for flowers." To this Dr. Czernick countered, "Please breathe into your words this time as you answer. Why does Tom bring you flowers?" This time I responded with, "I don't know why Tom brings me flowers." Undaunted, Dr. Czernick continued. "Breathe a single breath out through each word as you answer. Why do you think Tom brings you flowers?" And so it went, until my conscious mind stopped fighting and I found myself admitting that Tom probably wasn't trying to annoy me when he brought me flowers. There was most certainly a leading quality to Dr. Czernick's questions, but in listening to them afterward, it would be difficult to present a case against him for this. It could be argued that all therapists, especially those who practice hypnosis, are attempting to lead their patients toward the conclusions we think are best for them. It could also be argued, for that matter, that this power of suggestion is exactly what people are looking for when they seek hypnosis, such as in the case of smokers.

After a while, I lost consciousness. Yet I continued to mechanically respond to Dr. Czernick's questions, which were persistent and repetitive like the beating of a drum.

About midway through this period of unconsciousness, there was a moment in the taping when I felt Dr. Czernick might have administered something to me, had he been inclined to do so. I was in the middle of a statement and abruptly stopped speaking. Having no recollection of the moment now, I can't be certain why I stopped, but the strange thing was that Dr. Czernick did not appear to notice my faltering at all. In fact, he simply issued his next question along with another breathing instruction. This distracted me from whatever it was that had given me pause, and I simply resumed answering his questions while attempting to follow his instructions.

I should note here that since I left Dr. Czernick's office, I have searched all over my body and can find no evidence of a needle prick anywhere. I am fairly certain that I would have been able to tell if I had been given something—there would have been some visible mark, or if not that, then a slight discomfort that I would be able to detect. But even the most thorough search could produce no sign of anything having penetrated my skin. Furthermore, there were no other indications that I might have been administered a drug.

A few moments after this incident on the tape, there was another thing that I noticed. There was a change— very slight, imperceptible to most, perhaps—but I got the distinct impression that my replies were becoming markedly less confident. Another thing I noticed was that, at this point, Dr. Czernick's questions were gradually becoming more like statements. These statements were extremely positive and, on the surface, they appeared to be little more than positive affirmations. However, having listened to them several times now on the tape, I feel that they were predominantly in Tom's favor. For instance, Dr. Czernick would say, "Wouldn't you agree, Angela, that every gift, whether it be flowers or diamonds, is a gesture of love that should bring joy?" or, "Are you aware, Angela, that pleasing your husband is tantamount to pleasing yourself?" Toward the end of our session, his statements turned toward the therapy, with the clear objective of getting me, the patient, to embrace it.

None of this is especially unusual in any way, and I find myself feeling a little discouraged. Eleanor Dobbs would have had to be extremely susceptible to the power of suggestion for this therapy to account for her deep-rooted delusions about her husband. It is more likely that she had existing issues that Dr. Czernick's therapy only compounded. The only variable that remains unknown is whether or not she was exposed to any drugs that might have significantly enhanced the effects of his treatment.

I personally feel that Dr. Czernick's session had practically no effect on me whatsoever. Listening to the tapes helped me realize that I haven't put forth any real effort toward my marriage lately, but aside from that, which I already knew, it was pretty ineffectual, and even a little primitive. If I were actively trying to save my marriage, would I feel differently? Perhaps, but what I have seen so far does not seem to account for Dr. Czernick's incredible success in the field of marriage counseling. I wonder if he may have held something back because of my being a fellow therapist. I continue to puzzle over this enigma.

Tuesday, October 6, 2009

It was Tom's turn with Dr. Czernick this week. I'm not sure I will continue seeing him myself. I feel very disturbed and out of sorts.

At the mention of Dr. Czernick's name when Tom brought it up this morning, I suddenly had a flashback that I was being hypnotized. But I am almost positive that it was not the event itself I was seeing, but an extremely vivid dream. Whatever it was, it was frighteningly familiar, and I had the distinct impression that I had relived it over and over again since the event. Perhaps it was only a flashback of my subconscious state while being hypnotized.

The frightening thing—the thought I had in that first instant when the flashback occurred—was what Dr. Lang had told me about Zeldane's hallucinations. They were often replays of the actual events taking place during the time period that the patient was under its influence. I thought of the man whose house had caught on fire.

It occurred to me suddenly that if these dreams were actually hallucinations, they could be having the effect of hypnotizing me over and over again in my sleep!

But as the day wore on, I had the sense of how preposterous this idea really was. Working with Eleanor Dobbs intensified this impression. She is not responding at all to the deprogramming therapy. And yet, if she were still being hypnotized through hallucinations in her dreams...

After Eleanor left, I listened once again to the tape of my first session with Dr. Czernick. Hearing his bland voice reiterating the positive affirmations made it hard to defend my suspicions. I feel like I have been reaching somewhat in my effort to get something on Dr. Czernick. But why? Is it because subconsciously I am resentful of his success? Is my dissatisfaction with my marriage and my difficulties with my patients causing me to seek some kind of intrigue as a way of escape? I don't know that I can answer these questions objectively.

As for Tom, I must say that he appears to be trying especially hard to please me. He has not brought up any of his usual grievances, and we've actually been able to talk and laugh together in conversation. I suppose he, unlike me, is approaching the marriage counseling with the hope of things getting better between us. I wonder if Tom's session will be similar to mine. If only I could listen in on that one!

Tuesday, October 13, 2009

Despite my misgivings, I saw Dr. Czernick again today. This session went much as the first one had, except that his questions and statements were blatantly more focused on Tom this time. It was apparent that he was attempting to get me to look at things from Tom's perspective. His questions and statements were of a nature to encourage me to consider Tom's feelings rather than my own. He repeatedly delved into the past, when Tom and I first dated, but in a random manner, and I couldn't form a clear idea about where he was going with it, even in listening to the tape after the fact. No doubt he was trying to open my mind to Tom's point of view while reminding me of why I fell in love with him in the first place.

Here again, developing empathy for one's partner is a crucial part of maintaining a relationship and often will be taught in couples' therapy, but the way in which this was done is certainly questionable. There was a definite sense of being manipulated. But there's a fine line here, because in a sense, hypnosis is nothing at all if not the power of suggestion. I am not an authority in the field of hypnosis, but my understanding is that this power of suggestion is normally only as potent as the individual's beliefs in what is being conveyed. And indeed, I could feel myself resisting and rejecting some of the more self-effacing suggestions that Dr. Czernick put to me. If one went solely by the tapes, there would be little more than enough to raise an eyebrow.

But I continue to feel the nagging sense of alarm, especially since the peculiar interruption that occurred in the middle of my first session repeated itself in today's session. It was no more than a little blip in the proceedings, probably unnoticeable to anyone else, but I can't quite express the effect it had on me to hear it happen again. It was as conspicuous to me as a scream. But I know that it would be hard to explain it to anyone else and get the same response. It was once again about halfway through the session, at the peak of my unconsciousness. Something happened—I am certain of it—something distracted me in the middle of answering one of Dr. Czernick's questions. This time I made a small sound, no more than a gasp, really, but before I could protest further, Dr. Czernick instantly and smoothly filled in the gap with his next question and I, being in a state of unconsciousness, was easily distracted from whatever it was that had disrupted me. What was it that stopped me short and made me gasp? A needle prick would have that effect. And after the interruption, the therapy once again became more intense, with Dr. Czernick's comments becoming even more persuasive.

And yet again, I cannot find any evidence at all that I was drugged or tampered with in any way, either physically or psychologically. And in the end, even the hypnosis treatment has had almost no effect on me. I feel that my outlook is exactly as it was before.

Yet I can see a clear difference in Tom's behavior during this week since his session, which undermines my earlier supposition that Dr. Czernick was favoring him. When I asked him about his session, he said he couldn't remember anything about it. It would appear that Tom underwent the same treatment that I did, except Dr. Czernick must have given him suggestions favoring my point of view. And Tom, being more desirous of a reconciliation between us, and, too, being more susceptible to the hypnosis, has no doubt embraced the suggestions made by Dr. Czernick—much like Eleanor Dobbs had. How else could such a drastic change in his behavior have come about? He has been wonderfully attentive, asking me questions about even the smallest details of my day. And last night I came home to the most splendid, home-cooked Italian meal, with tortellini steeped in a fabulous white sauce. It is hard to remain indifferent when someone is making such a genuine effort. I can't help thinking of the man he was when we first fell in love, so many years ago. But I wonder how much of his behavior is the hypnosis and how much is really Tom. And does it matter? I don't know. Frankly, I am simply glad that things are going more smoothly between us now, so that I can focus more on what is happening in my practice.

Tuesday, October 20, 2009

Today I set aside the deprogramming therapy with Eleanor Dobbs and allowed her to simply discuss her feelings about her husband. There is an obsessive quality to her personality I hadn't picked up on before. This could be playing a part in her inability to grieve her loss and move on. Although she is still young enough, she doesn't even appear to consider the prospect of finding another man. It's like she is still *living* the memories, and seems satisfied to settle for that. Her connection with her husband appears to grow stronger with every day that passes.

The discussion once again turned to her sex life with her husband. As I listened to her, I struggled again to identify the motivating force behind her absolute compliance with all of his requests. I contemplated the source of her inflexible devotion. Night after night, she would crawl around on the floor, playing dead or chasing balls in a never-ending desire to please him. Why?

"...and he spread it all around the area," she was

saying. "I waited, perfectly still, until he gave me the command and then I rushed forward. Dogs love honey, and so I began lapping it up, licking all around his balls to get every bit that I could…"

"Why is it," I interrupted her suddenly to ask, "that you always played the part of a dog?" At her confused expression, I added, "Why not a cat?"

She wrinkled her nose. "He hated cats. He would never have had a cat."

"Okay, then how about a…bird?"

She snorted and just looked at me as if I were insane.

"Could you have played the part of a bird, do you think?" I pressed.

She thought about it. "No," she said at last. "I can't even imagine doing that."

"Back in the very beginning when this started—the night your husband first gave you the collar—had you ever imagined being a dog before?"

She thought about this. "No…" she answered slowly.

I took my time, too. I wasn't even really sure what I was looking for.

"Why were you able to play the part of his dog so well?" I asked.

She shrugged. "I don't know. I guess maybe…I *wanted* to do it well."

"Every time?"

"What?"

"You wanted to do it well every time—it was nearly every night that you did it once you got the collar, right—and you *always* wanted to perform well for him, every night?"

"Yes!"

"You never got tired?"

She looked at me and kind of laughed. "It's weird, I know, but I never did."

I was genuinely puzzled. "Did you never get sick? Too sick to play dog, I mean?"

She appeared to think about it and then shook her head.

I was silent a moment, thinking.

"Sometimes," she began, "I really thought sometimes... like...like I was a dog. Like maybe I was a dog in another life or something. I was comfortable with it. Everything he wanted me to do seemed natural. It seemed natural to have to eat dog food and beg for table scraps. Chasing the ball for him. All of it...seemed natural. When he would pet me, you know, when he would pat my head— I can't describe it. It was like I felt how a real dog would feel. He was my master and I wanted his approval. I *needed* it."

"You needed it...sexually?"

"No!" She shook her head emphatically. "I loved pleasing him that way, too, but what I needed was just to please him, period, as his *dog*." She looked at me dismally. "What am I now?"

I took a deep breath. "So your need to please him was your need...*as a dog?*" I repeated.

"Yes! It was like I had the needs of a dog."

"Had you ever had feelings of being a dog or any other animal *before* your husband gave you the collar?" I asked.

She thought about this, then shook her head. "I don't think so."

But we had run out of time. I felt certain I was onto something.

And I was preoccupied with thoughts of Tom. I

wondered how his session with Dr. Czernick was going. This week with him has been remarkable—his efforts are having an effect on me. He's so much like when we first met. I find myself thinking about him all the time now. I didn't think that I still had feelings for him, but clearly I do. Surely they are worth exploring.

Tuesday, October 27, 2009

I have not had the opportunity to listen to the tape of my session with Dr. Czernick today as there is simply too much going on, but I'm beginning to realize that I have been way off base about him anyway. It occurred to me today that my suspicions were really a kind of denial. Clearly I was not ready to look at my own issues, so I distracted myself with delusions about Dr. Czernick. I'm so glad now that I didn't confide in anyone about what I was thinking!

It appears that Tom's sessions have worked wonders. Unlike me, Tom has not been resisting his therapy. I am now wondering why I have been fighting it so hard. Perhaps I had some kind of misguided fear that I could not have it all. That I must give up something if I am to succeed at my practice.

In fact, with things so peaceful at home, I feel clearer than ever with my patients. I realized today, for instance, that Eleanor Dobbs suffers from a mixed delusional disorder, which brings about hallucinations that she is a dog. I'm not even sure anymore that these experiences she relates with her husband ever really happened. I have written her a prescription for an antipsychotic and we will begin cognitive behavioral therapy immediately.

I think today I had the epiphany that Tom has been

waiting for. It came in the form of twelve very stunning white carnations that were delivered here this morning. All day long, their delightful scent has acted as a reminder of how sweet it is to be loved. Tonight is the first night of the rest of our lives together!

Tom heard the front door, indicating that Angela was home, and he smiled. How long had it been since he felt excited to see her at night? Too long, and he had all but given up. It had become impossible to make her happy.

He felt a brief twinge of guilt.

But then he saw her expression as she came to him—her shy smile—and he was reminded of how she used to look at him when they first fell in love. It was worth the price, surely, he assured himself. The end would justify the means. He would use Dr. Czernick's therapy only so far as it was beneficial to them both. He would not take advantage of it or of her.

Angela's manner, so happy and appreciative, made him feel omnipotent, and a wave of protectiveness for her rushed over him.

Mostly there was relief. He could finally relax and trust his own instincts. He could be himself, without worrying that every little action was going to offend. Yet he promised himself yet again that he would not take advantage of her. He knew that with power came responsibility.

Tom noticed the arousal in Angela's eyes and he felt his heart jump. She came to him—willingly? Yes, he insisted adamantly as he pushed aside another wave of guilt. She was clearly willing—and *happy*.

Tom gently took Angela's face in his hands and brushed his lips over hers every so lightly and tenderly, almost apologetically. She pulled his head closer and kissed him back hungrily. Her response activated the various pent-up emotions in him, triggering an eruption that sent a harsh shudder through him.

His earlier guilt was suddenly buried under the anger and resentment that had been building and churning within him for all of these years. It was Angela who had brought their marriage to this point! His embrace turned almost violent in defense of his own actions, and he grasped her head firmly in his hands as he crushed her lips in an all-encompassing kiss. He felt her shudder in response, and it gave him a sense of power to have that effect on her. In turns, he kept alternating from tenderness to fury, and she responded to both equally. Everything he did seemed to fan the flames of her desire. Her response triggered his, and the kiss became an ardent embrace that left them both gasping for breath. And suddenly everything else was lost to the kiss; she kind of melted against him in a minisurrender as he held her steady in his arms, all the while continuing to ravage her mouth, even nipping at her lightly with his teeth. He could feel the heat emanating off of him, and even his breath seemed as if it might scorch her as it flared from his nostrils.

With every advance from Tom, it seemed that Angela became more pliant and yielding. Was this what she needed from him all along, or was it simply that he could now do no wrong? Tom was beginning not to care. Angela was clinging to him as if she needed him. For whatever reason, she needed him.

Tom struggled to control the overwhelming sense of power he felt over Angela. Her response filled him with confidence. He suddenly picked her up and carried her straight to their bedroom without interrupting their kiss. She appeared to be as consumed by the passion as he was. He felt he could kiss her for hours. Since she wasn't complaining that his face was too rough, or his body heat was too cloistering, or anything else she might have said before, he took his time, suddenly wanting to make up for all the lost years. He kissed her leisurely and thoroughly as he laid her out on the bed beneath him. It almost seemed as if he could erase the anguish of all the unhappy years of their marriage if only he could kiss her long enough. Surely that would heal both of their wounds and make it worth the price.

But with so much more pleasure to be had, Tom eventually became distracted from their kiss in his desire to touch Angela's body. His hands moved slowly and introspectively over her body, simultaneously caressing and probing, lingering over every nuance as if he were discovering her for the first time. Here and again he would carefully remove a piece of her clothing, clearing it out of his way decidedly and unapologetically. Where before there had been withholding and restraint, there now was utter freedom. Angela was his willing wife, for him to do with as he wished. He found that he wished to punish and please, both at the same time.

The scant clothing that remained was suddenly in his way. Tom tore at it fitfully. He wanted to see every single inch of her that instant. A part of him felt that he was fully entitled. All that had previously been forbidden or out of bounds was his by right. He would take all of it—and then some. Where before he had meekly accepted what little crumbs she tossed in his direction, he now would not be satisfied with anything less than all of it. He wanted to push the limits. Later, he would make it up to her, but for the moment he was still too well aware of a score to settle.

With this in mind, Tom bared Angela's body fully to his gaze, moving his hands over her body again and again as he drank in the sight of her. He loved the way she looked and wanted to set every inch to memory. Out of some misguided instinct, she tried to cover her nakedness with her hands, but he grasped her hands in his and placed them firmly at her sides.

"Let me see you," he said earnestly. He wanted to look at the woman he had married. And he wanted her to submit to him willingly. This was still a bone of contention for him. And yet he saw that it was shyness, not willfulness, that caused her reaction. "It's okay," he told her, wanting to put her mind at ease. "The sight of you brings me pleasure. It excites me to look at you here," he said, lifting her breasts gently in his hands. "And here—" he moved his hands down along the length of her stomach "—and here." He cupped his hands lovingly over her mound. "I love looking at you, Angela," he told her truthfully. He saw that his words had the desired effect, and she visibly relaxed.

From where he held her cupped in his hand, he could feel her wetness.

"Open your legs," he said in a husky voice, and he exulted when she obeyed. He leaned in to reward her obedience with a light kiss to her nether lips, but he became fully diverted and enthralled when he felt them tremble and part with his touch. He grasped her hips gently but firmly to hold her in place as he flicked out his tongue and licked the trembling flesh up and down along its parted folds. He once again felt a sense of power when she jumped and trembled. He slipped his tongue between her silken folds to capture more of the tantalizing taste of her. It drove him temporarily out of his mind, and he delved into her wholeheartedly, licking and sucking at her furiously, devouring her like a man half-starved. She shuddered and jerked, but he held her steady with his hands.

Tom knew well, after all these years, how to please Angela best—although it had been a while, it was something he would never forget—and she squirmed in delight under the effect of his administrations. But he refused to let her be satisfied—yet. Tonight, he wanted much more from her. He was suddenly overcome with an almost childish greed, and he felt gluttonous with power. He could have stayed and feasted between her legs for much longer, but he could see that she was becoming too excited. He would distract her with a slight intermission.

Tom, too, had become aroused to the point of impatience. Yet he had no intention of holding back his own pleasure. On the contrary, his efforts to enhance her pleasure would be more effective if he were to get some relief now. He wanted to keep her highly aroused and teetering on pins and needles, and to do that, he would have to maintain the upper hand.

"It's your turn," he told her, removing his pants and rising up over her. Without hesitation, she got up onto her knees and grasped hold of him with both hands. "Use your mouth," he groaned, feeling the tingling sensation curling up in his testicles. Angela took him into her mouth eagerly, delighted to reciprocate. She sucked and licked at him playfully, just as he had done with her, and was momentarily surprised and stunned when he grasped her head in his hands and thrust himself into her mouth repeatedly. As he released his warm fluid into her throat, she could do little more than swallow. But when he drew himself out of her, she only stared up at him in surprise. And yet, he noticed with an immense thrill that she was not angry but possibly even pleased. He was once again astounded by the immense change in his wife, and felt strangely humbled by the incredible power he had over her. It would please her no matter what he did! It was still so fresh as to have the ability to shock.

And Tom reminded himself yet again that he must never abuse the power. Even now, he had only allowed himself this release so that he could offer his wife extended pleasure. He had much in store for her, and after waiting so long for any intimacy at all, he couldn't bear to simply sample the great bounty that was there for the taking.

In spite of his orgasm, Tom was still aroused, but the desperate edge had been taken off his desire. Now he could take his time and they both could enjoy the pleasures to come.

Tom reached under the bed and pulled out the object he had hidden there earlier. Angela gasped when she saw it. She looked at her husband with a mixture of embarrassment and shame.

"You didn't think I knew about this?" he asked, waving the vibrator in front of her face. In spite of his newfound joy, a spark of anger flared up within him yet again. He could not help resenting the months—and even years—of neglect that he suffered while she secretly satisfied her own needs. With effort, he forced the anger back down. He knew that what he had planned for revenge would no doubt please her, too.

Angela stared at the vibrator remorsefully, but she remained silent. Tom softened somewhat, seeing that her expression was one of genuine repentance. And in that instant he was able to forgive her.

"It's okay," he gently assured her. "You're going to use it for both of us this time." Her eyes widened in surprise when she heard this, but she obediently took the vibrator from his hand. He could see that, although she was still embarrassed, she would not deny him. Yet it might have been the first time she ever touched it, considering how awkwardly she handled it.

"I want you to use it just like you used to when you were alone," Tom said. "This time, you'll be pleasing us both with it."

The vibrator Angela had chosen for herself was a finely crafted implement of pleasure. At a glance, it seemed rather ordinary, having the classic shape and feel of a medium-sized penis and testicles. But unlike a real penis, this simulated one was enhanced with a little appendage that jutted out from the lower front, clearly for the purpose of stimulating the clitoris while it was in use. Tom had been envious when he first saw it. Technology had surely outdone Mother Nature this time.

Angela rested back on the pillows shyly, clearly uncertain of how to proceed. Yet in spite of her obvious nervousness, there was a definite sparkle of excitement in her eyes. Noticing her uneasiness, Tom rushed himself to assist her. First he slid in between her legs, opening them wider and preparing a place for himself in the best seat in the house. Next he reached over and adjusted the lamp so that its light shone directly between her open legs. Not only would the light illuminate the event for his view but it would also bring a tantalizing heat to her exposed area that would enhance the experience for Angela. He lifted her hips up so that he could place several pillows beneath them. She was now in a more comfortable position to do what he had asked her to do.

Tom reached up and took hold of Angela's hand that held the vibrator. He encouraged her to bring the vibrator to her mouth.

"Get it nice and wet first," he said, staggered by the sight of her mouth opening to accept the vibrator. He stared in awe as together their hands moved the vibrator in and out of her mouth. He was unused to seeing her take anything in her mouth from this angle. He found himself pressing it farther and farther inside her mouth with every stroke, enjoying the sight of the rubbery testicles when they bumped against her chin. Angela watched Tom with as much amazement as he was watching her. And in the meantime, any remaining awkwardness or inhibitions were melting away.

"That's it. Get it nice and wet," Tom encouraged. "And in the meantime, show me how you get yourself ready for it. And I want you to do it exactly how you do when you're alone."

With the vibrator still being pumped in and out of her mouth, Angela reached her free hand down between her legs. She slid a few fingers up and down her slit, until it popped open to invite her in. With a little moan she slipped both fingers inside. Tom could hear the little slurping sounds of her arousal as he watched her work her fingers in and out.

"Mmm," he groaned. "May I check to see if you're ready?"

He pressed his free hand against Angela's and pushed two of his fingers in alongside of hers. She was soaking wet, and they both moaned together again as their fingers stretched her.

Why had she preferred to do this by herself? he wondered.

He pulled both their hands away. He wanted to see her use the vibrator.

When they pulled the vibrator out of Angela's mouth, it was glistening. Together, they brought it down between her legs.

"Turn it on," Tom said.

Angela flipped the switch and the thing suddenly came alive, pulsing and vibrating wildly in her hand. Tom let go of her hand so that she could work the head of it between her parted lips. He watched with mixed emotions as it wiggled and throbbed its way into her body. It was thick but only about average in length, which had puzzled Tom when he first saw it. At the time, he wondered why she hadn't chosen something supersized but now, seeing it lodged inside her, the reason became abundantly clear. In order for the little appendage at the base to have the most effect, the phallic portion of the vibrator had to be all the way in. Anything more than what she could actually take would render the clitoral stimulator useless. As Angela pressed the last bit of it as far as she could into her body, the little appendage at once began to vibrate and pulse against the trembling little nub that controlled her pleasure. Tom watched in awe as her flesh shimmied and trembled all around the throbbing vibrator. Once she had it lodged all the way in, Angela grasped hold of the rubber testicles at the base and simply held it in place in a kind of ecstasy. Tom stared, enthralled and a little envious of the mechanism in all of its glory.

Needing something to do with his hands, Tom reached out to caress and stroke Angela's body. "You like your little toy, don't you, Angela?" he asked, finding his voice at last. She only moaned and so he asked her again, more forcefully. "Do you like it, Angela? Say it."

"Yes," she admitted with a gasp. He pinched her nipples suddenly and she jumped.

"Yes!" she cried again, more loudly this time.

"Can you still enjoy it with me here?" he asked. When she hesitated to answer, he pinched her nipples again, a bit harder.

"Yes!"

"I want you to share this pleasure with me from now on," he told her.

"Yes!" she cried out again, seemingly incapable of more than that one word. But that one word was all Tom needed to hear.

"And you know, you can still give me pleasure when you satisfy yourself that way," Tom continued. Angela looked into her husband's eyes. The thick vibrator continued to throb and buzz unrelentingly inside her body. "You want to give me pleasure, too, don't you, Angela?" he persisted.

"Yes," she whispered, clearly teetering on euphoria.

"Good," Tom said, carefully pulling one of the pillows out from beneath her head. "Lie back just a little bit. Yes, like that." He lifted her legs up gently, so as not to disrupt the vibrator, and placed each of her ankles onto his shoulders. "Do you know how I want you to please me, Angela?" he asked.

Angela gasped as he rose up over her. He was roaring hard yet again, red and throbbing and standing at full attention. Her legs were forced high up in the air and spread apart as he moved in closer. It was not hard to imagine how he intended to take her. Tom watched her confusion turn to surprise, and then to interest. Yes, there was most certainly interest that he saw there.

Angela was certainly full of surprises, and Tom would know better than to make assumptions about her from now on. He noticed that there was doubt and fear in her expression as well as the interest, and it occurred to him that she probably never anticipated doing more than fantasizing about what he had in mind. But now she would experience it firsthand. There would never be a better time, for she was more aroused than he had ever seen her before. And besides, wasn't his every action guaranteed to bring her pleasure?

Tom was determined to find out. Having already planned this part of their night, he reached inside the drawer of his bedside table and pulled out a tube of lubricant. He applied it liberally, stroking himself in the process, until he was hard and glistening.

As he drew nearer to his target, Angela's legs were pushed higher up and farther apart. He could see by her expression that she was terribly aroused. She clung to the base of the vibrator, clasping it into her with both hands. Tom pressed himself up against her anus, thrusting forward gently but determinedly several times. Angela moaned as her tight entrance suddenly gave way and Tom worked the head of his penis inside her. She moaned again, more loudly this time, but in looking at her face Tom saw that she was experiencing her first orgasm, so he continued to push forward, only now and again pulling back the smallest bit to spread the lubricant around before making his next thrust forward. He could feel the throbbing vibrations of Angela's little toy through the thin membrane that separated the two parts of her, and it intensified the pleasure for him more than he could have imagined.

Angela was just coming down from the immense pleasure that had shaken her body in great, racking waves when she gasped, suddenly alert to the unsettling sensation of being stuffed to the breaking point. Tom could imagine how she felt; he could feel her body resisting him before gradually stretching to accommodate him. He was lost in the dizzying sensations as he squeezed himself into her. Angela appeared to be suddenly uncertain and afraid. She loosened her hold on the vibrator. She seemed momentarily flummoxed by the discomfort she was experiencing in being stretched to accommodate Tom as he kept pressing forward and breaching her. But then she seemed to relent, giving in once again to the raw, naked hunger for more as she pressed the vibrator even farther into her.

Tom had originally intended to prolong their pleasure in various ways but he was suddenly seized with a need that he could no longer control. He reminded himself that there was plenty of time to experiment in the future. They did not have to do everything all at once. He had the rest of his life to find ways to enjoy his wife from now on.

Tom wrenched his body up, forcing Angela to take even more of him into her as he now began to ravage her, enjoying her thoroughly, throwing himself into her in a kind of frenzy and knowing that she would take everything he gave her and more. Her whole body shook from the force of his thrusts and he knew that he must be hurting her but he could not seem to stop himself. He watched, transfixed as her breasts jerked and bobbed convulsively with the force of his thrusts. She cried out but he no longer heard her. He kept driving into her until the very last drop of his seed had been spent.

"How do you feel?" he asked somewhat remorsefully afterward.

"I'm happy," she said without the slightest hesitation. Any discomfort was forgotten. Tom clung to her protectively, pushing aside another pang of guilt. He would take good care of her. She fell asleep in his arms but Tom stared up at the ceiling most of the night, too deep in thought for sleep.

"Here are her tapes and journals," Tom told Dr. Czernick the next morning.

"Thank you, Tom. I appreciate you doing that."

"She almost had it figured out."

"I think she did figure it out, Tom, but on a subconscious level she chose this path over the other."

"Do you really think so?" As much as Tom wanted to believe this, it was difficult, knowing Angela as he had.

"Yes, I do," said the doctor. "Most people, I think, would choose happiness over the alternative if they realized that they had that choice."

"I would never—I mean, I could never do anything to hurt her," Tom said.

"You have no reason to feel guilty," Dr. Czernick told him. "Believe me when I tell you, Tom, there are men who would do unspeakable things to their wives if they were in your position. Many would be tempted to get all kinds of revenge on them."

"I've been tempted..."

"But you'll do the right thing, Tom," Dr. Czernick said. "I have no doubt of that whatsoever."

Tom shook his head. He still couldn't get over the way everything had changed. "She does seem genuinely happy," he said.

"She *is* genuinely happy, Tom," the doctor assured him. "And that's all that matters, right?"

Jimmy

"Don't go, Sara! Mom's right. You'll just be opening yourself up to potential evil."

Sara laughed, but she felt a strange twinge of anxiety in spite of the absurdity of her sister's words. She had never believed in all those evil-spirit warnings, but the old religious teachings were still a part of her. She would not let her sister know this, however. "I can't believe you still buy into all that stuff, Liz," she said.

"I'm not sure that I do," her sister admitted. "But why take chances?"

"I might ask you the same thing," Sara reminded her. "I seem to recall fornication being on the list of forbidden acts that will send you to the fiery pits of hell, but that hasn't stopped you. Does Mother know he moved in, by the way?"

"Mom is on a strictly need-to-know basis where my sex life is concerned," Liz replied. "But at least in my case, the crime would be worth the time. Anyway, I think God'll be lenient on the fornication thing. He understands. But what you're talking about is different. It's like intentionally sinning for something to do."

"Your arguments are so self-serving," Sara said with a laugh. But she didn't want her big sister worrying about her. "Look, this whole thing is probably just a scam. I'm only going because I want to get to know a few of the girls from my office who will be there. This is the first thing I've been invited to and it would be rude not to go. And it might actually be fun."

"You promise not to talk to any dead people?"

"I promise," Sara assured her, laughing. "I'm just gonna sit back and enjoy the show."

Liz released a loud sigh of defeat. "Well, just be careful," she warned, conceding in the end, just as Sara had known she would.

Sara herself hadn't a single misgiving about going; in fact, she was looking forward to it. She was delighted to have been included, but she was also rather intrigued to see what would happen.

On the night of the event, the atmosphere among the women—there were nine of them altogether—was alive with curious excitement. The women giggled sporadically at the smallest provocation, causing a chain reaction of nervous tittering throughout the room. Sara saw that the women from her office were already clustered into their own little group. One of them noticed her and excitedly gestured for her to join them.

"Hey! Hello," they chirped enthusiastically. Apparently Sara was not as invisible at the office as she thought.

"I never would have figured you for the type to be into this," Becky from Data Entry told her.

"Well, it sounded like fun," she replied, remaining neutral. She didn't want to insult anyone who actually believed in such things, but on the other hand, she didn't want them to think she was some kind of a nut, either.

"You're going to be amazed!" said Pam from Accounting. "I've been to a bunch of these before, but this woman is truly gifted."

Sara wore an impressed expression. "That's what I heard." She looked at Michelle, the receptionist, who only smiled shyly.

"I'm just here out of curiosity," she admitted with a little laugh.

"Okay, ladies," came a strong voice from the front. "If you'll all gather around the table and be seated, we're about to begin."

"Come on," Becky said to Sara. "You'll sit with us." There was an excitement in her voice that was catching. Sara's skin prickled with anticipation.

The clairvoyant's name was Margaret but she encouraged everyone to call her Maggie. She began with a rather long explanation of the spirit world and her philosophies about it. She had a careworn, almost pained look about her that added to her semblance of authenticity. She spoke of the spirit world as if it were more real than the one they were currently residing in.

Sara listened to Maggie skeptically. Everything she had been taught within the confines of her religious background—even those teachings she had rejected—rushed through her mind, contradicting each and every assertion the clairvoyant made. Maggie was explaining that the spirits she spoke to were actually people who had lost their earthly form, but still remained tied to Earth. Some were waiting for the right time to take on another life-form, while others simply chose to stay in the spirit realm. She compared them to angels—guardian angels—and claimed that they looked after the living. She explained that a spirit's connections with the people they left behind remained strong, although their interest in worldly concerns had, for the most part, disappeared. They had no thoughts for earthly or material things. This was why, Maggie claimed, they had such difficulty remembering names, and often attempted to identify people with only a letter from the alphabet. Sara had to restrain herself from rolling her eyes when Maggie concluded by adding that the letter a spirit gives her could apply to a first, middle or last name of a person. *Well, that sure makes it easy for you,* Sara thought to herself.

"While many of you will want me to find out if your loved ones are doing all right," Maggie continued, "the reality is that they come to me to offer you help, and ensure that *you* are all right."

Maggie claimed the spirits were gathering around her at that very moment. She asked the women to be patient with her when she appeared distracted as the spirits were constantly speaking to her.

Sara was becoming more and more anxious for Maggie to get on with it. But before she began, she lit a candle and said a short prayer.

Almost immediately after saying "Amen," Maggie singled out one of the women at the table.

"You," she said pointing. "What's your name?"

"Francesca," was the nervous reply.

"Francesca," she repeated. "There's a spirit here who is quite anxious to talk to you." Francesca's eyes grew wider. Maggie tilted her head to one side as if she were listening intently. "He keeps saying, 'Ladybugs. Ask her if she remembers the ladybugs.' He's giving me the letter E."

All the color drained from Francesca's face. She answered in a shaky whisper, "After my grandmother..." she looked around the room at all of the women as she emphasized the next word "...*Elizabeth* died, my grandfather and I went out and collected ladybugs. My grandmother loved ladybugs." Tears filled her eyes, but she laughed at the memory. She looked at Maggie again. "It seemed like I kept seeing ladybugs right after Grandpa died, too," she told her.

"That was him," Maggie confirmed. "He's telling me that he always sends ladybugs when he wants to get your attention."

Francesca laughed. "Is he... Has he seen Grammy?"

"He says they're together and they both love you. They're always with you, he's saying." Maggie smiled at her. "He wants you to be sure and always keep an eye out for the ladybugs."

Sara turned to look at Becky and the two stared meaningfully at each other for a moment, communicating their mutual amazement at what they just witnessed. It was quite extraordinary, and yet Sara wondered if it could have been staged.

But as Maggie worked her way around the table, it seemed that she always hit upon some link, or unearthed some undeniable and distinct tie that the person had shared with a loved one who had passed.

As Sara watched these proceedings, she wavered back and forth in her impressions—one minute convinced that Maggie was really communicating with the dead and the next wondering if she wasn't actually just making some very good assumptions based on the information she had gleaned from each of the women. She found herself critiquing the details that Maggie brought forth. Were they specific enough, or could they apply to anyone? She couldn't deny that some of the details were so specific that there was no disputing their validity. At one point, Maggie turned to one of the women and said, "Who's Amanda?" When the girl, taken aback, replied nervously that it was her best friend, Maggie, without even missing a beat, continued. "Could you please tell her that her aunt wants her to make up with her mother?"

Sara, like the rest of the women in the room, could not help but gasp in amazement.

"I'm only repeating what they tell me," Maggie kept saying.

Sara suddenly began to wonder what Maggie would come up with when her turn rolled around. Other than a few distant relatives that she had barely even known, there wasn't anyone in her life who had died.

Sara's heart felt as if it were going to leap from her chest when Maggie's gaze finally came around the table and settled on her.

"Jimmy," Maggie said, staring at her with an expectant look.

Sara felt her face heat up as she searched her memory for a Jimmy. A feeling of panic swept over her when she failed to locate one. She had never known anyone named Jimmy before in her life. She wondered if she should make something up. She shook her head, confused. "I…don't know any Jimmy," she said uncertainly. "Is it… Could it be someone I'm about to meet?"

"He's standing right beside you," Maggie said. "He's telling me that he came here to see you."

Sara felt an unreasonable sense of culpability for not knowing who Jimmy was. She looked at the clairvoyant apologetically. "I'm sorry…I don't know who it could be," she stammered.

"Mmm." Maggie turned her head sideways and was thoughtful a minute. "He's telling me you're kindred spirits."

Sara stared at Maggie. "I don't know what that means," she said.

"He's saying, 'We move in the same circles,'" Maggie continued, undaunted. "He wants me to tell you that he's looking out for you now and that you're going to be all right. He says you've had some pretty big changes in your life lately, involving 'R.' Whose name begins with an R? He's telling me that 'R' has uprooted your life, but that it will be all right. He keeps saying, 'Now, it will be all right.' Have you had any big changes recently?"

Sara stared at Maggie in disbelief. She could feel a tingling sensation working its way up the middle of her back like an icy finger as the light, feathery hairs on her skin stood up in alarm.

"I…moved here a few months ago and just started a new

job." There were murmurs of acknowledgement that these were, indeed, big changes.

"Was there anyone else involved in this move?" Maggie encouraged.

"Yes," replied Sara, stealing quick glances around the table at the amazed expressions of the women. "I came out here to live with my boyfriend, R-Ray." There were sharp intakes of breath all round the table.

"Jimmy keeps insisting that Ray is not the right man for you," Maggie said. Her blunt words only served to give her statement more credibility. "I'm just the messenger here," she added. "I simply repeat what they tell me." Even she seemed a little surprised by what she had just said.

Sara was stunned. Hers was the first spirit to convey such a negative message. Relatives, lovers and friends had all come forth with words of wisdom, comfort and love, but here was the spirit of someone she didn't even know giving her this piece of news, and in front of everyone, no less. She didn't know what to say. She felt a hand squeeze hers under the table and she looked up to see that it was Becky's. To her chagrin, tears were filling her eyes.

Thankfully, Maggie was already moving on to the next spirit. The women laughed at something Maggie was saying, but Sara couldn't concentrate on what was being said. She went through the motions, mirroring the responses of those around her for the rest of the reading, but she didn't hear another word. She was brooding about what Jimmy had said about Ray.

A sense of foreboding came over her. She had been so certain that she had gotten it right this time. Why else would she have uprooted her whole life to be with Ray? She had never been this sure about a man before. And she was so happy with him. They did nothing but laugh all the time that they were together, and she loved being with him. Everything was going so well.

She thought about their sex life and immediately brushed the thought aside. It was just that he loved her so much, she assured herself. He was so excited when he was with her that he couldn't control himself. That was a good thing, right? It meant that he was attracted to her. Anyway, what did that matter? Life was about more than just sex.

She tried to rid herself of the feeling of dread, but it seemed to have settled into her bloodstream like a poison. Again and again she reminded herself that the source of this supposed knowledge was a woman who spoke to dead people! How could she possibly let that affect her?

But it had affected her and Sara left the little gathering feeling as if she had been infected with something truly awful.

When she got home, she rushed into Ray's arms and immediately felt better. How ridiculous it seemed all of a sudden to let someone else—especially a false prophet, as her mother would have called the woman—predict your future! Sara clung to Ray, delighting in his warmth and goodness, and in that moment she was truly grateful for the teachings of her youth. Thank heavens she had the good sense to distinguish what was real from what was not.

As she examined Ray throughout the rest of that night, his look, his manner, everything about him was all that she had ever wished for. She could find no fault with him even when she tried.

By the time they went to bed that night, Sara was laughing at herself. She could not believe she had allowed herself to be affected that way. When Ray reached for her, she pulled him to her almost violently, clutching his hair in her fingers and spreading kisses all over his face. He immediately responded, delighting in her enthusiasm. She wanted him so much—needed him, even—that she was actually ready for him when he straightaway moved in between her legs and began making love to her. She clung to him eagerly, forgetting all of her earlier concerns as the desire escalated into a yearning she couldn't remember ever feeling before. It felt so good to have Ray filling her. The feel of him, so strong and hard, had all of her senses quivering with awareness. Losing herself in the sensations, she began undulating her hips beneath him. She abandoned all awareness but the pleasure. She could feel it building steadily as she mindlessly ground her hips against him.

With a low moan, Ray suddenly released himself inside her. Sara almost swore out loud, her disappointment was so profound.

"That was incredible," he said, covering her face with kisses.

But a short while later, when Sara was cradled in the warmth of Ray's arms, just like every other night, she reminded herself how fortunate she was to have a man as kind and sweet as Ray. She thought of the many things he did for her, listing them one by one as she waited for sleep. The surprise dinners, the sight of him outside chopping wood to keep a fire in the grate, the random love notes he left behind when he left for work—all of these were what made a relationship good. Sleep was a long time in coming, but she was content by the time she found it. A little smile played at the edges of her lips as she drifted off.

But after a while, the smile left Sara's lips and her brows furrowed in consternation. She turned her head from side to side and flailed her arms in an effort to push something away from her. She appeared to be having a vivid dream.

Sara's breathing became irregular. She was being kissed passionately—more passionately than she had ever been kissed before. Hands were moving over her body, exploring every inch of her. She responded to the kisses instinctively, sighing and moaning quietly as she became more and more aroused. The hands seemed to be everywhere at once, apparently trying to discover her through touch. Every now and again a finger brushed over her clitoris, and she whimpered when it moved away. She appeared to be agitated, as if her arousal were giving way to frustration.

Very slowly, in parts, she began to rouse from her sleep.

She lifted her arms and wrapped them around him. She had never known Ray to wake up and ravish her like this in the middle of the night before, but she was pleased. His skin felt cool to her touch and she let her hands roam over him. He continued to caress her as if he were touching her for the very first time. She moaned again as he reached between her legs and cupped his hand over her mound, clutching her firmly while one finger slid up in between and stroked her exactly how she liked.

Her hips began to rock lightly back and forth. She was surprised and delighted that he didn't appear to be in a hurry to climb on top of her, seeming content to simply please her. He kept teasing and tantalizing her with his finger while holding her securely in his hand. He stroked her skillfully, knowingly, and she absently wondered why he hadn't done this before. He was giving her more pleasure with his fingers than he had ever given her when they made love. Her arousal was calling her out of her sleep.

But something wasn't quite right. As Sara slowly became more conscious, even in her high state of arousal, she was becoming more and more aware of something being off, or different—something *wrong*. She came to this realization gradually, reluctantly, not really wanting to let go of the tremendous desire that was building up in her and yearning to be fulfilled. Another little whimper escaped her lips, this time of regret and disappointment.

"Shhh," she heard him whisper. "Just enjoy it, baby."

He held her even more firmly and his finger became more forceful and determined. His lips descended on hers once again, even more passionately, almost violently. She was temporarily distracted by the urgency of his response. She moaned, clutching him closer yet. He devoured her lips, sending new thrills through her.

But Ray had never ravished her like this.

And she could hear, in the background, quite clearly, actually, what she recognized suddenly to be Ray's light snoring.

There was another man making love to her in their bed!

With a sudden cry, Sara pressed her hands against the imposter's chest, but he was strong and held his ground.

"Quiet!" he told her. "Just let me satisfy you." But it was not Ray's voice that addressed her. She wasn't even sure that it was a voice. The sound seemed to be coming from inside her head!

"No!" she cried, struggling against him, and in the very next instant he was gone.

Sara sat up and reached for the lamp on her bedside table, frantically switching on the light.

"Wh... What's the matter?" Ray asked, waking suddenly and squinting his eyes against the sudden flood of light.

Sara looked all around them. There was no sign of anyone else in the room. She bent over the edge of the bed and looked underneath. There was no one there. But she had known there wouldn't be. Whatever it was had disappeared in a single instant. It had not moved away from her. It had *dissolved*.

"What is it?" Ray asked again.

"Nothing," Sara managed in a strangled voice. "I had a dream. Go back to sleep."

She switched off the light, trembling, her desire nearly forgotten.

Was it a dream? She couldn't believe that it was. It felt so *real*. But wasn't that what everyone said about their dreams?

Yet it had remained with her, even after she woke. It had

continued to touch and even talk to her. Characters in a dream did not follow you out of it when you woke up. They didn't struggle with you and try to quiet you.

But then, what else could it have been?

Her mind flashed back to the clairvoyant and the spirit who had supposedly spoken to her. Jimmy, was it? She could hear her mother's sanctimonious voice, cautioning her on the dangers of demon possession. She instantly rejected the thought. But she was suddenly cold all over, and a harsh shudder cut through her. Were there really such things as spirits and demons? Had she somehow exposed herself to potential evil simply by going to see a clairvoyant? Her mind balked at the possibility, but she remained uncertain.

Ray's breathing indicated that he had fallen back asleep.

Sara turned her thoughts to him and, as always, it had a calming effect on her. Her life with him, in the here and now, was what she believed in. He had resumed his gentle snoring and it eased her rattled nerves to listen to it. She thought about the man that Ray was, so kind and loving and reliable. And real. She tried to conjure up that feeling of happiness she felt in first coming here to live with him. After a while, the shock of whatever it was that had happened—she was beginning to think it really was all just a very realistic dream—faded, and she eventually drifted back to sleep.

Slowly, subtly and ever so gently, the hands began to once again make their way over Sara's body. They came as if out of nowhere, just lightly tracing over her skin at first, soothingly stroking her, subduing her with their tender influence. As she began to respond, the hands grew bolder, caressing her breasts possessively, cupping and fondling them, and even playfully pinching and pulling at the tips. Moving lower, they groped between her legs, assertively exploring the rest of her body. For the third time that night, the desire curled up within Sara, meandering in and around her insides, sharp and insistent.

Her breathing increased as the fingers began to once again work their magic, lightly circling and tweaking her clitoris until her hips trembled and swayed. Meanwhile the other hand kept roaming assertively up and down her body, sliding up over her breasts and creeping slowly down along her backside, brazenly exploring every part of her.

It was back.

Sara stirred restlessly in her sleep, once again disrupted by the persistent desire that kept rousing all of her senses. But she resisted being pulled from her sleep, conjuring images in an effort to enhance her dream instead. She pictured Ray taking control of her body like this, using just his hands—or possibly even his tongue—to tease and tantalize and torment her. With these thoughts of Ray mingling so faultlessly with the steady deftness of the fingers that now worked her clitoris, Sara drew nearer and nearer the brink of her long-awaited pleasure.

But in an unexpected turn, the fingers stopped and she heard the voice again. "No, Sara, it's not Ray!"

And suddenly the dream collided with reality.

Her mind, shocked beyond disbelief, was suddenly acknowledging the impossible. In fact, it suddenly seemed as if the impossible was the only plausible explanation. Some unseen thing, some otherworldly entity, was making love to her.

Was it a spirit or a demon? Why had he chosen her? What did he want? These questions drifted through her consciousness in a kind of blur, obscured by the thick curtain of exquisite arousal that still hovered and simmered in every fiber of her being.

The fingers once again resumed their efforts, moving over her clitoris with a precision and skillfulness that surprised her. The second hand, too, picked up where it had left off, once again cupping and squeezing her breasts, but this time pinching the tips more aggressively, as if to hurt. Sara automatically bit her lip to avoid crying out and possibly waking Ray.

"That's right," she heard the voice say mockingly. "We don't want to wake Ray."

Sara's heart started to pound with terrified excitement. She turned her head in Ray's direction in the dark, but he had not even stirred. She knew then that the voice was speaking to her from inside her head. She kept saying to herself, *This is not really happening.* But his fingers were working on her relentlessly, pulling her down. She felt weak and her desire was strong, but even so, she tried to resist.

"It *is* happening," the voice countered.

Another, third voice in Sara's head admonished her to scream.

"You don't want to do that," said the voice.

Clearly whatever it was could read her mind. "Who are you?" she thought.

"Open your legs nice and wide for me, and you'll find out."

"I don't have to listen to you!" she thought. But she opened her legs and allowed him to move in between.

She heard his low, rumbling laughter and shuddered. Abruptly, he plunged three fingers into her body and in spite of her wetness, she gasped.

"Sorry, Sara," he said. "But you're going to need this to prepare you for the little surprise I've got planned."

"What surprise?" she asked from inside her head. She meant it as an objection but it came out like an entreaty.

"Something that's going to ruin you for our friend Ray," he said, chuckling menacingly.

"What are you going to do?" she asked. "Tell me, damn you, or I'll scream."

"You're not going to scream," he said coolly. "You want this too badly."

"No," she insisted earnestly. "I love Ray. Why are you doing this?" Her hips were rebelliously gyrating over his fingers. She could hear the sloshing sounds of her body and she felt a sudden panic that Ray would hear them, too, and wake up.

"Never mind why," said the voice, while his fingers worked in and out of her aggressively. "I've got my reasons and you'll be no worse for wear. Except that you'll never be satisfied with Ray again." He laughed cruelly as he added this last.

"Please," she thought distractedly. "Please, please, please… this is wrong."

"Please…what, sweet Sara?" he asked. He kept thrusting his fingers into her as far as they would go.

Sara turned her head from one side to the next. "Please!" She spread her legs wider and jerked her hips up to meet his thrusts.

"You are going to tell me what you want," he told her. "All you have to do is think about it and I'll give it to you. You can start by admitting to yourself how much you want me right now. Maybe you want me even more than you ever wanted our buddy Ray over there?"

"No!" she thought so adamantly that she nearly screamed it out loud. "No! I…love Ray."

"Enough to stop?" he taunted her.

"You're evil," she thought, suddenly fearful again. But her hips seemed to possess a mind of their own as they rode back and forth on his fingers, which were steadily thrashing her insides.

"Oh?" he asked. "Evil, am I?" His fingers halted their thrusting movements and retreated almost all the way out of her, lingering just in between her two little lips. "I wouldn't want to corrupt you, Sara," he taunted.

Sara bit her lip. Her heart was going wild with a sudden panic. She could not account for the exorbitant need in her. The walls of her vagina were aching with yearning from the hours of frustrated desire. "Please!" she thought frantically. "God help me, please!"

"Please what, Sara?" the voice asked again.

"Please…just…oh, why are you doing this to me?" she wondered. "Why don't you just take what you want and go?"

She heard him laugh again. "Sara," he said in his most taunting voice, slipping his fingers all the way in and then out again. "Sa…ra," he repeated in a more singsong tone this time, teasing her like a child might tease another. With each syllable he pressed his fingers in and then withdrew again. "Saaaa…ra."

"Oh!" she cried inwardly. "Please don't stop."

"Please don't stop," he said, mimicking her tone as well as her words. "But what is it you want, Sara? Ask nicely for what you want."

"You bastard!" she thought.

"Nice…ly," he scolded, taking his fingers all the way out of her and once again leaving them just lingering at her quivering opening.

"Oh no, don't stop," she begged again.

"That's better," he reminded her. "But you have to also tell me what you want me not to stop. Tell me what you want me to do."

Sara hesitated for as long as she could. She hated him, whoever or whatever he was. But the aching desire in her was becoming painful. She had never felt anything like it before in her life. "I need him," she thought, and heard his wicked laughter. He could hear her thoughts, she reminded herself. Fighting him was pointless.

"Please," she thought, trembling with the effect that even her words were having on her throbbing body. "Finger me again." *And please make the aching stop,* she added to herself. And then other thoughts followed, frightening thoughts, thoughts she had never imagined thinking before.

It was an effort not to scream out loud with pleasure when

he complied, once again forcing his fingers in her all the way. "Yes, yes, yes, yes, yes…" she kept repeating in her mind.

"But there was so much more you thought about, too," he reminded her. "Are you ready for the rest of it?"

"Yes, yes, yes, yes…" She was now chanting the word over and over in her mind.

"Nicely," he reminded her.

"Please," she begged inwardly. But she could no longer remember what she wanted.

His fingers slipped out of her sopping body and she felt him shift between her legs. "Get ready for the ride of your life, Sara," she heard him say.

"Please," she thought.

He pressed into her opening. She gasped at the size of him.

"Raise your legs up nice and high, Sara," he instructed. She obeyed immediately. "Yes, like that. Bring them up." He grasped one ankle in each of his hands and then he gently but firmly pressed her legs toward her head. She felt the muscles in her thighs strain but she did not resist as he managed to bend her legs until her feet were on either side of her head. This position lifted her buttocks up high in the air. Up to this point he had only inserted a few inches inside her, but she could already feel the pressure of his thickness bearing down on her, opening her. Even with her extreme wetness, she felt that he was stretching her. "How does that feel, Sara?" he asked her.

"Yes," she thought. "Yes…yes…yes!" She had the urge to push her hips upward in an effort to get more of him inside her, but she couldn't move an inch in her present position. Her hands rested limply on the bed on either side of her. She was afraid to reach out and touch whatever it was that was doing this to her.

As he pushed farther and farther into her, she bit her lip hard to avoid screaming out from the pleasure. He was filling her so slowly and so completely. But still her body kept crying out for more. She wanted to be filled to the point of overflowing.

"Is that what you really want, Sara?" he asked, reading her thoughts.

"Yes," she said before she even considered what she was saying.

"You know the magic word, then," he reminded her doggedly. It seemed as if he were playing with her. There appeared to be no strain or suffering on his part at all. He held her down easily while working his way into her from above, almost as if he were floating. She realized that he could very well be hovering in midair between her quivering thighs.

"Please," she said again, pushing the reality of what was happening away. But it was not real, she reminded herself once again. It was a dream. Perhaps that's why her desire seemed to just keep building and building, never to be satisfied. Just like her dreams, perhaps this, too, would never reach fruition. Her desire was like something independent of her, something foreign, that held her body hostage while she looked on. Her hips remained high up in the air as she waited and yearned for release.

"Please…what?" he asked her, and suddenly she became infuriated with the waiting.

"Please fuck me all the way," she thought angrily. "Fuck me now, fuck me hard, fuck me deep…" Her train of thought was suddenly halted as he pushed himself into her and kept going, and it was more than she had ever dared imagine.

"Oh no," she thought. "Oh, good heavens, no!" Yet he kept filling her. Her feet were still pinned on either side of her head, leaving her hips trapped in midair. There was no escape. She was at her wit's end with numerous emotions ranging from pleasure to terror. "How much more is there?" she asked herself.

"There is exactly as much as you wished for, my greedy little girl," the voice told her. "I could've come to you in many shapes and sizes but you had to have to the mother lode."

Sara felt that perhaps she had bitten off more than she could chew. This thought caused her lover to laugh loudly inside her head.

"Nicely put," he said, withdrawing at last, but only long enough to prepare her for another thrust forward, once again going all the way to the hilt. "But we'll see how much of me you can swallow another time," he remarked. They were both quiet then as he began a steady pace of driving in and out of her with alarming vigor. With each forward thrust, she could feel his testicles batter her bottom, adding another dimension of pleasure to that region. She felt as if her entire body were being powered and driven by the large shaft running through her.

The intense desire was once again building in Sara with a frightening intensity. With each thrust it seemed to build higher, until she wondered that she didn't explode with her impending orgasm. What was holding her back?

"You'll get what you want when I get what I want," she heard him say.

"What do you want?" she wondered. He kept driving into her throughout their conversation. She was only half-aware of what was being said, as the terrible yearning seemed to curl into dangerous spirals of delicious anticipation that she feared might make her lose her mind.

"I want *you*," he explained. "To be my lover." He allowed what he was telling her to sink in for a minute before continuing, yet he never for an instant let up with his steady thrusts. "I'll be your secret lover and I won't even exist," he laughed. "How can you do any better than that?"

Sara was in no frame of mind to be negotiating. All she cared about at that moment was getting the relief she needed. She knew she would have to achieve some kind of release before she would be able to think again. Her desire couldn't just keep building up in her like this forever, could it? She didn't believe she would survive if it did. Already, she could feel an exquisite tenderness swelling her insides, causing them to cling at the intrusive thing driving through her with a kind of reflexive resistance. The sensations as her insides gripped him tormented her. She had reached the point of orgasm, but was somehow stuck there. Usually, when her desire reached this point, her release, like a giant wave, would break into a great rushing crescendo of satisfying pleasure. There was normally only a single precious instant of extraordinary euphoria in the transition between the building of pleasure and the climax, but that instant was somehow being stretched out indefinitely. She felt that it was too much for her to endure. Surely she would burst under the pressure. Perhaps she would lose her mind. She couldn't seem to get herself over the crest that normally she would never have been able to stop.

Yet the last shred of sanity that she possessed argued that to acquiesce with the demands of an entity that had the power to keep her dangling in this strange sort of sexual purgatory would be tantamount to selling her soul to the devil.

"I would be his sexual slave," she thought.

"And I would be yours," he countered.

If only he would allow her the release she needed. But her hips remained high in the air and virtually helpless to the exquisite battering that kept her hovering in a limbo of pleasure bordering on torture.

"The pleasure of the release I can give you will be better than anything you can imagine," he promised her.

"Ray," she thought.

"Ray's right here," he reminded her. "And he has no idea what we're doing."

"Oh, God help me," she thought miserably. "Very well, I'll be your lover."

"Say my name," he demanded.

"Jimmy," she thought.

"No, say it out loud."

"But Ray…"

"Whisper it. Just say it with your lips."

She felt a sudden fear, but the tantalizingly torturous sensation of wavering on the edge of release for so long was more intimidating than any potential fear. How many times had she wished the sensation she was feeling would last a little longer, she wondered ironically? Always it was so fleeting as to be unreal. But to experience it for an extended period was more than a person was meant to bear. It was like teetering just off the edge of a cliff. She would gladly plunge to her death rather than to remain indefinitely in midfall.

"Jimmy," she whispered tentatively, and in the very next instant, whatever it was that had been frozen in her was suddenly released in a gush of pleasure so powerful she screamed. Violent, racking tremors shook her body in large, tremulous waves of dizzying delight. Eventually the intensity of each wave decreased, and she was left trembling.

Sara was only partially aware of her surroundings. She vaguely remembered that Jimmy had exploded inside her at the same moment that she had found her own satisfaction, but it suddenly dawned on her that he had also, at some point, disappeared. The pressure on her legs had been released but they still hung in midair. Ray, who had been awakened by her scream, was reaching for her in the dark. If he noticed her odd position with legs all akimbo, he didn't mention it. She struggled to right herself, trembling violently, as Ray pulled her to him. She tried to push him away from her but he would not let her. His body felt so warm and she realized suddenly that she was shivering with cold. Jimmy had carried no warmth with him at all.

Ray clasped Sara to him, holding her firmly in the spooning position and she felt herself beginning to warm. "What is it, sweetheart?" he asked her in his husky, sleep-filled voice. "Bad dream?"

Sara couldn't speak. She was too overcome with guilt. That Ray was comforting her left her bereft.

"Baby? Are you all right?"

"Mmm." She didn't trust her voice.

He tightened his hold on her. Tears filled her eyes. But luckily, whatever it was that just happened had exhausted her. It was all she could do to remain awake. As she was losing consciousness, she heard a voice say, "Sweet dreams," but she couldn't tell if it was Ray or the voice inside her head. She simply surrendered to sleep without responding.

When Sara awoke the next morning she was alone, it seemed, and there were tears still on her cheeks. She was trembling again and very cold. The first thing she was aware of was an intense feeling of emptiness. She had an overwhelming longing, an acute aching that left her virtually starving for something she wasn't able to name. She was so weak that she couldn't seem to raise a finger on her own behalf.

Desolate, she looked around. It was ten o'clock! Ray must have gone to work. How had she slept so late into the day? She would have to call in sick at the office.

She made an effort to rouse herself but her limbs refused to move. As her mind became more alert, her sense of despair grew stronger. It seemed as if she had developed some kind of new, essential need, crucial to her survival, impossible to live without. She was staggered by the intensity of it. The word *addiction* came to her mind with an overwhelming surge of horror.

And then it hit her, with a force that terrified her more than death itself. The awful yearning, the brutal craving, the burning, aching desire that was spreading through her in curling, winding tendrils, like the smoke that streams from a cigarette, had its origin in her womb. She had this realization just as she heard the familiar chuckling inside her head.

"No!" she thought, but her objection instantly melted away. Her desire, and her overwhelming relief that he was there, superseded everything else. The swiftness with which this strange new need was taking hold reminded her of what she had heard about crack cocaine addiction, and how a single incident could bring it about. She felt instinctively that this was even more potent than that. Although the addiction seemed to have a firm hold of her body, she knew that its source originated in her mind. She remembered the pleasure she felt the night before and the need suddenly surged up in her, sending a violent shudder through her body, just at the thought. It seemed as though she had experienced a pleasure so intense that the mere memory of it was able to create deficits in those areas of her brain unfamiliar with how to achieve the same effect.

But even realizing all of this, Sara was already adopting the reasoning of the addict, pushing these realizations and her hope for a solution aside until such time, she promised herself, when she felt well enough to address them. For the moment, she must have relief. The incredible aching need was quickly penetrating the region between her legs, and once again dominating the forefront of her thoughts.

Jimmy was there with her, but why was he silent? What was he up to now?

"I thought I'd give you the opportunity to come to terms with the situation," he chimed in just then. "I've been waiting for you to wake up and call for me again."

She couldn't even put up a pretense of rejecting him. She felt him moving over her and she opened her legs wide. But she quickly discovered that he was not going to appease her need without making her work for it. She felt his hardness pressing against her lips and with dismay she opened her mouth to him.

"Why can't you satisfy me first?" she protested. "I'll do this for you after."

"You'll do it first," he told her. "I'll give you what *you* want after."

Her desire assaulted her like shards of glass scraping the tender flesh between her legs. It pierced her insides violently, demandingly, causing the membranes to rise up and moisten. *God help me,* she thought miserably. *I must get this over with quickly.* She gagged as he pushed himself against the back of her throat.

"Open your throat to me," he said. "If you swallow all of me, I promise I'll relieve you."

"I can't!" she thought.

"You can," he assured her. "You can, and you will, or you won't get what you need."

Sara tried to open her throat to him, but it seemed to have a mind of its own. It kept rejecting the massive appendage that kept pressing to get in. It suddenly occurred to her that she might be able to satisfy herself without him. Perhaps she could find something similar to him in size to use.

"You'll kill yourself trying," he warned her. "You can't get the feeling you're now craving without me."

"But I can't do this," she cried inwardly.

"You can," he told her. "Concentrate. Relax the muscles in your throat."

Sara tried to do as he instructed, but it was difficult to think about anything other than the screaming need between her legs. "It's so big," she objected, "and hard." It didn't seem possible. Yet she was getting nearer with each try. She had to do it. She simply had to. She couldn't even think about the alternative. She needed him. Later, she promised herself...but she abruptly turned her thoughts back to the here and now. For the moment, she could no longer delay her relief.

Sara tipped her head back as far as it would go and determinedly fought her gag reflex as Jimmy pressed forward. At last she felt the full, rigid thickness of him slowly filling her throat. She struggled to breathe through her nose, and realized she was panting from her exertions. He kept going until he was lodged deep within her throat, so deep that he could move in and out and still never fully withdraw. She strained her neck, holding her head at the perfect angle so that he could make better use of her. He was moaning and encouraging her. "That's it," he said delightedly. "Oh, Sara, your throat feels so good. Oh, yes, I can remember now why I always liked this so much. It feels so good to have my dick embedded in your throat."

"Hurry," she thought. "You promised."

"What are the magic words?" he taunted her.

"Please," she entreated. His thrusts were coming faster, pushing him farther and farther into her throat. She struggled to breathe, having all she could do to simply hold her mouth open wide while he had his way with her. He was so far inside her that his testicles began slapping at her bottom lip. In an effort to urge him on more quickly, she stretched out her tongue and licked at them.

Jimmy groaned loudly, seeming to like that, so Sara continued her efforts more eagerly. "You'll do anything for me now, won't you?" he asked.

"Yes," she began. "But you promised."

"Jimmy won't break his promise," he assured her. Up and down he moved along the walls of her esophagus as she dutifully kept lapping at his balls, impatient for him to decide it was her turn. It was difficult to keep her mouth wide open while he assaulted the deepest recesses of her throat, but the need in her wouldn't let her quit. The thought of his rigid thickness buried between her legs kept her going. She imagined the tip of him pressing against her womb, finding places in her that had never been discovered before and arousing that secret, mysterious thing that would lead her to higher and higher states of ecstasy. That thing, having been awakened, now cried out with a ravenous hunger that, if left unsatisfied, would surely be avenged. She simply had to feed it, and Jimmy was the only one who could help her do that. She needed him to quiet the thing again. Like an itch that simply cannot be reached at the surface, her need was buried deep beyond the realm of her own abilities.

Seemingly unaware of her plight, Jimmy kept driving himself deeper into Sara's throat, savoring every moment with relish. "Ahhhh," he moaned contentedly. "You're giving me incredible pleasure, Sara." He seemed to be mocking her, but then he added, "It won't go unrewarded." These words from him brought about another surge of uproarious need within her, beginning in her womb and radiating outward until it penetrated every part of her, even her mouth, which seemed to open even wider for him all at once. Her hips absently rocked back and forth, her little nether lips grasped at the air in desperation.

"Please, Jimmy," she thought, lapping more eagerly at his balls. "Please, remember your promise."

"Jimmy'll take care of you," he promised again. "*After* you take care of Jimmy."

Sara had long since lost the urge to gag and was, at last, getting used to the feeling of having her throat so thoroughly filled. It was still terribly intrusive and a bit discomfiting, but those sensations only increased her arousal and compounded her need. But there was not much more that she could do to enhance the experience for him. To simply keep her head arched and still, and her mouth held wide open for him, was all that was required. She had taken it a step further by using her tongue, to show him just how anxious she was to please him, and she could tell that he had been pleased. Her hands, though, had simply been lying on either side of her on the bed. She suddenly realized that she could use them to please him as well. She tentatively brought them up, feeling for him—for there was no visible evidence that anyone was there—and moving them up along his thighs and resting them on his buttocks.

Sara moved her hands over the firm, twin globes, experimentally sliding her fingers down in between his crack. He groaned loudly, and his thrusts into her throat came harder and faster. It was almost more than she could bear, and she gasped for air through her nose as she struggled to endure it. Meanwhile, to rouse him even more, she moved her finger down along the crease until it settled on his tightly puckered hole. She pressed her finger against the opening, gently at first, but as he grew even more excited she gradually applied more pressure.

"Oh, you are a dirty little girl, aren't you?" he moaned, clutching her head in his hands now as he literally ground himself into her wide-open throat. She wondered how much longer he could last as she kept pressing her finger against the entrance of his anus. She seemed to recall wishing for a lover who could go on forever. She silently prayed that wish wouldn't come true. Her jaw ached, her throat felt bruised, and her chin burned where his balls were battering her face. At last her finger breached the opening of his anus, and she pressed it deep inside. "Oh, you're a *dirty* girl!" he cried out again. He threw himself deep into her throat one last time and she thought she could feel his come slide the rest of the way down her throat. He remained inside her for much longer than was necessary, she felt, and his testicles twitched restlessly on her chin. She waited for him to recover with something akin to hysteria growing inside her. Her efforts on his behalf had partially distracted her from her own voracious need, but now her body was gripped in a frenzy of lust. With her own desire back in the forefront of her mind, the emptiness and yearning she suddenly felt struck her like a blow. She hated him in that instant, for moving in such a leisurely manner, taking his sweet time, knowing all the while how desperately she craved him because it was he who put the craving there to begin with!

She heard his chuckle and her resentment grew, even as his amusement further inflamed her desire. She trembled and ached everywhere, and every part of her was alive with wanting. As he pulled himself out of her throat, she reached to grasp hold of it, feeling the emptiness already. And she was overjoyed to find him as hard as if he had never ejaculated.

"Okay, now it's your turn," he told her. "Grab the headboard." She had no difficulty moving suddenly and scrambled to do as he instructed. She rolled onto her knees, spreading her legs far apart for him and grasped hold of the headboard as he had instructed. The cool air caused goose bumps to prickle and rise on the soaking flesh between her thighs. She was shaking uncontrollably, but she was sighing and moaning already in anticipation of what was to come.

She felt him moving slowly up and then down her saturated slit. She pushed her hips back in an effort to hurry him, but Jimmy firmly held the reins on the situation by grasping her hips. Holding her still, he moved himself unhurriedly up and down along her little lips, which by now had parted for him in a silent appeal. But still he lingered outside, only just wetting himself at her entrance.

"I need it," she reminded him. "I need it now!"

He responded by moving away from her lips, sliding upward

and coming to rest against her anus. He gently pressed against her tightly puckered hole.

"No!" she cried aloud. "You promised…please! Please," she repeated again, out loud this time, speaking calmly but with desperation in her voice. "Please, Jimmy, please fuck my pussy."

"And you'll let me have this next time?" he asked.

"Yes!" she agreed. "Yes, anything, just…please!"

Relief washed over her as she felt him sliding back down to where she needed him. She arched her back as he pressed into her, moaning loudly in ecstasy. With every inch that penetrated her, the terrible craving was diminished a little bit more while the pleasure was significantly enhanced. "God, yes!" she cried mindlessly. "Yes, Jimmy, yes!" And he just kept filling her, inch by inch, until it almost became too much for her and at last she felt that she might be satisfied.

With Jimmy inside her, pleasing her, the agonizing need was being quenched, leaving only the pleasurable part of desire to keep building and building. He was filling her so absolutely, stuffing her, stretching her until she thought she might burst, so there was, for the moment, little more that could be yearned for. She could hardly move, she was so full; all she could do was clutch the headboard for support while holding her body bent and spread open for him to do as he would. With every thrust from him, she felt her desire rise up higher and higher and higher, reaching impossible heights, taking her body over and leaving what remained a mass of trembling pleasure. When at last it reached its massive crescendo, she braced herself as it exploded within her, spreading little molecules of pleasure everywhere.

Immediately afterward, she was alone. Although she was shaken and confused by the experience, she suddenly felt better, overall. There was none of the horrible emptiness and craving that she had felt upon waking. She took in her surroundings and saw that it was two in the afternoon. She had not even bothered to call in at work!

Sara didn't encounter Jimmy again for the remainder of that day. This gave her a kind of reprieve, which she spent trying to think of ways to control the hunger if it rose up in her again and, alternately, denying that there was anything that needed to be controlled to begin with.

Her reprieve was short-lived, and by the end of the day she felt herself becoming depressed. The horrible, aching emptiness was returning. Ray was watching television.

There was suddenly the sound of laughter inside her head. "Maybe you can get him to join us."

At the sound of Jimmy's voice, Sara was once again thrown into the full spectrum of withdrawal symptoms—from the mental depression that filled her with dark, never-ending bleakness, to the physical symptoms that left her shaking and craving and weakened. She almost fell down where she stood.

"In the garage," she heard him say.

It took all the energy she could muster just to get there.

"Please," she began, struggling to remove her pants.

"I'll give you your fix," he promised. "All in good time." He was quiet for a moment, apparently considering his next move. "Over there," he said at last. "Ray's old motorcycle." He said this as if he were familiar with it.

Sara approached the bike, looking it over in confusion.

"Hop on."

Sara sat on the bike. She felt a thrill from the cold leather on her bare bottom. "Take off your top, too, Sara," she heard Jimmy say.

"But Ray…"

"As long as you keep quiet, Ray will never look for you out here."

She took off her top. New thrills and sensations were

building up within her. But she could hardly enjoy them with the violent craving that remained in the forefront. With horror, she realized that the need would take all her choices away in its quest to be satisfied.

Jimmy sat on the bike behind her. "Scoot up a little," he said. "That's right. Rest your feet on the running boards. And keep your hands on the handlebars. You're going for a little ride." She felt his massive hardness digging into her back. "Ahhh," he groaned in satisfaction. "Back in the saddle again!"

Jimmy grabbed hold of Sara's hips, lifting her slightly. She straightened her legs a bit, leaning on the running boards, to assist him. He reached up between her legs and played with her with his fingers. "Nice and wet," he remarked, pleased. She moaned. Soon he would be inside her and then everything would be all right again.

Jimmy wrapped an arm around Sara's waist, slowly pulling her back down toward the sitting position. She knew that he was bringing her down over him so that he could take her, right there, on Ray's motorcycle. She clutched the handlebars and closed her eyes, bathed in longing and anticipation. Soon the ache would be eased and the pleasure would begin.

But Jimmy only dipped in and out of her a few times to collect some of the wetness before maneuvering Sara so that it was her anus that was being broached as he pulled her hips down farther.

"No!" she cried. "Please, Jimmy, not that."

"But you promised," he said, pretending to be hurt.

"I need you the other way," she pleaded.

"But I need this," he countered. "And if you won't give me what I need, why should I give you what you need?" And as he spoke he kept jabbing at the puckered little hole.

"I already did something for you this morning," she nearly whined. "Is it going to be something difficult every time?"

"You'll learn to love all of these things over time, Sara," he said, causing a thrill and a horror to shoot through her simultaneously. More than anything, she was afraid of how she would be able to wait for her own pleasure. The incredible yearning left her feeling desolate.

"Please hurry, then," she conceded.

"You don't want me to hurry too much, though, do you, Sara?" Jimmy teased. "You might have been able to resist me if old Ray wasn't always in such a hurry." He settled both his hands on either side of her waist, just above where her hips curved outward.

"How many things like this are you going to make me do?"

"I won't make you do anything," he said. "I promise." And he kept pulling her hips down gently, and she could feel him beginning to breach her tight outer ring. But he was so large that her body kept resisting him, virtually bouncing him out before he got in. "Open," he demanded.

"It's too big," she complained.

"Arch your back as much as you can," he told her. "It will help me force you open."

She immediately did as he asked. Every second without him inside her seemed like an eternity. They struggled together, him pulling down on her hips and her pressing her hips out, until finally, with a triumphant groan, he penetrated the ring that barred the entrance and inched himself inside. Sara cried out loudly in discomfort.

"Shhh," he warned her. "You don't want Ray coming out here, do you?"

But the discomfort, for all its intrusiveness, literally wedging her open and filling her to the breaking point, actually eased the aching emptiness that had been causing the feeling of desolation. It seemed to somehow halt, or slow, the torturous anguish by diminishing the painful craving so that the discomfort of him taking her this way was preferable to the alternative. But he was not even half inside her yet and she felt that she would most certainly be rent in two. She clung to the handlebars and found herself instinctually straightening her legs here and again to raise herself up and escape him. But Jimmy had her in a secure grasp, with one hand on either side of her waist, buried in the soft tissue just above the hipbone. When she tried to escape, he yanked her back down even farther. She struggled not to cry out, as she was forced to take every bit of him deep inside her anal cavity.

"Up and down," Jimmy encouraged. "Go on, take us for a ride, mamma."

Grasping the handlebars more tightly, Sara tried to gain enough leverage to move up and down on Jimmy. Her foot suddenly slipped from the foot peg and she fell, crying out again as she fell down, hard, on Jimmy's lap. But realizing that she had to get through this or suffer the consequences, she shook off her discomfort and tried it again, this time with more success. If she was careful and watched what she was doing, she could determine how far down her hips would go and avoid the discomfort of taking him all the way in. He kept a firm grip on her waist, so she was aware that he could jerk her hips down whenever he wanted to. But for the time being, he seemed content to let her steer the ride.

Sara carefully began to ride him, using her legs mostly, but her arms, too, to piston her bottom up and down over his thick, rigid shaft. The discomfort of it never let up, but it was just bearable if she didn't descend too far down on it, and Sara repeatedly reminded herself of her reward if she persevered.

"Look out for the bumps," Jimmy warned suddenly, and in the next instant it was as if the bike had come alive. The engine wasn't running, but it was moving, and yet it wasn't going anywhere. But it felt as if it were traveling along a bumpy road.

It reminded Sara of a mechanical bull, the way it moved. She gasped as it shook and bounced between her legs. But she was determined to maintain control of it. She knew it would be much harder to keep her balance, but it was imperative that she try her best.

"Going into a curve," Jimmy warned, and sure enough, the bike tipped sideways, forcing Sara to lean back into him and tighten her buttocks in order to hold on.

"Ooooh," she complained, when her efforts caused him to penetrate her deeper, while thrashing about inside her.

"Looks like we have a jump coming up," she heard Jimmy say. There was amusement in his voice, and she knew he was enjoying this.

"No!" she cried, bracing herself. Suddenly it felt as if they were flying through the air for a few seconds before coming down with a hard landing that wedged Jimmy even farther up into her body. Sara bit her lip hard to keep from screaming. But she kept going, and rode through every imaginable condition without ever once losing her footing or giving up. Her backside burned from the intense activity and even her breasts ached from bouncing so aggressively in her efforts to manage the ride, but she refused to let up, knowing that she must go through this to get what she needed. There were moments when she felt she could not endure another minute, but somehow she made it through the entire ride.

And as promised, Sara, in her turn, got her fill of the pleasure that made it all seem worthwhile and, for the time being, anyway, satisfied her insatiable need.

But things could not go on like this forever. Sara realized this and yet she couldn't concentrate on the problem long enough to think of a solution. The need was coming every few hours now, regardless of where she was, whether it be at work or at home, and the things he was making her do were getting more difficult—and more risky. Sara was terrified of being discovered. And even if she could keep it a secret, her preoccupation with Jimmy made it impossible for her to function normally. She was late, distracted, disassociated, nervous and forgetful. She would disappear for long periods of time without an explanation. It was becoming impossible.

Sara decided to turn to the woman responsible for bringing Jimmy into her life.

"Incubus," Maggie said when Sara explained what was happening.

"Incubus?" Sara repeated, shaking her head. "What is that?"

"An incubus is a spirit, often an evil spirit, who seduces mortal women, sometimes causing them to go insane."

Sara's heart beat faster. "How can I get rid of him?"

"Well, I have to admit that this is the first one I've come across in my experience, but I've read quite a lot about them. It depends on why this incubus chose you, to determine what's the best thing to do. If I'm remembering right, you didn't recognize this spirit at first, did you?"

"No. I didn't know who he was. I still don't. I'm sure he's never been a part of my life before this."

"Well, then, he must be a part of someone's past who you're close to. It is rare for an incubus to simply choose someone at random. Usually they have reasons for what they do, most often reasons of revenge. They use sex as a tool to destroy the person they're after."

Sara sighed. "I can't imagine who that would be."

"Has he ever mentioned the name of anyone you know?"

Sara thought about it a minute. Had Jimmy said Ray's name before she brought him up? She couldn't remember. "I think he might have mentioned my boyfriend, Ray, but I'm not sure."

"That's right! The guy you moved out here for. I remember now. The incubus did bring him up." Maggie looked at Sara thoughtfully. "You're going to need the help of the person the incubus is after, so you'll have to find out for sure if it's Ray or not."

"Oh, God," Sara said.

"Can you tell when the incubus is with you?"

"Sort of. Sometimes."

"Well, be careful. Generally an incubus will try to avoid direct contact with those connected to their female victims. They'll come around when the women are alone, or when their partners are asleep or otherwise occupied and unlikely to be aware of its presence."

Sara thought about that first night when Jimmy came to her while Ray was asleep. "If it's Ray he's after, how do I stop him?"

"Ray will have to help you keep the incubus away until its influence is out of your system, which will mean he'll have to get you through at least one—and quite possibly more—of these sexual spells you told me about. Once the incubus leaves, you will have it out of your system."

"What if I have someone besides Ray do that?" Sara asked, considering rehab.

"It must be the person the spirit is after. The spirit can only lose power to the person it comes here for. It's as if no one else has any power over it."

By the time Sara got back from her visit with the clairvoyant, she was once again wild with need. A dark depression was beginning to set in with each new incident now, and she was afraid that she would not last much longer. All that Maggie told her only added to her depression. The power of the spirit seemed so much stronger than her. How was she ever going to fight it when she didn't even know for certain who it had come here for?

She felt Jimmy's presence suddenly and immediately halted her thoughts. They were becoming more and more hopeless and incoherent anyway, now that the desire was taking hold. Without hesitating, she mentally asked him what he wished of her, knowing without a doubt that whatever it was she would do it. There was no longer any objections or pleadings. She followed his directives to the letter willingly, even eagerly, knowing that it was the only way that she would get what she needed to survive.

It was several hours later when Sara was finally getting her end of the bargain met, having at last satisfied all of Jimmy's demands. She was grasping some kind of a metal pipe in the floor of her laundry room with both hands while Jimmy stood behind her, holding her legs up in the air. He was driving himself into her with the force of a powerful machine in long, even strokes that caused her body to jolt forward with every single thrust. Her body was naked and bruised, but the look on her face was one of pure ecstasy. She shuddered violently as the amazing pleasure washed over her.

"What the hell?" Ray's voice broke into the room like an alarm. Sara looked up and saw him watching her with an expression of absolute horror and disbelief.

"Well, hello, Ray," she heard Jimmy say from inside her head. And in the next instant he was gone. Her legs immediately dropped to the ground with a painful thud. She hadn't even had time to catch herself.

Sara looked up at Ray. This must be what they meant by "rock bottom," she thought. "Please…help…me," she whispered pitifully.

Ray rushed to her side. His eyes moved over her naked body, lingering confusedly over the bruises as he picked her up off the floor. "How…how were you just floating there, sideways, in midair?" he asked, clearly shaken.

"I need to get dressed first," she said.

When Sara had dressed and composed herself, she found

Ray sitting on the couch, staring at a blank television set. She sat down next to him and reached for his hand. He moved his hand away but met her gaze.

"What the hell was that?" he asked slowly.

"Do you remember, about a week or so ago, when I went to the clairvoyant?" Sara asked.

"Yeah." He was looking at her as if he had already heard enough.

"Ray, listen to me a minute," she said, more self-possessed suddenly than she had been since this began. "I'm not crazy and I'm not deranged...at least I don't think so." She looked at him pleadingly. "Something happened there. The clairvoyant said there was a spirit there who knew me...or something like that. Well, he followed me home, and...God! This gets so weird. I know you're not going to believe this but he...he... touched me in my dream...and I woke up." Her eyes grew wide suddenly. "Maybe you remember. It was that night I screamed and woke you up, too." Ray just stared at her, so she continued. "But...then we went back to sleep and he...came back. This time I couldn't fight him off." Her expression turned pleading when she saw the look of pain and horror in his eyes. "You have to believe me and please just let me finish..."

"What?" he gasped. He was incredulous but at least he was still speaking to her. "You're cheating on me with a *ghost?*" He laughed suddenly. "Who is he? Anyone I know?"

"That's the thing," Sara continued. "I went back to the clairvoyant today because I didn't know what else to do. He's been coming back whenever he wants and it's like I can't control myself anymore. Maggie—the clairvoyant—said he's an incubus and I could go insane if I don't get rid of him. She said they only come back for revenge, and if he hasn't come from my past then he must have come from the past of someone I'm close to."

Ray just looked at her.

"He says his name is Jimmy," she continued, shrugging. "I personally have no idea who—"

"Jimmy?" Ray interrupted. He was still looking at her with disbelief, but there was suddenly something like alarm in his face, too. "He told you his name was *Jimmy?*"

"Yes, he said his name is Jimmy." Encouraged by Ray's response, she added, "And he told the clairvoyant during that first reading to tell me that you weren't the right guy for me."

Ray's eyes moved sideways as he absorbed this. Sara watched him. His expression of disbelief was being replaced with something else. He seemed to be considering what she said.

"Do you know someone named Jimmy?" she whispered hopefully.

He was silent for a long time, as if weighing the possibility of something. He seemed reluctant to speak. "I knew *a* Jimmy," he said finally. There was another pause. "Once," he added.

"Was he…alive?"

Ray was starting to pale. "Yes," he said. "He was…someone I knew. But then he died."

"Someone you knew?" she repeated. "You knew a Jimmy? How did you know him? How did he die?" She was suddenly filled with hope—and questions.

"We grew up together. He was… Jeez! This is ridiculous!" he yelled, getting up off the couch suddenly and walking toward the window. "This is not possible."

"He was what?" she encouraged. "Please, Ray, I know this seems crazy but let's just pretend for a minute that it's really happening. Please, please…" She sighed, so tired of begging all of a sudden. "Please just tell me how you knew him."

"He lived next door to me and we grew up together," Ray began in a strange voice. He didn't turn to face Sara as he spoke, but just continued to stare out the window. "He made a big show of being my friend all those years but he was really just a pain in my ass." Ray appeared to be getting agitated just from talking about it.

"A pain in your ass…how?" Sara asked.

"He was always getting me into trouble, for one thing," he said. He turned and looked at her. "Or trying to take what was mine."

Sara stared at him. "What did he try to take from you?"

"He wanted everything I had, whether it was a toy, an answer on a test, a friend." He met her eyes. "My girlfriend." She wasn't sure if this last referred to her.

"Had he taken a girlfriend from you?" she asked.

"Yes."

After a moment's silence, she decided to go in another direction. "What was he like?"

Ray thought about this. "He was charismatic, but mean underneath. He loved to play pranks on people. And he was tough to shake. He'd get under your skin. I spent most of my years growing up trying to ditch him."

"That sounds like him, all right," Sara whispered suddenly, without even thinking.

They looked at each other. "Hold on a minute!" he said, rushing from the room. When he came back, he was holding a pile of books. "Yearbooks," he told her.

Sara was excited, in spite of herself. She couldn't help but be curious about the being who had so completely infiltrated her life in this short span of time.

"Here we go," Ray said as he flipped through the pages. "There!" And he tapped his finger on one of the pictures. "Is that him?" he asked her.

Sara looked at the picture. Smiling up at her was a handsome young man with that mixture of curiosity and self-assurance in his expression that gives adults cause for hope. On the surface, he looked like he was fun, perhaps even impish. But upon closer inspection, his eyes had the look of a much more sophisticated being, and his smile, at the right angle, appeared almost menacing. She had no doubt that she was looking at the young man whose spirit now haunted her.

"Is it him?" Ray asked her again, and she suddenly realized that he thought she had seen Jimmy.

"I haven't actually ever seen him, Ray," she said. "But I think this is him."

"You've never seen him?" he asked, surprised.

"No, never. He's always completely invisible." Sara flipped through the pages of the yearbook until she found Ray. He, too, had that look of optimism characteristic of youth, but Sara noticed that there was also anxiety in his eyes. She wondered what he was thinking about the moment that picture was taken. Was it Jimmy?

"Is the girlfriend he took from you in here?" she asked.

He pointed out the girl and Sara carefully examined her picture. She searched for something extraordinary in her look or expression but found nothing.

"She's pretty," she remarked.

"If you've never seen this ghost, how can you be sure it's him?" Ray asked, bringing her back to the subject at hand.

"Well, I can't," she admitted. "But I just feel like it must be him. It all makes sense. Look, why don't you just tell me the rest of the story. What happened to him?"

"He drowned."

"How?"

Ray sighed, obviously not comfortable discussing it. "Jimmy was always showing off. He wasn't even invited the day it happened but sure enough, he turned up. We were all swimming in this little alcove, one of those little private spots where just us kids went sometimes. We were having a good time, but then Jimmy had to stir it up." He laughed humorlessly. "He would just go around looking for ways to start trouble, goading everyone into these dangerous exploits. He'd do them himself, too, which is why it was so hard to say no. He was getting everybody riled up to the point where it wasn't even fun anymore. Then he found this one spot way up high, a kind of ledge in the side of the mountain, and he dared me to jump. When I wouldn't do it, he got up there himself. It was way up, and the water wasn't that deep. Sure enough, just as we all knew he would, Jimmy jumped." Ray shook his head in disgust. "When he didn't come up right away, it didn't really surprise anyone. That was another prank he loved to play…pretending to drown. We'd all seen it before, and some of us had even fallen for it, searching the water for fifteen, twenty minutes just to find him watching us, laughing, from behind a tree somewhere." He met her eyes again. "By the time we actually started looking for him…and found him…it was too late."

"Do you think maybe he blames you?" Sara asked.

"I don't really care," he said coldly. "I'm finished feeling bad for him."

"Well, the clairvoyant says you're the only one who can help me get over this. You can keep him away from me when this…thing comes over me—it's his influence, Maggie said—and I suddenly get this need. Like a drug. I've never felt anything like it before. It's like I have no control when it comes over me." Sara reached out to touch him and, although he brushed her away at first, she managed to get her arms around him. "I don't know how or why this happened but I love you," she told him. "I love you and I need your help."

She kissed his lips and looked into his eyes.

"How am I supposed to help get you over it?" he asked finally.

"When it happens, I get unbelievably…aroused," she said,

blushing. "I'll need you to be there in *that* way, and for a *long* time...until it's over." She was suddenly afraid. Here she was discussing her addiction to sex with a ghost and she couldn't seem to address the issue between her and Ray. Perhaps it was time to be completely honest with him. But the last thing she wanted to do was to cause him even more pain. She sighed in frustration, searching for the right words. "I think he...he...got to me because he found a weakness." She paused. "With us."

"I'm listening."

"That first night when he came to me, we had just made love. I was...frustrated because you finished before I did." Ray didn't respond, so she went on. "He got me excited again while I was sleeping, but when I woke up and screamed, he left. This left me sexually frustrated for the second time that night. When I woke up the third time, it was like I just wanted to get off, you know? I half thought it was probably all just a wet dream. But then, afterwards, it was like he owned me, and then I couldn't stop."

She had expected her words to upset him, but he appeared to be considering what she said.

"I thought you had gotten off that night," he said. "But I'll admit, it's really hard for me to tell. You seem to get these little spurts of...something, and then you slow down. I'm not always sure what's going on."

"Well, I guess I could be more expressive."

"So...has that been happening often, me leaving you in the lurch, so to speak?"

Sara blushed and shrugged. "I don't know...sort of... sometimes."

"How often?" he asked. His manner made it hard to be completely honest. If he had gotten angry or defensive, she might have found this conversation easier. As it was, he seemed genuinely sorry to learn that she was not being satisfied and interested to know how he could prevent it from happening again.

"I don't know," she said defensively. She bit her lip.

His expression suddenly grew alarmed. "You *have* gotten off with me, right?"

Sara looked away. To lie now, at this crucial point, would be terminal.

"But you acted like you did," he said, suddenly bewildered.

"I know, I know," Sara tried to explain. "I was so excited when I was with you at first that I just couldn't relax enough to…get off so I…faked it. And then, from that point, it just seemed like we got into this pattern where you finished before I could get there."

Ray just stood there, amazed.

"I'm really sorry. I know this is my fault."

"It's not all your fault," he said quietly. He sighed and shook his head. "But I really don't see how I'm going to be able to help you, considering this."

"The thing is, I know that you can get me there," Sara told him. "I've actually gotten pretty close a time or two. I'm just going to need you to hold back for as long as you possibly can. That's the only way I'm going to get through this. You're going to have to keep going and going and…going."

He thought about this and then nodded. "Okay."

"Okay?" Sara smiled. "Just like that, okay?" She laughed in spite of the fear and embarrassment and everything else that tormented her. Ray's manner, so all at once strong and steady and loyal and calm, made her believe in the impossible. She rushed into his arms. "I love you so much," she said, suddenly crying.

When she had recovered from this little outburst, she pulled away, wiping her eyes. "So what's next?" she asked, sniffing. "I guess we wait for it to happen again?"

"Wait for it?" Ray repeated, shaking his head. "No! We're not just going to wait for it. We're going to head it off at the pass."

"What?" Sara looked at him in surprise. "But…"

"Get your clothes off," he told her.

"But…"

"Now, or I'm gonna tear them off." He was unbuttoning his shirt while simultaneously kicking off his shoes.

"Shouldn't we wait until the desire hits me?" she asked. "I mean, if we wear ourselves out now, I don't know…"

"I know I've let you down in the past," he said, removing his pants. "But I'm not going let you down this time. You're not taking your clothes off—why?" He waited for her to start removing her clothes before he went on. "And you're going to tell me everything you're feeling as we go, so I'll know if I'm on track. Think of this as practice. When we're done, I'm going to know everything there is to know about making you happy."

Sara shivered, although she wasn't in the least bit cold. As she undressed, she looked up at Ray in amazement, wondering that she had never trusted him enough to confide in him before. To her surprise, the old, familiar, comfortable desire, desire born out of genuine attraction and lust, curled up in her.

Ray proceeded to make love to Sara in half a dozen or more different ways, switching positions and techniques as he found it necessary in order to keep himself going. And he did keep going, even after he was certain that Sara had been satisfied repeatedly, and until she literally begged him to stop. And even then, he refused to allow himself to be satisfied, knowing good and well that if he did, that would be the moment that Jimmy would pounce. And Sara felt so satiated and content that she imagined that perhaps it was all over, that it had been that easy.

Hours went by. Ray and Sara had gone to bed and they even made love again.

"I think I'm past it, Ray," she told him. "I've never gone this long without it happening before."

But Ray doubted that Jimmy would give up that easily, and he continued to avoid his own orgasm so that he would remain rock-hard and ready. The painful frustration he must have been feeling seemed to make him more sensitive to what Sara had suffered, and he held and kissed and comforted her more compassionately than he had ever done before.

It was several hours later, while they were both lying naked together in bed, sleeping, when the feeling came over her and Sara began to shake with her growing need.

"Ray!"

"I'm here, Sara," he told her. He immediately took her in his arms and held her there. "What do you need?"

"Love me."

"I'm gonna love you. I'm gonna love you all night." He grasped her face in his hands. "And you're gonna talk to me. Whatever you want—anything—you open your mouth and you tell me, do you hear?"

"Yes, yes, oh, Ray, please!"

Ray flung the covers down from over her body and moved in between her open legs. Sara was hot all over and soaking wet. He began by using his tongue on her, groaning miserably with his pent-up desire. She knew that it must be torture for him. She had felt his body growing hard the minute she first called out to him.

Even after having pleasured Sara so many times already that night, Ray attacked her clitoris with vigor, pleasing her in all the ways he knew she liked best. He was an extremely quick study, she discovered, practicing on her with the enthusiasm of an accomplished musician. His ministrations at first acted like an alternate drug to an addict, only just holding her desire at bay, but she relished what relief she could get. Her first orgasm shook her, but it did not entirely hit the mark. She looked at Ray in dismay.

"It's still there," she cried.

"Don't worry," he said. "I'm on it."

It was easy to see that she was in distress. Her entire body shook and she was flushed and hot, as if with fever. Ray used his hands this time, inserting three fingers inside her while using his thumb to stimulate her on the outside. He knew that she loved that. Meanwhile he used his other hand to stimulate other parts of her body. And he moved in close to kiss her lips.

"I love you, Ray," she whispered.

"I love you, too, Sara," he replied.

And this was what was different, she realized. It was not just the sexual release that she needed, but the real genuine feeling that exists between lovers.

Ray was able to get Sara through several more orgasms before he was obliged to finally enter her. When the time came, Sara noticed that he seemed reluctant. And yet she needed him inside her so badly. Each little orgasm had knocked away at the terrible hunger, but she felt that there was still so much left inside her. She craved the feeling of having him inside her. But she also knew that, in her present condition, she was far more sensual than she normally was. She was like something out of the wild. How would Ray be able to withstand the temptation and not give in to the pleasure? She knew that this was what was worrying him, as well.

"I'm sorry," she murmured as he drew up over her. "I know... Oh!" she cried out as he pushed himself into her. Her body instantly went wild. She bucked and thrashed against him, oblivious to everything but the intense pleasure building up in her. She tried to control it but she could not. She heard Ray's long, agonized groan and saw his pained expression but even this couldn't stop her. She wished fervently that her release would come and prayed that it would be the last one she would need this time around.

But before it was over, she ended up getting that orgasm and several more before the craving settled down and she once again felt sated and calm.

"Now you must let me satisfy you!" she insisted, but Ray was adamant that he continue to hold off for at least another day or so, until they were absolutely certain that Jimmy was gone for good. And Sara was once again impressed by the man that Ray was, and amazed and humbled by his love for her. She felt as if she were wrapped in a blanket of well-being when she was with him, where no harm could touch her. Everything that happened was behind her. Why should Ray continue to suffer so?

"I can't stand it for you," Sara said, seeing the discomfort and frustration in his expression.

"And yet you could stand it for yourself," he reminded her.

"I should have told you," she said. "I should have trusted you. To be perfectly honest, I was a little ashamed, as well. I felt that there must be something wrong with me that it took so long. I didn't want to ruin it for you."

"Then maybe this is a good thing," he said, with his usual positive, no-nonsense approach to things, which left Sara feeling safe and sound. "It's shown us that we can get through literally anything—even supernatural stuff—as long as we are honest with each other and work together."

And in that moment Sara knew without a doubt that she had found the man she would spend the rest of her life with.

The Incentive Program

2019

Georgia reluctantly gestured to an older gentleman in the front.

"So this…simulation program…you're saying it can actually predict the future?" he asked doubtfully.

"Yes, in a manner of speaking, I am," Georgia replied. She tried to contain her excitement over the program so that she could explain it in a more clear, concise manner. She simply *had* to get them to listen to her. "But if you'll just let me finish my brief overview of the program *before* asking questions, I'm sure it will clear up much of your confusion." She groaned inwardly as she saw another hand go up. She wasn't going to get very far at this rate. Biting her lip, Georgia motioned for the person to speak.

"But do you think a computer program is capable of considering all of the many human variables in its predictions?"

Donald was right. She should have put the pertinent information in the program outline. Not that anyone ever read those things, but at least she would have had the satisfaction of getting all the information out. She sighed. This was, in any case, a valid question that she could use to turn the discussion back to the points she wanted to make.

"If the program is given the proper information, yes. Our program has been fed every kind of statistical data on humans and human behavior that you can imagine, going back four hundred years. We've included statistics that cover all aspects of human life, from cultural, to economical, to psychological tendencies and behaviors. In addition, we've trained the program to configure the logical progression of human existence based on this data. Literally, we have given the program an education in human behavior that would be the equivalent of about two hundred scientists with doctorates in everything from psychology to sociology. And I'm only scratching the surface here. The details this program has…"

But several more hands were popping up so, with a sigh, Georgia selected one from among them.

"How does the program compute the behaviors into predictions for the future?"

"This program is interactive and ongoing. What we did was actually create an exact replica of our world—a kind of cyber world—that's running parallel to ours, but at an accelerated speed. We started with the statistical data from our world, past and present, as I stated before. But to simply tell you this doesn't really even begin to get you acquainted with what this program knows. We have collected and input literally *billions* of data files containing every single detail of human existence according to culture, gender, religion, status and so forth."

"How can a computer program process all of this?" Georgia searched the audience to see where this question originated. She didn't want people just yelling questions out at her, and wondered fleetingly if she should say something to nip it in the bud. But she didn't want to say or do anything to discourage them from the program, either.

"The program examines our present-day life—population, cultural issues and so on—and compares it to the historical data to analyze the logical, cause-and-effect tendencies in our life's progression. It uses its psychological skills to study these behaviors individually and culturally, and then calculates probable future behaviors based on its findings. Again, I'm oversimplifying here, but basically the program recreates an *exact* replica of the world that exists in conjunction with ours, but moving at an accelerated pace, so that we can get a glimpse of what most likely lies ahead for us in our future." In the stunned silence that followed, Georgia was able to pause for a moment before continuing. "In order to optimize accuracy, the program computes all activity on an *individual* basis. For every documented life in our current existence, the program was given a corresponding life. It has computed the effects of every human being on the planet!"

There was another moment of shocked silence, and then nearly half the audience's hands went up. Georgia motioned to a woman in the front.

"Are you saying that *we*...each one of us...is in that program?"

Georgia's mind raced as she thought about how to answer that question. She was well aware that her ideals as a scientist might not coincide with the ideals of those less enthusiastic about the program, but on the other hand, she was optimistic. How could anyone fail to be impressed by the program's capabilities, in spite of any seeming moral or purely emotional objections? Still, Georgia chose her words carefully. "*Theoretically,* yes, each of our individual statistics has been entered into the program. We represent, after all, the starting point for peopling the world in our program. We used data from census reports around the world. However, the program has assigned new identities to each individual."

"But it's still *us,* right?" someone asked. "I mean, couldn't people in your program be identified by their addresses? Assuming you don't change the names of streets, cities and states, too."

"We have changed other identifying factors as well, but it's important to remember that the program is not designed for the short-term." Georgia realized she needed to steer the audience away from this obviously touchy subject. "The purpose of the program is to help us see the impact we're having on the planet, and give us an idea of what life might be like for future generations."

Again there was thoughtful silence, followed by a flurry of hands. She selected one arbitrarily.

"How far into the future does this thing go?"

"We've just crossed into the twenty-fourth century."

More hands went up.

Georgia finally raised her hands in protest. "Perhaps it would be easier to simply show you the program," she suggested. "There is a screen already set up behind me. If you will be so patient as to hold your questions, I will run the program for you right here."

Georgia opened her laptop computer and began a flurry of activity on the keyboard. Within minutes, a picture popped up on the screen. It showed a street teeming with average-looking men and women. After a few seconds, the picture came to life and the people on the street resumed their activity, single-mindedly heading toward destinations unknown and unaware of any surveillance.

"The year is 2304," Georgia began. "At a glance, the changes are relatively subtle. You can see that the vehicles on the road are few, and considerably different from ours." She typed something on her keyboard and their view turned toward the road. "The program has generated all of this," she reminded them. "Although it simulates human life at an accelerated pace, we can view it at our own. The program is meant to be used as a tool that allows us to look ahead at some of the challenges we are creating with the decisions we make today." Georgia looked over the faces of the audience. "Just think of the potential benefits!" she exclaimed.

"How do we know that what happens in your program will really happen in the future?" someone called out from the back of the room.

"We don't know that for certain," Georgia admitted. "But we do know that this program is drawing the most logical conclusions based on real data. This program has been running for more than seven years and so far it has had an accuracy rate of ninety-seven percent!"

There was a gasp of surprise.

Georgia typed something else on her keyboard and the scene on the screen changed to a place in the desert. A city could be seen far off in the distance. "At any given time," Georgia told them, "we can look up a day in the future and get a good idea of what may well be happening in *our* world on that day."

As if to prove her point, she caused the picture to change again, this time to an ocean view with tall buildings forming the skyline. "We can look at how people live. The individuals in the program—literally billions of them—are living simulated lives to ours and our offspring's and, in the process, showing us the impact we could be having on the world."

"What about chance, or unexplained phenomenon?" someone else asked. "Without advance knowledge of these things, it seems as if your program is little more than science fiction."

"This is real," Georgia countered. "These people are living simulated lives, it's true, but as far as we can see from the last seven years of its running, the statistics created by the program have mirrored own our real-life statistics during the same period socially, economically, ecologically…"

"How do you know that?" another person asked.

"From the data." Georgia typed something on her keyboard and the screen changed again. A statistical data sheet appeared.

"You can pull up the statistics for any given day," she told them. "I'm going to enter the date for a month ago yesterday. On the left it will compute the program's stats for that day and on the right it will list our real-life stats. These are just an overview of major world statistics. We can formulate lists that are much more detailed and precise. But this list configures automatically, making it simple to compare the two worlds at a glance. It tells us things like the number of births, percentage of birth defects, injuries, health trends, deaths, the job market, crime and so forth."

"And this is all based on…what, exactly again?" someone asked.

Georgia sighed, trying to hide her impatience. "It's based on the program simulating our world and our lives. The individuals living in this cyber world are psychologically programmed to behave exactly how we are most likely to behave, according to genetics, our environment, etcetera. It then estimates what effect our behavior will have on the world." As Georgia spoke, the computer appeared to be calculating, and now a series of numbers popped up on the screen. "These figures list the statistical data for both worlds as of last month," she explained. "Note how close the statistics are running side by side, right down to the number of babies born. As I mentioned before, after running the program for over seven years, we can see that it is maintaining an average of ninety-seven percent accuracy."

"So what about the future…how far did you say this thing got in the last seven years?"

"We are now into the twenty-fourth century," she said.

"Can we see the statistics for then?" asked another. There were murmurs of agreement throughout the audience at seeing this.

Georgia entered the dates, wondering if it was wise to show them this. The last thing she wanted to do was to turn them off the program. But this was exactly what the program was designed for, she reminded herself. "If we had more time—which I'm hoping we will have after this meeting—we could examine each and every cause and effect that brought our cyber world to this point," she said as the screen flashed a series of new numbers. "But for the moment, let us just suppose that this is something like what we are looking at in the future." She highlighted the various areas on the screen with her selector tool as she spoke. "These are the stats for the last five years of our online world, bringing us to September eighth of the year 2304. Believe it or not, wood burning is still the preferable method of heating. Solar is not an option because there is no longer enough sun. There was initially a very slow response to global warming." She took a deep breath before continuing. "You may have noticed that the number of deaths is extraordinarily high for this time period." She tapped the word *deaths* on the screen and it caused another page to appear. This page detailed all of the deaths by gender, age, location and cause. At a glance, it was clear that the highest number of deaths, by an alarming margin, were among women.

"Based on all of the current data we have on our existence—global warming, disease, genetics and so forth—the program has predicted that women will be hit the hardest by the various effects of global warming."

There was a moment's silence, and then a woman from the audience asked, "What did you say the accuracy on this program was so far...ninety-something percent?"

"Ninety-seven," Georgia told her.

"Can you break that down by year?" someone else asked.

Georgia had dreaded this question but felt that, with a little luck, she could turn this, too, around to her advantage. She typed something on the keyboard and another screen popped up.

"Yes," she answered. "The program is able to compute the statistics from its world daily, whereas our real-life statistics can, at best, be computed weekly, depending on what they are, while others can take months or even years to collect. And this is another great thing about the program—it allows us to enter new data at any time. Each time our real-life data is entered, the program computes the accuracy rate." As she spoke, the percentages were appearing on the screen, showing the breakdown by year.

"It appears that the highest percentage was in the first year," one man observed. "The percentage seems to get lower with each passing year."

"That is correct," Georgia admitted. "However, this program is interactive, so by feeding it the correct statistics as they become available the program, is able to go back and correct itself, redirecting its steps so that it is once again back on track and in sync with our world." There was a murmur of voices and she perceived that this last bit of information had cast a negative shadow on the program, so she spoke up quickly and loudly in an effort to get her point across. "We fully expect that the accuracy level will go back up once these program adjustments take effect. You can see in the last year the accuracy rate has already risen point three percent."

"But what if it doesn't go up?" someone asked. "What if the accuracy rate just keeps going down? Even at the rate of a half a point a year, it would be below zero long before that date you showed us on the screen."

"He's right," someone else agreed. "Anyone could make predictions a year or two in advance."

"The purpose of the program is not—" Georgia tried to interject, but she was interrupted once again.

"I think we all understand the purpose of the program and what it's capable of now, Ms. Warner," said a voice from the front, and Georgia saw that it was the chairman speaking. "You did an excellent job of explaining it. Thank you. With the time remaining, let's run through the costs of continuing the program." Georgia met his eyes. He seemed a kindly man, and she had the impression that he wanted to cut the presentation short to make it easier for her. But she felt that if she could just have a little more time to explain, she might be able to convince them.

However, it would not do to argue with the chairman. She pulled up another chart on the screen and went over the staggering amounts of money it would take to keep the project going. She explained the numbers dejectedly. The audience was polite and listened attentively, but she knew that she had lost them. She had not aroused the kind of enthusiasm she needed to get the additional funding.

Georgia had imagined the meeting going so differently. She had fully expected the investors to be impressed and excited by the program. She should have known better. These people were not scientists. She tried to hide her dismay as she concluded her presentation.

"I'm taking you to dinner," Donald announced afterward. "For a job well done."

"I'm pretty sure we're not going to get the funding," she told him.

"Probably not," he agreed, having watched from the back of the room. "But you know there'll be something else. There's always something else, around every corner."

Georgia looked at him. "How can you say that? How can you so easily abandon this project when we've worked so hard?" She turned away, not really angry with Donald but at the world in general. She sighed miserably. "I just don't get it. It cost them millions to get to this point. We didn't even know the project's potential back then. Why were they willing to invest in the program to begin with if they were just going to abandon it halfway through?"

"That's the way it works," he told her, shrugging. "Investors get bored. They get excited about new theories and ideas, but they'll pick apart an experiment that's actually unfolding." He was much more philosophical about it than Georgia. "These guys aren't scientists. They're not really looking for any kind of achievement. We're just expensive entertainment for them."

"Well, I'm tired of entertaining them!" she exclaimed, suddenly sick to death of the subject. "Where are you taking me? It better have a full bar this time!"

But no matter how much Georgia drank, she couldn't shake off her disappointment. She felt as if she were losing a part of herself. Or worse, she was being forced to kill it.

For the first night in nearly seven years, Georgia went to bed without logging on to the program and checking in on her cyber world.

"So how long do we have?" Georgia asked when Donald told her the inevitable news the next morning.

"We've got the rest of our contract, through the end of the year," he said. "Just enough time for me to finish that addition to my house, maybe take a vacation with the wife and kids. Look into some options for our next project."

Georgia stared at him. "You're going to abandon the project early?" she asked him, incredulous.

He shrugged. "What's the point of going through the motions? It's over, Georgia."

"Uh, we're being *paid* to go through the motions," she reminded him.

Donald laughed. "Once you get used to how all this works,

you'll catch on," he said. He formed a tube with his hands and placed it in front of his mouth. "Earth to Georgia," he said in his best robot voice. "The funding has stopped. Beep. Nobody cares anymore. Beep."

Normally his nerdy behavior would make her laugh, but not this time. "*I* care," she said stubbornly.

"Well, I care about getting us another gig," he told her. "Life goes on."

"Some lives won't," she muttered.

"They're not real lives, Georgia," he said, catching her drift. "I wish they were. Maybe then you could find out what our next gig is going to be."

"I've got five more months on this project and that's where *I'm* going to be," she said stubbornly.

He laughed at her. "Suit yourself."

When Donald left, Georgia approached her workstation gloomily. She logged on to the program without enthusiasm. For the first time in years, she wasn't on pins and needles to see what was happening. Since she last logged on—apart from the brief encounter at the investors' meeting—more than twenty-four hours had elapsed, which meant that nearly forty days had passed in cyber world.

What will happen to them? Georgia wondered miserably. She paused, perplexed by the question. More to the point, what would happen to *her?* She had no life outside of the program. She had given up everything for this project. It was all she thought about anymore.

The program made a humming sound when it was updating, and hearing the familiar drone gave Georgia a tiny thrill in spite of her depression. She perked up a little, recovering her interest in what was happening in "her" world.

When the program finished updating, Georgia opened the fields that she secretly kept bookmarked. She held her breath now as she waited for her own special little corner of cyber world to be located. In a moment, life appeared on the screen like a movie in progress.

They were inside an apartment. A dark-haired woman in a bathrobe stepped into view, carefully taking sips from an over-filled coffee cup. Georgia watched as Cassie logged on to her own computer to check that day's news, just as she did every morning. Cassie took another sip from her cup just as the headlines appeared on her screen, but when she saw them she dropped it, spilling coffee all over her floor.

Georgia gasped in surprise when she saw the headline, too. It happened! It really happened! She couldn't believe it. Everything had been building up to it and the pundits had been saying it was only a matter of time for many months now, but even so, it was hard to imagine. Even the fact that people had already been more or less participating without the "incentive program" didn't make it any less shocking. To think, even with all that had happened in the past three centuries— global warming, the horrible epidemic and all the unimaginable consequences that followed—that such an incentive program could actually be ordained by the government, with tax breaks to go along with it!

Georgia wondered how Cassie would react to the news. It was hard to tell what she was thinking from her stoic expression as she read every word of the news article. Her shattered coffee cup remained on the floor where she'd dropped it.

Georgia tried to predict what Cassie would do. Would she sign up for the program? Surely she must have thought about it. As shocking as it was, it made a certain kind of sense, too, considering what the world had come to. Things were very different in the twenty-fourth century, although Cassie was like a throwback from the past. Perhaps that's why Georgia related to her so well. Cassie reminded Georgia of herself.

Georgia was suddenly excited. What would Cassie do? Why, oh, why couldn't this news have come out a week ago? Now Georgia would actually have to wait to see what would happen next. Yet even in the minutes that passed while she watched Cassie read the news article, Georgia knew that time in her virtual world was steaming ahead at a rate of an hour and a half per minute. Georgia only needed to update the program again to meet it. But she lingered for the moment, waiting for Cassie's response.

But aside from dropping her cup of coffee, Cassie appeared to have no reaction. She turned off the computer and began cleaning the coffee from the floor. Her face remained impassive. Georgia continued to watch for a bit, preferring to hold off for as long as possible before updating the program. She knew from experience how frustrating it could be to keep updating and updating in anticipation of something happening. She'd wasted entire days doing that. Particularly through the epidemic, which kept Georgia on pins and needles until she was certain that Cassie would be one of the survivors.

"I've got a surprise for you!"

Georgia jumped, nearly falling off her chair, at the unexpected voice coming from behind her. "Christ!" she exclaimed.

Donald laughed. "What are you doing?" he asked.

"Working on the program," she snapped irritably. "What do you think I'm doing?" She quickly closed the window she was in.

"Sorry. Didn't mean to scare you. But I've got some exciting news."

"Well? You've got my attention."

He laughed again. "I might have something here to cheer you up. Don't get your hopes up too much," he warned. "It's still under scrutiny, but there's a team of scientists who are conducting a number of studies that are similar to the one we've been doing here. They contacted me because they were impressed with our work. I'll be meeting with them next week. And two other organizations left messages but I've yet to get back to them." He smiled at her smugly. "It seems we made an impression on the science community, at least. At this rate we'll have our new jobs lined up before this contract is even up!"

Georgia just stared at him. This was supposed to cheer her up? It was good that people were interested, she supposed, but the thought of terminating the program was still too difficult for her to accept. She was not ready to even contemplate it.

"Well!" Donald said. "I expected a little more excitement than that." He dropped the papers onto her desk. "I went to a lot of trouble to get this information because I thought you would at least be curious."

"I am," she murmured unenthusiastically. "I'll look at it. Thanks, Donald."

"Still mooning over your little program?"

Georgia glanced at her computer, wishing he would leave. She was dying to know what Cassie was doing at that moment. "I guess. I feel like I have to keep working on it for now, you know?"

"Yeah, I suppose," he conceded, although she could tell that he was lying. She wondered that he never became more involved in the project. "You don't mind if I don't hang around, though, do you?"

"Of course not," she told him truthfully.

"Well, be sure and look over that stuff I left, will you?" he reminded her as he headed for the door. "I know there's a few things in there that will appeal to you."

"Thank you, Donald," she said more sincerely this time.

"Hey, I wouldn't have half these opportunities if you weren't around," he said with a laugh. "I need you to make me look good."

"See you later," she called as he walked out the door.

Georgia brushed aside the documents Donald left her so she could run another update on the program. Normally she would have hours of data entry to squeeze in between her obsession with watching the ongoing saga of the world she had helped create, but now it seemed there was no immediate necessity to keep up with that. It gave her a little pang to realize she was already adopting Donald's careless work ethic about the program, but on the other hand, it would give her more time to watch Cassie.

She sat back in her chair and waited.

In the short time that had passed since she had first updated, perhaps twenty minutes or so, Cassie had put half the day behind her. Georgia found her sitting in her office, working on her computer. Something in the way she sat there, with her back unnaturally straight and nervously glancing toward the door intrigued Georgia. She zoomed in closer so that she could read Cassie's computer screen. The words *Incentive Program* immediately caught Georgia's eye. Upon further inspection Georgia saw that Cassie had, in fact, already registered her profile. She was now perusing other profiles in the program. Georgia cursed. She had not wanted to miss a moment of this. She promised herself she'd go back and catch what she missed while Cassie was asleep.

Georgia's heart began to beat a little faster as she looked over the profiles with Cassie. She sat on the edge of her seat, her whole body alive with excitement. She shook her head in amazement when she saw how many profiles matched. There were more than three hundred of them!

Georgia had to admit it made sense. The men far outnumbered the women since the epidemic, and she supposed that the changes in behavior, given the circumstances, were to be expected. And yet, it seemed that mankind had, in many ways, moved backward, not forward. The violence, the kidnappings, the aggression—if not for their advanced technology and sophisticated appearance, she might have thought she was watching Neanderthal man. Many of the events of more recent years had left her aghast and wondering. Most of the women who survived the epidemic didn't dare leave their houses for fear of what might happen to them. This left them as isolated as the men. Participating in the government-funded incentive program would give these women a chance to choose their own fate, while offering them protection and even saving them thousands of dollars in tax deductions. All of the men in the incentive program had to submit to scrutiny and approval by the government, not to mention that they would be held accountable if any harm came to the women they met through the program. And the men, too, had more options with the program. They could either join individually and be paired with other men by the program, or they could join as a group. Cassie was presently perusing profiles of men who had signed up in the program together. Silently Georgia approved of this. Surely the men would cope with the situation better if they already knew one another, especially if they were friends.

Georgia was mildly surprised to see that many of the men were joined up with relatives. It seemed that it was more tolerable for a man to share a woman with a man he was related to.

As Georgia watched, she was becoming more and more frustrated with the way Cassie was rushing through the profiles. She merely glanced over them quickly and bookmarked the ones she liked. At times, Georgia wondered at her selections. Some of the better choices, in Georgia's opinion, were carelessly being passed over. Georgia would have put more thought into it, if it were her. But then again, there were so many. It was pretty overwhelming.

"Shit!" Georgia murmured as Cassie passed over yet another profile that she had been favoring. "Your taste in men sucks," she murmured. Cassie just kept heedlessly bookmarking the profiles that appealed to her. Every now and then Cassie would glance nervously at the door to her office, to ensure that no one was coming.

The next profile to come up featured an especially attractive threesome. You could see at a glance that two of the men were brothers. Their eyes, which were startlingly blue and intense, had a sad quality to them that brought about an instant response in Georgia. The brother who stood in between the other two men—Craig, the profile said his name was—was the one who held Georgia's interest. In his eyes, she perceived an innate kindness, and in his smile a cheerful manner that shielded a deeper sorrow. It was as if he was calling out to her.

"There!" Georgia cried out to her computer screen. "That one!" At that very moment, Cassie clicked on their profile to get a closer look. But just as she did with all the profiles, Cassie gave this one no more than a cursory glance before clicking back to the main page. Georgia had had only enough time to read the first line of their greeting, but that was enough to intrigue her even more. *Three good friends looking for a fourth.*

However, Cassie was already forging ahead, arrowing down to the next profile on the page.

"What?" Georgia cried in outrage.

As if she had heard Georgia, Cassie suddenly paused, and then arrowed back up. Georgia held her breath as she watched Cassie bookmark Craig's profile.

"Yes!" Georgia cried.

And so it went, for the next hour or so, until Cassie—with Georgia watching every step of the way, cursing the computer when a decision was made that she disagreed with—bookmarked the profiles of no less than thirty-seven groups of men. Most of the groups consisted of three, but there were a few that contained four and even five men.

Once the preferred profiles had been bookmarked, Cassie, with her usual organized and methodical way of doing things, sent each of the groups a message. To Georgia's surprise, she didn't even personalize the message for each individual group, but rather, simply cut and paste her first message and sent it to each of them.

Her message read, *Hi. I saw your profile on the site for the incentive program. I just signed up today. My profile has been created if you would like to check it out. Have you received many responses so far? Cassie.*

Cassie leaned back in her chair with a sigh. Her sigh seemed to say, *Now I will have to wait for the responses to come in.* But Georgia smiled, because nearly two days had passed in Cassie's virtual world during the time they had spent perusing the profiles. She hit Update and waited excitedly.

Dawn was breaking in cyber world when the update was complete. Georgia saw that they were once again in Cassie's apartment. She could see the light slowly penetrating the blinds. She maneuvered her view to Cassie's bedroom, to verify that she was, in fact, still asleep in bed.

Satisfied that nothing significant was happening at the moment, Georgia tracked backward in the program to where she had only a moment before left off. Then she perused Cassie's activities in fast-forward mode, until she next saw Cassie settle in front of her computer. Then she stopped to see what was happening.

Just as Georgia hoped, Cassie was logging back on to the incentive program.

And there were responses!

Every profile, it seemed, or nearly so, had responded to Cassie's message. A few had responded twice. The men were clearly eager and they didn't make any effort to hide it. Georgia read their responses along with Cassie and watched as she replied, but there was one message in particular that she was looking for. And there was nothing exceptional in any of the messages that diverted Georgia's attention from the one she awaited. She waited impatiently for Cassie to get to it.

At last she caught sight of his name in the heading of the next message, and she squealed excitedly as Cassie opened it.

——Original Message——
From: "Craig Holbrook"
To: "Cassie Michaelson"
Sent: 9/23/2304 3:15 p.m.
Subject: Re: YOUR PROFILE ON THE INCENTIVE PROGRAM
Hi Cassie,
Thanks for writing. As you might have noticed from our profile, two of us travel for work most days, so if you try to contact us and don't get an immediate response please be patient. We will respond first chance we get. I already looked at your profile and I think I can speak for all of us when I say that you seem like a very special person. You've definitely piqued my interest. You're the second response we've received and hopefully you'll work out better than the first, who lives halfway across the country. I will forward these messages to the guys. So what would you like to know about us, Cassie? Craig

Georgia read Craig's message several times over. She felt a little disappointed. It was a very nice message, and yet it lacked the enthusiasm of some of the others, which were filled with personal information or pressing for an immediate meeting. But on second thought, she felt that perhaps this was a good thing. The men in this strange new world had become a bit too desperate. Yet given the circumstances, it seemed rather cheeky of this one to act as if he had all the opportunity in the world when they both knew that he did not. Georgia was even more intrigued.

Cassie seemed intrigued, too. She went back to Craig's profile page and took a good look at the picture of him and the other two men in his group. She zoomed in to get a better look at Craig. Georgia's heart beat a little faster as she watched.

Georgia and Cassie read the three men's entire profile this time. Craig was a civil engineer who went on the road to visit customers for servicing and maintenance. He appeared to be the spokesperson for the group. He described himself as "self-assured but not self-confident." He said he was easygoing, but Georgia had already surmised this from his e-mail. He said he valued women, even before the shortage, but he stressed that he was not willing to settle. His was the only profile that "strongly agreed" with the statement that he "had high expectations." Georgia raised her eyebrows at this.

Craig's best friend was Steve. Steve was described as "a good guy" with a "great sense of humor" and as the "best-looking out of the bunch." Like the larger portion of the population, he worked in a computer factory, programming various systems from a small cubicle. In his free time, he was into sports and playing poker. Steve and Craig had grown up together.

Peter, Craig's brother, was a pilot. Craig described him as "a good guy" who was "serious" and "reliable." Overall, the least was said about Peter.

After reading their profile over several times, Cassie went back to the message page. She replied to Craig as follows:

——Original Message——
From: "Cassie Michaelson"
To: "Craig Holbrook"
Sent: 9/23/2304 6:07 p.m.

Subject: Re: YOUR PROFILE ON THE INCENTIVE
PROGRAM

Hi, Craig,

I read the profiles for you, Steve and Peter. Can you tell
me something more about yourselves that isn't there? I am
a little nervous about all of this, and it would help if I could
get to know you better. I am curious about one thing...how
do you choose who to team up with for something like
this? It must be strange for you. Were you on one of the
other sites before the incentive program was approved?
Do you know of others who have done this and how it
worked out? I'm sorry if I'm asking too many questions. I
am very unsure about how this all happens. Cassie

Georgia felt this response was rather unexciting, as well, but
on the other hand, what did one say in this situation? She
sighed dreamily, wondering how Craig would answer Cassie's
questions. Then she suddenly remembered that more time had
elapsed while she had been looking over their profile with
Cassie! And, too, she had backtracked in time to get there. She
hit Update and waited, noticing now that time was quickly
passing in her real world as well, and she had done nothing but
watch Cassie all day. But she had to see what Craig would
answer next. So she followed the same pattern as before—
updating, then going back to where she left off and fast-
forwarding in motion so she could pick out the parts she
wanted to watch in real time.

It didn't take Georgia long to find what she was looking for.
She hit the real-time button just as Cassie was opening her
message from Craig.

——Original Message——
From: "Craig Holbrook"

To: "Cassie Michaelson"
Sent: 9/23/2304 8:15 p.m.
Subject: Re: YOUR PROFILE ON THE INCENTIVE PROGRAM
Cassie,
We welcome all your questions. We expected them. What's not in the profile? I'm practical and probably the most laid-back, Steve's the life of the party, and Peter is focused and intense. We are all loyal types who are there when you need us. We are new to adopt this concept and quite honestly a bit skeptical about getting involved. We are, however, realists and, with a great deal of discussion, willing to make a go of it. I seem to have been selected to be our mouthpiece but all three of us are committed to it. Steve wants to know what you meant in your profile by "this could be exciting." Peter would like to know why you joined up. I think he's having a hard time believing women do this because it's the "right" thing. Please don't be too concerned about our questions, either. We all believe in being up-front and honest about everything. Looking forward to hearing from you again. Craig.

Georgia was taken aback by Craig's honesty. She smiled as she read his words again. She waited impatiently to see what Cassie would reply.

——Original Message——
From: "Cassie Michaelson"
To: "Craig Holbrook"
Sent: 9/23/2304 8:23 p.m.
Subject: Re: YOUR PROFILE ON THE INCENTIVE PROGRAM
Hi, Craig,

There is something very nice about the tone of your messages. It sounds like you three have put a lot of thought into this. I have, too. I have been thinking about it ever since the debate over the incentive program began. With everything that's been happening, I have been afraid, frankly, to go out with a man without some kind of protection but, outside of the program, there is none. And women can only participate in the program if they are willing to accept multiple partners, as you know. So I guess you could say I didn't think I had much choice. For one reason or another, I never got married, and now it looks like I might have held out too long. Who could have guessed this would happen? Steve sounds like a card. Tell him I said what does he think I meant by "could be exciting"? You seem like fun guys. One of the things that caught my interest is that two of you are brothers. Are you close? Do you think it will be better or worse, sharing a woman with your brother? This all still feels so strange to me. I have to admit that I don't know how it's supposed to work. They have some real-life stories posted online from people who are doing this already, with advice on how to make it work. Have you read any of those stories? I guess I have given you enough questions for now. I don't mind you asking me questions, either. I look forward to hearing back from you. Cassie

Georgia was equally surprised by Cassie's candid remarks. This was going to be interesting. She fast-forwarded through all of Cassie's other daily events until she found her reading another message from Craig.

——Original Message——
From: "Craig Holbrook"

To: "Cassie Michaelson"
Sent: 9/23/2304 10:30 p.m.
Subject: Re: YOUR PROFILE ON THE INCENTIVE PROGRAM
Hi back again,
You seem to be quickly becoming more at ease with this. I like that. Steve and I are very close even though he's much better-looking than I am and usually steals all the girls' hearts. I haven't read any of those stories online. I think this type of thing would have to be worked out on an individual basis with us communicating about what we think would work best. We might have to set some ground rules as we go along. Your profile said you're willing to have children. How many? I was thinking nine would be great for a baseball team. Steve and I have both always wanted children. Peter's not sure, given the state this world is in. As far as sharing a woman, we men have shared women for hundreds of years, in my view. Just ask any woman how many men she has slept with. This concept is not new and the fact that it's being promoted by the government makes it even more acceptable. Although I do realize there is still a stigma attached to women who do this. Some people will always stick their heads in the sand. Says a lot about your strength to step up for it. Let's talk again soon! Craig

Georgia found herself smiling as she read Craig's message. She watched with interest to see what Cassie would write back.

——Original Message——
From: "Cassie Michaelson"
To: "Craig Holbrook"
Sent: 9/23/2304 10:38 p.m.

Subject: Re: YOUR PROFILE ON THE INCENTIVE PROGRAM

Hi, Craig,

I enjoy your messages. Your attitude seems really healthy. I like the way you look at things. I'm not sure I'm "at ease" with this per se. I would say I am becoming accustomed to the idea. Your manner is definitely making it easier. I agree with having ground rules. I am just wondering what they should be. Any ideas??? I do not recall saying that I wanted children. Was that in my profile? Oh, maybe it was. I have always wanted children, just maybe not as many as you, lol. But I would have to really give it some thought in this situation before I made that kind of commitment. But there is time for that, right? Cassie

There were so many things that Georgia wished Cassie would write, so many questions she would have liked Craig to answer. She sighed in frustration to only be a spectator in this. Meanwhile, there were many other e-mails from the other men in the program, and Georgia watched halfheartedly as Cassie answered each of them. But all of her thoughts were of Craig and Steve and Peter. She continued to watch the other correspondence mostly just to gauge their importance to Cassie, and to ensure that no one was moving ahead of Craig. She was pleased to find that Cassie appeared to prefer Craig, as well.

After answering all of the e-mails, Cassie went to bed. Georgia once again jumped ahead to Craig's next message, which Cassie discovered upon waking the next morning.

——Original Message——
From: "Craig Holbrook"
To: "Cassie Michaelson"
Sent: 9/24/2304 6:35 a.m.

Subject: Re: YOUR PROFILE ON THE INCENTIVE PROGRAM

Good morning, Cassie,

It's nice having you to wake up to in the morning. As you can see, I'm an early riser, which means I'm also usually early to bed. I thought about all of this a lot more when I went to bed last night. Having a real-life, tangible candidate for this suddenly makes it seem so much more real. I was thinking of some of the issues that might arise. Although the relationship would ideally be doled out in equal parts to all three men, we do realize a closer bond would most likely arise between you and one or even two of us. But it's important that none of us be left out either socially or sexually. To my way of thinking, this would be the most important hurdle to overcome and unfortunately this may fall on your shoulders as it is your feelings that will determine who gets what. As with all issues, it is our belief that there are no problems, there are only solutions and we are willing to do what's necessary to make this work. You would without a doubt be spoiled to the core. The three of us are each successful in our jobs and financially sound (although I have to admit not very materialistic). We are always up to something, usually outdoor activities. Steve and I were on the rowing team in college and Peter played a lot of baseball and wrestled. All of us take our health seriously, and we each cook and eat well. A big part of us staying healthy includes downtime and so we make time for that, as well. You asked before what brought us together. Maybe it's that we seem to agree on so many things. About these ground rules, how about we take turns throwing one back and forth? Sound good? I'll start. Rule #1. Cassie can veto anything that us guys come up with, but she has to be a part of resolving the matter. Okay, your turn. Craig

For some reason this message caused Georgia to laugh, and to her surprise, she heard Cassie, who was normally so serious, chuckling right along with her. Craig really did have a very appealing way of approaching things. Georgia was glad to see that Cassie appreciated his thoughtful manner as much as she did. And she also noticed that Cassie had singled out his message from the many in her in-box, yet again, to read first. She watched excitedly as Cassie replied to Craig.

——Original Message——
From: "Cassie Michaelson"
To: "Craig Holbrook"
Sent: 9/24/2304 8:09 a.m.
Subject: Re: YOUR PROFILE ON THE INCENTIVE PROGRAM
Hi, Craig,
I have to admit that with every e-mail from you I like you more. I can tell that you are a considerate and thoughtful person by the way you are already thinking of your friends' feelings. I couldn't help but think when I read it that, if the situation was reversed, you might be one of the few guys who could actually pull it off with multiple women partners! I have thought of those same issues, as well. I am the sort of person who wants everyone to be happy and I am aware going in that this situation would be difficult for the men involved. To be honest, that was the biggest drawback about the program for me. I have also been thinking about how hard it might be to make multiple partners happy, not that it wouldn't be worth the effort, but I was wondering if it could be done. I do take this situation seriously and I would only do it with the intention of making a genuine effort, especially if I was being, as you say, "spoiled to the core." I wouldn't want to let anyone down. But I'm very

encouraged by your determination and your positive, make-it-work attitude. I find that extremely attractive, and I want you to know that I am the same way. As for the rules, I LOVE the idea. Although I am confused by your first rule...do you mean I will always have veto power over your three votes? Please explain. And in the meantime, here is my first rule. RULE #2. In everything, we will first and foremost always try to make it fun. How's that? Cassie

Georgia clapped her hands together with delight. She congratulated Cassie on a response that was better than she could have done herself. Everything she said was perfect. Georgia watched her with renewed admiration. She had an old-fashioned, practical attitude that appealed to Georgia. And her solitary lifestyle which had been, until lately, made up primarily of her work, was also something Georgia could relate to.

Many of the other candidates were quickly being sifted out. Some of the men were becoming too aggressive for such a new acquaintance. Others had already become blatantly sexual. Cassie instantly terminated all future correspondence with those. Georgia continued to monitor the remaining candidates, but she was confident that there were no real contenders for Craig.

Georgia glanced at the clock and gasped. Her workday had elapsed and she hadn't done any work. She could suddenly see what Donald meant. When it was no longer imperative to keep going, it was terribly easy to let the work slide. And yet, Georgia reminded herself that the sooner she stopped entering data into the program the sooner it would lose its accuracy and run off course. But what did that matter? She could not keep the program running without the funding. And anyway, she found herself unable to move away from the screen. It wasn't every day that a woman came across an event like the incentive program! She simply had to keep watching. It felt like all she had. She fast-forwarded, yet again, to Craig's next message to Cassie. He must have been working on the road that day because he did not answer her until later that afternoon.

——Original Message——
From: "Craig Holbrook"
To: "Cassie Michaelson"
Sent: 9/24/2304 3:32 p.m.
Subject: Re: YOUR PROFILE ON THE INCENTIVE PROGRAM
Cassie,
Pleasing several women??? I'm not saying it's impossible but it's not an endeavor to be taken on by the strongest of my gender and live to tell the tale. I'll leave it at that. Of course, what I meant is that you would have the veto power over issues dealing with you and the four of us. But in other matters your vote would count for one, just as with ours. Everyone loved your Rule #2. You used the term "multiple partners," I see. So let's explore this a little, shall we? Is there a part of you that is a little intrigued by this? RULE #3. Always be honest. Craig.

Georgia read along as Cassie typed her reply to this message. She wondered what Cassie would say to Craig's last question.

——Original Message——
From: "Cassie Michaelson"
To: "Craig Holbrook"
Sent: 9/24/2304 3:45 p.m.
Subject: Re: YOUR PROFILE ON THE INCENTIVE PROGRAM
Craig,

So are you saying that you would not be intrigued with the prospect of having multiple partners if the situation was reversed? Remember your Rule #3! Back to this veto power thing, what kind of issues are you referring to? Can you give me some examples of things I would have veto power over versus things I would just have a single vote in? Since we are being honest, and yes, I love the idea of us always being honest with each other, I will admit that I am a bit intrigued by this. Who wouldn't be? I'm a little apprehensive, too, but the excitement is there. But I don't know yet how it will all play out in reality. Now, for another rule: RULE #4. All four of us must be equally committed to each other and the relationship. I thought of this one because it occurred to me that you three would have to be committed to each other as well as being committed to me. And each of you would have to accept that I would have a commitment to the others. Do you agree that this makes sense? Do you think that we are ready to talk on the phone? And would I be talking to just you or all three of you? Do you share everything in these e-mails with Peter and Steve? Cassie

This was happening so fast. Georgia was on the edge of her seat. Yet she hadn't eaten anything all day and she was exhausted. She forced herself to stand up and nearly fell down. One of her legs had fallen asleep from being in one position for too long. She stretched, glancing back at the screen longingly. But luckily, she had access to the program from her computer at home, so the most logical thing to do would be to go home and get comfortable before watching more. She opened the refrigerator at the office but there was little inside that wasn't covered in mold. It wouldn't do to stay longer. She was already getting weak from hunger.

Georgia was suddenly thrust into motion, rushing around

absently to get just the bare necessities done before leaving the office for the day. Then she stopped for fast food on the road and ate it in the car. She knew it was insane, to be so connected to Cassie's life—far more connected than she was to her own, in fact—but she couldn't seem to control herself. It was as if Georgia were living a part of Cassie's existence, a part that was more intriguing to her. She almost choked on her cold, tasteless sandwich when she realized suddenly that Cassie's existence *was* more important to her than her own! She hadn't taken the slightest interest in her own life since the inception of the incentive program. She was forced to think about this as she drove the rest of the way home.

Georgia felt depressed when she walked through the door of her apartment. What was she doing, allowing herself to become so involved in a program that wouldn't even exist in a few months? She moved listlessly through her apartment, noticing for the first time how messy and unappealing the rooms were. She pulled off her work clothes and quickly covered up her neglected body in sweatpants and a T-shirt. When she was finished, she glanced at the computer longingly. She had promised herself in the car, during that moment's revelation, that she would avoid the computer for as long as she could once she got home. And although she had known she wouldn't be able to hold out for long, she had expected that she would be able to find something else to do for a few minutes at least. She told herself that she would have to wean herself off the program slowly. Yet, looking around her dismal apartment, she wondered how she was ever going to give the program up. What else did she have?

She moved toward the computer as if being drawn by an invisible force. She made another promise to herself that she would read the information Donald left her first thing in the morning. Perhaps there was something in there that would pique her interest enough to lure her away from Cassie and the program. These thoughts reassured her as she logged in and updated the program.

She felt the blood once again warming her veins as she forwarded through the events of Cassie's life, searching for the next correspondence from Craig.

——Original Message——
From: "Craig Holbrook"
To: "Cassie Michaelson"
Sent: 9/24/2304 4:19 p.m.
Subject: Re: YOUR PROFILE ON THE INCENTIVE PROGRAM
Hi, Cass,
Do you mind if I call you that? Yes, I share and discuss all of our e-mails with Steve and Peter. It's what we agreed upon. And yes, if the roles were reversed we would all be intrigued with the idea, too. But to be honest, finding one woman for the three of us has been hard enough. Fantasizing about having multiple women is just cruel at this point. I came up with that first rule because I wanted you to feel in control. Your body is yours, and if us guys come up with something that involves you—let's say sexually—and you're not on board with it, then you should always have the right to veto it. An example might be who you sleep with, or when. As you might imagine, three healthy males in the prime of their lives could probably wear you out. We agree with your Rule #4. As well, we think a phone connection would be great. Not quite sure if you're ready for it, but we would prefer a virtual call to kick things off. We want to see you as well as to hear your voice. Are you shy? Of course we would be delighted to talk to you in any format you desire. RULE #5. Everyone gets some alone

time with you, including yourself (we're talking about social
time, not sex). You're up. The boys

Georgia's introspection was instantly forgotten upon reading
this message from Craig. Her earlier excitement came back in
a gush. Craig and "the boys" were becoming real to her. She
could see that it was the same for Cassie. She waited impatiently
for her to answer. Cassie actually got up from her computer
and walked around before responding. She seemed nervous and
Georgia could imagine why. Craig made things seem so easy
while at the same time making them easier by being so
thoughtful and kind. But the practicalities of the situation were
frightening. Cassie, like Georgia, had been completely without
a man for a very long time. It had to be overwhelming to contemplate suddenly having three. And in spite of Craig's easygoing manner, it really was all happening very fast. In a few
minutes, Cassie became composed enough to respond to
Craig's e-mail.

——Original Message——
From: "Cassie Michaelson"
To: "Craig Holbrook"
Sent: 9/24/2304 4:50 p.m.
Subject: Re: YOUR PROFILE ON THE INCENTIVE
PROGRAM
Craig, Steve and Peter,
I figured it was probably time that I start addressing all of
you in these e-mails. I have to admit that I find myself
looking forward to hearing from you. I have stopped
e-mailing all of the other candidates. Maybe I shouldn't tell
you that. I don't mind you calling me Cass. I like it. I under-
stand your veto rule now, and I agree it is necessary,
although I have to say that I don't care for the idea of

picking and choosing between you. It seems like it could be a rather cruel thing to have to do. I remember in school reading about how in historic times men in some countries had multiple wives and how some of those wives were passed over and ignored. I could not bear to be that way. It seems like a lot of power to have over others. I want our relationship to be, as much as possible, like a traditional relationship between two people. But maybe this is un-realistic. Even among those relationships, I know that there was a high failure rate. I can't wait to see you and hear your voices, as well. Yes, of course we should do the virtual call. As I'm reading these messages, I'm trying to imagine what you are really like and what your reactions are. It would be wonderful to communicate in 3-D, so to speak. I like your Rule #5. It was very considerate of you to think of that. I am having difficulty coming up with more rules. We might need to get into this a little more before we know what kinds of rules we'll need. I'm going to pass on putting a rule in this message. Will you forward me your virtual code and a good time to call? Cass

Immediately after the message was sent, Georgia hit Fast-Forward and watched Cassie in high speed trying to stay busy between checking the computer for Craig's next message. It didn't take long for him to get back to her with his number, but he suggested she wait until Peter got there before actually calling. They had about two hours to wait, as Peter was still working. Cassie looked dejected. But Georgia merely pressed Fast-Forward once again. So much had happened in such a short span of time that Georgia was getting farther and farther behind in the future events while she watched. In the back of her mind, she was aware that Cassie and the boys might actually be together somewhere by now, but she desperately wanted to see the events unfold as they occurred. As much as it tempted her, she resisted her urge to sneak ahead and peek at where all of this would lead. She was always aware that the program was moving ahead at an accelerated rate while she lingered to watch the details.

She stopped fast-forwarding when she saw Cassie entering Craig's code for their virtual call. Both she and Cassie took a deep breath as they listened to the first ring.

"Cassie!" Craig's voice was just as Georgia had imagined it, gentle and kind. He smiled up at Cassie from her computer screen. "Right on time. Say hello to Steve and Peter."

"Hi, Cassie," both men said at once.

"Hi." Cassie stared back at the three handsome men like a deer caught in the headlights.

Craig chuckled. "We're all a little nervous, but I can only imagine how you must feel, Cass." He paused a minute. "We can take this as slow as you like, you know. Give you a chance to get used to us." Cassie smiled at him. Georgia knew that Cassie must be overwhelmed, seeing the three of them all at once. She was a bit overwhelmed herself! She found that she couldn't pull her gaze away from Craig's piercing blue eyes. They seemed to touch something deep inside her, stirring it to life.

"Give her a minute to absorb it all," Steve told Craig. "I'm sure she didn't expect us to be so good-looking in person." Cassie laughed when he said this and, encouraged, Steve said to her, conspiratorially, "I get credit for that. I told these guys, 'You can't put your best picture online or she'll be disappointed when she sees what you really look like.' That's why we chose that one where Pete and Craig look so goofy. We figured it'd be a pleasant surprise when you saw that they didn't really look like that. Of course," he added to Craig and Peter, "I didn't expect it to have this effect on her. Look, she's speechless!" He reached over and messed up Peter's hair. Cassie laughed again, a spontaneous burst of merriment that caused all three men to smile—even Peter, who initially seemed a little put out over getting his hair messed up.

"There," Craig said. "Do you feel a little better now, Cassie?"

"Actually, I do," she told him, still laughing at Peter, who was trying to fix his hair the way it was before.

"You have a wonderful laugh," Craig told her. "We were sitting here talking before you phoned about how down to earth you seemed in your e-mails. In person you seem even more so. We really appreciate that."

"Thank you," Cassie said. "You guys are very easy to be with, too."

"So, how are you?" Craig asked.

"I'm okay. I guess I did get a little stage fright there for a minute. How are you guys? Peter?"

"Good, Cass," Peter piped in. "It's so nice to meet you. I've been looking forward to this since your first e-mail. We're just a bunch of ordinary guys, so don't worry."

"Yeah, we're house-trained and everything," Steve added. Cassie giggled.

Disregarding Steve, Peter continued. "By the way, Cass, a good friend of mine graduated from your alma mater the same year you did. He was in a different field of study from yours, so you may not remember him. Gerald Blake. That doesn't ring a bell, does it?"

Cassie visibly relaxed. "I do remember Gerry!" she said, pleased by this connection. "He was kind of a quiet guy most of the time, but every now and then he came out with something that surprised us. How is he? Do you see him often?"

"He works for the same company as my brother. He's part of our outdoor crew, camping, hiking...that kind of thing. He's

doing well. When I mentioned you to him, he said he remembered you as being someone who was pretty special. He was
sure you wouldn't remember him, though. He'll be glad to hear
that you did."

And here they began a detailed discussion about each of their
jobs, what they did and how they felt about it. Georgia watched
and listened with fascination, comparing Cassie's comments
with what she herself might have said. She couldn't help
thinking that all three men together made up the perfect man.
Craig was sensitive and thoughtful, while Peter was more
intense and focused. Steve made everything fun. It was thrilling to watch. As always, Georgia was mindful that something
even more exciting could be happening while she sat there
watching them talk to one another. Time was constantly racing
ahead in the program but, although she was dying to see what
was coming next, she didn't want to miss a single detail.

When the call ended, Cassie stood in the middle of her
room, alone. She stared straight out in front of her, unseeing,
yet with her eyes appearing to look directly at Georgia. Georgia
wondered what Cassie was thinking. What emotions had the
computer program produced in her for this scenario?

After a while, Cassie turned back toward her computer.
There was a small smile playing around her lips. She sat down
and began to type.

——Original Message——
From: "Cassie Michaelson"
To: "Craig Holbrook"
Sent: 9/24/2304 9:17 p.m.
Subject: Re: YOUR PROFILE ON THE INCENTIVE
PROGRAM
Dear Craig, Steve and Peter,
I really enjoyed talking to you. Now that I've heard your

voices I want to see your faces *in person.* Now that I've met you, so to speak, I get the impression that Steve, you're the funny one, and Peter, you're the serious, more sensible one, and Craig, I think you're the one who keeps everything going smoothly. Of course, I am generalizing here. You all seem to have these characteristics to some degree because you can appreciate them in each other. How did I do? Do you agree? Cass

It took only a moment or two for the guys to answer.

——Original Message——
From: "Craig Holbrook"
To: "Cassie Michaelson"
Sent: 9/24/2304 9:29 p.m.
Subject: Re: YOUR PROFILE ON THE INCENTIVE PROGRAM
Hi, Cass,
Okay, we knew by your profile and picture that you were attractive but in person you're simply a dynamic person with the wholesome qualities that we appreciate as well as find attractive. Yeah, you've got us pegged. We call Peter "Pops" a lot. He doesn't have a great deal to say, but he is always right on target when he does. And he was impressed with you, as were all of us. You seem to be an easy laugh, so you may want to take some time to adjust to Steve slowly, or you may tear a few stomach muscles. He can sometimes get Peter and me in stitches. Personally, I found you captivating. I love that you don't appear to play games or beat around the bush. You seem straightforward and honest and those are qualities we three appreciate. Each step we take is an opportunity for this to fail but I have to say (for the three of us) that we are

growing attached to you. I hope we're not being too forward here. If we are, just say the word. We will slow it down. Let's talk again soon. Your boys.

Georgia was trembling. She couldn't seem to move. A strange ache was growing inside her, but she hardly noticed it. She waited impatiently as Cassie read and answered Craig's mail.

——Original Message——
From: "Cassie Michaelson"
To: "Craig Holbrook"
Sent: 9/24/2304 9:36 p.m.
Subject: Re: YOUR PROFILE ON THE INCENTIVE PROGRAM
Boys,
You are sweet and I have no problem with you telling me how you feel, no matter how forward it may seem. I want to see you in person now. I was thinking of where we could all meet, and I realized that I have not gone out to a nightclub since the epidemic broke out. I used to love to go dancing. I haven't dared go lately, though. Do you guys like to dance? Would that be a fun night for you? I know I would feel safe going anywhere with you. Speaking of which, what do you enjoy doing for fun? Do you go out much? Cass

In another moment they responded.

——Original Message——
From: "Craig Holbrook"
To: "Cassie Michaelson"
Sent: 9/24/2304 9:39 p.m.

Subject: Re: YOUR PROFILE ON THE INCENTIVE PROGRAM
Cassie,
Dancing it is! Saturday night would work for us. All three of us are willing to do at least a little dancing. Peter the least. We're not sure what to call what Steve does, but he always seems to have fun. I love to dance, so your suggestion hit home with me. How about dinner first, and then off to a night of dancing? Peter suggested Anthony's, seven o'clock. What do you think? Talk to you soon, Craig

Georgia was itching to jump ahead to Saturday night but she waited for Cassie to reply first.

——Original Message——
From: "Cassie Michaelson"
To: "Craig Holbrook"
Sent: 9/24/2304 9:51 p.m.
Subject: Re: YOUR PROFILE ON THE INCENTIVE PROGRAM
Craig,
This Saturday? Two days from now? I'm suddenly nervous. Are you always this agreeable? Of course it's a date! I have never been to Anthony's, but I have heard very good things. It will be wonderful to be able to get out for a night of dinner and dancing. It has been ages. I can't wait! Cassie

Before Cassie had even signed her name, Georgia fast-forwarded. She saw that she was passing correspondence between the parties in the two-day interim, but Georgia forced herself to pass through it to get to Saturday night. Later she would go back and read each and every detail, but for the moment she couldn't wait another minute to see what was happening on their date.

She did not release the button until she saw Cassie rushing through her apartment to answer the door. Cassie was wearing a stunning red dress that showed off her figure while flaring out at the bottom when she moved. It was perfect for dancing. Georgia was particularly aware of her own slovenly appearance as she watched Cassie make one final adjustment before pulling open the door.

Each of the boys held a dozen roses in their hands. Cassie laughed delightedly as she let them in.

The sight of the three of them took Georgia's breath away, and no doubt Cassie's, too, as they filled her tiny living room with their overwhelming presence. Georgia was suddenly aware of the ache that had been steadily growing inside her. It seemed to underscore the emptiness of her life with each throbbing pulse that reverberated through her, pounding its awful force outward to her extremities and leaving a clammy film on her skin and a bitter taste in her mouth. How she longed to be Cassie in that moment! What she would give to trade places with her. She couldn't drag her eyes away from the scene. Her own life seemed more distant and inconsequential than ever. Even to get up and relieve herself seemed too much of a distraction to merit.

Georgia remained glued to her computer screen so she wouldn't miss so much as a meaningful glance or gesture. She particularly watched Cassie now with a more critical eye. She wondered if Cassie comprehended the enormity of what was happening to her. These three incredible men, each so sweet and with so much to give, offering everything to her. Somehow, in a world where so much had gone wrong and so many had suffered, Cassie, it seemed, had been singled out by the gods. She even looked prettier suddenly, sparkling like a diamond under the constant glow of affection the three men kept showering on her.

By the time they made it to the dance club, it seemed to Georgia that the four of them had formed an unspoken bond of mutual friendship and respect for one another. The attitude of the men was what impressed Georgia most. This was not an ideal situation for any man, and yet these three managed it with a grace and optimism that astounded her. Theirs was the perfect combination of personalities for the incentive program, it seemed. They each cheerfully picked up where the others left off, even as a good-natured kind of competitiveness was developing between them. They were able to joke and laugh about even this, and Cassie, obviously sensitive to their feelings, made a noticeable effort to treat them all equally. She doled out her growing affection in measured increments, so that it was difficult, even for Georgia, who knew her so well, to determine which man she actually favored. The men were relaxed and enjoying themselves. And as for Cassie, it was as if she were floating on air. She might have been with her own brothers for how completely at ease she appeared to be.

Even so, Georgia saw that Cassie trembled when Craig, who was the first to ask her to dance, took her into his arms and led her onto the dance floor. He chose a slow song and Georgia could see that he, too, trembled as he pulled her close. They danced for a while before either one spoke.

"I love how kind and considerate you are," he said close to her ear—so close that his breath caused her hair to flutter. She seemed surprised, and pulled back just enough so that she could look into his face.

"That seems a strange comment, coming from you," she remarked with a smile.

"Why coming from me?"

Georgia was struck by the comfortable intimacy with which they spoke to each other. Their gazes were steady as they talked.

"Because you may be the most considerate person I've ever met," Cassie told Craig.

He laughed. "Maybe that's why I appreciate that quality so much in another person."

She laughed, too. "How do you mean? In what way am I considerate?"

"You know," he told her. "I see how careful you are to treat each of us individually yet the same. You seem to be making an effort to give us your affection in equal parts. I can't help being reminded of a mother with her children. It would be very tempting for a less considerate woman to play games and pit us against each other."

Cassie stared at him a moment, silent. The song was ending.

Craig smiled. "Thanks for the dance, Cass."

He kept hold of her hand as they walked off the dance floor.

The next song was lively and loud, and Steve took hold of Cassie's hand before she even made it back to their table and pulled her out onto the dance floor. He danced well, staying in tune with the music, but his movements were just animated enough to illicit giggles from both Cassie and Georgia.

"Are you always this happy?" Cassie yelled over the music.

He smiled, and for the first time Georgia noticed the sadness behind his eyes. "You have to make the best of every moment," he told Cassie, and Georgia believed that he really meant it and lived his life that way. He leaned in close and spoke into Cassie's ear. "When you do that," he said, "things can't get any better."

"I'm glad you're here," Cassie blurted with a smile.

Steve leaned in again. "So am I," he said, stealing a quick kiss on her cheek before pulling away with a wicked grin. When he saw that she was still smiling, he threw his arms up and spun his body around, gyrating wildly in time with the music. Cassie threw her head back and laughed out loud.

Of the three, Peter seemed the least comfortable on the dance floor, although he was a suitable dancer. Yet there was an awkwardness in his manner that seemed to indicate he would rather be doing something else.

"You're a good dancer," Cassie told him.

"Thanks," Peter said, visibly relaxing. "I try to keep up with those two, you know." He smiled, nodding his head in the direction of Craig and Steve.

"It sounded earlier like you're the one who's difficult to keep up with," she said, referring to their conversation at dinner where the guys were praising Peter for how well he did just about everything.

"Ah, those guys are just really lousy at most things," he joked. Cassie laughed.

"You're very fortunate to have each other," she said.

"I know it!" he said, quite serious suddenly. "I'm glad to have them, especially tonight." He paused a moment, as if unsure about whether he should continue. "Those two are the only two guys I could imagine doing something like this with," he admitted. "And I know that they're the only reason I'm here with you now."

Cassie remained silent.

Peter smiled. "Jeez," he said. "I didn't mean to get all serious on you like that."

"I don't mind it at all," Cassie told him.

The group alternated between talking and dancing until closing time, and Georgia lived every moment of it with Cassie. She remained riveted to her computer screen throughout, unwilling to fast-forward through a single detail. But her eyes were drooping and there was little of the night remaining. She was exhausted and she felt like hell. Yet she had to see how the date would end.

As she watched the men escort Cassie home, Georgia felt that she might have been watching a scene from a date four or five centuries previous. The men were so polite and courteous, it called to mind early America with their ideals about courtship. But Georgia supposed that this return to chivalry was a natural result of evolution. The playing field had become more competitive now, and while some men would take the low road, turning to violence and other means, the superior men would naturally evolve into something more appealing to women. She couldn't wait to see how they would handle the good-night kiss.

Craig, Steve and Peter escorted Cassie to her door together. Georgia wondered if the men had agreed to it ahead of time because it was so seamlessly carried out. Cassie turned to face them, uncertain.

"May we kiss you good-night?" Craig asked her.

"Yes!" she said, beaming.

Craig stepped forward first. The other two discreetly looked in another direction. Craig took Cassie in his arms and kissed her on the lips. Although it was not an overly passionate kiss, it was a kiss to stir, but he was mindful not to linger too long. Afterward, he took an extra moment to look down into her face. She stared up at him. "Thank you for tonight," he murmured softly. "I had a wonderful time."

Peter stepped up next. "I had a great time, too, Cass," he said. "And I think I was enjoying myself too much to remember to mention how absolutely beautiful you look." As Craig moved away, Peter touched her face gently, caressing the line of her jaw where it curved into her neck. He brushed his lips over hers lightly at first, and then pressed them more firmly over hers. It was evident that he was struggling not to ravish her. Cassie shivered.

"Okay, okay," Steve interjected. "We don't want her to freeze to death out here while you two are mauling her. Here!" He opened his jacket and captured her inside, wrapping his arms tightly around her. "There," he said, snuggling up close to her while effectively trapping her inside his embrace. "That's better, isn't it?"

"Uh...it's not even cold outside, Steve," Craig reminded him. "You're probably suffocating her." But they could hear her giggling from inside Steve's coat. This encouragement was all Steve needed to squeeze her even tighter. He maneuvered himself a little so he could find her face. Then he kissed her, again and again, making loud smooching sounds all around her face. But she stopped laughing suddenly and looked up at him. He stopped laughing then, too. He leaned in slowly and pressed his lips on hers, flicking his tongue out over her lips to get her to open them. She did, and he dipped his tongue inside. Georgia was the only one to notice this little intimacy, however, because she had zoomed all the way in as close as she could get. Craig and Peter were still standing behind the two, waiting silently. With visible effort, Steve finally managed to pull himself away from Cassie.

"Good night," he said, his voice jagged with emotion.

"Good night," Cassie whispered back. She looked at Peter and Craig. "Sweet dreams to each of you, and thank you for a wonderful night!"

Georgia watched until the men were gone, aware once again that even more events had taken place while she'd been watching. Perhaps they had even spent their first night together. A ripple of excitement rushed through her at the thought. But she was so tired. It was already time for her to go back to work! Yet why bother?

But she was not ready to abandon the project in spite of the fruitlessness of it all. If she didn't go in and enter more data, the program would simply start breaking down sooner, putting an end to the lives of Cassie and the boys. She could not bear to let that happen. She got up and stretched. Her body ached everywhere.

Besides, she told herself, once she was at the office and began the data-entry process, she could easily sneak in a few hours to watch the rest of it unfold. If she didn't stop now, she sensed that she never would.

She pulled her hair back, threw on her clothes and somehow got herself back to the office.

This time she heard Donald when he came in. She had just attached the disc containing the updated data to the program and was about to sign on and see what was happening.

"Did you get a chance to read over—whoa! What the hell happened to you?" From the expression on Donald's face, Georgia could tell that she looked every bit as bad as she felt. He looked at her in alarm. "For crying out loud, Georgia, close down the project right now. Get some rest. Take a vacation. You need to move on."

"I know, I know," she agreed. "I will."

"You will? Is that why you're installing more data?"

Georgia forced a penitent smile. Secretly she wished he would leave so she could get back online and see how Cassie was progressing. But to her chagrin he lingered.

"I want you to look over the information I left you," he said. "You've been so wrapped up in this outdated mode of looking at the future through a computer-simulated program that you don't even realize we're on the cusp of actually seeing the future firsthand." When he finally got the response he was looking for from Georgia, he gave her a smug smile. "That got your attention, eh?"

"What do you mean?" Georgia asked, thinking she must have misunderstood him.

"Time travel, baby," he confirmed. "That's where it's at now."

"What? *Actual* time travel?" A thousand questions and ideas popped up in Georgia's head all at once. "Has a hypothesis on how it could be accomplished actually been accepted for testing?"

"Read the information," he said. "It's all in there."

When Donald left, Georgia immediately fished through the papers on her desk for the ones he'd left. There were more than forty pages of information, so she scanned them quickly. Her heart began to beat faster as she discovered that the time travel barrier had, in fact, already been breached in an earlier experiment. In this new project that Donald had found, they would test the parameters of time travel, possibly discovering ways to send something tangible, such as a robot, into the future to collect data. As she continued to peruse the file, she saw that it included hypotheses for sending living matter into the future, as well.

Georgia could hardly believe what she was reading. Time travel! Her mind conjured all kinds of scenarios, most of them placing her in a fixed time and place in the future.

This brought her thoughts back to Cassie. Georgia had to catch up with Cassie and the boys. She updated and immediately began scanning, intentionally passing by all kinds of interactions in her search for that one specific event. As she fast-forwarded through Cassie's life, Georgia tried to imagine how she would handle the situation if it were her.

If I were the centerpiece of this little dance, she thought, *I would take control of the floor.* She knew that the guys would want to lead by instinct, but she felt it would have to be Cassie who held the reins in this potential minefield of emotions. Her eyes looked sharp, suddenly, as she caught sight of Cassie packing an overnight bag. The moment she had been waiting for had come. But still she kept forwarding the scene ahead, until Cassie at last stood just outside the door of what could only be Craig's house.

Before Cassie could raise her arm, the door flew open and Steve appeared.

"Hello, gorgeous," he said with a large smile. "We've been looking forward to this for a long time." He opened his arms and when she stepped inside, he grasped her in a huge bear hug, literally lifting her feet off the ground.

When Steve released Cassie, breathless and flushed, Craig stepped up and took both of her hands in his. He just stood back and looked at her for a moment, smiling, and then lifted her hands to his lips. He tenderly kissed the sensitive flesh on the insides of her wrists.

"I'm so happy you're here," was all he said.

Even Peter could not contain his joy in seeing her, and she actually cried out from how fiercely he squeezed her.

"Welcome," they all kept saying.

Everything within was tidy and comfortable, although the decor was quite plain and masculine. As they showed her around and attempted to make her feel at home, it was obvious to Georgia that all three men had formed a strong attachment to Cassie, and she to each of them.

"Everything's so nice," Cassie kept murmuring.

Steve took her bag to her room while Craig and Peter led her into the kitchen for a glass of wine. Georgia noticed that they had food cooking on the stove.

"Something smells wonderful," Cassie observed.

By the time Steve returned, the wine had been opened and poured. All four held up their glasses.

"To us," said Craig.

"To us!" the rest of them agreed enthusiastically.

They discussed the meal the men were preparing for a few moments, but it didn't take long for the subject to turn to the sleeping arrangements.

"I put your bag in the spare bedroom," remarked Steve casually. "Later, I'll show you how to get to the tunnel I dug from there to my room."

They all laughed.

"I'm glad you brought that up, actually," Cassie began, a bit nervously. She looked at Craig. "I know in your last e-mail you said there were no expectations and I appreciate that. But I think each of us has expectations anyway." Her glance swept over each of them. "I want all of you to be as happy as I am."

The three men looked at each other, clearly impressed by this little speech.

"Tell us what's on your mind, then, Cassie," Craig said.

"Well, tonight, for one thing!" She laughed.

"What about tonight?" Craig encouraged.

Cassie took a large gulp of her wine. "I have been thinking a lot about how we should go about this. You've all agreed to leave the choice to me. That is, I suppose, the only way it can be. But before I decide, I would at least like to get your input. I was hoping we could work this out together."

The guys thought about this.

"The problem, of course," Steve chimed in, "is that each of us, given the opportunity, would say, 'Pick me tonight.' We'd get all competitive. Peter'd probably let it slip about Craig's sex-change operation. Or Craig would leave Peter's rash ointment prescription out for you to find."

This got everybody laughing.

"I'm just saying it could get ugly," Steve remarked.

"What kind of input were you looking for, Cassie?" Peter asked. "Oh, and, I don't have any rash ointment, by the way."

"Oh, sorry, Pete, I just thought, you know…because of the rash," said Steve.

"Okay, Steve," Craig interjected. "Continue, Cass."

She smiled, surprisingly calm, considering. "You're each very special to me. I know it may seem hard to believe, but I want to be with each of you equally. In a strange way, I've come to think of you as each individual parts of one relationship. It's the only way I can do this, to look at it that way." She paused. "The truth is, I can't just pick one of you tonight. No, don't interrupt until I get this out. I can't bear to think of two of you lying in your beds alone all night while I spend the night with the chosen one. I know that's how most nights will be, but for tonight, I..." She seemed to be searching for the right words. "For tonight, at least, I want to split the night into three equal parts and spend a third of it with each of you. If you'll have me," she added at the end.

The men were speechless for a moment.

"And you'd like us to determine the order?" Craig asked finally.

"Yes," she said solemnly. "Let's go into this with our eyes wide open. We said honesty first, right? I don't want to choose between you tonight. I am committed to all of you, and I want to be with each of you."

Georgia's mouth was wide open as she watched. She couldn't believe how much Cassie had changed, how assertive she'd become. And she noticed that all three men regarded Cassie with admiration and respect.

In the end, they decided that Craig would get the first shift with Cassie. Georgia felt there was a certain correctness in that and apparently so did everyone else. They all seemed to be satisfied when they announced their decision to Cassie. After Craig would come Steve, and then Peter last. Cassie was radiant and seemed remarkably at ease all throughout dinner, but when the time came for her and Craig to retire, Georgia saw that a shudder vibrated through her. Craig saw it, too, and he reached out and took hold of her hand, squeezing it reassuringly.

Alone in his bedroom, Craig took Cassie in his arms. She brought her arms up and around his neck, pressing her breasts hard against his chest. Both moaned as the kiss grew more passionate. But Cassie pulled away.

"I would like to change," she said.

"Sure, Cass," said Craig. "The bath is over to your left. I've already put your bag in there for you. Take your time. I'll be here waiting."

Cassie walked into the bathroom and closed the door behind her. She leaned back against it for a moment, as if she had grown weak, when all of a sudden she noticed something on the wall in front of her. She stood up straight then, taking a step forward. "Oh, my God," she whispered. Georgia followed her gaze and gasped.

There, hanging on the wall, was a stunning silk negligee with intricate lacework over the bodice. It was revealing, but tastefully so, and from the expression on Cassie's face, Georgia felt that she approved. Attached to the negligee was a note that read, "Your choice."

Georgia knew that by "Your choice," Craig was telling Cassie that she could wear the gown or not, according to her own preference. It was just another way of letting her know that he was looking out for her.

"Not bad, Craig," she heard Cassie murmur under her breath.

"Not bad, Cass!" was Craig's remark when she emerged from the bathroom a short while after, wearing the exquisite gown. His expression and tone of voice told her that her appearance was a lot better than just "not bad."

With the happy assurance and glow of new lust, Cassie approached Craig. She even succumbed to the whim of slowly twirling herself before him. Craig let out a low whistle of appreciation. He, meanwhile, had changed into soft, cotton pajama bottoms that accentuated his toned hips and thighs. Aside from these, they both were wearing enormous smiles. Craig's eyes kept moving over Cassie, drinking in the sight of her in the negligee he had picked out for her.

Craig closed the distance between them and took her face in his hands, but he stopped just inches from her lips to gaze down into her face. Trembling with desire, Cassie brought her arms up around his neck and pulled him down the rest of the way. Suddenly Craig let loose and ravished her mouth in an all-consuming kiss, holding her so close that Cassie gasped.

The kiss was smooth and passionate, as if it had been rehearsed, and Georgia watched breathlessly as Craig's hands moved down to the small of Cassie's back, where they lingered with enough pressure to cause it to arch slightly. The two seemed to fit perfectly together. There was none of that awkwardness or discomfort that often accompanies first intimacies, yet their excitement was apparent. Cassie was the most confident and at ease that Georgia had ever seen her.

When the kiss finally ended, both were left breathless. Craig pulled back just slightly, peering down at Cassie with his kind smile as he brought his hands back up to either side of her face. But the smile gave way to a more serious, determined look. Suddenly he began moving his hands very leisurely over her, using his thumbs to kind of massage his way down along her face and throat and breasts. It was easy to see the effect his touch was having on Cassie. Her entire body responded as a shiver of pleasure coursed through her. Even her toes curled upward as she seemed to fall back on the flats of her feet. Craig kept teasing her breasts over the thin, silky negligee, apparently pleased with the effect it was having on her. He caressed and squeezed them until her eyes closed and her head rolled back in ecstasy.

"Here," he said, pulling the sides of the negligee up. "As beautiful as this looks on you, I want to feel your skin."

Cassie lifted her arms to allow him to remove the nightgown. With her fully bared before him, Craig seemed stunned. "My God," he whispered.

He resumed his love play of her breasts again, this time on her bare skin, groaning low in his throat as he captured the feel of her for the very first time. Then he moved his hands over her abdomen and down around her hips in an effort, it seemed, to feel every inch of her. Cassie arched her back and went on tiptoe in response. She gasped when his fingers reached between her legs and mingled in the rich moistness that was clearly crying out for his attention. This evidence of her desire seemed to push Craig over the edge because he suddenly picked her up and, in a fluid movement that gave evidence of his lean strength, he settled her onto his bed in a sitting position with her legs apart. Then he slid between her legs and kneeled before her. Cassie rested back on her arms and allowed him full access to her body. He dipped his head and gently captured one taut nipple between his lips, running his tongue all around it and then pulling it into his mouth. Georgia watched his mouth working over Cassie's breast, and she could almost feel the delicious sensations of having her own breasts handled in such a manner. He took turns suckling each nipple, back and forth, until he had Cassie crying out with pleasure. Encouraged by her reaction, he extended his kisses lower, covering her stomach and then even lower still, until suddenly his face was buried between her legs. Cassie squirmed and writhed beneath him as he worked his tongue in and out of her, and then up and around. He kept pleasing her with his tongue untiringly, never once letting up until Cassie's body went suddenly rigid and afterward fell back limp.

Craig rose up then and pulled off his pajama bottoms, finally releasing his turgid erection in all of its glory. It stood high and inflamed and proud. Cassie reached out for it as he approached her, stroking it lovingly in anticipation.

In spite of how he had prepared Cassie's body for him, Craig still had to work his way into her, purposefully doing so at a calculated and leisurely pace. He clutched the back of her head firmly and held his face within inches of hers, letting his lips hover just above hers, so that every now and then he could lightly brush them over hers for a soft kiss. She wrapped her arms and legs around him, and both of them sighed in unison when he was fully inside her.

Like a well-oiled machine, the two moved together, grinding out their pleasure in a single, uniform motion. Every now and again, Craig would slow momentarily, apparently reining in his excitement so that he could better please Cassie. She clung to him, moaning lightly as he made love to her. Craig allowed his hands to roam all over her body and, when he saw that she loved being touched like that, he increased his efforts, using his lips, as well, and kissing and stroking her breasts and shoulders and face.

As they both grew more excited, Craig's thrusts came harder and deeper, and it was clear from the tension in his powerfully muscled buttocks that he was not holding anything back. Cassie accepted all of this eagerly, lifting her legs even higher to open herself to him. This sent Craig over the edge, and he suddenly lost all of his former tenderness and became almost violent as he drove himself into her. Cassie took the last little bit of his control when she cried out with her orgasm. Then Craig threw himself into her one last time and bucked his hips several times in climax.

They remained joined, with Craig just off to one side for a long time after. Still watching, Georgia thought they had fallen asleep. But after a while Craig spoke.

"You're everything I've ever wanted in a woman," he told her.

"I hope I can always be that," she said.

He let his fingers roam through her hair, playing with it absently. And then they did fall asleep.

Georgia hit Fast-Forward until she saw Craig stir.

"Cassie," Craig whispered, kissing her lips and her ears and everything in between. "Cassie."

"Mmm, Craig?" Cassie woke with a start. "What time is it?"

"Time for the second shift. If you still want to. It's up to you. I hated to wake you but you said that was what you wanted."

"Oh." She looked sad for a minute, but then she sat up, waking. "I did say that I would," she said apologetically.

"No, don't you feel bad," he scolded. "Your choice, remember? I was only asking because I wanted to make sure it was what you still wanted. We'll understand, whatever you do." He kissed her lips several more times. "I'm going to miss you," he added.

Cassie got up and stretched. "Are you sure you're all right with this?"

"This is what we agreed upon and this is what we'll do. Are you all right?"

"Yes, I think I am. Or I will be. I just have to get used to it."

Cassie grabbed her overnight bag and slipped into the bathroom to clean up. When she came out, she was wearing a thick robe. She approached Craig. He reached out for her and held her close to him for a long moment. Then he kissed her.

"Good night, Cass," he said.

"Good night, Craig. Sweet dreams."

Georgia watched Cassie leave Craig's bedroom with admiration. She was actually going to do it! The house was quiet, as everyone had retired. Cassie made her way quietly into Steve's room and closed the door behind her.

He was sitting on his bed watching television. When he saw Cassie, he jumped up and turned it off. He approached her tentatively.

"Hey there." He smiled. "I didn't know if you'd come."

"I told you I would," she reminded him.

"Yeah, but you could've wigged out at the last minute."

Cassie laughed. "No, I couldn't," she said more seriously.

"Come on in," he said, motioning her toward the bed. "Get comfortable." She sat on the bed.

"I know it's probably hard to just switch gears all of a sudden, so why don't you just sit back and let me help you relax?"

"How are you going to do that?" Cassie asked him with curiosity. But she sat back on the bed as he instructed and rested her head against the headboard.

"You'll see," he told her, opening a drawer in his nightstand and fishing around inside. "Ah," he said. "Here it is!" He squirted something into his hand. "Now prepare to be impressed."

"I have a feeling I'm going to have to always be prepared for that around here," she said. "You boys are full of...oh... ahhh...uhn." She threw her head back in ecstasy. "God, that feels so good!"

Steve was rubbing her feet, vigorously and energetically. He enclosed one of them completely in his large hands, kneading and pummeling it with his strong fingers. Cassie was so overcome by the sensations, she couldn't speak. Eventually he moved upward to massage her ankle, and then her calf, and so forth, thoroughly and vigorously moving his way up her leg until he reached the very top of her thigh. Her robe had fallen open, exposing her nakedness to him. Cassie did not close it back up.

Cassie's leg, by this time, was trembling from the effects of Steve's hands, and her breathing had quickened. Georgia watched keenly to see what he would do next. His hands were still working over the flesh of her thigh, moving round and round in a circular motion. Very cautiously and inconspicuously, almost as if it were accidental, Steve let his pinky finger periodically brush up against Cassie's clitoris. He did it lightly at first, and quite casually. Meanwhile he kept massaging her upper thigh, and just every now and then, his finger would reach out and caress her. Each time he did it, Cassie's body would jolt the tiniest bit in response, and she would let out a little gasp. But just as she was beginning to really enjoy his little game, Steve suddenly started working his way back down her leg in the other direction. His lips twitched when she sighed in disappointment.

Once he made it all the way back down to her foot, Steve switched to the other foot, taking his time and massaging her thoroughly as he inched his way up her other leg in the same manner he had the first. When at last he reached the top of her thigh, he once again went through the pretence of accidentally brushing up against her, this time with his other pinky finger. Cassie giggled.

"What?" said Steve. "Oh, pardon me!"

They were both smiling now. But when he brushed against her again, she boldly caught hold of his hand, and pressed it between her open legs.

The smile left Steve's face. They looked at each other a moment.

"I take it the massage worked," he murmured in an undertone.

Cassie laughed in spite of herself, but she looked as if she would throttle him if he told another joke.

"All right!" Steve announced decisively. "The goddess has spoken." And with that, he took her head in his other hand (he kept his first hand right where it was) and crushed her lips in a hungry kiss. Cassie arched her body up toward his invitingly, as if she could never get enough.

Suddenly it was as if a dam had burst, making their passion escalate out of control. Steve finally set aside his reserve of always trying to amuse, and for the moment let his own desires take over. He buried his fingers in Cassie's hair as they kissed, one moment simply luxuriating in its lush softness and the next grasping it and using it to jerk her head back so that he would have better access to her lips and throat. With his other hand, he alternately squeezed and massaged the throbbing mound between her legs. They rolled about the bed heatedly, and in the tumult of their embrace Steve somehow ended up beneath her. When the kiss ended, Cassie was sitting on top of him. Her robe had fallen open but, suddenly shy, she began to close it. Steve stopped her.

"Please," he implored her, as if it were his last dying request. "Don't deny me."

With a smile, Cassie pulled the robe back and let it fall off her shoulders.

"Heaven help me," Steve murmured, drinking in the sight of her. She was sitting on top of him without anything on. "Oh, shit," he suddenly groaned. "Heaven only helps those who help themselves, and here I've left all my clothes on. No! For God's sake, don't move! Not one inch! I can do this." Steve struggled to remove his clothing with Cassie sitting naked on top of him. "No, don't help me!" he'd cry when she'd try to move a little out of his way to assist him. "I've got it." Even Georgia was laughing hysterically with how much trouble he was having, but he would not allow Cassie to budge an inch in any direction as he stripped off every single piece of his clothing, including his shoes.

"You are an extremely talented and agile man," Cassie remarked when he was finished.

"That's why I did it," he said, grinning. "I wanted you to see how agile I was."

"Oh!" said Cassie, pretending to be disappointed. "And here I was thinking of staying right here where I'm sitting. But if you'd rather show me some more of those stunts you can do…maybe a few acrobatics…"

Steve laughed. But then he grew suddenly serious.

"I'm sorry, but I can't just sit here looking at you any longer," he said. And he was, quite obviously, painfully aroused. He touched her then, tentatively at first, but then more aggressively as his hands moved up and down over her body, lingering on her breasts. "Just look at you," he murmured.

In response, Cassie lifted her hips just enough to allow his erection to pop into position beneath her, then she lowered herself slowly over the top of it. They both moaned as she descended. His headboard was right in front of her, so she reached out and grasped hold of it, positioning her breasts so that they were stretched out right above his head. He continued caressing them gently. She began to move her hips up and down on him, slowly, leisurely, rocking her hips as she went. Steve watched her as if mesmerized, as if he still couldn't believe she was really there. All the while his fingers kept moving over her breasts, lightly and lovingly. Georgia watched them, mildly surprised. There was no discomfort or urgency. And they never once looked away from each other or changed positions. Cassie just kept moving up and down, up and down, in a nice, leisurely manner, rocking her hips as she went, moving forward as she went up and jutting backward when she went down. And Craig just kept caressing her breasts. Their eyes remained locked.

But eventually, as was bound to happen, Georgia noticed that Cassie's movements were growing faster and more urgent. She kept hold of the headboard, throwing her head back periodically in pleasure. But her gaze never left Steve's; even when her head was tossed back, she would cut her eyes to the side so that they were still glued to his. Neither one would look away. It was as if they had made a silent pact. And even when Cassie's face contorted with pleasure and she cried out, she still maintained eye contact with Steve.

Once her pleasure subsided, Cassie's movements became less regular. Steve's hands glided slowly down along the sides of her waist until he reached her hips, and then he suddenly grasped hold of them, almost fiercely. Cassie stopped moving altogether for a moment. She still looked into his eyes, and he into hers. They were silent and still.

Very slowly, Cassie suddenly began moving up and down again, but this time Steve used his hands on her hips to assist her. He guided her movements, allowing her to move exactly as she had been doing before but with more force this time, pulling her hips down and back when she moved downward and jerking her hips forward and up when she moved up. As they continued in this way, in perfect rhythm, he began using more and more force, especially when he pulled her hips downward, so as they progressed he was eventually slamming her hips down into his. Cassie grasped the headboard tighter, crying out with every downward thrust. Her breasts heaved and bounced about wildly. Steve jerked her hips up and down so forcefully that it seemed his strength alone was driving her now. In those last manic thrusts, he lifted his own hips up to meet hers as he yanked Cassie's hips down. Georgia could hear their flesh slapping together even over the noise of their cries. Finally Steve slammed their bodies together one last time. And still, their eyes remained fixed on each other.

"Christ!" Georgia murmured as she watched them.

Cassie collapsed over Steve and he wrapped his arms around her, squeezing her tight.

Neither one spoke for a while.

"Are you tired?" he asked at last.

"A little."

"Get some rest."

"You don't have any more jokes?"

Steve brushed her hair aside and looked into her face. His expression was strangely serious. After a long moment, he said, "No more jokes tonight." And he kissed her.

They rested together in each other's arms, but neither one slept. Georgia pushed Fast-Forward, scanning the screen for activity. She stopped when she saw Steve get up. There was an alarm beeping quietly.

"It's time," he said with a sigh. "You still up for it?"

"Why does everyone keep asking me that? If I say I'm going to do something I do it," she said, but it was kindly.

"We all agreed ahead of time that if you had a hard time going through with it, you know, we just wanted you to know it wasn't written in stone."

"I do appreciate that," she said.

"We care about you," he said quietly. "You know, we want you to be okay."

Cassie looked at him and Georgia saw that there were tears in her eyes. "Me, too," she whispered. "I want you to be okay."

Steve nodded.

She grabbed her overnight bag and went in Steve's bathroom to get cleaned up again. Georgia wondered how Peter was going to top this.

Peter was stretched out on his bed, fast asleep. Cassie slipped into his room quietly and stood watching him for a moment. She approached his bed cautiously. There was an open book resting on his chest. Curious, Cassie reached for the book and carefully slipped it out of his grasp. He suddenly started, waking.

"Cassie!"

"You don't have to get up," she told him. She sat on the bed. "How are you?"

"Great!" He looked around. "I must have dozed off."

"Reading always makes me sleepy, too," Cassie said. "What were you reading?"

"A classic," he said. "From 2062."

"Wow!" Cassie said.

"Oh, I have books dating much further back than that. And now with all the reprints and comebacks, I'm always finding new, older stuff. It's great. I just picked one up yesterday for you."

"Really? For me?"

He got up and fished through some items on a nearby desk. "Here it is," he said, handing it to her.

"*'Enchanted: Erotic Bedtime Stories for Women,'*" she read. "Hmm…" She looked up at him with a wry smile.

"Remember the other day when we were talking about books and you mentioned fairy tales?"

"This doesn't look like the fairy tales I was talking about," she remarked, but she was still smiling.

"That's because these tales are for grown-ups," he informed her. He sat on the bed next to her. "When you told me your favorite childhood memory was being read bedtime stories, I couldn't resist getting this book to read to you one night. And then, when tonight happened…I guess I figured by the time you got around to me you'd need a bedtime story to help you relax." He looked at her shyly. "I could read you Byron instead."

"No!" she cried, laughing. But then she grew serious. She perched herself back on one of the pillows on his bed. "Okay, I'm ready," she said with a little smile.

Peter settled in the bed next to her. He began flipping through the pages. He cleared his throat. "Okay," he began. "I don't know what any of your sexual fantasies are…" He looked at her and added, "Yet." Then he resumed perusing the book. "But we can just work our way through the stories and see what happens."

Cassie touched his arm. "Thank you," she whispered. "It was a wonderfully thoughtful idea to read to me."

"You're welcome," he replied, distracted by her eyes for several moments before turning back to the book.

He cleared his throat again. "*'Beauty and the Beast,'*" he announced, giving her one more quick glance before delving into the story with enthusiasm. His voice was rich and expressive, and he read well. Cassie leaned back and watched him while he read the bedtime story to her. Georgia couldn't resist watching, too, as Peter brought the classic tale to life. Even the sensual parts he read with a grave seriousness that made Cassie's eyes glow.

"So she preferred the beast!" sighed Cassie, wide-awake by the time he finished.

"Of course," replied Peter. "That's who she fell in love with."

"Mmm. Interesting," reflected Cassie. "In the original tale, the beast changes into a prince in the end, as a kind of reward to Beauty, for seeing more than just the beast's appearance."

"But if she truly loved the beast, why should he have to change?" wondered Peter.

"True." Cassie thought for a moment. "I wonder…" she began.

"Hmm?"

"The fairy tales…they're extremely old-fashioned, and yet…it's almost as if they've really captured the ideals of people for all time."

"What do you mean?" Peter asked.

"Well, for instance, the idea that if you fall in love with someone they'll change for you…that hope, or belief, or whatever it is has stuck to this day. People seem to really expect it!"

"Do you think that those really are people's ideals, or just how we're taught to think?"

"I don't know what I think. That story got me feeling all fuzzy inside."

They laughed.

"I was hoping for that effect," Peter admitted. He leaned in close and took her in his arms. "You know that I want you," he said huskily, and his desire was obvious in his face and manner. He positively trembled with his need and his eyes burned so hot that Georgia wondered at his control. "But I want you to know also that I would be perfectly happy to just hold you in my arms if you've had enough of being mauled for one night."

Cassie stared back at him in openmouthed wonder, but her desire was clear to see, as well, and her eyes burned just as hot as his. She reached out a hand and lightly touched his face. "That, right there, is why I have decided that I don't want the 'choice' any longer. From now on, I'm passing that responsibility over to you boys. I think I want to stay in the room you've prepared for me and let the three of you decide who comes to me. I don't care how you do it. You can pull names out of a hat, for all it matters to me. All I know is that I can't choose between you. I want all of you equally, I truly do. I don't even know how that's possible but it's how I feel. It's like, in my heart, you're each parts of one love."

"You decided all that just now?"

"Yes."

"Why?"

"Because I was suddenly glad that I wasn't the one who put you last tonight. And in that moment, I realized that I didn't want to ever put any one of you last."

"But I'm glad I got to go last," he told her. "It means I get to wake up with you."

It was suddenly too much for Cassie, and tears spilled from her eyes onto her cheeks. Peter kissed the tears away. And all of a sudden there was nothing but their desire for each other; it consumed all of their thought and energy.

Georgia stood up abruptly, but she couldn't quite pull her gaze from the screen. Cassie's robe had fallen open and Peter was ravishing her. Georgia's mind was racing with ideas. With effort, she turned away from Cassie and Peter to find the information Donald left. Glancing around, she became aware that it was dark outside. Another day had passed and she had done nothing but watch, obsessed with a future that didn't even exist. But it *might* exist! She searched more eagerly for the papers.

This time, Georgia sat down and carefully read over every word. Time travel was possible! And if she had anything to do with it, it could be achieved in her lifetime. For the first time in her life, her interest in science came second to her interest in her own life. She finally saw science for what it was—a means to an end. She wanted to learn how to travel into the future because she *wanted* to travel into the future. There was someplace out there that she wanted to go

As she closed the office for the night and drove home, for once Georgia thought about something other than Cassie. She thought about what might happen—to her! She thought about the new time-travel project she had been offered and the many opportunities that came with it. But there was only one program that interested her now. It was what captured her interest the most since the first hint of it had been introduced into her consciousness. It was the only thing that made sense to her anymore. And no matter how many projects it took to get her there, she knew she would always be working toward that one final goal. It was something she would spend the rest of her life trying to achieve if she had to. She would find the Incentive Program.

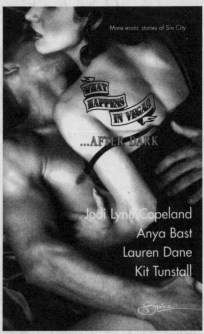

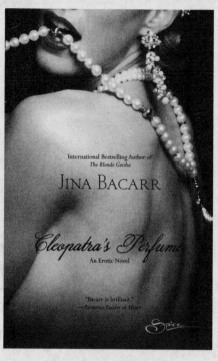